VARGAS HAMILTON

LIFE IS A GAS

DAVID COCKLIN

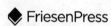 FriesenPress

Suite 300 - 990 Fort St
Victoria, BC, V8V 3K2
Canada

www.friesenpress.com

Copyright © 2018 by David Cocklin
First Edition — 2018

ISBN
978-1-5255-1063-2 (Hardcover)
978-1-5255-1064-9 (Paperback)
978-1-5255-1065-6 (eBook)

1. FICTION, ESPIONAGE

Distributed to the trade by The Ingram Book Company

Cheri !

Welcome to the wild ! side !

VARGAS HAMILTON

LIFE IS A GAS

DAVID COCKLIN

Find that bit of VARGAS within you and cherish it... then nurture it... and set her free !

31 oct 18

TO ALL THE WOMEN OF THE WORLD,

AND THAT BIT OF VARGAS HAMILTON IN EACH OF YOU

Vargas slipped slowly back into consciousness. Her head delivered a pounding rhythm of pain that danced effortlessly with her heartbeat. She felt the cold embrace of the concrete floor against her cheek, and grimaced at the discomfort in her arms. Her hands were tied behind her back at the wrists, and her elbows were similarly bound and pulled together.

She rolled onto her back, crushing her arms slightly in the process, and yanked herself into a sitting position; a sort of sit-up without any upper body support. She tilted her head back and tested the quality of the knots holding her arms. They were not only sufficient, but seemingly overdone. *Amateurs*, she thought.

She sat there for a while, trying to let some strength seep back into her. She brought her knees up to her chest and lunged forward so the momentum would help her stand. It felt good to have the blood running up and down again, instead of back and forth. Her shoulders ached. She paced back and forth in the small holding cell, waiting for the opportunity to re-claim her freedom.

Sometime between the gradual clearing of her head and the realization that she was voraciously thirsty, the door to her cell was kicked open and two undistinguished captors entered. They were dressed in the usual black garb, with scarves and sashes dangling about them. They both had automatic weapons and a belt full of military accoutrements; knife, transceiver, flashlight, bullet clips, and of course, an iPhone. One of them held a metal chair and swung it vigorously onto the floor beside her. He yelled in some foreign language, which she translated internally to:

"Excuse me ma'am, would you be kind enough to sit down so we can enjoy some fruitful discussion surrounding your visit to our area, and your current endeavors herein?"

His companion moved in from behind, and grabbed her roughly by the shoulders. He positioned her over the chair, before shoving her down onto it. The force of his push sent her backwards and brought the chair, along with her, onto the concrete floor. Her elbows and shoulders shot fresh pain up through her neck. *Christ, my head hurts,* she thought. The guards clambered forward and grabbed her again, hoisting her and the chair into a sitting position. They made more kind comments in their language, and laughed a bit. Vargas managed a curled lip to acknowledge that she understood their humor.

"I'm gonna kill you both," she hissed softly, "in just a few moments."

The two men looked at each other as if to demonstrate that they could not understand English, but then the taller of the two bent over her and brought her head close by gripping and pulling her hair from behind. His other hand went to her breast and cupped it in a rough molestation.

"We are going to have fun with you, bitch. You will be a pleasure to chat with."

His hand moved up and down the front of her shirt, once again fondling her left breast. The intrusion stretched her shirt and popped the top two buttons, leaving the garment slightly open and askew, exposing her upper chest. The guards saw her chest tattoo simultaneously, looked at one another, and laughed. The tall one released his grip and turned to close the door.

Vargas leapt to her feet and delivered a violent kick straight to the jaw of the smaller man beside her, knocking him sideways into the cement wall. He crumpled to the floor as she turned her attention to his startled companion. She lunged forward and used her body as a battering ram to drive him backwards into the cell door, catching him off guard and unprepared. He spun around just as her forehead crashed into his nose with an unnatural cracking sound, confirming she had broken it. *Christ, that did not help my headache.* She brought her knee upward with all the force she could muster and delivered a crushing blow to his groin. His hands were unsure which injured area they should cover; nose or balls. Either way, he left the rest of himself unprotected. His head was tilted back as his hand tried to confirm the mush on his face. Vargas stepped back and sent a side kick full throttle into his exposed Adam's apple, and the party was over for him. He sunk limply to the ground, dead and gone.

She turned quickly to the smaller man, who was up on one knee and just beginning to recover his senses. Her left knee came up violently into his lower jaw, snapping his head back and driving him against the wall again. He crumpled to the floor and Vargas brought her knee down across his throat, applying her full body weight until he joined his colleague in the after world. *Seventy-two virgins for you guys, no doubt!*

She turned and sat down, leaning against the smaller guard, and feeling along his belt for the knife it held. Once she located it, freeing her hands was easy enough, but she was unable to reach up to cut the ropes lashing her elbows. She glanced back over her shoulder, seeing his dead face, and let a smile cross her lips. She plunged the handle of the knife into the dead guard's mouth, clearing a few teeth out of the way, and lodging it in his now dormant throat. It stood there hard and erect. She chuckled at the thought. *How appropriate!* She leaned back and rubbed the ropes holding her upper arms against the exposed blade until they succumbed to the sharp edge.

Rejuvenated by her rather easy escape, she stripped off the other man's belt and swung it over her shoulder and across her chest, keeping her torn shirt in better order. She picked up his automatic rifle and cautiously exited the cell. She didn't know what was out there, but she figured time was short. She hurried silently down the corridor.

The first door she came to was closed. She ignored it and moved to the next, which was slightly open. She peered through the cracked entrance and saw four men engaged in elevated chit chat, manning a radio receiver. *What the hell,* she thought, and stepped into the doorway, pushing the door wide open in the process. The first two fell to her burst of automatic spray and she dove forward in a soft roll as a third man returned fire. She straightened her body, now prone on the floor, and send a short burst of three or four bullets into the soft frontal lobe of his brain. The radio operator looked at her, frozen. As she got up, he finally came to his senses and reached clumsily for the handgun parked on his belt. Too late. Vargas had time to switch her weapon to single shot mode and send a gift right between his eyes, before he even got his weapon un-holstered. She then turned to the radio and plugged two rounds into it as well, just in case.

She knew the sounds of gunfire would rouse any other terrorists in the compound, and she darted towards the doorway. Just before she cleared the room, she saw it from the corner of her eye; tall and white. She raced back to pick it up and spun the lid off, dumping a handful of pills into her palm. She pushed some into her mouth and chewed through the crunch and grind. *Tylenol. Perfect!*

She heard footsteps running up the hall and she dropped to the floor, crawling to the doorway and peering out from her prone position. She returned her weapon back to full automatic and leaned out into the hallway. The three bad guys were dead before they ever saw the woman lying on the floor in front of them.

She jumped up and ran down the hall, discarding her nearly empty rifle and picking up a new one as she passed, along with a Type 64 silenced pistol from the holster of one of the dead men. *Chinese weapons,* she thought. *That's a new twist.* She didn't dwell on it, but parked it in her mental filing cabinet for future access.

She turned left at the end of the hall, moving briskly past her old cell and her ex-roommates, until reaching another dead end. She looked out the window cautiously and saw the grounds clearly for the first time. She was on the second floor. This was a large compound, and there were terrorists scurrying everywhere, chasing down the reason for the sudden gunfire. It was easy to spot the commander. He was standing with hands on hips, perusing the confusion and calamity of the situation. Several men came forward to receive instruction, accompanied by the obligatory waving of hands and shaking of fists.

She spun and let off a short burst, which brought down the unsuspecting guard that had rounded the corner behind her. The sound of renewed fire brought attention to her window, and when she looked out again there were several faces staring back at her. She pulled back just in time, as several rounds came crashing through the glass and bit into the ceiling along the corridor. The guard she had just shot caught a few ricochets, just for good measure. She slid back to him after the initial gunfire subsided and found a couple of grenades attached to his tunic. She had seen the jeep below the window, and visualized that as her most likely mode of exit.

There was the crash of numerous footsteps heading toward her from around the hall corner. She popped one of the grenades, reached around the corner, and bowled it down the hallway. She ducked behind the dead guard, using him as a shield against the blast. *Poor guy, definitely not his day.* The grenade explosion caught the charging troops with enough force to knock off a few and drive the rest back to the safety of the radio room. The concussion left a distinct tingling in her ears. *Christ, I'll definitely need more Tylenol.*

She seized the moment, lifted the dead body over her shoulder, plunged forward, and threw it through the window, clearing out the glass and metal frame. She dove out after him, Type 64 pistol in one hand and the grenade in her other. She released it mid-air as she landed and rolled under the jeep. The blast stunned the courtyard momentarily. Then she was up and in the driver's seat, glancing at the ignition. *Keys? Yes!*

She started the ignition and jammed the jeep into gear, racing for the obvious exit from the compound. Shots rang out, and the twang of lead on steel was unmistakable. The vehicle easily broke through the compound gate and she was in full flight down the dusty, bumpy road. By the time the terrorists mounted a motorized pursuit, she had nearly a minute head start; plenty of time!

After about five minutes, she came to a steep incline in the road, accompanied by a sharp cliff drop-off on her right side. As she rode over a rise in the roadway, with a sharp left turn at the bottom of a small hill, she gunned the jeep. It was clear that she could not navigate the turn at this speed. She dove out the driver's door as the vehicle plunged over the side of the cliff. It floated out into the afternoon air like a warm balloon, before crashing in a tangled mess, some five hundred feet below. Vargas rolled with the momentum of her jump and clutched desperately at the rocky road, as her torso bounced towards the precipice. With toes dug in and fingers scrapped raw, she managed to stop herself inches before eternity swallowed her.

She quickly rose and climbed up the hill on the opposite side of the road, putting some distance between her and the point where her previous captors would soon be arriving. They did. Her smoldering vehicle was far below and the terrorists cheered like little kids as they looked at the situation, somehow feeling they had gained a victory, instead of recognizing the whole-hearted battering they had actually received as a community, at the hands of this single, formidable lady.

More instructions were given, the context of which Vargas could only guess at from her lofty hiding spot. The pursuing vehicles moved back towards the compound, but two men and a small car were left behind to confirm her perceived demise. One terrorist began the climb down towards her wreck, ostensibly to verify the existence of a body, while the other began climbing the hill directly towards her. *Thank you, China, for the Type 64.* She plugged him gently in the head with a blast from the silent pistol, then leapt back to the road to commandeer the car, bumped her head during the haste of entry, and sped off. It was all so silent that the descending terrorist was completely unaware of what was transpiring. *Christ, my head still hurts.* It would be close to an hour before the man in the canyon would discover the lack of a body, return to find the car gone, and notify the main compound. She would be long gone by then.

Vargas leaned back onto the soft leather of Colonel Younger's easy chair. *What a life,* she thought. She was relaxed, rejuvenated, and revitalized. Two weeks in Aruba had done wonders. Well, two weeks less the three days that were cut short, following two days of debriefing from the compound escape. Handsome meals and tasty men, supported by the sun and sea, was the cast of characters that eased her pains and syphoned the stress from her tight body. *Thank you Casa Tua.* While she was a little pissed at the abrupt end to her eleven-day *fourteen-day* vacation, she was especially impressed with the fact that the agency had sent a private jet to collect her.

Thursday morning delivered properly poured Mimosa's, fresh shrimp cocktail, and a Gulfstream G200. *Now that's what I call a "special brunch."*

She had planted herself in Colonel Younger's office when she arrived, and was now waiting for anyone to walk through the door. Soon enough, a young lady came in with a silver flask of coffee and a creamer on a sterling tray. She parked it on the credenza and asked Vargas if she would like a cup.

"No thanks," she said. She didn't want to say what she was actually thinking: She never drank anything she hadn't seen in raw form, or watched her adversary drink before her. Not that Colonel Younger was an adversary, but Vargas was not familiar with his operation and could not verify his security. Who knows who had access to the coffee flask? She realized she was being a little paranoid, but better alive than dying!

Soon after the young lady left, Colonel Younger walked in with a robust shove of the door, followed by four other men. Two of them went straight to the coffee trough, obviously veterans of the colonel's office. Another man slowed and glanced in several directions at once, before closing the door gently behind them. The fourth man was calmer and had his eyes glued on Vargas. She returned his stare, in the least offensive or aggressive mode she could muster, careful not to seem alluring. She hated that type of BS. After a few moments, he dropped the stare and shuffled onto the chesterfield across from her. Colonel Younger stood behind his desk and waited impatiently as the coffee hunters dragged their quarry to the couch. The doorman remained by the door, scanning the room.

The colonel moved in behind the chesterfield and looked at Vargas with a soft smile.

"Vargas Hamilton," he said. It was as if he had just discovered her in a video game and was introducing her to his playmates. "Gentlemen, meet the most dangerous woman in the world."

That perked them up. *Christ,* Vargas thought, *how corny was that? I always thought of myself as kinda sexy, in a combative sort of way.* The colonel moved around the edge of the couch.

"Sorry, Vargas, I just wanted them to get the stereotype out of their heads so we can move forward with this meeting." He smiled.

"Fair enough, Colonel," she replied. "I'm sure they'll just think of me as another suit and tie now," she mused. Her smile was littered with ambiguity. He smiled back, not sure if she was appreciative of the compliment.

It didn't matter. The men all looked at her as if she had suddenly appeared in the room through some unseen portal. She looked across at coffee-man number one. He was staring at her ample bosom. *Of course! Bloody men,* she thought, *it never changes.* Vargas slid her hand back and forth across her chest, which caught the man by surprise and drove his stare up to her eyes.

"All the danger is right up here," she said, pointing at the side of her head.

She wore that sarcastic little look that one gives a child with his fingers in the cookie jar. The man immediately shifted his gaze to the coffee table.

"Gentlemen, Vargas is here because she is going to take front line action on this threat. It's plausible and tangible, but we have not yet verified the details through TIS."

TIS was Telecommunications Information Systems, and Vargas was never impressed with them. They usually overstated the facts to inflate their own importance, while letting the small but imperative details slip quietly under the radar. Every report from them was to be questioned for both authenticity and accuracy. She wondered inwardly if they should have a separate department reviewing the information department!

"Vargas, this is Sam Ryder and James Sanders from Military Intelligence." She knew they were MI, of course. The old adage that military intelligence was an oxymoron was probably never closer to the truth.

"They will run through the situation and provide details on where things are at. By the way, sorry to pull you out of Aruba, but this threat needs our best operative. The concerns go all the way up the flag pole to the White House."

"Good afternoon, gentlemen," Vargas offered with a slight nod.

Younger stepped back and pushed a button somewhere down in the bowels of his desk. The blinds began to whir shut as a projector screen rose from the mantle behind her. She stood to turn and watch the show.

"Fleming, keep watch on the other side of the door, please." The muscle man standing inside the closed office door nodded. Vargas guessed this was above his clearance. He turned and exited without fanfare or embarrassment.

She had not yet been introduced to the calm gentleman sitting on the sofa, and he had not said a word, or even changed his impassive expression. No problem, she knew that would come when appropriate.

Ryder and Sanders rose in unison and walked to the screen. The PowerPoint began, and Ryder cleared his throat. She wondered which one would be the voice, and guessed Ryder drew the short straw. The face of a ruggedly handsome man came onto the screen. Perhaps European or South American; definitely not Arab. Vargas held an extensive repertoire of faces of interest to the agency, but had never seen him before. Her photographic memory was one of her formidable gifts, and she had an amazing recall of people and places. This guy was definitely not on her flash cards!

"Armand Creusa," Ryder began. "Born in either Albania or Romania, depending on which friendly intelligence group is describing him. He's been off our interest list up until now because he was a small-time, local player. Drugs, money laundering, human trafficking—you know, the good stuff. We have no record of him ever entering the US, but feel certain that he was in Los Angeles. Of course, detecting arrivals and departures is usually about as accurate as the TSA guard who pats you down with a magic wand. Saving America, no doubt."

Vargas smiled. *MI guy making jokes. Hey, maybe he isn't a total loss after all.*

Ryder continued. "Like I said, he's been a good little bad guy, up until a couple of weeks ago. Running through the usual pitter-patter of activity, one of our analysts noticed some strange signs at one of the training camps we monitor. The satellite images showed some unusual activity in North Africa."

Vargas saw Sanders click the button for the next slide. *Aha, that's why they needed two guys to handle the presentation,* she thought. *Operating the pointy stick and the little push button at the same time is too complicated for one person.* Her head still had a dull ache.

Ryder used the pointer stick to pinpoint some images on the

next slide.

"There is heavy traffic on the edge of a terrorist training camp, which is unusual enough, but there was what appeared to be a gun battle, with accompanying explosions and a car chase. It looks like someone was being held there and managed to get away. We're trying to nail him down as we speak. It shouldn't take long. Looks like blonde hair and a four-pointed star tattooed on his chest."

Vargas suddenly realized the event under scrutiny was actually sixteen days earlier. Yes, that was her jumping out the window and racing off in the sand-colored jeep, but she had definitely not seen Mr. Creusa there, and she had no idea she was on satellite TV. The commandant she saw looked nothing like him. She wondered who in the room actually knew it was her in the satellite images, wreaking havoc on the compound and escaping.

They couldn't tell it was a woman? They could read the tattoo on her chest but not see the two breasts poking out of the shirt? She wondered who knew that it was actually her they were trying to 'nail down'? Surely, Younger was aware. Or was he? She decided to keep quiet for now. And who is this calm gentleman on the couch? She glanced at him. He was looking at her, either aware that she was aware it was her in the satellite shot, and gauging her reaction, or sizing up her demeanor towards the on-going presentation.

She looked back at the screen, a little self-admiration bringing goose bumps to her arms. *Okay, the loose shirt does sort of hide my 'stuff'.* She wasn't prone to bravado or conceit, but this situation highlighted exactly how far apart the CIA and Military Intelligence were in their relationship. They were like roommates hanging panties on the doorknob whenever they were engaged in some special activity. *Fuck ups!*

Ryder continued, Sanders always on cue with the next slide. She assumed they actually rehearse this over breakfast?

"There was a seventeen-minute window in the satellite feed and we lost the guy escaping." *The gal escaping,* she corrected to herself. "Shortly after that, when we were back on line, there was what appeared to be several trucks arriving at the facility. They were actually a series of containers on flatbeds."

Sanders clicked up the appropriate slide.

"Inside the containers were a number of individuals. That in itself wasn't amazing, but when we tracked some of the container numbers, we realized the units had travelled via cargo vessel from Los Angeles, to Shanghai, and finally to Algiers, all without being unloaded. That's a sixty-day voyage, or more. These men, and possibly women, had been in the containers for that long and showed no ill effects. If such a safe habitat container has been created, well, we can just imagine the uses. They could move people and equipment long distances. We've been aware of containers stuffed with unfortunate souls in the human trafficking supply chain, but those are usually short lived voyages, and often end with a percentage of the occupant's dead. But these were fresh, vibrant, healthy individuals, as far as we could tell. They are seen embracing one another and moving directly to physical activities without any recovery period."

Sanders clicked up the next slide. *Okay*, Vargas thought, realizing there had to be something more than a Cadillac container involved here. *Where's the punch line?*

"But that's not the key point," Ryder continued. "While this piqued some interest at the analyst level, and inspired a closer look, the real discovery was that there were large canisters concealed in the end walls of some containers. Watch this."

Sanders clicked again and a series of satellite images time lapsed across the screen. One of the canisters, about the size of a fire extinguisher, was carried to an open field, and several cattle were brought into a corral. One person was brought out and tied to a post inside the corral, clearly in the same environment as the cows. He was obviously *persona non-grata* for the terrorists, and appeared to struggle as he was manipulated into place. The terrorists all put on some type of mask, though not a standard, bulky gas mask. It looked almost like the regular dust masks that populate the streets of Tokyo.

The canister was pointed at the corral and the valve was opened.

It was difficult to tell, but it appeared that it was opened for only a moment. The cattle fell like dominos almost immediately. Only three cows remained standing, though a little panicked with the on-going demise of their friends. The prisoner continued to struggle against the ropes holding him in place, but he appeared to be unaffected by the gas. The terrorists soon removed their small masks without hesitation, and began jumping about with some jubilation. It seemed to be a successful test.

Colonel Younger interceded as Ryder and Sanders tried to regain their place in the presentation process.

"This was a target-specific gas in a huge outdoor environment, with no apparent residue or random spread. It projected where pointed, and evaporated quickly after delivering its intended damage. The hostage was only a few feet away and showed no apparent harm." He paused for dramatic affect. "A devastating weapon, already equipped with a delivery method, and already proven able to evade current security protocols in America."

The room sat silent. Chemical warfare wasn't a new phenomenon, but this gas certainly had some special qualities. The fact that it was being danced around the globe without consequence was a major concern as well. Sanders clicked a couple of times. The face of Armand Creusa retuned to the screen.

"This is the man that handled the canister," Ryder continued. "We thought he might have joined the vessel in China, but the containers were buried within the deck board stack, and he could not have accessed them there. He definitely boarded in Los Angeles. Several subsequent tests were run, and the results for the poor cattle were always the same."

Ryder looked at Younger to indicate he was done, perhaps waiting for some undelivered applause, as though he had been the one to discover the new weapon being discussed. Sanders clicked one final time to bring up a blank white screen, and Colonel Younger reconnected with the media button, pushing the room back into its original form. Sunlight flooded the room, and everyone made a few adjusting blinks to re-focus.

The calm guy on the couch was looking at Vargas again. She was beginning to not like him.

"What do you think, Vargas?" the colonel asked. "What's your take on the scenario?"

Vargas stepped forward, moving closer to Ryder and Sanders, looking towards the spot where the screen had been moments earlier.

"I think the gas is lethal to cattle and not humans. Perhaps even to other forms of animal life, but somehow not to people. At least not in its' current form. I can't say how that works without having access to forensics on one of the dead animals, but I'm trying to piece together what kind of effect this could have on the world"

Ryder laughed and looked at Vargas. "A cow gas? Is that your input?" He put his hand on her shoulder. It was a mistake.

Vargas grabbed his right hand with her left and bent his wrist awkwardly in an excruciatingly painful embrace. Ryder reached out for his offended arm with his left and Vargas applied a little more pressure, bringing him to his knees.

"What the fuck," Sanders stammered as he reached out for Vargas, somehow hoping to assist his partner. She grabbed his left hand with her right and quickly applied the same agonizing grip. Sanders also went to his knees, both men now helpless and sucking deep breaths, as they pondered the future use of their wrists.

"Easy, Vargas," the colonel hummed, palms down to calm the situation.

Vargas flipped her left wrist abruptly, sending Ryder backwards onto the floor, and lifted her other hand to bring Sanders to his feet. She brought him close, manipulating him like a puppet, and looked him in the eye. She reached in without his awareness to snatch the Beretta 92 from his shoulder holster, and then turned him around in a pirouette before bringing him back to his knees and letting go. Ryder spun around and reached for his gun but froze as Vargas slipped off the safety of the Beretta with an audible click, and pointed the barrel straight at his head. Both men relaxed backwards, happy to be free from her grip and embarrassed at their predicament.

"Vargas," the colonel said, raising his voice, "they are on our side."

"Lucky us," Vargas replied. She lowered the gun, clicked on the safety, and tossed it to Sanders. He fumbled it a bit but managed to catch it. She turned and saw the still-calm gentleman reclined on the couch. "Any comments from you?" she asked in her best sarcastic tone.

He held her stare. He wasn't nervous in any discernable way.

"If you're here, with this much at stake and the highest powers pulling the strings, you must be one hell of a warrior. No comment from me." He smiled. She smiled back and let out a little huff. "As a matter of fact," he continued, "we've come to the same conclusion, but we weren't prepared to vocalize that yet." He snickered a bit and looked over at the two operatives now gathering themselves. "But I guess the cat's out of the bag now!"

Colonel Younger thanked Ryder and Sanders for their presentation, stifling his desire to laugh at their folly. "We'll take it from here," he told them. "Give my regards to Colonel Marteau when you get back to the Pentagon."

As they headed towards the door, Vargas said "Hey!" They turned. "No hard feelings guys, it was all instinct."

She reached up and started to unbutton her shirt. The two looked at each other and then back at her. The gentleman on the couch was also curious and leaned forward to see what was going to happen. She undid the top four buttons and pulled the lapels back, showing the curve of her breasts and the top of the lace bra that held them. But her lady parts were not where all eyes were focused. Her chest bore a black outline tattoo, the same one as the person escaping in the satellite images.

"It's the morning star," she said calmly. "It reminds me of my ancestors."

V argas flew home to New York in the Gulfstream G200. Colonel Younger had left it at her whim for twenty-four hours while she checked in, packed some clothes, kissed whoever she was kissing these days, got a massage, and of course, a mani-pedi from her go-to gal, Maria. She never asked why Vargas showed up with huge chunks of nail missing, or why her feet were a little torn up. *Good girl. Christ, it's tough to eliminate North African road dirt once it embeds itself under ones' nails,* Vargas reflected.

She took an inventory of her travel bag, all of which fit into the over-shoulder briefcase, that carried no papers. This was the seven-day emergency pack, as she liked to call it. Three shirts, two days each, and a third day for the least used one. Two pairs of pants, no skirt or dress needed for this trip. Three underwear and three socks, packed under the same protocol as her shirts. Two lace bras, she wore nothing else; one never knew when there would be a revelation of sorts, whether by choice, or by force. One light jacket, usually worn during travel. One sweater which could serve as a forth shirt, or a liner for the jacket if temperatures got cool. Disposable toothbrush and toothpaste -she hated when her teeth got crusty- a brush for those long golden locks, and the accompanying hairbands to keep them in order, one lucky lipstick, nail clippers, a small make-up bag which also housed her phone charger, an iPad and iPhone, sunglasses and just enough room for her favorite friend. She had a full carry permit for her concealed weapon, a 9mm SilencerCo. Maxim 9, with integrated silencer, and several fifteen-round magazines. Normally it was tucked into a belt holster on the small of her back, even though that made it a little uncomfortable for plane rides.

Although she had her own plane this time, she still had to clear security and would probably be using a commercial flight somewhere along the way. Certain countries frowned on such handguns, but Vargas had the required credentials, those elevating her slightly higher than air marshal status, with authority to carry and access her weapon in all circumstances. Sometimes, the pilot was informed about her status and asked for a short face-to-face before departure, to feel her out, so to speak. She always respected that, and recognized their ultimate responsibility for the passengers. A few times, the pilot asked her to surrender her weapon for the duration of the flight, but she never would. A couple of times, she compromised by flying in the cockpit with the captain, and on one particular flight, with the captain refusing to allow her to carry on board, she leveraged her position with the agency to get the captain changed. He was not happy, but screw him! The passengers were unaware of what was going on, and they were not happy either. The PA system claimed they were delayed due to technical issues, which was technically correct.

During her flight back to Washington, Vargas drifted off, and felt her memories returning to past operations. She loved working in the field. Unbeknownst to her at the time, everything she did in her whole life, from eleven years old on, was preparing her to be the go-to agent she was. Most people at the agency had only heard of her; this quasi-mystical lady who took on all the tough dirt. She kept a low profile and avoided any relationship that required her to reveal her actual occupation. To those who knew her socially, she was the daughter of a rich daddy, happy to wander through life on his cards and cash. That was the easy way to explain her lifestyle and frequent travel, without any questions about what her job was or how she supported herself. The 'rich daddy' was actually the agency, and the funds used to support her cover had been acquired in an operation that also affected her personally, in a negative way.

Four years earlier, she had broken up a major arms deal in Accra, between some unsavory American scum and an African dictator. The lines of investigation stretched across three continents, through the US, Russia, and West Africa. The pot of gold was seized on a vessel at the Tema Container Terminal, which she and four other agents boarded under the cover of night, climaxing their three-month operation with resounding success. Seventeen hundred fifty-three hand-held weapons, eight surface to air missiles, one hundred four hand held rocket launchers, and sixty-four crates of various rounds, all packed up with $12.7 million US in cash.

This was still a small cache though. The wars raged on, and this particular dictator would probably end up getting weapons from the US, or Russia, or China, depending on who he made future commitments to. She knew it was all rather hypocritical, but what wasn't?

Somehow, this deal was important to the government, because the Russian mafia was also involved, and there was a distinct desire to prevent the forging of any relationship between American gangsters and the Russian mobs. If Vargas and her team successfully drove this deal bad, it would put the limp on future co-operation between the international bad guys.

It was only Vargas and Tom Keller from the agency, along with three support agents from the elite ATF team, that scuttled their deal. Keller didn't make it. Vargas always carried around some guilt about that. He had no family, and no one she could comfort in an effort to alleviate her own pain, so she just carried it around like a small imaginary back pack, and called upon it whenever she needed to get angry, quick. Several agencies were involved in credit-taking after the fact, though. Vargas didn't care. She had slipped away silently.

Several days later, back on home soil and checking in online to catch up on her banking, she faced one of the few times in her life that left her surprised and speechless. Her account balance was $12,726,409.17.

"It's yours," Assistant Director Sean Malone told her. "It's our thanks for your great work, and in a way, a kind of selfish stab at keeping you wrapped up with the agency. As long as you're with us, it's yours to use."

She wasn't sure how to handle it all back then, but she got over the pandering his comments had delivered and sank into a comfortable lifestyle—whenever she wasn't in the field facing the constant threat of death or dismemberment. She never told anyone about the cash, and as far as she knew, the agency didn't either.

▶ ▶ ▶

Vargas arrived back in Washington after a short nap on board, and felt pumped and ready to rock-n-roll. She glanced at her Rolex Oyster Perpetual Lady-Datejust with an 18K gold president bracelet and cornflower blue dial. It was almost cocktail hour.

Vargas strode into the waiting area outside the assistant director's office and smiled at Beverly. Beverly had been the AD's PA before Vargas ever showed up, and they liked each other. Vargas represented a strong female image, and Beverly, who was a very attractive woman as well, appreciated her obvious status in their male-dominated world. She wasn't exactly sure what Vargas did, but she knew that she had the respect and attention of everyone there. She noticed the cuts and bruises from time to time when Vargas came by, but always kept her thoughts to herself. They bantered during those few minutes, whenever Vargas was waiting for the AD, and they had done that about six times a year for the past five years. Other than that, they never had contact.

Despite the down time in Aruba, Vargas continued to have a dull ache in her head. She wasn't sure what caused it, but it was more than exploding grenades and goofy agents.

"He'll see you now," Beverly said, following a little buzz on her phone.

She raised her eyebrows in a friendly goodbye as Vargas walked into the impressive office. A few minutes later, Beverly received the call for coffee and San Pellegrino, which she brought in swiftly. It was water for Vargas, who sat comfortably on the Tudor chair facing the door. Vargas didn't worry about drinks served by Beverly; anyway, the bottle was sealed.

The AD chatted a bit and quizzed Vargas about the little episode with Ryder and Sanders in Colonel Younger's office. She was surprised that the story made it all the way up the chain. She explained that Ryder had grabbed her shoulder and she went into self-preservation mode.

The AD laughed. "God, I wish I'd been there to see it!"

After a few minutes, the door opened and in walked her old friend, the calm gentleman from the last meeting with Colonel Younger. She realized he must have informed the AD about the episode. That made sense.

"Vargas, meet Tom Clemenson. He runs a rather special department for the White House and asked specifically to meet you."

"We met," Vargas said.

"Relax, Ms. Hamilton," Tom Clemenson said. "The meeting with Colonel Younger wasn't the time to begin our relationship."

Begin our relationship? She replayed the comment back to herself. *That's a pretty strong assumption.*

He moved forward and offered his hand. She hesitated for a moment before taking it. Vargas always shook hands like she meant it, because she did. He returned her grip with a warm and firm clutch, but void of any macho clamping like many guys did.

"Thirty-two. A striking woman, and a dangerous one to be on the wrong side of." Clemenson released her hand and walked to a table by the window. Vargas was still uncertain about this man, although she was definitely a little flattered. "You scored off the charts in every category at the farm, and have parlayed that into a significant success rate in the field." He hesitated for a minute, moving back towards her. He looked into her eyes. "I hope the extra cash I sent your way has helped."

He was certainly making it clear that he knew everything about her.

"So, you're my fairy godfather," she said, letting that realization sink in. "It's been a blast."

He smiled. "Best money I ever spent," he said. Vargas was enjoying the flattery. "I think you are the person I'm looking for, Vargas. Do you mind if I call you Vargas?"

"Not at all, Tom," she replied, in what she felt was a cool retort.

"You can call me Mr. Clemenson, or boss, if you like, but Tom remains the property of my family and friends."

"Since you're not my boss, Mr. Clemenson it is. I have no doubt you've earned that. And no, I don't mind if you call me Vargas. It's a name I'm proud of, and pleased with." *Why, Vargas, you've surely endeared him with your little butt kiss.*

"Cut the bullshit. I am your boss, from today on. You just convinced me of that."

Vargas looked at him, trying to catch some sarcasm or other sense of gamesmanship, but there was none. He looked back with complete authority, and they both knew it.

"Okay, boss, here I am." She was intrigued. She glanced at the AD, who winked and stood up.

"I've got a lunch with the director," Malone said. Vargas realized that would be John Brenmar, Director of the CIA. "I'll leave you two some space to get further acquainted." He swept some papers into an old leather satchel before heading towards the door. "Nice seeing you again, Tom. Let's catch up soon."

The two men shook hands, and Tom Clemenson put his free hand on Sean Malone's shoulder. "Thanks again for the intro, Sean. My regards to John."

Vargas looked on. *Okay, Clemenson's on a first name basis with the director of the CIA and gets favors from Malone, and shit, the AD calls him Tom. What am I getting into… and why don't I know him!*

Clemenson turned his attention back to her and used a wave of his hand to ask her to join him at the same small table by the window. She walked over with purpose, trying to project comfort and composure, despite her feelings of uncertainty. She wasn't sure why she felt intimidated by him.

Tom Clemenson started to lay it out. "Let's relax a bit and get things straight. No intimidation intended." Vargas wondered if he was somehow reading her thoughts. "And no cloak and dagger stuff. I have an important job within our country, and I am extremely cautious about who gets to see inside my walls. I've been watching you for almost three years, and following you intently for the past eighteen months." He paused to see if she would react negatively. She didn't let on. "I get daily reports on your activity and, while I haven't tapped your phone or installed cameras in your house, I do crunch every piece of data I can find. The bottom line is, I'm looking for a key field agent, someone I can trust with extremely sensitive material, under unbearable conditions, in extremely volatile situations." He pursed his lips slightly, leaving his last words to sink in.

"I have to be honest, considering a woman has stretched my sensibilities." *Here we go,* thought Vargas. "But the more I've seen of you and your character, the more I feel I've embarrassed myself for entertaining such notions." He paused again. Vargas kept an attentive poker face. "The big chunk of money was a test. You've handled it perfectly, using what you need to enjoy down time, and never letting it cover your head with self importance. You've handled every field op with precision, proven to be inventive and resilient, you're results driven, and seem to be both patriotic and impervious to some of the BHR that flies around here." He recognized that she probably was unfamiliar with the acronym. "Bureaucracy, hypocrisy, and red tape." They both smiled.

"Back to the bottom line, Vargas. I have followed eight operatives from three different organizations over the past four years, in order to find two that can help me fulfill my mandate. You're my number one choice, and I need you to agree and commit to me before you know anything about what's involved. That's a big leap of faith. It means leaving behind your current role in the CIA, and basically losing your current existence. You will relocate to Washington, and have no contact with anyone you know now, not even Sean Malone."

Vargas looked at him. He was dead serious. What was she getting into? She already knew she was going to say yes, she just didn't want to jump too quickly. She thought of a million questions but realized that they didn't matter. If they were unimportant enough that he could give her an answer, then they weren't worth asking; if they were pertinent and responsible questions, he wouldn't be able to respond.

"I'm in."

"All the way in?"

"Straight off the diving board," she replied. She thought a little humor might be appropriate, just to keep it human. "I just hope there's some water in the pool."

He smiled and stood up, handing her a card with a name and address.

"Be there tomorrow at four AM. Do whatever you're told." He also handed her a new ID card, but without a name on it. It was red, and unlike any she had seen before. "This gets you in everywhere in the United States of America, or our protectorates. Never abuse it. The magnetic strip works in unison with your right thumb print." Vargas wondered how he got her thumbprint. "Hold it accordingly when you swipe. There's a number on the back. It connects with our action office and can bring you immediate relief or support, almost anywhere in the world. Use it for weapons, accommodation, transport, cash, or anything else. You'll need it."

He tossed her a set of car keys and turned to leave.

"It's parked in the garage, spot one-seven-five. Drive carefully. By the way, the address on the car key tag is your new residence. Head there from here. You'll find additional information on your kitchen counter. Absorb it and burn it. Your old place is history; you can never go back there."

He left the room, leaving the door wide open. She sat there a little stunned. Had she just committed the foreseeable future to this man she didn't really like when they first met? Was she giving up everything that had come before? No more Sean Malone or Beverly. No more Chrissy and Mike, her next door neighbors. No more Wendy at Starbucks, or Max, who so efficiently filled her car with gas, even though it was a self-serve station. No more pedicures from Maria. Wait, that was too much. Maria was her only confidant! He must have known she was going to accept, otherwise the whole card, car, and accommodation thing would not have been laid out.

She saw Beverly peeking in, trying to look nonchalant. Vargas smiled. She stood up and walked in a bit of a daze towards the door. She slipped her hand into her pocket and pulled out a fresh fold of hundreds, probably a couple of thousand dollars, placing it on Beverly's desk as she passed.

"Get some lunch on me."

She left, realizing that she would possibly never see her again. She felt somehow strange, as if real change had just grabbed her by the scruff of her neck and was dragging her out into a new world. There were many surprises coming, she realized. For some reason, her head didn't hurt at all. That was the first time in months!

IV

Vargas strode purposefully across the parking lot floor, her footsteps echoing against the assortment of vehicles jammed into the honeycomb slots. She was looking for spot one-seven-five, which should be on the first floor, but the highest number she could find was one-six-five.

After what she felt was enough time dwelling on the situation, she decided to re-enter the building and speak to somebody who knew the multi story lot a little better. She considered that her new boss might have been wrong, but quickly discarded that notion. Tom Clemenson was never wrong, she had no doubt about that. The attendant at the front desk of the elevator lobby fielded her question as if it was the most natural thing.

"Ahhh... one-seven-five, ya, that's the seventeenth floor," he said matter-of-factly. "There are only six spots on that floor, ma'am. Guess you must be pretty important."

Vargas looked at him. *Christ, is he a mind reader too? Of course I'm important.* "Nope. Just a little old support worker here at the big company," she replied.

The attendant smiled and shrugged, pointing to the last elevator. Vargas pushed the button. No response. Then she noticed the swipe card reader to the side and used her new red card to initialize it.

Another reader waited inside the elevator, but there were no buttons to select a floor. Vargas swiped again and the door closed. She felt the sudden acceleration of the elevator as it surged downward to what she now guessed was floor seventeen—underground!

This was not the ordinary parking garage. There were only six numbered slots, but each had two, three, or even four vehicle spots. She turned the corner at one-seven-three, cutting close to the bumper of a very sexy, brand new BMW M8, and spotted her stall. One-seven-five. Two vehicles sat quietly there. One was an Audi R8, red Coupe, full carbon package, with the V10 studs clearly planted on her front fenders. Beside it was an Audi S8. Not just a regular one, but an MTM S8 Talladega, flat black, with limited chrome hardware.

She reached in for her key, wondering which door was going to pop open, and was happy to see the lights of the R8 flash. She slipped into the driver's seat and leaned back in the leather cockpit chair, which was surprisingly comfortable. The entire cockpit was, to her further surprise, very roomy. She pressed the brake and turned the ignition, bringing the car to life with a thunderous rumble. *Holy shit*, she thought, *almost like good sex*! She popped the emergency break, slid the shift sideways to put it in gear A1, and slowly inched out onto the parking garage driveway.

She followed the series of exit signs, card swipes, elevator ride and gate openings to the service road, and then followed the road east, connected with the George Washington Memorial Parkway, and headed towards Washington.

The R8 screamed along the highway effortlessly, and she lost track of the speed she was going. There was a navigation package on board but, Vargas grabbed her iPhone and read her new home address to Siri. She came through as always, and Vargas was on her way. Suddenly, there were bright flashing lights and the wheezing sound of a state trooper siren behind her. *Shit, I'm going about one-ten*, she realized. She eased off the accelerator, letting the R8 decompress automatically, and pulled onto the right shoulder.

The state trooper approached her cautiously, with his hand on his holster, even though it was still clipped shut. He hesitated before approaching her window, and she figured he was probably waiting for feedback on his license query. He suddenly stood up straight and walked a little too briskly up to the driver's window. Vargas tapped it down and tried to put on her *who-little-old-me* face. It wasn't necessary.

"Really sorry to bother you, miss. Safe travels and let me know if you need an escort."

Holy heavens, this new job is pretty hefty, she thought. "No need, officer. I'll keep it more reasonable. Thanks." And with that, she raced off the shoulder, leaving a slight skid mark across the officer's bow, and sailed back onto the expressway.

Vargas followed Siri's instructions as she offered them in her usual sexy monotone. She knew she would have to change her for a male voice at some point. *Okay, Key Bridge, right on M Street, right again on Wisconsin Ave., and finally left on South St. Thirty-one-fifty. A pretty fancy address for a secret agent.* She pulled up to the parking entrance and was greeted by an elderly security guard, with a small patch over his left eye.

"Good evening, Ms. Hamilton."

"Good evening to you," she replied, somehow not surprised that he knew who she was.

"I have an envelope for you." He went back into his guard cabin to retrieve the brown sealed envelope. "Just follow the left side up to spots 87 through 90, they're yours." *Four spots,* she thought. *That should suffice for my two cars.*

Vargas parked in spot 88, leaving plenty of room on both sides of the R8. No sense having a neighbor accidently bump doors with her new baby. She opened the envelope. Inside were keys, lots of them. She identified a spare key for the R8, two for the S8, two that appeared to be for her mailbox, one that was not immediately ascertainable, possibly for a locker or something, and two sets with FOBs attached, obviously for her apartment. PH4, they said. *Nice, a penthouse.* There was also a sheet of paper with a hand-written note:

Good evening Vargas,

Enclosed are the keys to your residence; I hope the place meets your needs. There is further information on your kitchen island. Please review it and destroy it at your earliest convenience. Don't forget your appointment in the morning. Please be on time.

The cleaning lady, Emma, arrives every Tuesday and Friday promptly at nine. She has a key so you do not have to worry about accommodating her. If there is anything you need, you can ask her—I repeat, anything. She will shop as well. The kitchen is fully stocked, however, and I don't believe there will be anything needed immediately.

Enjoy the status, transportation, and accommodation upgrades. You will earn them. I'll see you in my office at ten AM.

Sincerely,
Mr. Clemenson

He did have a sense of humor after all, and very fancy handwriting. *A lot of practice to get that,* she thought. *And where the hell is his office?*

Vargas open the double door entrance. "Hello Mr. Grand Piano," she said as she entered the foyer. It was a spectacular residence. She toured slowly, floating a bit as she sank quietly into this lap of luxury. She counted three bathrooms on the main floor before even thinking about ascending the winding staircase. The kitchen area was huge, with side by side Wolf gas ranges and the accompanying Sub Zero built-ins.

She popped open the wine cooler and pulled out the first bottle she touched. A Chateau Boswell Russian River Valley Chardonnay from California. Clean, crisp, and perfectly chilled, it was an ideal match for her current euphoria. Following her tour, she reclined on the long living room sofa and nearly faded to dreamland. It had been an immensely long day.

Just as she felt the call of slumber beckoning in a soft whisper, she remembered that there was additional info for her on the kitchen counter. She jumped back into focus and raised her weary body. There were two envelopes. She opened the smaller, bulky one first. Inside were several pieces of identification: A District of Columbia driver's license, complete with the new address; a United States passport, also updated; membership cards for the prestigious Metropolitan Club and Equinox Sports Club; a medical insurance card; an American Express Centurion card; and a book of vouchers for Wiseguy Pizza. She wasn't sure about the last item, but figured it would all be revealed at some point.

She parked envelope one and carefully opened the second one. It contained another note, but this time a printed message:

Memorize the following information and destroy this message.

EMERGENCY NUMBER 301-555-2222
REAL EMERGENCY NUMBER 301-555-2223
EXTRACTION NUMBER 301-555-2224
SAFE HOUSE: 3650 DENT PLACE NW
PASSCODE: THE GREAT EIGHT
YOUR CODE NAME: COLESTAH

Vargas grabbed her iPhone and Googled 'Colestah.' She skipped past Wikipedia automatically, as it now saturated every web search entered, half the time with false or clouded information. She went to the second entry: 'Colestah, Yakama warrior woman, well known as a medicine woman as well.' *That will work,* she thought. *Keeps some focus on the native side of my ancestry.*

She rolled the sheet with the printed message into a long straw and dipped the end into the flame being coaxed from the Monogram Wolf range. It caught instantly and she bent it gradually until the soft orange heat had consumed the paper, and then dropped it into the sink. Done. She reflected on the note once again. *A hockey player passcode, a native code name, and a safe house. Why not? And numbers for emergency and real emergency, whatever that meant, and an extraction number. When an extraction is needed, a phone is not always sitting close by.* She laughed to herself. All in all, a pretty sweet transition. She would have to let it all sink in later. Right now, she needed some sleep.

Vargas strolled through the house again and easily located the master suite. It was larger than necessary, with various furniture not usually found in one's bedroom, like a sofa set with a corresponding television, a desk with a computer, and various printers and add-ons. Beyond the bedroom and sitting area was a passage leading into a closet filled with clothing, a huge wardrobe dressing area with a make-up table, fully stocked, a shower room like a rain forest, and private compartments for all other bathroom activity. *This will do,* she thought. She nodded in approval, threw a quick glance around the room to ensure no obvious Clemenson cameras, and added a small skip to her step as she went back towards the bed. She reached out to touch the various clothing as she passed. *I wonder who picks out this stuff. Better not be Clemenson!*

Vargas took everything off except her panties, set her iPhone alarm for 02:30, and crawled between the sheets. The bed was large enough for four, but she wondered if she would ever have even two in it. She missed the occasional cozy night with a warm lover. As she drifted to sleep, she had one final thought. She was pretty close to the Baked & Wired Café, and she had heard so much about Rita's Creamed Coffee Cake.

As Vargas slid into a deeper sleep, her new direction in life delivering both trepidation and anticipation, her mind skipped backwards. She remembered fragments of her past, some of them best forgotten.

Hers had been a reckless childhood, full of events and occurrences no child deserved. She had buried most of it. She often wondered how much the CIA really knew about her past, or what Clemenson knew. She had only told her story once, and that was at a time of great sorrow, and to a young lady who had no idea what was coming.

It was shortly after the arms deal mission in Accra; shortly after Tom Keller died and ingrained himself in her mounting guilt; and shortly after she had a bundle of dollars dropped into her bank account. She had decided to get a mani-pedi. It always seemed to bring her spirits up. For some reason, on that day, Vargas had an unrelenting need to tell her story. It was almost like she had to tell it to confirm to herself that it was real. Things had become so blurred. The past was a series of episodes, a selection of half truths and perceptions. She somehow knew that articulating it would help her deal with it.

"Hey, what's up Maria?" Vargas had said cheerfully as she walked into the salon, slightly ahead of her 2:30 appointment.

Everyone knew her there, perhaps because she always seemed a little audacious, or maybe because she was a stunning female. More than likely, it was just because she was a huge tipper. Most of the folks working in the salon were gay. They were a particular cluster of gentlemen who found some joy in life by taking care of ladies, creating beauty where possible. And of course, the ladies loved it. There's something unassuming about having a man touch your hair for reasons other than personal arousal. It also helped that these dudes were quite simply the best hairdressers around.

Maria, on the other hand, was Vargas' favorite because she accepted the unruly condition of her fingers and toes without comment; other than the occasional, 'Holy shit'! Vargas always had a good laugh with Maria. She was someone completely distant from her dynamic life, yet somehow privy to her inner world.

Sure, Maria knew there was something out of the ordinary with Vargas, but she never tried to extract more than was offered. Vargas liked that. It actually allowed her to be more open with Maria, more than anyone else in her loose circle of acquaintances. Her cocktail buddies in New York were always kept at a slight distance. Vargas always avoided detailed conversation about her past. Even with the occasional lover, conversations were concentrated away from her.

When they first met, Maria had offered Vargas a glass of chilled white wine, before there was even a discussion of what she was looking for. Hell, she could have been selling lipstick! Maria didn't care; she had walked through the door, a new face in the world, and nothing said 'Hello' better than a glass of wine, even though it was still morning at the time.

Initial treatments were a little routine. Vargas was guarded in her comments, and Maria reticent to pry. Quite symbiotic. In retrospect, Vargas realized that it had been herself who first broke the barrier between social chit chat and professional information, not Maria. Vargas was so isolated, so deep in her cover facade, that she was longing for a face, a person, with whom she could be unguarded, and completely honest. She was definitely getting comfortable with Maria.

The fourth or fifth time Vargas slipped in for a mani-pedi, she realized she was spewing out details and dissertations that were beyond her normal protocol. Maria always listened closely, completely unsure whether to believe the winding tales, but eventually unable to find any reason not to. Vargas was larger than life.

Vargas was feeling particularity isolated that day. The episode with Tom Keller was still raw, and she needed someone to share with; some way to release some of the anxiety she was harboring. Maria moved from slightly obscure acquaintance to obvious choice, pretty quickly. She had already heard fragments of Vargas' adventures, and was surely void of contact with the various agencies, and off the radar as far as the CIA was concerned. Plus, she was genuinely pleasant, forthright, and intelligent.

That morning, Vargas was exhausted by the final mission wrap up and trying to ignore the raised eyebrows stretching Maria's face as she began work on the slightly tangled mess of her toenails. She suggested to Maria that they get a drink together, outside the salon.

Maria looked up her with a quizzical expression and nodded. "Sounds good," she said. "Maybe you can explain these damaged nails." It was slightly sarcastic, and brought a smile to both ladies' lips.

Maria had one more customer, so Vargas waited, chatting in an endless banter with the hairdressers, always with a hint of sexual innuendo bouncing around the room. The ladies in their chairs, hair wet, foil and fragrance amid the chopping of scissors, were equally amused with the repartee.

Maria finished up, slipped into her street clothes quickly, and headed to the front.

"Let's roll," she said, pushing the glass door open ahead of Vargas.

"Ciao, boys," Vargas winked. She followed Maria out the door, the accompanying goodbyes from them fading into the past.

"Where we heading?" Maria asked as they slid into Vargas' Impala rental.

"I've got just the spot," Vargas replied. She reminded herself that not everyone liked scotch. "Do you like scotch?" she asked.

"I love it." Maria smiled back. "Especially Glenfiddich."

A little bit of a common and slightly bland single malt, Vargas reflected, but certainly a popular one.

"And where did that particular taste emanate from?" Vargas asked, keeping the conversation flowing.

"My dad always drank it," she replied without hesitation. "He always had a straight Glen when he got home."

"Your past tense leads me to assume he is no longer with us," Vargas said.

"Unfortunately, not," Maria said, without any obvious sorrow. "He died some time ago."

"How old are you?" Vargas asked. She was suddenly worried that maybe Maria was younger than she thought.

"Thirty-four," she replied. "How about you?"

"Ya, I'm early thirties too," Vargas replied, knowing Maria would appreciate her choice of 'early' rather than 'mid'.

They pulled into the Jack Rose Dining Saloon, which was, at the time, her new go-to spot in Washington. They slipped downstairs and grabbed a booth. Glenfiddich Fifteen for Maria and Lagavulin for Vargas. The Lagavulin was a little pricey, but the occasion called for it, and Vargas was still wallowing in her new-found wealth. Doubles. Vargas had already decided she was going to divulge the truth to Maria, to drop off her story and some of the unbelievable episodes it contained. Maria had no idea what was coming. She thought they were out for a little lady-like chit chat.

"I work for the CIA," Vargas said, without drama or emphasis.

Maria laughed, just a bit. She looked up at Vargas, who did not smile. Maria realized she was serious.

"Like, the government CIA?" she asked, stating the obvious.

"Exactly like that," Vargas replied, still without any change in expression.

"Cool. Are you doing surveillance of something?"

"Nope. I'm a field agent." Vargas kept up the matter-of-fact tone.

Realizing this was not just a bit of beauty salon humor, and reassured by the look on Vargas' face, Maria let her mouth drop open a bit, suddenly putting together all the 'wilderness' effect that seemed to haunt Vargas' toes.

Vargas unloaded. Ten years of secret rendezvous, hidden agendas and fabricated history was mounting on her. Tom's death was tugging at her constantly, and she just needed to share her reality with someone. She didn't want to be like Tom; a hero's death and no one there to mourn. No one to even shed a tear. She needed a human connection. It was essential to her sanity.

Maria seemed like the perfect sounding board. Her lifestyle was rather tepid, with the occasional fling, but little else of note apart from the birth of her niece, who was significantly celebrated, as she was the first of the 'next' generation.

"Maria," Vargas began, feeling comfortable about her decision to unload, "I am someone completely different than what I have always said."

Maria looked at her. She didn't look surprised. "No kidding."

Vargas laughed. There was no way that Vargas' condition would reflect a young lady living the business life in New York.

"Like I said, I work for the government."

"I sort of guessed that, or something dramatic like that. I mean, who else comes into Washington a dozen times a year? I never thought it was to get a manicure. I mean, I never thought you were an agent or something like that, but I always figured you were a government type."

They both chuckled.

"I'm not sure why I'm telling you my tale, young lady, but somehow I feel I can trust you."

"You can," Maria replied. Vargas recognized it as completely honest and sincere. "Lawyers, bartenders, pedicurists. Completely trustworthy, and not in that order," Maria continued. "The things my clients tell me would make your eyes water, but I never share that. It's part of my job to have big ears and a little mouth."

Vargas thought about it for a moment. Her brain working at the excessive speed it does.

"When I was ten, my father killed my mother," she began. Maria looked up, recognizing that this was indeed a revelation of sorts. No doubt, Vargas wasn't what she seemed. "He was a son of a bitch. He hit her, he hit me, he hit the dog. Nice enough when normal, but bourbon always brought out the worst in him—and bourbon was his best friend."

That rested heavy on the table for a minute. Maria looked on, expressionless. Vargas was encouraged by her lack of pandering, or artificial sympathy. Vargas wasn't the only one with a tough childhood. Maria asks no questions, she sensed that Vargas would reveal what she wanted to, when she wanted to.

"So, I killed him."

Maria wasn't ready for that. "Jesus...," she finally said, letting the word come out as part of her exhale.

"He had this gun. When he got really drunk he'd wave it around, threatening us, especially me. Ranting about what a little burden I was, and how I ruined their wonderful life together. You know, usual shit."

Actually, Maria had no idea.

Vargas continued. "Anyway, my mother always jumped in to protect me. She used to tell him I was the only good thing he ever gave her. I always liked to hear that. So, on this particular night, with the gun waving and the threats coming, he hit me across the face. I was screaming, my mother was screaming, the dog was barking; it was a mad house. She lunged at him. He hit her with that gun, sent her sideways into the counter, and her head cracked against it. I still remember that sound."

Maria could only stare. Vargas had a distant look, like she was reliving it, transported back to the moment.

"So, what happened?"

Vargas looked at her, refocusing. "She died."

"Christ. That's terrible. That's crazy. What happened to you, did he attack you again?"

"No," she said, relaxing back into her booth. "He collapsed beside her, holding her and telling her to get up. I think he realized she was dead, but couldn't really connect with the possibility."

"Wow, that's really crazy. What did you do?"

"I picked up that gun, pointed it at his head, and shot him; three times."

Vargas said it in such a distant and reflective manner, that Maria wasn't sure if she meant literally or figuratively.

"For real?"

"For very real," she said. "I also spat on his body later on. It was lying quietly in the casket, some of his bar buddies milling about, my mother in another room in the same god-damn place. Only the Stark County Juvenile Prosecutor's Office could figure that out. I slid up to the casket and kneeled, pretending to give a shit. I saw one of the exit wounds on the side of his head, so carefully camouflaged, and then I spat on him. I don't know if anyone saw me, but I felt so much better after that. I told my mother about it when I went over to her casket. I swear she smiled. I turned eleven a couple of weeks later."

Vargas paused. She had spewed out that entire portion of her life in what amounted to one big sentence. Maybe that was because the events were not what was tangling Vargas up. They were details of the past, but long ago accepted. Her current dilemma was part of something else. Maria showed nothing but a raised eyebrow.

"I was a ward of the state, no relatives, no caregivers. They sent me to a reform house for five years. Three bedrooms in that house, and always between seven and nine young ladies, all under sixteen."

Vargas glanced at Maria. She was fully captivated by the story, a sympathetic edge to her expression, still waiting for the tale to unfold.

"It wasn't too bad. It was a make-or-break type place. Either end up a really bad criminal, or seize the opportunity to reform and make something of yourself. Both types ran through there. I used it all; the anger, remorse, shock, even self pity I guess, and I channeled everything into becoming someone nobody would be able to take advantage of." She hesitated. "I mean, there were lots of roadblocks to that, but I tried to turn every obstacle into a challenge that would help me grow stronger, even when there was some older brother offering to help me shower. Fuckers!"

Maria recognized that this was getting much more than just personal. She liked Vargas, she liked her a lot, but she wasn't sure if she was ready to be her sounding board.

Vargas sensed her trepidation. "Hey Maria, sorry I'm venting. I've just never articulated it so clearly before. A shitty past, I guess, but everyone's got their own issues."

Maria relaxed, more comfortable that Vargas wasn't going to fall off the emotional edge. She had never seen her even remotely vulnerable, but she recognized that this was more than a mere chat.

"Listen Vargas, I don't know how much you want to tell me, but I can promise you that whatever you reveal will be kept only in my heart."

Vargas smiled. So personal, yet so sincere.

"It's just time I unloaded a bit," Vargas said. She looked at Maria.

Maria reached cross the table and took her hand, squeezing her fingers. "Rock and roll," she said, smiling slightly.

VI

T he alarm whirred softly at 02:30, and that was enough to bring Vargas back to the real world. She slid her finger across the iPhone, returning the room to silence. She reflected on her dream, her recollection of the conversation with Maria. It was funny, she thought, how the conversation was more vivid than the events surrounding her parents. Maybe she was blocking those memories out a little harder. *Whatever*.

She headed for the shower, then threw on minimal make-up and grabbed flats, slacks and a blouse from the vast wardrobe. She finally slipped on a jacket, with definite plans to go through the clothing in more detail later. She pushed her cards and cash into her pockets, completely unorganized, and took the keys for both house and vehicle from the pile on the counter. Breakfast was a granola bar and a bottle of orange juice, which she shook to life as she headed for the elevator.

"Good morning, young lady." An elderly man smiled to her as he stepped off the arriving elevator.

"Hey, hey," Vargas responded, smiling in turn. She wondered why such an elderly gentleman was just arriving—it was after three AM!

He breezed past her, a distinct bounce in his step, and approached the door next to hers.

Vargas climbed onto the elevator and hit RC. She pulled the card that Clemenson had given her from her pocket. It showed only the name 'Abigail', with an address in Brookmont, Maryland. It was an easy run, straight up Canal Road and then MacArthur Blvd. With no traffic so early, she was soon flying along, and arrived a little early. The R8 certainly didn't allow for a stealthy entrance.

Vargas walked up to the nondescript building, with a plain metal door, and looked for a bell. There was none. She knocked and waited. No response. She knocked again, louder, and still no response. Finally, she pounded on the door with a little force and stepped back, anticipating its' opening, with the possibility of an angry occupant.

"You're early," said a soft voice from above.

Vargas moved back further and glanced up. She saw a small face, surrounded by a large bush of fuzzy red hair, and a twinge of sarcasm, staring back.

"I'll be down in a sec to open up, just need a sweater." She didn't wait for a response. Vargas could hear her huff under her breath as she walked away. "What is Clemenson doing to me?"

A few moments later, the door swung open and Vargas was greeted with a broad smile, too big for the rather tiny face, and an invitation to enter. Abigail clutched her sweater closed with her left hand, and extended her right.

"I'm Abigail, Miss Hamilton, welcome to the Den."

Vargas took the offered hand with her usual firm but distinctly non-aggressive grip. "Hello, Abigail. Nice to say hi at such an early hour."

"Clemenson loves setting these things up early. I guess he thinks it is somehow more dramatic or something. Probably has you heading over to his place around ten or so, instead of setting us up at eight and him at two. What's the big deal?" Abigail blurted it all out in a single breath and Vargas smiled at the observation. She had the feeling she was going to like Abigail.

The redhead led her through a softly lit office and down a narrow corridor past several closed doors. Vargas figured her living quarters must be upstairs. At the end, on the left, she stooped to use a key that was hanging around her neck, and opened another steel door. She stepped inside and snapped on a row of switches, which woke up the flickering fluorescent lights. Both ladies squinted a bit as the harsh light came to full brightness.

"You first arrived at the Den, and this is the Dungeon," Abigail said casually. She strode purposefully across the room to a small rack of computers, flicking a power button there as well.

Vargas sensed the door swing closed behind her, and took a couple of steps sideways so she could scan the room. Abigail was punching some kind of communication into her electronic friend at the back of the room. It was a large room, perhaps twenty by forty feet, and contained several long tables, a series of cabinets along one wall, and a large window against the left side. Vargas could not see through the window, as it was black on the other side, and the reflection of the Dungeon lights created a mirror effect. She moved further into the room.

"Grab a spot over there," Abigail said. She pointed without lifting her head from the screen, towards a steel bench table with a few chairs surrounding it.

Vargas walked around the table and sat down on the other side, where she could keep Abigail in full view. Suddenly two cabinets opened automatically, obviously remote controlled. Vargas jolted up and spun to face them.

"Easy Colestah," Abigail whispered. "It's all safe in here. This is a sanctuary of sorts. Safest room in America that doesn't involve the presidential seal."

She chuckled at her own remark and returned to her computer for a moment. She picked up a small stack of documents from the open cabinet, and walked over to the table where Vargas was still standing. A printer whirred into action and she sat down. She plopped the documents on the desk.

"Sit," she said. "Please."

Vargas relaxed and sat down. Abigail had used her code name, so that obviously meant she was senior enough. It was no accident that she had done so. She had also referred to Clemenson without the Mr. in front, so that indicated she was either friendly with him—which seemed unlikely, as he appeared a difficult person to be friends with—or she had worked with him long enough to know she was entrenched and valued.

"Here's your first assignment," Abigail said nonchalantly. She slid a two-inch-thick folder across the table.

She raised a hand held remote and clicked twice. A large screen lit up just behind Vargas, and she spun to watch it before having the opportunity to open the file. A rather handsome face popped onto the screen, which Vargas recognized immediately.

"Armand Creusa," she said, noticing Abigail raise her eyebrows in surprise. Vargas continued, realizing Abigail had full clearance. "I got the scoop on him yesterday in Langley, from two guys with MI."

"Ryder and Sanders," she asked? Vargas nodded. "Assholes," Abigail said, then added an apology for her choice of words. "It amazes me how these guys got to where they are. I guess it justifies the need for our unit!"

Vargas thought about that. *Our unit.* She wasn't sure yet what it was, but said nothing.

"Look, I know it's all new and a little bit cloak-and-dagger right now, but you'll catch on soon enough. Here's the intro lecture. I've given it before and sadly, I'll probably give it again. That usually means someone's been lost out there. It's no fun."

Vargas noticed Abigail's change in expression to one of genuine sorrow, but she quickly recovered. It was obvious that she had suffered some loss, either personal or operational. Either way, Vargas decided to leave the matter in the drawer—for now.

"We are referred to as PT1, or Presidential Team One. Very few people even know of our existence, let alone our mandate. We cover any issue that crosses the president's desk, from any agency, foreign or domestic. Anything that either gets mucked up by other agencies and leaves the president in panic mode, or when some issue garnishes his utmost concern, he can redirect it to us. But only he can do so. When a new president is sworn in, after the standard intros and affairs, he gets a sit down with Mr. Clemenson, the head of the CIA, the head of the NSA, and the head of the FBI." Now she used the Mr. when mentioning the boss. "These are the only five people that are supposed to know about PT1, plus any past presidents, or past directors of course. The sitting president is briefed on any ongoing assignments, and fully informed on what he can expect from us. Any questions?"

"A thousand," Vargas replied. "But you go on for now, whatever you're authorized to tell me." She smiled.

"I'm pretty authorized." Abigail returned the smile. "It's not a big organization. You, me, one other operative, and Clemenson. That's it. "Of course, I don't know if there is another PT1, or PT2. As far as I know, we are it. You can imagine that we get the crazy stuff, and the really important stuff, which also usually means the really dangerous stuff."

Vargas raised her brow a bit, but she had expected nothing else. She tingled with the idea of dangerous missions. That was her high, her addiction. She was cautious of course, and rigorously trained to go along with her natural abilities, but it was her instinct and fearlessness that made her what she was—the best agent in the world. At least that was her humble feeling.

"Clemenson says you're probably the best agent in the world." Vargas mentally thanked her new boss. "And I've gathered your entire file from everywhere you've ever been, any place you've ever touched." Vargas looked up with a little surprise. "It's my job," Abigail continued. "I am an information cauldron, but I'm also your confidant, Ms. Hamilton."

"Whoa," Vargas said. "I do appreciate that, Abigail, but that Ms. Hamilton stuff will have to go. I've got this premonition that you and I are going to have plenty of communication, so Vargas works, or even 'V', and there are only a few people in the world that have ever called me that."

"Okay, Vargas, thanks for that. Maybe 'V' will come later. Guess I'm just moving forward at a cautious and unassuming pace until we are fully acquainted. And we will be."

Vargas smiled. She wondered if this lady really knew *everything* about her, about her past.

"I am your liaison, your eyes and ears when you're in the field, your contact point at home, your assignment provider, your guide, your friend—whatever is needed." *Clemenson's right hand,* Vargas thought.

"But, I'm not Clemenson's spy, I'm just his right hand," she continued. *Good call, Vargas.* "I work for you. He uses me as a conduit to the agents, but does not interfere too much once the assignment is in motion. By the way, we refer to them as PAT's, like a person's name. I think it originally came from 'Presidentially Activated Task' or something like that. Anyway, I will activate you when a new PAT comes in."

"Who decides on who gets what PAT?" Vargas asked.

"Clemenson, I guess. I don't get that info. Maybe the president himself." Vargas nodded. "PT1 is not like other agencies, and I know, I used to work for several. By the way, I was also recruited by Clemenson. Fourteen years ago."

"Christ, how old are you?" Vargas asked. "I mean, you look like you're about thirty, max."

Abigail laughed. "Everyone's a little confused by my appearance. I'm actually forty-four."

"That's crazy. Good for you, you look great. I guess you'll have to reveal some of those aging secrets one day." Vargas threw the compliment with an easy grace, and Abigail appreciated it. It added to the nice little start they were sharing.

"PT1 was formed in the sixties, in the thick of the Cold War, long before any of us were involved. I think it was a temporary organization originally, but it's more active than ever right now. I don't know if that's because there is so much BS happening with terrorists, or whether it's just a reflection on the inadequacies of our other various agencies. It was always run under the auspices of the CIA until about four years ago. That's when it became independent and began answering directly to the president, through Clemenson. Anyway, I'm sure you'll get some old stories from Clemenson along the way; he's been around for about twenty-five years. He used to be a special advisor with the CIA, but now he's independent."

Vargas wanted to believe it was terrorists driving the need for PT1, but realized it was probably the internal bickering, secrecy, and ineffectiveness of the disjointed agencies tasked with protecting the free world, so to speak. A gentle reminder of the institutions that spawned Ryder and Sanders!

"So where are all the other PT1 agents Abby?" Vargas asked.

Abigail looked at her. Vargas wondered if she was going to skirt the issue, or be straightforward.

"Originally, PT1 was a CIA sub-group, and agents were selected on a case by case basis. As the PAT's became more classified, certain agents were permanently assigned to the team. There have been eleven specific PT1 agents before you. Five have retired and moved on the other roles in life. Unfortunately, five have been lost in the field as well."

Vargas noticed her heightened emotions as she revealed that info.

"That's ten," Vargas said.

Abigail popped up her drooping head and looked straight into Vargas' eyes. "One remains unaccounted for," she said.

Vargas tilted her head, and raised an eyebrow, in an unmistakable request for more detail.

"He disappeared in the jungles of Colombia some four years ago. Despite extensive searches, intel gathering, and strong-hand tactics by local authorities, his whereabouts remained undetermined. He is assumed dead, but his body was never recovered. That left him in MIA status," she explained. It was Abigail's turn to provide a raised eyebrow.

Vargas took that to mean, 'I've been straight with you, but don't ask for further details'. She decided to let it rest.

"Well, thanks for the honesty," Vargas closed that conversation.

Abigail moved on with her planned intro, without skipping a beat. "You get all the perks that go with the importance of the job; no one wants you stressed over non-operative issues. The lifestyle is a great cover for you too. I mean, what endowment fund baby would want to be an agent?"

Vargas wondered if that was how the rest of the world saw her now. An endowment fund baby?

"Okay, enough on the intro, we'll get to know each other really well, really fast, once you hit the ground with this PAT. Before that, we have to take a look at this Creusa dude, and then I have a few things to give you."

Abigail went through the Creusa file, and it was similar to what Vargas received back at CIA HQ, with one key addition: Creusa was located in China, and was in the middle of preparing a shipment, probably cattle gas, as it was being called. Vargas would be heading there tomorrow.

Following the full briefing, Abigail smiled. "Now for the good stuff, and don't ask me who comes up with this crap. I only know it's been a lifesaver before, so pay attention."

She promptly ran through a list of accoutrements that Vargas would have access to. These were special weapons, some tested in the gun range behind that mirrored window to her left. That clarified that little mystery for Vargas. The list included miniature communication devices and various other operational enhancements. She felt like a kid in a candy store. Vargas reviewed the assorted weaponry and recognized that they were all meant to support her activities. She picked up a mini KAHR P380 Pistol – about as big as a half-pound cigarette lighter, thinking it would be a good support weapon.

Abigail also pointed out the mini plastique patches, wrapped in gum foil. She explained that there was a ten-foot blast radius, so it was definitely not a stealth weapon. Vargas had only to gently fold the green portion into the white portion and throw it. The blast was on impact.

They continued their briefing for a while, but soon realized it was after nine. They had been at it for the past five hours, and it was time to get on the road for her meeting with Mr. Clemenson. Abigail filled her in on the exact location of his office, and reminded her that her red card would allow her access. As Vargas departed, Abigail handed her an earpiece, with an integrated transmitter. She explained that it ran through cellular lines anywhere in the world, and Vargas could stay on line with her throughout her operations. Vargas could access information instantly, provide feedback in real time, and channel communication to other points through Abigail. Vargas tucked it into her pocket.

With many thanks, and a mutual appreciation for their professionalism, Vargas was off. She accelerated the R8 out onto MacArthur Blvd, back-tracked to Chain Bridge, and drove across the Potomac to get to her next meeting.

Abigail watched her go. She knew Vargas would do okay. It was her sixth sense about people. She returned to the Dungeon to clean up and prep for the other new operative on PT1, Brendan Dunkirk. He was due around noon.

VII

A s Vargas neared Chain Bridge, her phone rang. Her ring tone, Bob Dylan's 'The Groom Still Waiting at The Alter,' came to life. She answered through the car's panel. Clemenson's voice came over the speaker.

"You enroute, Vargas," he said in a monotone, without a hint of question to it, almost as though it was a statement of fact.

"Yup, fifteen minutes out."

"Change of plan," he waited for a response, she waited for him to continue. "Re-direct to the White House. Straight to the situation room." Then he was gone.

Ahhh, okay, Vargas thought as the R8 screen flashed, 'call ended'. *I guess I'll just walk into the White House and have the Secret Service escort me to a little morning brunch with the president. Perfect.* As she reflected on the situation, she thought about the red access card Clemenson had given her. 'This gets you in everywhere in the United States of America, or our protectorates. Never abuse it,' he had said. She was going to find out exactly what weight it carried. Did everywhere, mean *everywhere*?

She stayed on MacArthur, went down Canal to Whitehurst Freeway, and over to K St. With a quick turn on 17th to Pennsylvania Ave., she was there—eleven minutes after the call with Clemenson.

Vargas approached the front gate and waited for the staff to meet her vehicle. Two guards immediately approached either side of her car, with mirrors to view the undercarriage. She realized she still had her Maxim 9 pistol.

"Good day, Ma'am," the young man said without further explanation. Vargas handed him her red card and he immediately stepped back, coming to attention.

"It's good, guys," he barked at the others. He pointed to a separate driveway, just to the right of the main road. He handed back the card. "You can use that at the gate over there, ma'am."

Vargas smiled a little at his discomfort, but not enough to embarrass him. *Damn, this card is good,* she thought.

"Thank you, young man," she replied, coy and cute. She realized she was a lovely sight for young men, and pushed her shift to the right twice to engage reverse.

She backed up, then swung the car over to the indicated gate, watching the soldiers behind her staring in a little wonderment. She pulled up, held the card with her thumb over the biometric scanner, and swiped. She wished it worked with her left thumb too, it wasn't easy to reach across her body and up through the R8 window. The gate swung open and she sped up the driveway, a little faster than necessary.

Two rather burly men, Secret Service obviously, were waiting. She always wondered why they use the word 'secret' when it was so obvious who they were. One of them pointed to what was an obvious parking spot, and she pulled in, again a little faster than necessary, breaking sharply and giving a final rev of the 525 HP engine before shifting to gear A1, engaging the parking brake, and shutting her down.

"Welcome to the White House, Ms. Hamilton," he said. His hands were clasped behind his back, making it obvious that there would be no handshake.

He did not frisk her, and she left the Maxim 9 safely tucked into the holster behind her back, just beside the hidden pocket concealed within her belt, containing a sharp Exacto blade and a lock-pick pin. Essential tools for the poor captured counter-espionage agent. She was surprised she was able to enter the White House while armed.

"Let's go," she replied, hoping to come off as equally inhuman as him.

He turned and went fast paced up the stairs and in through the double doors. Agent two followed her at a safe distance. They marched down several corridors and turns, before the agent stopped in front of a large door. He knocked twice and opened it before receiving a response. Vargas walked in. The situation room. *Christ, this is good shit.*

Thirteen seats surrounding a large polished wood table with a gold ribbon edge. Six chairs sat on either side with one more at the head of the table. Only five of the thirteen were occupied. Vargas kicked her nervousness into the bottom of her left boot and strode forward. She recognized three of the people: The CIA director, the president, sitting at the head of the table, and Clemenson at his right.

Vargas stood there awkwardly, unsure of her next move, when Clemenson rose and began walking towards her.

"Gentlemen, Vargas Hamilton." He held out his hand as if proudly displaying Nefertiti's tomb to the prying eyes of a group of Egyptologists. Vargas didn't like it. *Perhaps I should curtsy,* she thought, but she didn't. She smiled without opening her mouth and remained in her position.

The president stood, seemingly discerning her discomfort, and spoke over Clemenson's approach.

"Welcome, Ms. Vargas. Tom, let's skip the full routine and get her parked somewhere." She immediately liked the president.

"Yes sir," Clemenson replied. "C'mon Vargas, grab a seat here."

He pulled out a chair on the same side as him, second from the last. She slid into it with a nod, indicating her appreciation for the offer, and sat upright, surveying the table. Three men sat across from her, one with five stars on his epaulettes and several pounds of ribbons and medals clinging to his left breast. She congratulated herself for discerning that he must be the general. The two others were in dark suits, funeral attire for sure. She glanced over at the president, who was wearing a white starched shirt, open at the collar, and a charcoal blazer. *Smart look,* she thought.

"Ms. Hamilton," the president began.

"Vargas works," she replied, suddenly realizing that she had both interrupted the head of her nation, and interjected a casual mode that was not yet called for. *Yikes! Fucked that up.* She cringed inwardly, all eyes now gaining some lightning bolts.

"Okay, Vargas," he replied without missing a beat. "Call me James."

"Thank you, Mr. President," she answered. *Shit, I'm striking out here.*

"Vargas, you're here because Tom has put a lot of faith in you." *You mean Mr. Clemenson,* she corrected him with a little inward sarcasm. "We're going to run through a few things, and then get some dialogue going on this situation." He gestured towards the opposite side on the table. "General Danforth, Chairman of the Joint Chiefs of Staff." Danforth nodded slightly. "John Brenmar, Director of the Central Intelligence Agency."

He stared at her with no emotion. "Nice to see you again, Vargas," he said. She wondered if he was pissed because she doesn't work for him anymore. He probably took credit for 'producing' her. Anyway, with that cold stare, she wouldn't play poker with him late at night.

The president continued. "And General Alexander O'Keefe, Director of the National Security Agency." Surprisingly, he was not in uniform.

"Good day, gentlemen," she said in her most official voice. It empowered her to know she could take any of them out, before they even put down their coffee cups.

Clemenson, who had re-seated himself during the introductions, stood again.

"Vargas, these gentlemen have received the same briefing you did from MI." He paused. "And I guess you got the updates this morning."

Vargas looked straight at him and nodded. "Yup."

"General O'Keefe has just delivered some additional news, and it's put a lot of pressure on us to get some real response going." He stopped talking, without re-introducing the NSA director.

The general clicked a remote and a picture came on the screen. It was a killing field of cattle, hundreds of them laying dead on the green pastures that were supposed to feed them.

"That gas wiped out four thousand head of cattle in a few minutes," the general said. "With only a few hundred survivors, and not a single other causality anywhere else, not even a bird. Christ, even the squirrels walked through the mist with impunity."

"Where was this?" Vargas asked.

"Heilongjiang Province in northern China. This was on a ranch built to provide cattle for the Russian market. China claims a freak outbreak of sorts, and the international fallout from the WHO and others brought it to our attention. Satellite activity of the region shows a fully healthy heard reduced almost entirely to a pile of glue, within four minutes." Vargas wondered if the entire country of China was under constant satellite surveillance. Probably.

The general walked through all the aspects of the scenario and laid out everything they knew. Brenmar, her former boss from the CIA, punctuated things a bit with some insightful comments, but also some silly bravadoes. That annoyed Vargas, since he had never been on the front line. The info had been disseminated and the conversation was producing nothing new. *Boring, let's get going*, Vargas thought.

Clemenson jumped in. "Vargas, we need you on the ground in China. You'll have the full support of any of these gentlemen, and direct contact access." He slid an envelope down the table.

Christ, he likes envelopes. She opened it. The names of the three men and the president were typed out, along with a phone number for each. She flashed a mental photo of it. Also in the envelope was a small list of addresses and passwords that were undoubtedly safe houses in China. She flashed another mental image of that.

"Memorize that information and destroy it," Clemenson barked.

Vargas looked up at him. She returned the pages to the envelope, and slid it back to Clemenson. He didn't reach out for it.

"You need to memorize that info," Clemenson repeated.

"That's already done, boss," she replied calmly, knowing the entire room was a little aghast.

Clemenson reached slowly for the envelope and tucked it into his portfolio bag. He looked at her for a moment to be sure she wasn't kidding. "Okay, let's get moving. There's a jet waiting for you at Dulles. Landshark Aviation, ask for Rogers. It will take you via LA, Honolulu, and Fusa, and then on into Beijing. Your contact from Chinese intelligence will meet you there and bring you up to speed on where this is heading. Keep me informed, Vargas. I think you can see the level of interest here. Get these fuckers before they unleash more gas. We need to know what the hell they're doing."

Vargas was more than a little surprised to hear the 'F' bomb, but realized it did have the effect of slapping an exclamation point onto the proceedings. She had a few questions but figured that this wasn't the time to ask them. Clemenson could respond later once outside this power vortex.

"Let's roll," she said. She stood without formality and headed towards the door.

Christ, I've been sitting here with the president and my Maxim 9 pistol. This red card sure is something special. Before reaching the door, Vargas turned back towards the president, who was collecting his papers.

"Don't worry, James, I'm on it." She pushed her way out into the hall, leaving everyone in the room with raised eyebrows. She liked the president, and she complimented herself of the nice exit. After all, he did say to call him James.

Vargas shot straight back up to Abigail's. She wanted those special support weapons with her on this trip. She arrived unannounced, admired the Austin Martin in the driveway, and pounded hard on the door, remembering the last time she knocked like a lady. After a minute or so, Abigail opened the door.

"Hey Colestah, what's up?"

"Heading out. Thought you'd be briefed. Anyway, I'd sure like to carry some of those gadgets you showed me earlier. One never knows when a little plastique can come in handy."

"Ya, I saw the PAT details roll in just after you left. C'mon in and I'll get you a little bag of goodies."

Vargas slipped through the doorway and started down the hall towards the Dungeon.

"Hang in here for a sec," Abigail said without much drama. "Got some stuff going on in the back."

That made Vargas, the supposed priority, a little curious. She moved down the hallway just the same, as soon as Abigail turned into the Dungeon. She waited outside the door. *Christ, maybe she has a dude in there or something.* Abigail opened the door with a bag full of goodies, and was surprised to see Vargas right in front of her.

"Hey, Colestah," she said. She closed the door behind her, almost too quickly.

Vargas saw the figure of a tall gentleman inside with his back to her, but his head tilt assured her he was aware of the unexpected interruption. She brought the toys out in front of him, so he obviously knew about PT1, and the accompanying secrecy. She figured he must be her counterpart. Who else could it be?

"Shit, sorry Abbie. I didn't realize you had company."

"Work is never done," she replied. She started walking back towards the front of the Den. Vargas thought it a little odd, but said nothing.

"Here you go: A full bag of goodies for the casual secret agent. The Speedline and suction cups aren't here right now. Please don't lose anything. Inventory reports are a pain in the keister."

Vargas smiled. "No worries, I'll guard them with my life."

"More like they'll guard *your* life," Abigail replied. "Hook up with the transceiver once you get on the ground in China and we can follow along together. I promise not to talk your ear off.".

"Guess that earpiece works in China as well," Vargas said.

"You betcha. Yilu Ping An."

Vargas looked at her. "Yi-who ping-what?"

"It's Chinese," Abigail said. "Safe journey. I can probably help you with the language once you're on the ground there. I don't speak it fluently, but I can get along." That was pretty god damn impressive.

"Okay, Professor. I'll ring ya when I'm in the land of the dragon."

The R8 took off towards the Capital Beltway and Dulles Access Rd. It was only one o'clock and traffic was already building.

Vargas inched along the Beltway, careful not to ride the bumper in front of her, and anxious when the vehicle behind her got too close to the R8. Her mind ambled back to her dreams of the night before, the recollections of her revelations to Maria. A tingle climbed up her back and buried itself in the base of her neck. A vividly clear memory of her formative past exploded inside her head. She had detailed some of it to Maria, but the entire recollection flashed at lightning speed through her brain—details, smells, words, moments.

She often wondered why she wasn't more traumatized by the events of her young life, but she wasn't. The psychiatrists had probed and analyzed, scrutinized and studied, but Vargas just wasn't screwed up by her past. They determined she had buried the events away, but she had repeatedly told them what she knew in her heart; she was over it.

School had been amazing. Without the constant tension that her parent's marriage delivered, she was unfettered in her desire to learn. Her photographic memory was developing rapidly, and her performance at school was way beyond the curve. After a couple of years, she was already a full grade ahead of the other girls. By year four, at the age of fifteen, she was through high school and taking college courses on her own.

She also excelled in the martial arts training program that was available to her. Her instructor was amazed at her development over a very short period, and eventually considered her his prize pupil. That was her life. Eight hours of school a day, five hours of Krav Maga or Aikido, food, bath, and sleep. All that left little time for friends.

Although unrecognized at the time, the most fortuitous event of her young life was a decision by Stark County to allow her to accept the college scholarship she earned. That meant living on her own, and it was through her Krav Maga instructor that she was able to accomplish that. Instructor Pearlman. He was too old to be truly considered a father figure, but perhaps a grandfather. He was an Israeli, long retired from the Mossad, but endlessly skilled in the art of self-defense and aggressive attack. He had always been a little distant and aloof with the delinquent girls he trained, never really letting a close relationship develop, but when Vargas moved into the dojo, that all changed. He provided her both special intensive training, and some enlightened observations on her life and future.

She was still just sixteen, but Sensei Pearlman successfully lobbied Stark County Juvenile authorities to release her under his guardianship. He arranged employment for her at the dojo. She provided training and mentorship to young female students, cleaned up at the end of each day, and of course, jumped to do anything else he asked of her. In return, she received a small wage and a rather Spartan room above the dojo. She reported weekly to Stark County, as did Instructor Pearlman.

Vargas thrived. She completed college in two years, just before her eighteenth birthday. She was also invited to test for her black belt before she turned eighteen, one year after obtaining her brown belt. She was the youngest female ever to receive it. By the time her obligation to Stark County ended on her eighteenth birthday, she was a smart, beautiful, articulate woman—and skilled fighter.

Despite his failing health, Instructor Pearlman continued her training, moving on to specialized techniques for delivering lethal force to an attacker, including certain actions and strikes that would render them permanently disabled. Vargas also moved on to a postgraduate program in political science. Everything flowed smoothly during that time; life was good and harmonious.

Things were shattered with the news that Instructor Pearlman was nearing his last breath. He had known for some time that his disease would eventually defeat him, and he had planned his passing with great care. He sold the dojo to a land development firm for considerably more than he expected. This provided comfortably for his family.

Before he died, he introduced Vargas to Mr. Alders, an aging friend of his from his youthful and active past. He was an ex-CIA agent, a long time contact, who had also retired quite some time before. He was still connected to enough people at the agency though, that he could open some doors for Vargas. Instructor Pearlman encouraged her to apply to the CIA, considering her a perfect candidate to be a field operative. She promised to do so, even if it was only to appease the wishes of a dying man.

His passing was much more traumatic for her than anything else she had experienced, but he had led a full and valued life, which left Vargas sorrowful, though not bitter. His was a life that most only dream about. Instructor Pearlman also left a small inheritance for her. She was surprised but eternally grateful. Armed with her freedom, a small stake, a post-grad degree, and lethal fighting skills, she reached out to Mr. Alders.

He did open some doors for her, and she bounded through them, impressing anyone and everyone with whom she came in contact. Her psych profile was rock solid, her IQ hit 152, even after a second testing, and her combat skills made the other candidates look like amateurs. Her aptitude for calm during chaos was superior. Twenty-two years old and with full agent status, her first field assignment was underway. She was three years ahead of anyone else in her graduating class. Even though she found herself once again with no friends, no family, and no attachments, she had long ago learned to be happy, living with herself.

► ► ►

Shit! "Sorry!" she said only with her lips as she glanced in the rear-view mirror. A man in some late model sedan was sitting with his hands raised in a standard 'what-the-fuck-are-you-doing' sign. She realized she had been daydreaming and now sat a hundred yards behind the car in front of her. The line behind her must have been honking for a while.

I always felt the only job we have during a traffic jam is to follow the guy in front of you. Guess it's my turn to be the jerk!

VIII

Vargas cleared the security gate at Dulles with her red card and swung up to Landshark Aviation. It would take her a few trips to realize she could bypass customs almost anywhere using the card. This enabled her to get going fully armed and without confrontation.

Once inside the hanger, a short, stocky man with dirty dungarees waddled over to the car as it came to a stop. She dropped the window.

"You Rogers?" she asked.

"Nope. He's up top in that jet," he said, pointing to one of the three jets housed inside the huge hangar.

"Where can I park?"

"Just leave me the keys and I'll take care of it."

"Sorry, amigo, no one touches my baby but me," she replied with a smile and a little wink.

He smiled back. "Put it over by that blue Merc, but you'll have to leave the keys."

Vargas revved up the R8 and burst towards the wall beside the Mercedes, stopping abruptly and maneuvering in close to the back wall. She grabbed her bag of goodies from the passenger seat, jumped out from the low-lying vehicle, and snapped the 'lock' button without looking back. She strode towards the jet housing Rogers, as Mr. Dungarees moved on an interception path towards her with his hand out. *He's expecting the keys, no doubt.*

"No worries, young man." She smiled without losing a stride. "It should be more than safe right there."

"What if I need to move it?" he said, gradually raising his voice. She was already past him and pushed him out of her reality.

Vargas climbed the six stairs up into the jet. She peeked in and then entered. *Wow, this is some set up.* The interior of the Gulfstream V was stunning, and much larger than the G200 that Colonel Younger had provided her.

She stood in the galley upon entering—full kitchen and pantry with an accompanying lavatory—and then turned right, through the bulkhead into the passenger room, past a closet with some freshly dry-cleaned uniforms covered in plastic, and on into open space. There were two tables, each with a small screen embedded in the wall beside it, and two armchairs for each. They looked like luxurious card tables. Through another bulkhead was a sofa along the port side, seemingly with four separate seating spots. Opposite the sofa was a credenza with a large screen TV and several drawers. The last portion, which was leveled down to sitting height, had a cut out base and a chair slid under it, with a computer and printer on top. *Perfect little desk to help me stay in touch.* Through the last bulkhead was another couch, but obviously a fold out one, morphing into a comfortable looking double bed. Beyond that was a bathroom, complete with a shower… and Rogers. He finished some type of repair to the light socket, and looked up without surprise as she peered in.

"Grab the corner there and push," he said as he stepped out of the bathroom, pushing through the doorway and brushing lightly against Vargas She didn't mind. Vargas realized the bed was not fully closed and she reached out to help complete the task. "Thanks," he continued. "Rogers." He offered his hand.

"Just Rogers?" she asked, taking it.

"That's it. Always figured one name was enough." He chuckled. "Reality is, because I only use one name, people remember it more clearly." He was folding up the last little hand towel. "Kind of the reverse of what you'd expect." He let that be absorbed for a second, then continued. "I'm going out on a limb here, but I assume you are Ms. Hamilton."

She liked Rogers. "Ms. Hamilton departed when I was very young," she smiled. "I'm Vargas."

He looked back and smiled. *Nice smile.*

"Fair enough. I guess we're both comfortable with our names." He pushed by her, out into the office area. "You'll appreciate that bed after about six hours. C'mon up here and settle in."

He motioned her forward and reached into the top drawer of the credenza, pulling out another brown envelope. *Clemenson's envelopes. Jesus.*

"You're supposed to get this once airborne, but I think now will do. Grab a seat over there," he said, pointing at one of the armchairs behind a card table.

Rogers moved forward towards the cockpit. *Shit, I guess he's the pilot too,* Vargas realized, just as Mr. Dirty Dungarees peered in from the top step.

"What's up, Martin? We're ready to push off," Rogers said.

"I need the keys for her car," Martin said.

"Did you ask her for them?"

"I did, but she just said something about nobody touching her baby."

"So?" Rogers replied. Martin looked on, waiting for Rogers to request the keys. "Get down there and pull those blocks out of the way. We're already a little behind."

Martin tilted his head, a little incredulous, and turned to descend the stairway. "Unbelievable," he huffed, loud enough for both Rogers and Vargas to hear.

Rogers smiled at Vargas and shrugged before pulling the door shut, arming it, and shuffling into the cockpit. *Yup, I like Rogers.*

As the plane initiated her twenty-minute climb to thirty-five-thousand feet, Vargas tore open the envelope. Inside was a bio sheet on her Chinese counterpart. *Wow, now that's a good-looking man,* she thought. She didn't really have a thing for Asian men, but Ang Qiangguo was special. He was definitely Asian, but looked like he might be from mixed parents. He had a strong angular face, deep dark eyes, and a head of thick black hair that gave him a mysterious, perhaps even enigmatic appearance. *Perhaps he's from Singapore; Malay, Chinese mix. He's probably short.* Vargas scrolled down the bio. Height 190. *Mmmm... That's about six-three. Nice.* Weight 95 Kg. *That's like, two-ten. Probably muscle,* she reflected. His field name was Wancheng. *I'll have to look that up.*

She read every detail: Orphaned at a young age, showed special intelligence with an aptitude for combat, and was moved to a specialized school as a young teenager. Following his general education, he moved on to the Guoanbu, the Chinese Ministry of State Security, where he received special training in espionage, explosives, and counter terrorism. He had numerous field commendations and a history of success wherever he went. He actually sounded like a male version of her! She wondered what he saw in *her* bio.

The envelope also contained a hundred thousand Yuan, Chinese currency, which was about fifteen thousand dollars. There was another page with new coordinates and a meeting time: 02:00 - Stealth. *Okay, straight to the battle zone, and keep it quiet.* The bottom of the page said: 'Memorize and Destroy,' as usual. Vargas stepped up to the galley and put the page in the sink. She knocked, and then opened the cockpit door.

Rogers sat reading a chart of some type, the plane obviously flying itself, and glanced back at her over his shoulder.

"What's up?"

"You have a light?"

He reached in his pants pocket and pulled out a gold DuPont. "Spin sideways."

Vargas went back to the kitchen and incinerated the sheet with the bio and rendezvous co-ordinates. *Nice lighter,* she thought as she juggled it a bit in her hand. She returned the lighter and went back to the office area. *Let's try this communication thing,* she thought.

She rummaged through her bag of goodies from Abigail, slipped the transceiver into her ear, and pressed the tiny "contact" button. Nothing. She tried a couple more times before giving up, realizing that it was using a cellular network, and nothing like that was available at their altitude.

She pulled out the desk chair and turned on the computer. There was Wi-Fi on board so she could at least check her emails. The computer sprang to life and requested a password. While Vargas pondered what that might be, she noticed the swipe slide on the side of the computer. *No way*, she thought. Out came her red card. Swipe, she was in. The screen popped up a. 'Greetings, Colestah,' with the cursor flashing in the search bar. She navigated to the CIA internal web site, to which she had next to top clearance. She typed R-O-G-E-R-S and hit enter.

He was a veteran operative, specializing in aviation, transportation, and the supply chain. If you needed to get something, get somewhere, or get back, he was the man. A good guy to know. She didn't go through things in detail because he was right on the plane. She leaned back and perused his agency history quietly, as if reading a sleepy summer novel.

Suddenly the cockpit door opened and Rogers came strolling out, stopping in the galley to grab a bottle of water.

"You want something?" he called down the cabin.

Vargas lunged forward on her chair and hit the sleep button on the computer. No sense letting him know she was checking up on him.

"All good here, unless you have a nice twenty-one-year-old Belvenie," she replied, not completely without hope that he did.

"Rocks?"

"Just one, thanks."

She was almost tempted to ask for something even more obscure, but figured it wasn't the right approach. If he did have it, it would look like she was testing him, if he didn't, it would look like she was trying to embarrass him. She decided to shut up and enjoy her scotch.

Rogers brought her the glass, complete with a generous portion of Belvenie and a single ice cube.

"Port wood finish," he said, handing her the glass and raising one of his own for a little clink. "About three and a half hours to Vandenberg AFB, our first fuel stop."

"Shit, I need some clothes," she replied. She hadn't taken the time to return home after Abigail's.

"Well, I've got scotch, cigars, caviar, and even duct tape under that sink, but no women's wear." He laughed. "Just jot down a list and I'll have it waiting in LA." He spread his arms a little as if it was a simple request, like a simple request for a twenty-one-year-old scotch.

"Thanks," she said, then reflected for a moment. "Duct tape?"

"In case the plane breaks down," he replied, shrugging it off as if it was a normal maintenance item. *I like Rogers*, she thought.

Vargas sat down at one of the card tables and pulled out her iPhone, opening her notes app. She began dictating a list of items and sizes she needed, and the phone recorded her requests accordingly. It took her a few minutes, but once she reviewed the list, and corrected 'decoder sent' to 'deodorant,' she was done. She went back to Rogers.

"What's your email?"

"Rogers@Rogers.gov."

"Christ, you have your own government domain name?" He just smiled. Vargas forwarded the note with her requirements and verified that Rogers had received it.

The stop at Vandenberg AFB was short. Rogers handed off a package to some military type official, who then tried to peek inside the plane. Vargas kept her back to him, not sure if anyone needed to know who was on board. *Just as that gentleman had in Abigail's Dungeon earlier in the day*, she thought. Her requested items were delivered by a bright and cheerful young lady, who referred to Rogers as 'boss', and kept up a nearly constant chatter. She probably had a blast shopping in Los Angeles for the various items. Rogers eventually ushered her back down the stairs and out of their lives, at least for a while. Once fueling was complete, they were off again, headed for Hawaii and Hickam AFB.

Hickam was uneventful. A quick stop, some more document exchanges, and some fresh Pacific air. Vargas had completed all her research and pre-deployment planning enroute. The basic plan was to get to China on time, find Wancheng, and follow him around. She chuckled a bit to herself, reflecting on the fact that she had a long-standing wish to visit Hawaii, but somehow this was not how she had pictured it.

Rogers got the plane up to cruising altitude again and came back into the cabin. He reached into the fridge and brought out a nice salad plate, complete with cheeses, veggies, and other nibble foods. They both snacked, washed down with some red wine and San Pellegrino. Vargas hadn't eaten in nearly twenty-four hours. It was good and healthy, a perfect meal.

"We've got about seven hours to go," Rogers said as he stood up and stretched a bit. *Pretty nice body going on there*, she thought. "I'm going to grab a quick nap. Let me know if we hit anything," he said with a smile.

"Only if it's bad." Vargas winked.

Rogers went into the back room and popped the bed open. He lay down on top of the covers, and Vargas could soon hear him snoring away. Normally she didn't like snoring, but this time it was almost soothing, like a lullaby dragging her towards sleep. It had been a long day since her early morning rise to meet Abigail, and fatigue was setting in. The additional Belvenie also whispered thoughts of slumber into her head, and she went to the back room. Rogers was laying on his back, sleeping with a rather content look on his face. She crawled up onto the bed beside him. He tossed a bit and popped one eye half open.

"Hey," he said.

She looked at him. She was tired but he looked pretty good right now. She lifted herself up onto an elbow and leaned in close to his face. "Hey."

Their first kiss was extreme, and clothes were soon flying. He pulled a condom out of the top drawer of the bedside table. Vargas wondered if he was confident or just prepared; she didn't like to be predictable. It didn't matter, he felt good and she was content to let him lead the passion. She usually liked to be in charge, to control the tempo, but she was tired and enjoying the feelings of pleasure from a relaxed and passive position. It didn't last long, but it lasted good. *Christ, I needed that.* There was no chit chat after; there was nothing to say. They stayed wrapped up together and drifted off with ease.

Vargas woke when she felt the plane shift into a soft descent. She cleared her head. Fusa. Rogers was not there. *Thank god he woke up in time to land,* she thought. She wrapped the sheet around her body and went to the cockpit. It was dark outside. "Good evening."

"Good night," he replied, sliding his finger over to the clock on the dash. 8:30 PM. "We're about half an hour out of Fusa. We'll only be on the ground for about forty minutes."

"How long to Beijing from there?"

"I'd say three hours on the nose."

"Shit, I've got a little meeting at 02:00; don't want to be late."

"We should get there before one. There's an hour time difference."

"Perfect," she said. "I'm heading to the shower."

"Watch out for turbulence." He cracked a smile and she did the same, closing the door on the way out.

Vargas went back to the bed and laid down. She decided to forget the shower, realizing there would be enough time between Japan and China. She drifted off into a semi sleep, thinking about Wancheng and what lay ahead for them.

They touched down in Beijing at 00:40 local time. Vargas was prepped. She swung the bag of goodies from Abigail over her shoulder, further burdened with several clips for her Maxim 9, which was now in the belt holster behind her back. She tucked her ESEE Strike Knife in its Kydex sheath on her right ankle. She jotted down her destination coordinates on a post-it, and grabbed a bottle of Bloody Mary mix from the fridge, though it was not exactly the breakfast of champions. A car was waiting. She pushed past Rogers with a gentle touch of his shoulder and jumped down the stairs.

"Your things will be in your hotel room when you get there," he said. Vargas wondered when that might be. "Go get 'em." He gave her a thumbs-up from the top of the stairs. He said nothing sentimental, realizing, like her, that their little romp together was nothing more than a shared release. Vargas definitely liked Rogers.

She returned the thumbs-up, barking over the Jet engine hum, "Thanks for the lift." She turned to get in the car, handed the driver the co-ordinates, and also plugged them into her iPhone GPS.

"We're heading here. I don't know how far it is. Let's move."

The driver looked at her. She wasn't sure if he actually understood. She thought for a moment, but discarded the possibility that they would send a driver who didn't speak English. The car took off.

Vargas plugged the transceiver into her ear and hit 'connect.' In a few seconds, Abigail was on the line.

"Go," she said.

"Good morning, or is it afternoon?" Vargas said. She didn't wait for a reply. "Just hit the ground in Beijing and I'm with a driver, but I'm not sure he speaks English." Before Abigail could respond, the driver turned off the highway onto a much smaller road. "Hey, follow the GPS," Vargas yelled at him, her sense of danger sparking her adrenalin.

"Wo zhidao qu nali de jiejing," he said.

"You get that, Abigail?"

"He says there's a better route; a faster route," she said. "Send me a photo and I'll confirm with Guoanbu data." *Smart gal.*

Vargas reach over the seat and snapped a photo when the driver turned his head. She texted it to Abigail.

"Here you go. I need an answer quick." She didn't respond. "Hello?"

"Hang on, just a sec," Abigail said. "Chen Hui, that's him. Oh, and he speaks perfect English. Tell him, 'Jiang yingwen.'"

Vargas called him by name and repeated the sounds out load, "Yang ying when."

The driver smiled. "Okay, Colestah, just making sure you're on your toes," he replied in perfect Oxford English. "I didn't know you speak Chinese."

Vargas let him think so. Abigail whispered into her earpiece, "I just said, 'in English, asshole.'" *I like Abigail.*

He knew her field name, so that confirmed he was on the right side.

"We need to be there ASAP," she told him.

"02:00 Stealth," he confirmed back to her.

Vargas relaxed back into her seat, the Maxim 9 slightly uncomfortable but always reassuring against her lower back.

"You have a tracker on me?" she asked Abigail.

"Nope," Chen Hui responded.

"Not you. I'm chatting with my landlady here."

Abigail confirmed she did have a ping on her, and repeated that she would ride the PAT with her all the way. They would wake, eat, and sleep at the same time.

"I'm in the Dungeon, doors closed, locked in," she said.

It was a first for Vargas, having a shadow, but she could easily see the advantages of having real time support, information, and intelligence while actively engaged.

"Sweet to have you along for the ride. You have a ping on Wancheng as well?"

"Yup. Looks like he's a couple of hundred feet from the rendezvous point, but he's stationary there. Maybe he's waiting for 02:00." It was already 01:44.

Chen Hui closed his lights and stopped the car about five hundred feet from the destination. He turned and looked into the back seat.

"Stealth, remember?"

Vargas lifted the door handle and climbed out into the warm night air, sliding Abigail's bag of goodies over her shoulder and across her chest.

"You coming?" she asked her driver.

"My instructions are to wait close by. Guess this is it." He handed her a small disc. "Push hard on the top of that and I'll get a distress signal. If I get it, I'll be there double time, and not in stealth mode."

Vargas nodded, both in comprehension and appreciation. She didn't say a word. She switched her iPhone to silent, dimmed the brightness to minimum, and set off towards the rendezvous point.

She was beside an old factory complex with several buildings. Dusty roads confirmed there wasn't much activity happening in the area, and the exact coordinates were just in front of the main entrance. No Wancheng.

"You still have him beeping?" she whispered to Abigail.

"Hasn't moved an inch," she replied.

Vargas looked at her phone. 02:02. "I'll give him three more minutes, then I'm heading to him."

"You're the boss," Abigail said. "I'm just along for the ride."

They sat in silence. *Three minutes, less time than it takes to soft boil an egg.* "Any movement?"

"Nope. Still stuck in one spot."

"Probably not by choice," Vargas replied. She moved cautiously from the cover she was using.

She stuck to the side wall of the building as Abigail texted the exact coordinates of Wancheng. Vargas followed them on her screen and soon arrived at the side of another building. She could hear some chatter around the corner, and a faint whir of helicopter blades. Her hand went to the Maxim 9. She crouched down low and peeked around the edge. She figured it was much less likely that her movement would spark interest if it were low to the ground.

Two men stood chatting, dressed in military garb, but not really looking official. They appeared much too casual to be soldiers. A light flickered above her and she looked up. The window illumination oscillated a few times, but it was too high to see in. Vargas returned her attention to the guards. She put her gun away, kicked some dirt out beyond the wall, and stumbled forward as if drunk.

The guards snapped their guns to fire mode and looked at her as she came closer. They bantered a bit in Chinese and laughed. Vargas knew they wouldn't find it funny in a few seconds. As she neared them, her right hand went out like a cobra, fingers straight out, and nestled perfectly in the Adam's apple of the first victim. He never knew it was over until…well, he just never knew. The second guard was frozen. *Amateurs. Where do they find these guys?* She leapt up in a semi flip, and her arm went around his neck upside down, so that his head protruded from beneath her arm and looked at her back. She flipped over and heard the unmistakable crack of breaking bones as he fell limp to the ground below her, his own weight breaking his neck. She dragged them both around the corner and moved to the building entrance.

She pried the door open a bit. There were two more guards inside, about twenty feet beyond the entrance. One glanced up as she backed up and let the door close with a distinct click. She knocked on it. Her hand went to the ESEE knife and slid the five-inch blade to life. The door was opened abruptly by the disturbed guard, and Vargas swiped the knife in a single broad stroke across his neck, partially severing his head. The second guard straightened up from his leaning position, and her throw left the knife stuck in his forehead, before he realized there was fresh air coming through the doorway.

Vargas collected her knife, placing her foot on the guard's nose to gain leverage as she pulled it out of his head. She wiped it on his shirt and tucked it back onto her right ankle. She reminded herself that the knife was indeed an excellent weapon, as she moved silently towards the staircase.

There didn't appear to be a main floor, only half a flight of stairs heading up. She covered the twelve steps in three silent, cat-like pounces. At the top was a long hallway. No guards. She pulled out her iPhone and relocated Wancheng. She moved along the wall until she was apparently on him, calculating that he must be inside the door to her left. Vargas pulled her Maxim 9 and tried the door handle gently. It wasn't locked. She pushed it open slowly and peered inside. At least eight men were inside what looked like a classroom, performing various functions, not the least of which was torturing Wancheng. They all looked up at her with surprise. That was enough for Vargas.

She dove forward, getting off three shots from her gun, all of which found their target, before landing in a roll that ended in a crouch behind a metal desk. She toppled it over, just as automatic weapons returned her greeting. Vargas waited out the initial storm of gunfire, certain that the ricochet of so many rounds would take down at least one more combatant, and hopefully not Wancheng. She was right; two men were struck in lower limbs by the stray rounds.

Once the initial response quieted a bit, she remained in a crouch and pushed the desk forward on its side. As she passed a second desk, she dove under it and squeezed off two more rounds. Two more dead. She rolled to the next desk as more bullets found the spot she had just vacated, and jumped up, delivering two more deadly shots to put the ricochet-injured guards out of their misery.

The room went silent except for the whiz of sucking breath coming from the only enemy still alive. Vargas silenced him with a little puff from her suppressed pistol. *Christ, it's like I'm at the shooting gallery in an amusement park. Hope there's a big teddy bear for the winner. Oh ya, Wancheng!*

He was hanging from his wrists, electrodes clamped on his nipples. *Ouch.* He looked at her as she stood in front of him.

"Colestah, I guess?"

Vargas smiled, a sense of humor at this point meant he was a tough cookie. She unclamped him, unsheathed her knife, and jumped a bit to swipe through the ropes above his head. He landed without falling and started to loosen the ropes around his wrists, finally assisted by another swipe of her blade.

"You owe me," she said with a wink, and headed towards the door. Wancheng was behind her. She turned right to return to the exit.

"No, this way," he said.

She looked at him. Solid build, with just a little blood dripping from his discolored chest, holding an automatic pistol he borrowed from one of the dead interrogators. *Definitely a sexy look,* she thought. Then chastised herself for allowing her focus to drift.

"Lead on," Vargas replied.

They moved quickly down the hallway until the end and kicked through a double doorway, where a railing stopped them. They looked out onto a huge open-air courtyard, perhaps half a football field long, with various people scurrying around like chickens. There were three helicopters, all just dancing in idle mode.

"That's Creusa." Wancheng pointed to a man running across the yard towards a helicopter. "He's got the latest formula for the gas. It's supposedly new and improved."

"We need it." Vargas leapt over the railing and slid down the side of the wall, using the building features as a makeshift ladder. It was only twenty-five feet or so. She dropped the last fifteen. Wancheng was impressed and followed her.

"I'm going for Creusa, grab us a lift if you can," and she dashed across the open terrain.

Six rounds left. She ran in a jagged pattern and took out several enemies as she sped towards the helicopter. She ducked behind a pile of boxes as more automatic fire headed her way. She grabbed a new clip from her bag of goodies and slapped it into place.

Just as she looked up, two men moved in from behind with their guns about to unload into her. They both went down like slabs of meat. Vargas looked over to her left and saw Wancheng. He smiled, blowing a little breath across the top of his automatic pistol like some cowboy in a Western movie. *Smartass.* She smiled back.

Vargas negotiated her way closer to Creusa as he boarded one of the choppers. She holstered her Maxim 9, leapt up on a fuel drum, and jumped with an outstretched arm to grab the chopper's landing skid, just as it lifted off. She hoisted herself up so she rested with the pad in her armpit, and relocated her gun, as the helicopter moved vertically. She squeezed off a few more rounds during the initial ascent, striking combatants on the ground. She saw Wancheng fighting his own battle. As she tucked the Maxim 9 back into her belt holster, she saw him climbing into one of the other helicopters.

Vargas used both hands to pull herself up onto the landing skid, ignoring the significant distance between her and the ground, and relieving the pressure on her arm. She reached up for the door—too far. The bird cleared the buildings and began darting forward through the still night air. It was still climbing as well. Vargas reached in her pocket and pushed the button she got from Chen Hui. She didn't know if would help, but she figured it couldn't hurt, especially since the stealth part of the mission was long gone. She returned the button to her pocket and lifted one foot onto the skid, raising her body to window level. She peered in.

Creusa sat holding a large metal case, clutched in both arms. The pilot was busy to her left, but the co-pilot was staring straight at her and about to squeeze off a round into her face. She ducked and the window above her blew out as the bullet shattered it. *Fuck.* She looked under the chopper and saw the external cargo hook. She leaned forward and grabbed it, swinging her body out and underneath as another bullet pierced the door frame and bounced off the landing skid. Now she was hanging from the bottom of the bird, dangling a little out of control at about a thousand feet. She tried swinging her legs to reach the far side skid, coming closer with each motion and finally catching the edge with her right foot. This left her in a vulnerable position, and with some uncertainty about her chances of survival.

She saw the foot stepping from the chopper door onto the skid and figured a pistol would soon be pointing at her. *Yup, there it is.* Suddenly, her would-be assassin lurched forward and slumped down onto the skid, dead. The round intended for her shot up through the cockpit instead. She looked over and down a bit. There was another chopper, a pistol pointing out through the side window, and Wancheng clearly visible through the glass, with that bloody smile on his face.

Vargas swung back the other way and used the dead co-pilot as leverage to swing up and regain a grip on the relative safety of the landing skid. She pushed him off. She climbed back up, onto the skid, and looked cautiously through the now disintegrated window. Creusa sat there smiling. The metal case was open and he held a large canister in his hand. His other hand was on the door handle.

"If this goes out the door it will be the end of the cattle industry in China," he said, a little too smugly.

Vargas thought about it. *Probably not, even if it hits in central Beijing it can't cover that much ground before it dissipates.* She swung her Maxim 9 up and dropped him with a quiet gift just in front of his left ear, before he even flicked his wrist. The pilot looked at the now deceased Creusa, and then back left over his shoulder at her. She pointed the pistol at the back of his head. He was clutching at his leg and wincing.

"Abigail, how do you say, 'land this mother fucker' in Chinese?"

"It's a little more polite, but try, 'Xianzai denglou zhe jia feiji' for best results."

Vargas reached in and lifted his comms set. She screamed out Abigail's instructions, stumbling through a crude rendition, and jabbing her Maxim 9 menacingly.

"You bet. Heading down now," the pilot replied in perfect English. Vargas began to wonder if everyone in China spoke English.

He set down on a deserted stretch of road and looked at Vargas. She waved him out of the chopper with her gun. He slid out cautiously with a significantly pained look on his face. Vargas saw the blood oozing from his left leg, and realized he had been the recipient of the bullet meant for her. He collapsed to the ground.

"Where were you taking him?" she asked, using the gun to indicate Creusa.

"I don't know," he stammered. "He was giving me instructions as we went."

Vargas looked at the wound in his left leg, just above the knee. It looked like the femur had been smashed as well. She leaned over him and brought the gun up next to his crotch, resting her arm on the injured leg.

"What was your destination?"

He winced painfully at the pressure from her arm and the precarious position of her weapon. "Okay, easy. We were heading to Miyun," he said. She knew there was no way he was lying. Ha had to know she wouldn't be reluctant to put an end to his happiness, even though it was clear that he wasn't going to survive for much longer.

Vargas heard the second chopper moving in for a landing and stood to greet Wancheng as he jumped down, leaving the rotor running.

"Guess we're even," she screamed a bit, over the swoosh of the rotors, referring to his earlier marksmanship.

"Nope. You owe me one," he replied with a wink. He pushed past her to chat with the downed pilot. She noticed he still wore that same damn smile.

"What did you do to him?"

"Nothing, his co-pilot managed to take out his leg by accident. I was just encouraging him to tell me where they were heading. He says Ma-Jung or something."

Wancheng turned to the pilot and spoke in Chinese. She couldn't make out anything except the word 'Miyun.'

"You getting this, Abigail?"

"Not everything, but sounds like our informant is giving up a few more details. Seems Wancheng is telling him that he'll let you at him if he doesn't talk." Abigail snickered at the thought of Vargas as the bad cop.

Vargas let them chat for a bit while she went to the downed chopper and recovered the metal case and canister of gas from Creusa. He sat just like she left him, a smug look on his face, with dead eyes taking in the scene. She snapped a photo of his dead face for proof of death. She heard a soft hissing sound as she tried to secured the vial back inside the case. She listened as the gas expanded out into the early morning air. Either the canister had been compromised when Creusa fell limp, or he had punctured it before she shot him. Either way, the gas was loose. She felt sorry for any cows in the immediate vicinity. She tucked the canister into its' case and went back to see how Wancheng was doing.

"We've got a pretty clear destination," he said, "but it seems our pilot doesn't really fancy you."

Vargas walked over and elbowed between Wancheng and the pilot. She brushed close to Wancheng, letting the adrenalin of the battle heighten her other senses as well. She looked into his eyes and knew that he felt it too. She wanted to lean into him and share the excitement. Perhaps if the pilot wasn't there, she would have. But he was there. She reached down as he cowered a bit, and undid his belt, pulling it off after unclipping his holster and phone holder. She wrapped it around the top of his leg and pulled tight. He winced. She took out her knife and punched a hole through the leather strap so she could fasten it tight as a tourniquet. She hoisted him to his feet despite his cries of pain, and pushed him towards the waiting bird.

"Show us," she said, keeping her hand on his back and his arm over her shoulder. He started walking, actually hopping, towards the chopper. Vargas redirected him to the passenger side. Wancheng jumped back onto the controls.

Just before she climbed in behind the pilot, a black Merc sped up to them and slid to a stop. Vargas looked over at Chen Hui. He smiled and walked over to her.

"Give me the old one," he said, handing her a new tracking button. "Inventory control."

Vargas took the button and pocketed it. She handed Chen Hui the case containing the canister.

"Perfect timing, Chen Hui. Get this to the techies ASAP. It appears to be leaking. I guess it got punctured, but maybe they can break it down and find some kind of antidote or whatever." She turned and spoke to Abigail. "Guess you heard that, the Chinese have the gas sample we needed, or at least what's left of it. Let Clemenson know."

"Already did that," she said. *No kidding.*

Vargas looked back at Chen Hui.

"Get here a little faster next time." She smiled.

"Stop travelling by helicopter," he replied, backing away with the case to return to his car. She gave him a thumbs-up and the bird lifted straight up before powering forward towards Miyun.

Wancheng looked at her. "I don't think they'll get much info from that canister you gave Chen Hui." He said it matter-of-factly, with neither innuendo nor certainty.

Vargas sat snuggly beside Creusa's dead body, with her gun pointed directly at the bleeding pilot, who was now riding shotgun. She looked forward at Wancheng. He was still topless, fully concentrated on the instructions he was getting from the wounded man beside him. The man was clearly still worried that her wrath was heading his way.

"Give me your shirt," she told the ex-pilot, jerking her gun to emphasize that it was not a request.

"What?" he said.

"You know what can happened when you hesitate," she said, pointing the gun a little more menacingly at his good leg. He got the shirt off pretty quickly.

Wancheng looked back at her, holding her gaze for more than a moment.

"What?" she said, shrugging.

"Nothing," he replied, "But thanks."

"Who said it's for you?" She smiled. "Maybe I just like guys shirtless." She nodded her head forward, indicating his own bare torso. She found Wancheng to be a sexy guy and felt more stirrings inside. *Christ, I'm glad I ate and slept on the flight over*!

"Maybe under other circumstances."

"These are pretty crazy circumstances," she said, shaking the gun to inspire some haste in the prisoner. He handed the shirt to Wancheng.

"What's with you two?" The ex-pilot looked at Vargas, puzzled.

Vargas didn't like him, and that wasn't good for him. He was a weasel type, looking out for himself regardless of the cost to others. A cheap mercenary with little training. No personal character and no professional quality. Suddenly she flashed on the terrorist who had killed Tom Keeler. She looked him straight in the eyes.

"Shut up," she said, closing the conversation.

A while later, they were closing in on the yard the ex-pilot had identified. "That's it, over past those floodlights."

"We'd better go in low," Wancheng said to Vargas.

"Get very low," she replied. "I'll disembark and head in by foot. No idea what's waiting for us. You can bring them Creusa's body. Just pretend you're this guy," she suggested, once again pointing her gun at the ex-pilot.

"And what about him?" he asked.

He was already near the end. He had lost a lot of blood and was barely clinging to consciousness. Vargas didn't want him to slowly bleed to death. She lifted her Maxim 9, gently squeezed the trigger. "He's coming with me."

Wancheng just shook his head, recognizing that she was pretty crazy. "You're callous."

"Awe, and I thought you found me cute," she replied. "What's the difference if I kill them while running through a field or sitting in a chopper? Besides, he was about to bleed to death."

"Look there," he pointed to a small field.

"Get ready. Let's make it fast so nobody on the ground spots the drop."

He moved the chopper into place about ten feet off the ground. Vargas climbed between the seats and kicked open the opposite door, pushing the dead passenger out, and jumping down after him.

The bird flew off with Wancheng and Creusa along for the ride.

"You there Abigail?" A little hesitation. "Abigail."

"I'm here, I'm here. It was slow, I went for coffee"

Slow? Shit, I wonder what perks her up. "No worries. Just wanted to know if I was still under your umbrella."

"Always," she replied. "Unless I'm with the president."

"You still have a feed on Wancheng?"

"Sure do."

"Can you send it to me again? I seem to have lost it." A little flash on her screen told her Abigail had done so before she asked.

Vargas was enjoying having Abigail's support. She felt in her pocket for the button beacon and pressed it. She figured Chen Hui must be a long way off, and a head start would bring him into play sooner rather than later. Wancheng appeared as a small flashing blue circle on her phone and she started chasing it down, after rolling the dead body into a small drainage ditch. The body didn't have much cover, but at least it was hidden from the road.

As Vargas began the short hike in on foot, Wancheng eased the chopper down onto the field. Several men were hustling towards him. He exited. It was obvious that they thought he was with their team. He urged them to check on Creusa, even though he knew he was obviously long dead. They pulled his body out and Wancheng explained that a crazy American woman was responsible, and that she got away with the canister. They hustled him towards the entrance to the main building, but a group of men exited it before they got there, and headed towards him.

"What happened?" one of them asked in English. He was not English though, maybe Russian or Polish.

Wancheng pretended he didn't understand. One of the other soldiers spoke up and recounted Wancheng's story. Several of the men looked at him.

"Ask him for the password," the foreigner demanded.

The Chinese guard asked Wancheng for the password.

Wancheng realized his ruse was up and decided to get the show on the road.

"How the fuck should I know," he replied. He hit the ground with his automatic pistol screaming out a blur of bullets towards the gathered crowd. Blood was flying, and the crowd scattered. Wancheng rolled behind a couple of fallen bodies and ducked away from the return fire.

The group of officials who had exited the building raced back inside, hands covering their heads as they crouched. Wancheng stood and managed to cut down a couple of others before he felt the bullet pass through the left side of his neck.

He went dizzy and lost consciousness for a moment. His hand went up to his throat and then pulled away so he could see the damage. Massive amounts of blood covered it. He slid his sleeve over his hand and reapplied it to the wound. He realized he was losing blood too fast.

Several guards grabbed him and lifted him up. One securing him on each arm, but they didn't need to; he was already weak from the loss of blood. The senior guard pulled his knife and raised it over his head, ready to drive it into his chest. It wasn't the way Wancheng planned to leave this world.

In a flash, the senior guards face jerked sideways as a bullet struck him just below the eye. The guard holding his right arm was gone in almost the same instant. Then the left arm went down from a direct strike to his forehead, as he turned to locate their attacker. Wancheng slipped to one knee, and two other guards felt the fury of Vargas' firepower. She reached him in a moment and dragged his body around the corner for cover.

"Now we're even," she said. She looked at his neck, realizing that it was extremely bad. "Just a flesh wound. Let's get you out of here."

"There's a group of foreigners in that building. Must be buyers or something. We've got to find out what's going on," he stammered, pointing across the yard to a smaller building with the name 'SVG Chemicals (China)' above the door.

Vargas unslung her bag of goodies, jammed three clips into her back waistband, and pulled off his shirt. "I guess you're just destined to be topless."

She returned fire to someone behind the stairway as she dragged him closer to the wall. She saw another round strike through his upper arm, missing the bone but ripping his skin apart. "Fuck," she shouted, jumping up slightly to return fire and drag him further behind cover.

She rolled up his shirt and applied the bulky part to the throat wound, tying the loose end sleeves around his neck. "I don't think it's a main artery," she whispered, but Wancheng was already drifting towards unconsciousness.

The arm strike was a flesh wound. Vargas thought about plugging it with dirt to stop the bleeding, but figured the possible infection was not worth the risk. He certainly didn't need to compound his situation with a future bout of tetanus or lock jaw. She knew she had to get him some real help soon. She leaned him against the wall and took off her own shirt. She wrapped it around his arm and tied it off tight. Wancheng was barely conscious.

"Hold on to this," she demanded, handing him the ends of her shirt.

Wancheng looked at her, then down at her lace-topped bra. "Nice underwear," he said, their shared innuendo continuing despite the circumstances He wore that same goddamn smile. He leaned his head against the wall. "Find out what's going on in there," he whispered before closing his eyes.

Vargas changed out her Maxim 9 clip. She wasn't sure how many rounds were left in the old one, but didn't want to risk a miscount. With fifteen fresh rounds, and figuring that there was only a dozen of them left, she felt confident she had more than enough. She handed Wancheng an automatic pistol, removed from one of the dead assailants, and left him there. "Back in a flash," she said. It wasn't clear whether he heard her.

She looked around the side of the building. There was a garbage bin and a water pipe along the outside of the wall. Together they looked quite a bit like a ladder to Vargas. She was on the roof in a few seconds and moved quickly to the front. She was too far away for accuracy with the Maxim 9, but saw no other choice. She peered over the edge and tried to determine who all the guys were. Soldiers, guards, terrorists? She aimed and fired off a silent round. One down, then another. The muzzle flash didn't help though, and soon there was lead flying all around her. She raced back to the drainpipe, shimmied down, and bolted around the back of the building, appearing on the other side within a half minute. Two more soldiers caught her bullets before the rest realized the attack had changed focus. Meanwhile, Vargas raced back around to where Wancheng was, to renew the attack. To her surprise, Wancheng was gone! The obvious questions zipped through her mind. What happened to him? Did they get him? She didn't see anybody.

Sweat poured down her front, soaking her body. She was tired, but the adrenalin was fueling her muscles. She wasn't sure where the last two or three soldiers were, so she broke for the door of the building, letting their muzzle flashes give her a good idea. She tumbled forward and came up in a single knee position, steadied herself with one deep breath, resting her elbow on her knee, and squeezed off three shots as her body rotated at the waste. The yard fell silent.

Vargas went to the front door and pried it open. No one there. Suddenly, she heard a shot behind her and spun around in time to see another soldier falling. She looked to her left where the shot had come from. Wancheng! *Eventually I'm gonna have to wipe that stupid grin off his face.*

"You owe me," he whispered. "Go on."

Vargas swung open the door and headed up the stairs. She changed out her clip again, kicked open the only closed door, and hit the deck. Several shots came flying out of the room, all of them over her head. Vargas cracked off eight rounds in quick succession, taking out six of the eight men in the room. She realized they were not pros. The two remaining men, who had been cowering behind the others, threw down their weapons and put their hands behind their heads. They both had western features, perhaps even American.

"Don't shoot, Christ, take it easy. We're not armed," one of them whined. Vargas knew she had nothing to worry about. She stood and pointed the Maxim 9 straight at his head. The other survivor had his eyes closed. The look on the man's face when he saw her was priceless—sweaty, dirty, and bloody from Wancheng's flow, dressed in a lace bra, with a pistol pointed at him.

"What the…" His words trailed off. The other survivor opened his eyes and did a similar double take.

"Easy boys, you don't want to get me upset." Both of them averted their eyes and moved away as she walked towards them. "Who's in charge?"

"He is," the one who had his eyes closed said. Vargas dropped him with a quick shot to the face, then a second round to impress his still breathing companion.

"Jesus Christ. What are you doing?" the other man screamed, panicked and holding his hands out in front of him. "Don't shoot."

"He said you were the boss," Vargas replied calmly. "So, we had no need for him anymore."

The man looked at her like she was crazy. Well, maybe she was. Just a little.

"What do you want?"

"I want to know everything about that toxin you folks are chasing up here. Where it's made, what it's for, who has it, who's going to use it. You know, little stuff like that." She moved in closer, not more than five feet in front of him.

He held up his hands. "Look, I'm just a courier here, I don't know…" Before he could finish the sentence, she put a bullet through his left hand. He grabbed it and spun around in pain. "Fuck, fuck, why? What did you do that for?"

"If you don't know anything, I don't need you. We're going to go one limb at a time until you tell me what you know, or until I'm convinced you don't know anything." Vargas put another shot into his left shoulder.

He howled. "Fuuuuck…Okay, okay… What's the question?

"What's your mother's maiden name?"

He looked at her, his chin pulled inward in both pain and confusion. Vargas pointed the gun at his knee. "Kennedy," he shouted. "Her name is Kennedy."

"Is?" Vargas repeated. "You mean she's still alive?"

"Yes, yes, she's still alive."

"Give me her address."

"What!" Vargas pointed the gun again. "Okay, okay… Ahh… 540 Dunton Drive. It's in Blacksburg, Virginia."

"You get that, Abigail? Check it out. If it's a lie, I'll drop him."

"Who are you talking to," he said, squeezing his hand against his chest.

Vargas turned her head and pointed at her ear. He could see the small steel insert. "Home," she said. "You sure it's Virginia?"

"Ya, yes, yes… Blacksburg."

"Okay, easy," Vargas said. He was beginning to hyperventilate.

Abigail came back on. "The info's good. Mary Scarlett Kennedy, born October 12, 1945."

"What's your mother's birth date?"

"What?" Vargas raised the gun and fired a round just past his right ear. It bounced off the wall behind him and clipped the lamp on a table nearby. Vargas recalculated. Firing at cement walls probably that wasn't the best idea. "Ah, October, in October, the twelfth."

"What year?"

"Shit, ahh… 1944."

"You mean 1945," Vargas asked.

"Shit, ya… Forty-five, sorry."

"That's okay," Vargas said. "Now sit down and stop whining." She walked towards him, forcing him to retreat to the desk nearby. He sat down with a plop and a grimace. "Here's the deal: I have no time to waste. My colleague is lying in a pool of blood downstairs, and I need to get him out of here ASAP. But I need some answers first. So, I ask a question, you answer. If I think the answer is good, I ask another. If I think it's bad, I shoot one of your body parts and ask the question again." She paused. "You follow the rules?"

"Jesus Christ, who are you?" He lifted his arms in some kind of useless self defense posture.

"No, that's a question," she fired another round into his left elbow. He flew out of the chair, swearing relentlessly and making other sounds Vargas could not readily identify. She gave him a moment to get use to this new pain. "Back in the chair!" He jumped back into it. She knew he was ready to spill everything. "I told you my friends dying and I have no time for BS. Where's this gas made?"

"Shit, right here, right around the corner. At least that's the intention"

"What about Los Angeles?"

"There's a storage point in LA, there's a blending lab in Long Beach."

Vargas slid a pen and paper to him. "Right down the address." She was hoping he wasn't left handed.

He looked into her eyes. "I do not know the address." He paused, almost crying at his inability to reply, half expecting a fresh round to enter his body somewhere.

"Okay, how about a general area."

"I know it's near the Queen Mary. Pier GE I think, ya GE. But the chemists are in NOLA, I mean New Orleans."

"I know what NOLA means. What do you mean the chemists?"

"Look, the chemists figure out the mixture. They blend it and package a sample in LA, that's a control point. Then it comes here for production. Christ, lady, I don't know all the details, I'm just a broker."

"You're doing okay," she said calmly, "but you've got lot's more to tell me."

"Look, whatever, just get me to a hospital."

"Soon, soon. So, what are we doing in China?"

Any will he had to hold back was gone. His left arm was almost severed and numb from the broken nerves. His brain had shut down the pain to prevent him from passing out. He slid his jacket off his chair and wrapped it around his elbow before leaning back.

"Can I have a smoke?" he said, ready to take another bullet to get a puff.

"Sure, you light up and tell me all about this cow gas."

"Cow gas?" He looked up. "Are you kidding me?" He rummaged for his pack in his jacket. Vargas looked on but said nothing. "Fuck, you don't even know! You think we're killing cows? Holy fuck." He tilted his head back and looked at the ceiling, drawing a huge puff from his Marlboro. Vargas could have sworn she saw him smile.

"Enlighten me," she said, feeling a little out of control for the first time in a while.

He leaned forward on his chair, grimaced at the pain his change in position brought, and looked her in the eye. "This is DNA targeting gas. Christ, cows?" He spat out the words as a rhetorical question. "Who the fuck wants to kill cows? This gas can be formulated to kill anything. It can be tweaked to attack any DNA." His smirk was a little annoying, and her raised eyebrows reminded him of the situation. "Sorry, sorry… This gas can be tweaked to kill humans, or just men, or just women, or just tarantulas, for Christ's sake. It can be targeted to just Asians, or Caucasians, or your next door neighbor. You getting this? Any identifiable DNA strand can be integrated with the gas."

Vargas was beginning to get the point. That was why certain cows survive; they were a different breed, and therefore immune to the DNA-specific gas!

"Who's got it? What the hell are we doing in China?" she demanded.

He leaned back in his chair, once again scrunching his face in obvious pain. He took another long drag on the cigarette.

"Look, son of Mary Scarlett," Vargas continued, "I'm pretty sure she wants to see you again, and I'm trying to accommodate that, but you have to give me some detailed info here."

"Colestah," Vargas heard her name called out. *Chen Hui!*

"In here," she screamed, so he would know the room was safe.

She looked back at her prisoner. "What's your name, Kennedy?"

"Phillip," he said, a sad look in his eyes.

"Look Phillip, I'm pretty sure you don't want Guoanbu interrogating you," she reflected on that for a second. *Shit, maybe you would prefer their interrogation to mine!* "You need to give me everything right now or I can't protect you." Somehow, after delivering three bullets into this man's left arm, her statement came across as a little disingenuous.

"Protect me?" He looked at her like she was crazy. Vargas raised her eyebrows again "Ya, ya, okay. Look, I need a hospital, I need some attention."

Vargas stood up and walked to the window. "Abigail, you getting this?"

"Loud and clear," she replied. "Does not sound good!"

"No shit," she replied. Kennedy looked at her like she was crazy, talking to her ear piece. Vargas ripped down a small curtain framing the glass, noticed a swarm of cars outside, and returned to Phillip Kennedy. He didn't look very happy, even though Vargas was now trying to help him. She grabbed his arm, despite his screams, and wrapped it tightly in the cloth, using the tail ends to form a sling around his neck. He was sweating profusely and obviously close to unconsciousness. She just needed a couple of minutes.

"You okay?" said Chen Hui. He marched across the room with a shiny blue windbreaker and her bag of goodies. "Here, put this on." He handed her the jacket, and as she reached for it, he hesitated for a second, savoring the view.

Vargas smiled and put her hands on her hips, her Maxim 9 pointing directly at Hui Chen's crotch.

"You sure you want to go there?" she asked.

Chen Hui smiled and handed her the jacket. "Wancheng told me you'd be needing something."

"Shit. How is he? Where is he?"

"We just loaded him on the chopper. He's in pretty bad shape. Looks like he lost a lot of blood. The only thing he said was 'upstairs, bring Colestah a jacket.' Who's this?" He nodded towards Kennedy.

As if on cue, the helicopter rose up past the window. It was almost full light outside and Vargas tried to see Wancheng but could not. Only the co-pilot was visible.

"He's our Whitey Bulger," Vargas said, looking over at Kennedy. He knew what she meant. Bulger was one of the biggest storytellers the police ever nailed. He had informed on the Italian mob in Boston, and was instrumental in bringing about their collapse.

"Who?" Chen Hui asked, completely missing the reference.

"Never mind," she said. She returned her Maxim 9 to its holster and zipped up the jacket, then swung the goodies across her shoulder. With the gun away, Kennedy relaxed noticeably. "We need to get this guy to a hospital as well, but it has to be a secure one. He has a lot to say."

"No problem. Same one as Wancheng, but we're going by car. No more birdies available."

"That's okay." Vargas shrugged. "I'm enjoying my conversation with him." She looked at Kennedy, who rolled his eyes. "Looks like our first date is going to continue for a while."

"You okay?" Chen Hui asked, pointing at the fresh blood covering her hands.

"Oh shit, that," she said, wiping them across the curtain holding Kennedy's arm together. "No worries, it's his." Kennedy grimaced again at the pain.

As they left the room, Kennedy in tow, and feeling lightheaded from the blood loss, Chen Hui suddenly stopped in his tracks. He used his foot to turn over a body that was lying on its side.

"Friend of yours?" Vargas asked.

"His name is Mr. Lei, or was Mr. Lei. He's on the most wanted list at Guoanbu." Chen Hui took out his iPhone and started snapping a few pictures. "You're going to get some accommodation for nailing him."

"Bull," Vargas said. "Credit for that is of no use to me. Let's just agree that you took him out during the rescue mission." She marched

Kennedy out the door.

Chen Hui smiled.

The ride back to the city center took some time, and Vargas had the opportunity to chat with Kennedy. What a fountain of information he was. Abigail recorded everything. *Thank god for her,* Vargas thought. *What a nightmare writing up a report would be.*

The gas was almost ready to mass-produce; there were just a few adjustments to be made in the formula base. The producers and patent holders were Americans, somewhere in New Orleans, but the main production and distribution would come out of China, where reporting on chemicals and production was far less stringent. A lot of money had already exchanged hands on that. Vargas smiled at the fact that Mr. Lei wouldn't be spending much of it.

The containers were used to ship the gas samples from Los Angeles to China, and then on to any point in the world. The trip they had already identified at the CIA was the test run—apparently a huge success. But the producers were not planning on selling the gas; they were renting it out for huge sums. If a terrorist group in Palestine, for example, wanted to take out a specific individual, they need only to get a DNA sample—a hair, a cigarette butt, a toothbrush, anything that had a DNA signature. The producers would then create a batch of gas for that specific DNA source. All the terrorists had to do was release the gas in a certain vicinity of the victim. Kennedy mentioned within a half mile, but Vargas just didn't believe that was an effective range. How could the gas remain concentrated over such a huge area? He indicated that a single spore would be lethal, while remaining completely harmless to others.

This stuff had unlimited options. It could be used to target any specific person, race, or other group where the DNA string could be isolated, even by a single molecule. *Jesus, they could wipe out everybody with blue eyes if they wanted, or every field mouse.* It was unimaginable.

Kennedy explained that the process for harvesting revenue from the gas came from being selective on who could acquire it. Each batch that left the production line was unique for only one purpose, as agreed with the producers. The key to maintaining that originality was a chemical masking agent that was added to the gas. The DNA binding agent was part of the manufacturing process, but once produced, it became integrated with the DNA map, and indistinguishable as a separate component, preventing any laboratory breakdown of the chemical composition. That way, they protected the world from any maniac who wanted to wipe out an entire race or species. It was nice to know our bad guys had a conscience.

Kennedy was basically an interpreter and liaison for a potential buyer from Europe. He shuttled back and forth to witness the various tests and verify the product integrity. He confirmed they were on the verge of a final, workable formula. There was a buzz about actually testing it on humans—that was the next step—but he didn't know who or where yet. The more he talked, the crazier the story got.

They pulled up to a hospital. Chen Hui jumped out and yelled something across the driveway. A team of medical people and a stretcher bed emerged. Several men, looking quite a bit like Guoanbu officials, surrounded the stretcher and Chen Hui. Vargas watched them wheel Kennedy away. He was barely conscious.

"Thanks for sharing some time," she said with a little wave. "See you soon." She figured he didn't truly appreciate her sense of humor.

In a few minutes, Chen Hui returned to the car.

"Come on, let's get you to your hotel," he said, returning to the front seat.

"Not yet," Vargas replied. She started towards the hospital entrance. "I need to see Wancheng."

"He's out of it," Chen Hui replied as he jumped to keep up with her. "You can see him tomorrow."

"It is tomorrow," she said. "You coming, or do I have to find him on my own?"

Chen Hui already knew there was no point in arguing, so he escorted her up to Wancheng's room. She never would have gotten through the security without him, unless of course she dropped them all, but she knew that would not meet diplomatic protocol.

He was right; Wancheng was completely out of it. Vargas moved beside the bed and turned her back to Chen Hui before unzipping her jacket. She reached behind to unclip her bra and slid it off, pulling the straps out the jacket sleeves before re-zipping. She wasn't sure if Chen Hui realized what she was doing, but she didn't care. She rolled her bra up into a ball, leaned in against the bed, and reached under the covers. She slid the lace garment under his gown and down into Wancheng's groin. *Shit, he puts that Asian men theory to shame.* She left it nestled close, and backed up to leave. She smiled, hoping he would find it when he woke up.

Vargas hit the hotel completely starved and exhausted. The young lady at check-in had given her a rather wide-eyed once over. Vargas was surprised. Hadn't she ever seen an attractive blonde with a little blood and dirt, an oversized windbreaker, and disheveled hair, checking into the presidential suite? *What's happened to today's youth?*

It was only four o'clock. Her clothes were neatly hung in the room, as Rogers promised. It was the first time she'd seen them. There was some pretty nice stuff, which reflected well on that little butterfly in California, who must have done the shopping on crazy short notice.

She stripped off, dumped her earpiece on the counter, and pushed the shower on full flow, as hot as she could stand. It burned a little at first, but the aches and pains in her muscles, not to mention the blood in her hair and on her hands, appreciated the situation. The built-in bench was inviting, and Vargas sat down in the horizontal and overhead streams, closed her eyes, and thought about Wancheng. *He better make it through, if only so I can crush that freakin' smile!* She laughed to herself. After a half hour of beautiful heated water, she stepped out to get a toothbrush. It was freezing when she left the hot stream. She quickly jumped back into the warm flow, and brushed vigorously enough to erase the taste of the battlefield. She thanked God that Abigail could file a report; she would have been way too exhausted.

Vargas finished up, slipped her earpiece in, and dressed in some casual slacks and a soft blouse—no bra or panties. She wasn't going out and wasn't feeling particularly sexy. Slippers completed her ensemble for the elevator ride to the lobby. First, two double Belvenie, one rock, at the bar. No twenty-one on hand, but a fifteen-year-old would do. Some creepy businessman from Spain tried to engage her in conversation. He was half drunk and playing the big shot.

"Fuck off," she said, loud enough for the bartender and the two other patrons to hear. He turned away. No one else talked to her, not even the bartender. She tossed the last half drink down with one swig. "Presidential suite," she said, and headed to the restaurant.

"You have to sign, miss!"

But she was already gone.

There were a few people eating a late lunch, or perhaps an early supper, but the restaurant was basically empty. Vargas sat down at a table for four.

"Is Madam expecting someone else," the young waiter asked, with unmistakable sarcasm, hoping she would move to a smaller table.

Vargas looked up at him and smiled. He might have been twenty-five.

"Fuck off," she said.

He recoiled and stormed off in a huff. Vargas was too tired for this shit. She got up and went back to her room. She picked up the room service menu and laid back onto the plush mattress, but she was asleep before she finished reading the appetizer list.

She woke sometime very early, long before the sun rose, stripped off the pants and blouse, and slipped back under the covers. Sleep was elusive. Wancheng's face danced in her head. She smiled inwardly as other things danced there too. It took a while but she drifted off, dreaming of flying cows and Mrs. Mary Scarlett scolding her for being so abusive to her son.

She finally woke again around six and called down for room service.

"Eggs, over medium, none of that runny shit please. Bacon, ham, hash browns, pancakes, and rye toast." She hung up. "Christ," she said aloud. "You'd think I was at Denny's, all the way over in China."

It didn't take long for the food to arrive and she stuffed herself, even though they just didn't make bacon the same in China. She lay back down, thinking of Wancheng again, before drifting back into a full, deep sleep...for about an hour!

Chen Hui rang her room around eight that morning. She was half asleep, but still feeling almost completely rejuvenated.

"You want to see Wancheng?" he asked.

"Is he okay?" She suddenly felt a little anxious.

"Says something about wanting the matching set. You know anything about that? He said you would know."

"I'll take care of it. Be down in a few minutes." Vargas could already see that bloody smile on his face.

Vargas grabbed fresh underwear from the drawer and threw on the same pants with a new shirt. She liked the first blouse, but it was a little wrinkled from the previous evening's service as a nightgown. She grabbed the old matching panties from yesterday. She thought about rinsing them, but decided against it. She tucked them into her pocket.

Chen Hui confirmed that Phillip Kennedy was also in survival mode, although there remained some question as to whether or not his arm could be saved.

Vargas reflected on her handy work. "They might have to chop it at the elbow," she said, "but the shoulder was a baby wound."

Chen Hui just shook his head.

They strode into Wancheng's room. He turned his head slightly and opened one eye. He tried to smile but it was clear his neck was not happy with that. He forced a swallow. Vargas nodded at him. He opened his other eye.

"Can you give us a few minutes, Chen Hui?" she asked nicely.

Chen Hui noticed the softness in her voice; it was a new side of her. He didn't say anything, just backed out of the room with a little 'thumbs up' to Wancheng. After he left, Vargas moved over to the bedside. She looked at the bulk bandage around his neck.

"Anything to make me do all the work, right?" she said, smiling with her eyes.

He smiled too, but it wasn't that sarcastic one, this was genuine. He nodded.

Vargas held her fist up in front of his face and let the panties fall, keeping a grip on one small part of the band so they would dangle suggestively.

"Where's the bra?" she asked coyly. He didn't say anything, but let his eyes look down towards his body.

"You want to shut down for a few minutes?" Abigail whispered. Vargas jumped, letting her panties fall onto Wancheng's face. *Fuck, Abigail is still there.*

"Christ, you been there all night?"

"I have, post shower, through drinks, and sleep. And yes, you do snore on occasion."

Vargas slid the earpiece out of her ear and said, "Later." She pushed the 'contact' button to close it down. She put the transceiver into her pocket and leaned back towards Wancheng.

She retrieved her panties and let her hand slip under the cover, slowly crawling along his gown, until she reached her bra. Obviously, he had seen it and then placed it back down there. She looked at him and smiled. He rolled his eyes as her hand moved under his gown and found its destination. She lifted the cover over her head and move down towards her hand—to reclaim her underwear, of course. *This could take a while*, she thought.

► ► ►

"Wheels up as soon as you get here," Rogers said over the cell phone. "Some folks in Washington are anxious to see you."

"You taking me all the way?" Vargas asked, with a little double entendre thrown in. She hoped the answer was yes.

"Nope, you've got United 804 out of Tokyo at five o'clock," he replied. "Gets you into Dulles at about three-thirty today. Twelve and a half hours. That's a lot faster than I can make it."

"Probably, but your inflight service is obviously superior!"

"Well, we still have a four-hour flight from here to Tokyo," he replied suggestively. She liked Rogers.

Vargas threw the un-touched wad of Chinese money at Chen Hui as she jumped out of his car and up onto Rogers' plane.

"The exchange rate at the hotel was lousy," she said with a wink. He looked at it and shook his head before climbing into his car, slipping the shift back into drive, and speeding off.

Beijing to Tokyo was indeed complete with full inflight service.

▶ ▶ ▶

United 804 touched down in Dulles right on time. Vargas was rested, well fed, and briefed. First class on United wasn't bad. It wasn't Rogers Air, but it wasn't bad at all.

Of course, there was a Clemenson envelope waiting for her at the Narita first class lounge, and most of Phillip Kennedy's comments were confirmed. She knew he wouldn't lie. She had boarding instructions for Narita, using the red card to swipe past security and the accompanying metal detectors, and arrival instructions for Dulles. As was becoming a habit, she also received fresh currency in the form of fifty crisp US hundreds. The last page of the stack of papers in the envelope carried a big yellow happy face with a blue halo above. The words 'YOU ARE AN ANGEL' were written below. *Clemenson*, she thought. *Just when you think he has no humor. Christ, I wonder if he knows what I did to Kennedy and Creusa, never mind losing that gas sample.*

At Dulles customs, Vargas went to the far end, just past the global entry kiosks, and spotted the blue and white door as instructed. She swiped her red card and it opened. Two men on the other side jumped up from their papers.

"Good day, Ma'am." The younger one looked like he was deciding on whether or not to salute.

"Jesus, don't salute," Vargas said. "Just get me over to Landshark Aviation." The two men hustled out ahead of her, almost fighting over her shoulder bag, and helped her into the government town car. "And get me there in one piece."

"No problem, ma'am. Just sit back."

The R8 was sitting right where she left it, and Mr. Dungarees looked up as she approached. She considered making a sarcastic remark about how it all turned out okay, but refrained. She was obviously maturing. She noticed a small scratch along the front bumper spoiler. *Curious*, she thought, *looks like someone lifted the car. I hope Mr. Dungarees wasn't a bad boy.*

"You weren't playing with my car, were you?" she said.

"Nope, definitely not," he replied.

"Looks like someone's been prying up the front a bit," she said, squatting down and rubbing her hand along the markings.

Dungarees walked over and looked. He crouched and ran his hand along the scratch as well, either because he didn't believe her or because he was concerned about it. Vargas figured she would assume the latter for now.

"A couple of dudes were in here looking at it yesterday when I walked in from lunch." She looked up, waiting for more details. "I didn't see them touching it, just some young guys taking a look I thought." He shrugged and walking back towards the tool bench.

"They work around here?" she asked.

"I don't know, never seen them before." He was back at work on his project. *Curious.* Vargas didn't like snoopy people, and she didn't believe in coincidences.

As she drove by him on the way out, she asked, "What did they look like?"

"Shit, I don't know. One Chinese guy and another kid. They all look alike to me." He caught himself on the racist comment. "I mean kids—kids all look alike."

Vargas pursed her lips and shook her head, but said nothing. *Asshole.*

The car screamed back out onto the Dulles Toll Road, up to Curtis Memorial Parkway, then hit a dead stop; either construction or an accident. Either way, Vargas couldn't really keep the president waiting. She cut over to Lee Highway and made it in from there. It took her a little over an hour, which wasn't bad.

She moved through the gate and entry process at the White House like a veteran, more or less leading the security team as they hustled to keep up. They started to ask her to wait and knock before entering but it was too late, she pushed the door open. Clemenson and the president were there, snuggled up at the end of the table, exchanging whispers and chuckling at something. When Vargas entered, Clemenson stood up.

"Welcome home, Vargas. Great job over there."

"How's Wancheng doing?" she asked.

Clemenson was a little surprised at her first comment. "As far as I know, he's okay," he said. He placed a file on the table.

"I'd appreciate a confirmation, if and when possible, boss," she said, extending him at least a little respect in front of the president.

"Just buzz Abby once we're done here. I'm sure she's got the full scoop."

"Will do." She nodded and walked up the far side of the table, standing a few chairs down from where the two men were.

"Sit, sit, Vargas," Clemenson said.

"Good afternoon, Mr. President," she said before pulling out the large leather armchair.

"Good day, Vargas," he replied. "Seems you've been pretty active over the last few days." That was a huge understatement, and she was sure neither of them wanted too many details.

"Seems like we've got a good lead on what's going on. It's a lot worse than cow gas though," she said.

"It's crazy," Clemenson said. "Look, the president has given this top priority. Everything we need to get a handle on this. I still think one operative—you—can get better results than sending an army of agents out there to rustle the grass."

"I think you're right, boss."

"Vargas," the president said. "Stopping these maniacs is obviously crucial, and if we can get the chemists who are creating this toxin alive, it would be a real bonus." *Christ, he wants that gas for the good old US of A.*

"Noted, Mr. President. If possible, of course."

"Abigail gave a detailed account of what transpired out there," Clemenson said. "But only the battle details, and Kennedy's disclosures, of course. How did you get him to talk?"

"He seemed co-operative, sir. He was wounded and needed medical attention. Most of his disclosures came during the trip to the hospital." She thanked Abigail internally. There was no need for the gory details to be part of the report.

"Too bad about Creusa. Abigail says he caught a stray bullet just as you were about to capture him. Would have been nice to get him under the spotlight." Clemenson looked at her. She wasn't sure if he knew the truth and was buffeting it for the president, or if he just didn't believe it and wanted to see her reaction. Either way, it didn't matter.

"Yup, a real shame, sir." A double thank you to Abigail.

Clemenson sat back down and slid the file to Vargas. It was info on New Orleans, and a general disclosure of the accumulated details they knew so far. They all reviewed it together. It was mostly a re-hash, probably for the president's benefit. She could have gone through all this enroute to Abigail's in the morning.

"Head up to see Abigail first thing in the morning, she's got details on the NOLA setup, at least what we have determined so far, which isn't much. There are only a few places that we think could be ground zero. Get down there and figure it out. We already have a man on the ground in LA." Vargas figured it was he mysterious man from Abigail's Dungeon, no doubt.

"I'm on it," she said. *These guys are unbelievable. It's like they're playing a video game or something!*

"Vargas," the president called as she was about to open the door. "I know we're just sitting up here like dummies, but we're here to help in any way we can. Use that number to call me if you need to." *How did he know what I was thinking?*

Vargas thought about her reply. "You're definitely not dummies, Sir." She hesitated, with her hand on the door handle, and looked back at the president. "Thank you, James." He smiled. She looked over at Clemenson. "Later, boss." He smiled too.

S he opened up the R8. It needed no coaxing. She flew off the White House grounds and headed back to her penthouse, straight along K St. One point six miles; seven point five minutes, with traffic. She arrived at the gate and slammed on the brakes. The parking attendant looked up from his iPad and waved, reaching to lift the gate. Vargas held her hand up in a 'stop' signal and slid the shift into reverse. *What am I going to do up there alone right now?* she wondered. She revved up in reverse and then broke, double shifted, and spun the car forward, fish-tailing slightly on the four-wheel drive. She was pretty sure the attendant hadn't seen that before.

She floored it back out South St. to Thirty-first, up to Q St, right over to Florida St, a little check off on T St, and over to Eighteenth. Left turn up the block, and she pulled up right in front of Jack Rose Dining Saloon. She parked in the metered spot, popped open her 'Parkmobile' app, and headed inside. Before descending into the whisky cellar, she registered her R8 with the app and paid her parking. It was a great tool.

Vargas had visited Jack Rose's almost every time she was in Washington, which was fairly frequent. It was her go-to spot before and after assignments involving visits to CIA headquarters, or for lengthy chats with Maria.

There were a few people dining in the booths to her left, and a couple more sitting at the long bar enjoying their preferred whiskey. Vargas definitely wasn't in chat mode, so she slipped into the last seat—seat thirteen, as she liked to refer to it.

"Good evening, Ms. Hamilton," a rather husky and elderly gentleman greeted her. "It's been a while."

She smiled, so nice to be remembered.

"How've you been, Art?" she asked. They had spent more than a couple of evenings kicking around life's adventures over a rare scotch, and occasionally, an ice cube.

"Lagavulin?" he asked.

"Think that's a little strong and peaty for the pallet tonight," she said. "I remember a nice Glenfarclas from last time, or maybe it was the time before that." She chuckled.

"Oh ya," Art said, cracking a grin himself. He remembered her consuming several doubles and spilling her beans about daddy's dollar legacy. She didn't seem too happy about having the burden of a trust fund. It left her without ambition, she had lamented.

"Forty-year-old single malt. Had to replace the bottle you killed last time." Another chuckle. "Luckily," he said as he grunted with the effort required to move the sliding ladder so he could locate the bottle on one of the upper shelves, "we have a new one, just waiting for you."

Of course they did—at eighty-eight bucks a shot. He picked up the bottle, descended, and returned.

"Launched at the Speyside Festival in two thousand ten. Pretty special stuff. You hanging out with us tonight?"

"A double please." She ignored his conversation starter. "No ice."

"Enjoy," he said. He poured her a glass, probably at least a triple.

He was a veteran bartender and recognized that conversation was not on her menu for tonight, at least not yet. Several doubles sometimes changed that.

"Perfect," she replied. She sat and caressed the glass with both hands.

He was a good bartender. He knew a nice long drink for Vargas meant a nice big tip. She kept her eyes on the drink as Art moved off down the bar to polish up some glasses and chat with others, who were a little more social.

First sip, and another. *Perfect.* She was thinking about Wancheng, wondering if he would make it back to field ops. *Jesus, I wonder if he'll be able to talk again.* She was happy she had said goodbye in such an intimate fashion. He had saved her life several times, even if she had returned the favor. It was rare to meet someone who not only took those same crazy risks, but was also a superior warrior. Just being alive after all the shit they'd been through in their careers was proof of that.

Vargas reached into her pocket and hit connect on the transceiver before sliding it into her ear.

"Hey there," Abigail said. Vargas wondered if she actually lived with that receiver in her ear.

Vargas laughed. "How is it that you are always on line? I mean, don't you sleep? What about when you're in that Dungeon?"

Art looked down the bar at her. He wondered if she was talking to herself. Vargas didn't care.

"Whenever you click connect on the transceiver, it beeps in my own ear, and I know you're there. It's only off when I'm with the president."

Of course, the president, I believe I knew that. "How do you know it's me? You must have some other contacts as well." She thought of that mystery man from the dungeon.

"Different beeps, pretty simple. And I'm a light sleeper. It all works out."

"Well, I have to say, it's a great comfort having you there. Sorry if I included you in some personal stuff by mistake. Guess you've already become so familiar, I forget your hanging in my head."

Abigail snickered. "I don't mind, I thought you handled yourself well; I mean during those personal moments."

Vargas didn't blush. She would have if she gave a shit, but she didn't. Abigail knew what she was and what she did. She was probably the only one that really knew the truth. Killing people for a living brought immunity to any reservations about giving head.

"Coming up there in the morning," she said.

"I heard." Vargas knew she would have. "Let me know when you're on the road and I'll whip up some breakfast. We can chat over, what was it? Eggs over medium, no runny shit?"

Vargas laughed. The room service guy probably didn't truly understand the significant difference between over-easy and over-medium anyway.

"Bacon and pancakes?" Vargas asked.

"With ham and rye toast," Abigail replied.

"Thanks." Vargas turned serious. "You heard from China. Any news on Wancheng?"

"I haven't heard today, but last news was that he remains in semi-intensive care. Don't think there's any life-threatening component left to the injury, it's just a question of getting some healing under-way. Look, Vargas, he's tough as crap, and I'm sure he isn't letting a little thing like a bullet in the neck slow him down."

Vargas appreciated the reassurance.

"If you could double check when convenient and let me know tomorrow, I'd appreciate it."

"Will do."

"By the way, thanks for a little doctoring on the Clemenson report. I wasn't sure how much heat I was in for."

"I told you from the start, I'm not Clemenson's puppet, I'm *your* partner. I work for you, and I'll always do what's necessary to protect you and support your PATs, even if that means cleaning things up a bit for Clemenson. And anyway," she added, "he likes things clean."

"Cool," Vargas replied. She appreciated her loyalties. She certainly had proven both valuable and trustworthy. "See you in the AM."

Vargas returned her focus to the bar and noticed it had filled up significantly. She finished off her third double, or triple for anyone counting, and paid the bill with her Amex Centurion Card. Five hundred twenty-eight, plus ten percent tax, plus a three hundred dollar tip, for a grand total of eight hundred eighty dollars and eighty cents. Not bad for a pre-dinner drink, she reflected. She knew that was why Art poured her tall doubles.

She headed back to the penthouse, painfully aware of her limited sobriety, and navigated through the parking ordeal. She dropped off her Beijing wardrobe near the laundry basket, even though she hadn't worn much of it yet, and went to rummage through the fridge for a snack.

Surprise! There was a nice little lobster platter already prepared, chilled with lemon butter, surrounded by a dozen oysters on the half shell and some accompanying marionette sauce. There were also some other small dishes of condiments, a salad of spinach stems, cooked al dente, and of course, a pineapple mouse to cleanse the pallet. There was also a note:

> I'm sure you'll be hungry after your vacation; hope
> you enjoy the food. I left a nice Sauvignon Blanc on
> the shelf above. Very best, Emma.

A cleaning lady no doubt, but she was obviously more than just a duster. She pulled out the wine—Seresin, New Zealand. Vargas picked away at the platter while plugging into a CNN re-run of their in-depth story: 'Targeting Terror- Inside the Intelligence War', with Jim Sciutto. She felt there was some interesting stuff, but a lot of BS too. She knew first hand that if people really knew how limited the intelligence gathering was, they'd be a lot more nervous, as most of it comes after the fact.

Vargas crawled into bed before ten and woke up early. The sun was not yet shedding light on the day when she slid on her jogging gear: UA 'Fly By' capris, Eclipse sports bra and 'Fast Fly' half zip outer jacket, topped off with brand new Nike 'Free' 5.0 iD running shoes, gravel grey with a charcoal 'swoosh', with her name, VARGAS, printed in white across the tongue. It was a nice touch. She slipped her iPhone into the side arm pocket, penthouse key, some cash, and ID into the back-zipper pocket, and headed out onto South St., up Wisconsin to Grace, and over to the Tow Path, heading away from the city center. After Key Bridge, she shifted onto the Capital Crescent Trail, and ran along the canal all the way up to the Boathouse at Fletcher's Cove, before turning around and retracing her steps. About two point seven miles each way.

On the way back, she took Wisconsin up instead of down and crossed the canal to the Tow Path on the other side, jogged two more blocks to Jefferson, and crossed back over to the Baked & Wired Café, and her little pink framed doors. She headed back home with Rita's creamed coffee cake safely tucked in a plastic bag, bouncing along with her pace. She knew it would be a test for her not to eat any before she headed out.

▶ ▶ ▶

"I'm ten minutes away," Vargas announced, reconnecting with Abigail via the transmitter as she headed up MacArthur.

"Pancakes going on now, eggs when you get here."

"You are an angel," Vargas replied, and re-focused on the road. She disconnected and found it funny that her words were exactly what Clemenson had written about her under the happy face on United 804.

She pulled up to Abigail's with the R8 announcing her arrival as usual, and saw the little red head peek out of the door before she got there.

"Hurry up," she said as she headed back into the room, leaving the door jar.

Vargas pumped up her pace a bit and pushed inside, closing the heavy steel door behind her, listening for the click of its locks. Abigail was across the room standing in front of her laptop computer, waving at her to come forward. Vargas shrugged as she moved over to see the screen. Wancheng! And his nice smile, the good one.

"He only has two minutes. The doctor wasn't happy about him chatting," Abigail said.

"Hey there, Colestah. Still keeping me waiting?" He made the statement firmly tongue-in-cheek.

"Christ, I'm starting my day with your sarcasm again," she retorted. She smiled with obvious joy at seeing him.

Abigail pointed with her thumb towards the stairs leading up to her apartment. "Eggs," she said. Vargas didn't really hear her.

"How's your neck?"

"Well, they say no shirt-and-ties for at least a month." He chuckled. She did too.

"Looks like you're out of bed."

"Yup, walking around like a regular person again."

"Where's your robe?"

"In the wash."

"Where's my underwear?"

"Oh, I gave those to the doctor. Definitely fascinated." Wancheng smiled again.

"Shit, they're no good without me there to …ahh…handle them." She winked mischievously.

"Oh, that's how it works. I'd better get them back from her then."

"Her?"

"Ya, my doctor's a lady. Anything wrong with lady doctors?"

"Only if she's fondling my underwear." They laughed again.

They bantered back and forth a bit, reminding each other that they'd be long gone without the other's intervention. The connection wasn't secure so they couldn't discuss any work related issues, but Wancheng did confirm he was pushing to get back on duty. Vargas thought that was a little crazy, since he was wincing every time he blinked.

"I'm sure you'll be back running around in no time," she lied.

"Gotta go, I think they're going to transplant some flesh to my arm."

"What? It didn't seem that bad."

"Nope, just kidding," he said, letting that sarcastic grin resurface.

"Good luck," Vargas said. "Looking forward to seeing you again. Besides, if you die, how am I gonna save your life?"

Wancheng smiled. "Guess we owe each other," he said, and pushed the screen blank.

Vargas stood there watching the blank screen for several seconds.

"It's getting cold, Colestah," Abigail yelled down the stairs.

V argas sped back out the Dulles Toll Road towards the airport. She hit 'contact' and was soon chatting with Abigail.

"Thanks again for the face-to-face with Wancheng, Abby," she said.

"You bet, Colestah. By the way, United 495 is confirmed. Arthur Petite will meet you. He's driving a sliver C230 and he'll greet you by name. He'll get you into town, and there'll be a briefing in Matt Wagner's office. He's the local head CIA spook. Seems a few of his guys have been chasing down some leads already."

"Got it, United 495, Arthur Petite, Silver C250, Matt Wagner. Super. Christ, I hope they haven't screwed things up down there. I'd prefer they just stay out of the way."

"Good luck. Make contact when you get rolling." Abigail was gone.

The evening flight to NOLA was smooth on United 495. Abigail had fed her well, with both food and info, and she was languishing in semi consciousness. The album 'Blood on the Tracks' was kicking out of her earphones. 'Idiot Wind' was her favorite, but 'You're A Big Girl Now' was keeping her aware of reality at the moment. Her mind returned to Wancheng. She definitely liked him.

As expected, she was met by her contact and his silver Merc.

Vargas moved directly towards him.

"Ms. Hamilton?" he asked.

"That's me," she replied, happy to keep it formal.

"Arthur Petite," he said, holding out a stubby little hand. It looked like it had just changed a tire, or perhaps something much worse than that. She gave him a fist-bump instead.

"Three-ten is totally jammed," Petite said as they swung out of the airport onto Airline Dr. "Better just stay local all the way in."

Vargas didn't care. She was relaxed and still reflecting on her past few days.

As they pulled up to a red light at Roosevelt Blvd. in Kenner, a black sedan suddenly pulled alongside in the left-hand lane. Two Asian men burst from the passenger side, back and front doors. Automatic fire crashed through Arthur Petite's window and, unfortunately for him, his face. Vargas brought her hands up to cover her own head, as if her forearm was going to stop a Type 54, 7.62 mm Chinese bullet. *Fuck, my Maxim 9 is in my bag!*

Vargas swung her door open to generate some attempt at flight, and then felt the blow coming before it actually reached her. It was a gun butt, or blackjack, or good damn sledgehammer. The dim evening sky turned to grey, then black.

▶ ▶ ▶

When she slowly eased back into consciousness, it was dark. Her head was pounding. She gradually focused on her surroundings. Her hands were cuffed behind her back, there were four men in the car, and they all had automatic pistols, the previously noted Type 54s. The fact that they knew exactly when she was arriving, and exactly who was collecting her, was disturbing. She reminded herself she would have to keep one of them alive, at least long enough to tell her how they got their intel.

The car sped along a lonely dirt road somewhere out on the bayou, with drainage ditches on both sides, the headlights illuminating a short distance ahead, but otherwise deep black. With no moon and no stars, she figured it must be overcast. The partially open windows let the crunch of dirt road and whistle of wind fill the car. With her hands behind her back, Vargas reached down for her belt, into the slot pocket, to extract the lock-pick pin she housed there. She raised her voice to complain about her treatment, eliciting a laugh from her captors, and providing cover noise for her activity. The cuffs were off in a flash, but she kept her hands in position, carefully returning the pin to her belt compartment. She knew it wasn't the time yet to engineer her escape. She wanted to see where they were heading. *I wish I had that damn transceiver on.* She managed to glimpse a small road sign that said '57 Houma' as they sped past, but otherwise the trip was void of any reference points.

The men spoke in Chinese, a little heated at times, with the occasional glance in her direction. The word 'bitch' thrown about from time to time. The one to her left kept his pistol pointed at her rib cage, like he was frozen in position.

Suddenly, the man on her right, who seemed to be the senior among this comedy of kidnappers, removed his pistol and waved it at the driver, then at Vargas, very much looking like he was going to pull the trigger. She didn't know what they were arguing about, and didn't care, unless it was about whether or not to kill her. Either way, it was time to act.

Vargas brought both her arms out rapidly at the same moment. Her left hand hitting the arm of her guard, driving his hand and his gun northward, as his finger squeezed the trigger. The first round scattered out of the barrel, removing the top of the head of the poor, quiet, and unassuming gentleman in the passenger seat. Her right hand grabbed the arm of the agitated ringleader, and she threw her shoulder into his face. She pushed up and out with her right leg to gain control of his arm and his weapon. Her left foot came up and gave a straight kick to the face of her guard, momentarily stunning him as she maneuvered the leader's pistol and turned it on him. The sudden burst caught him directly in the chest, ending his career.

The driver slammed on the brakes, already too late for his survival. Vargas used the leader as an airbag as they plunged into the back of the front seat. The driver jerked forward, still unable to unholster his weapon—or maybe he didn't have one, she couldn't tell. The leader was a little stunned from the rough landing against the seat, and no doubt her right elbow driving into his nose didn't help. His eyes teared immediately, and Vargas repeated the elbow action just to be sure, still holding his weapon in unison with him. She wondered which one she should keep alive, before determining that the leader probably knew more.

She twisted his hand clockwise to release his grip and took his weapon, spinning around and leaning back against her previously breathing guard. She looked the leader in the eyes, holding his surprised stare, and pointed the gun at the back of the driver's head. Without so much as a glance at him, she kicked off two rounds. The leader threw his hands up in front of him, screeching out something in Chinese, certain that he was about to get the same treatment.

Vargas lowered the gun and placed a single round in his upper thigh, straight through it actually, just to keep him occupied. It reminded her immediately of the helicopter pilot back in Miyun, though his had been an unintentional ricochet. The injured leader grabbed his leg with more howling, and Vargas kicked it once, just to remind him she was running the show. He sucked in a few breaths and looked up at her, somehow a little more focused. Vargas reached behind her and opened the driver side back door, letting her former guard spill out onto the dirt road. She climbed out after him, grabbing his gun instead. She noted at least seven rounds were left and kept it pointed at the leader as she bent over to look back through the doorway.

"Out," she said in a clear and crisp instruction, waving the pistol to reinforce her request.

He fumbled for the handle, still grasping his wounded leg. Vargas saw headlights in the distance. It wasn't the best time for company. She moved around to the passenger side, dragging the guard's body around so the oncoming folks wouldn't see him, and opened the passenger side front door. The leader still hadn't managed to extricate himself and his limp leg from the car. She yanked the nearly headless passenger from his seat and let him roll onto the ground, and with a lifting kick, into the drainage ditch. She grabbed the leader's shoulder to give him a boost as the oncoming vehicle approached.

She was hoisting him up to get him into the passenger seat when several rounds flew past. Unfortunately for him, one found his head. She happily noted that it was better his than hers. The oncoming vehicle slammed on the breaks and Vargas dove behind her car, letting her dead informant crumple in front of her. The hail of fire continued to rain.

She peered under the car towards the new vehicle, now fully stopped across the road from her, and saw several sets of legs clambering out. She squeezed off three rounds, removing the ankles of three assailants, then taking out two of them completely as they hit the ground.

Vargas grabbed the former leader and rolled his body on hers, just as two men sped around the front of the car with guns blazing. The Chinese not-so-bullet-proof vest took the fire, except for one. As she lifted the dead man up on top of her, she felt the bullet crash into, and through, the fleshy underside of her forearm. She squeezed her hand into a fist, confirming nothing was broken. She raised her pistol and took out the first on rushing attacker with two more bullets, then noticed both assailants were white. She then aimed at the second as well—no ammo! *Shit, only eight rounds in this scrap. Where's my Maxim?*

He slowed and moved over above her, smiling at her predicament and savoring the prospect of putting an end to her time among the living.

"Fucking bitch," he said. She wondered why everybody was so hostile.

His hesitation was a mistake. Vargas reached under her pant leg and found the handle. She drove the ESEE knife blade straight up into his groin as she moved laterally to avoid the oncoming bullet. He sunk to his knees as she pulled the blade out, and tried to straighten up to continue his attack, but it was too late. She arched forward in a sit-up motion, and her blade dug five inches through his neck, severing the jugular vein, the carotid artery, the thyroid cartilage, and the mass of muscle and nerves that held the body and head together.

Vargas shook off the bullet-riddled Chinese leader, stood up, and leaned back against the car. She reached inside and dug into her bag for the Maxim 9. Thankfully, the local guys carried Glock 22 .40 side arms—not enough force on the rounds to pass through his body and into hers. They were the same ones used by the Louisiana State Police, but then, that goes for half the police in the country as well. Looked like nine dead dummies; four Chinese and five Caucasians.

As she began to relax a bit, she heard a distinct rustling sound on the other side of the car, and went back into survival mode, hitting the ground and rolling out towards the back of the car. Her ex-guard remained there, providing some cover if she needed it. There was more rustling, then a moan. She looked around the corner and saw one of the Caucasians pulling himself along the road with a partially severed foot. *Oh ya*, Vargas recalled, *I forgot about you. Must be getting old.*

She reached into her pocket and brought out the transceiver. Abigail's voice came across almost instantly. "Hey there, Colestah. I've been wondering where you were."

"It's been an adventure so far, a real nice welcome to the Big Easy, though a little unexpected."

"Can you elaborate?"

"Later, right now I need your ears. I have a new and fresh, well slightly damaged, version of Philip Kennedy."

"Wow. Okay, I'm listening."

Vargas stood and walked out into the space between the two cars, looking down at the poor guy. He looked up, probably wondering who she was talking with.

"How you doing?" she asked, as though they were friends

meeting at the corner diner for lunch.

He looked up, half conscious, grimacing with pain, sweat pouring off his dusty brow. "Just great, thanks."

Vargas could appreciate the sarcasm. After all, it wasn't everybody that could smile at the face of such pain. She moved forward and placed her left foot on his ankle, applying a decent amount of pressure, feeling the skin and bone shifting apart. He screamed, waving his arms in futility towards his lower leg.

"I'm not sure about the foot, but I'm pretty sure we can save your life." She squished his ankle again. He screamed.

"Who the fuck *are* you?" he managed to say.

"That's your reply? Wow! I'm the fucking bitch that's standing on what's left of your ankle!" She applied even more pressure to his poor leg. "And I need some answers."

"Okay," he yelled, once again with a futile attempt to reach down to his ankle. "What? What?"

"Here's my offer. I'll wrap up your ankle and get you into this car." She patted the vehicle he had arrived in. "And speed you gently to the nearest hospital. How's that sound?"

He looked at her, waiting for the punch line. "And what's my roll," he finally said.

"I knew we'd get to that." She glanced skyward, then back down at him. She raised her knife outward, examining the blade. There was some blood, and perhaps some other body material, from her last victim, still dripping from it. He looked at it too. "I need some answers."

He started to say something, but before a single word could escape his clenched jaw, she held up her finger to her lips and gently pressed her foot down again.

"Before you say anything, let me clarify what I need answers on. She held her palm out towards his mouth to ensure his silence. "Let me tell you that I need these answers in a clear and forthright manner. Now, let's assume that I ask you something that you don't know the answer to. What do you think happens then?"

He hesitated a bit, looking up at her with a silly expression. He didn't want to reply, hoping that she would somehow just be gone.

"You step on my leg?"

"Shit! I'm already doing that." She applied some pressure, eliciting a muffled howl from him.

"I don't know! Is this a guessing game?"

He still had a sense of humor. Vargas sort of liked him, in a combative, murderous sort of way.

"Here's the deal. I ask, you answer. The first time you say 'I don't know,' I drive this ESEE blade into one of your other body parts. By the way, this method has proven very effective in the past."

"But what if I don't know the answer?"

"As just mentioned, I stab you in a joint."

She smiled, letting go of his ankle and bending to help him to his feet, or more correctly, foot. He leaned on her for support, weary of the blade in her right hand, as she walked him, or rather hobbled him, around to the passenger side of the car. Once he was in the passenger seat, she reached over to grab the keys from the ignition and left him, circling the car to look in the trunk. Bungee cords, perfect! She took a short one and wrapped his lower leg, tight, cutting off the blood flow. She didn't want him passing out during their chat.

She dashed over to the other car and grabbed her goody bag, still sitting on the floor. *Amateurs.* She holstered the Maxim 9. *"You see what happens when you don't keep me close?"* she imagined the pistol saying. She leaned in further to pick up the cuffs, which formerly held her wrists. At that point, she noticed the blood from her pierced forearm dripping a little more vigorously. She didn't need that. She glanced into the front seat, still occupied by the driver. He had a jacket on. *No good.* She reached down with her knife and cut the polo shirt off one of the dead Caucasian attackers, ripping the last part with her right hand. She glanced up. Her informant was still sitting there, paying full attention to his injured ankle.

"I'm going to need a medic, Abigail," she said casually.

"What's the nature of your injury?"

"Mine's a forearm flesh wound, stitches will do, but my friend here, Phillip Kennedy number two, has a nearly severed foot." She didn't wait for Abigail to question that. "Casualty of battle, unfortunately."

"Yes, I can imagine," she replied. "I just heard that battle ongoing, underneath your foot I believe." Vargas smiled. Abigail never seemed upset or surprised by what was happening in the field.

"We'll need some serious clean up on the highway as well... there's a definite cluster-fuck of dead individuals."

"Okay. Doctor first."

Vargas used her knife to fashion a cloth strip she could use to wrap around her wound, reconnected with the handcuffs, and returned to her guest.

"Give me your hands," she said.

"You think I'm going to..." He couldn't finish the sentence.

Vargas brought the handle butt of her knife into his right cheek, probably not breaking the bone, but definitely making a statement.

"Your hands."

He reached up and rubbed the damaged area before complying. Vargas hoisted his wrists and locked them, passing the cuffs through the grab handle inside the door. She wrapped another bungee cord once around his neck and pulled it backwards, clipping the hooks together behind the head rest. He gurgled a bit, but his protest confirmed he could still speak.

"There we go," she said, closing the passenger door. She moved around to the driver's side and slid in, looking again at her passenger. "All set?"

A bigail directed her to a safe house somewhere outside the city. They rumbled along for a half hour, dancing in and out of conversation. The car was steaming, or smoking, and the left rear was almost flat. Vargas chuckled at the fact that her, her passenger, and her vehicle, were all in need of some repairs. On arrival, she assisted her travelling companion towards the front door as a large, rather young-looking man rumbled down the steps to help. Bo, the housekeeper, as he was officially called, was like a kid in a candy store, probably experiencing some real field action for the first time.

The doctor and his nurse had arrived a little before them and immediately attended to the two combatants, Vargas first of course. Treatment consisted of hot water, sterile instruments, small head shakes of concern, bandage wraps, painkillers, and a buried desire by the doc to ask a pack of questions about how all this happened. Bo hovered around the physical repair work like a bee on a flower, more of a nuisance than anything. Once Vargas was stitched—four on top, nine below—they turned their attention to Riley, aka Phillip Kennedy the second, and tried to stabilize his ankle. Everybody, except the poor man himself, knew it was the end for the unfortunate, drooping foot. They froze it, packed it up, and applied an air splint, expecting he would hear the fateful news later at the hospital.

Then they turned their attention to his left elbow, recently pierced with the sharp tip of her ESEE blade. She only had to strike him once; he was a fountain of information after that. As before, Abigail collected, correlated, compacted, and disseminated the entire disclosure, in speedy fashion, all done before Vargas could even test her newly wrapped forearm.

"Let's go," she said to Riley, at the very moment the doctor indicated he was finished. He looked at her. The doctor looked at her. Bo looked at her. "What?" she said. No one said anything. She repeated her instructions, providing a slight push of Riley's back. "Let's go."

"I thought you were taking me to the hospital. I told you everything."

"What do you think *this* place is?" she asked.

"He really should rest a bit," the doctor said. "He needs that foot properly taken care of."

Vargas looked at him with her best 'mind-your-fucking-business' look.

"Doc, I appreciate your efforts here, and the fact that it's the middle of the night and everything, but Mr. Riley and I have an appointment to keep." Vargas reached out to Riley and slipped an arm under his to provide support.

"Bo, do you have a car here?"

"I've got a motorcycle. A Kawasaki KMX 200." He beamed with some pride.

"Shit, that's only 200 cc's Bo, and what, twenty years old. That's not going to get me and Riley here, all the way out to the bayou." Bo looked down a little sheepishly. "How about you, Doc? Anything I can borrow?"

"What's wrong with the car you arrived in?"

"It's wounded as well," she said, without elaboration..

"I only have my car."

"Perfect, it'll do." Vargas held her hands out for the key.

He stumbled for his words, only half sure that she was serious. "But I need it to get back. Ms. Robelette," he pointed towards the nurse, "needs…"

Vargas cut him off. "Keys!" He reached for his pocket. "Abigail, can you please ensure a ride home for the doc and Ms. ahh, what's your name dear?"

"Robelette, Nancy Robelette," she said, almost as if it was someone else's voice.

"Cute," Vargas said. "My friend Abigail is going to make sure you get home safe and sound. Thanks so much for your help tonight, you're a life saver." She took the keys from the doc and turned her attention back to Riley. "Now!"

"Who's Abigail?" Nancy Robelette asked.

"A little voice in my head," Vargas replied as she dragged Riley out the door. As she reached the car, she turned around. "Bo!"

He came stumbling out the front door. "Yes ma'am?"

"Hop in, you're driving."

His eyes jumped open. "Yes ma'am," he said with some excitement, and started towards the car. Then he stopped. "What about the house? I have to close it up."

"Fuck it," Vargas said, flipping him the keys.

She slid into the back passenger side with Riley beside her, his hands cuffed through the pull handle again.

Riley had provided a significant amount of information about the ongoing development of the gas, and more importantly some uncomfortable insights into how they knew about Vargas, her trip to NOLA, and poor old Arthur Petite.

Only Vargas, Abigail, Arthur, and his office knew exactly what flight she was on, and who was collecting her. Assuming that none of them was leaking info to the other side, that meant some microphones or other listening devices were planted somewhere. Riley said the intel came from the Chinese, but that didn't really make sense. It had to be someone on this side of the world. Vargas figured time would reveal all.

His original answer had brought the blade of her knife down into his elbow. He clarified his reply from, 'I don't know,' to, 'It came from the Chinese.' Vargas had applauded his corrected version and hoped the elbow wasn't too badly hurt. He did use some vulgar language when responding, but she, uncharacteristically, let that slip by. *I'm definitely maturing,* she reflected.

His information on the local setup was much more detailed. Riley was just a soldier, but there was no hierarchy within their group in terms of secrecy, and it seemed that pretty much everyone knew everything. One thing was for sure: The test facility was deep in the bayou and guarded by at least twenty men.

The head guy was known only as Mr. Pitts. That's all. Riley was sure it wasn't his real name, but that was all any of them knew him as. He was from Texas somewhere, San Antonio or El Paso, he couldn't remember. Apparently, he had lived in Singapore, or somewhere in Asia, for several years, and was fluent in Chinese. Anyway, he always arrived by airboat, and he had a crazy one, bright red cage over a white motor with royal blue seats. There were three passenger seats up front and a driver's chair behind. The thing moved swiftly and effortlessly through the swamps and bushy terrain. Riley had no idea where the other end of his journey was. All the samples went back and forth with him; nobody else touched them, except the chemists.

The chemists also came in on the airboat usually, with or without Mr. Pitts, and they always had their faces covered with chemical masks. It always made Riley nervous to see that, but everyone had been reassured that there was no danger. The masks were to disguise their identities. Sometimes, without clear reason to Riley, a helicopter would come and drop off or collect a chemist, but the gas always went on the airboat with Mr. Pitts.

There were always four or five Chinese guys hanging out at the facility. They changed out occasionally, but there was always someone. Vargas figured that might not be the case this particular evening, picturing the four bodies back on a dirt road. Riley didn't know their role or responsibilities, even at the threat of a punctured kneecap.

"Christ, we never talk to those guys," he had said. He figured they were probably just there to keep an eye on things for the Chinese connection. He didn't know the connection, and they never came to the camp.

The Chinese team had gone to collect her from the airport. All he knew was the buzz about some bitch—he took that back when Vargas raised her eyebrows—some *lady* raising hell in China, and was now heading to NOLA. They had gone to collect her and bring her back to the camp. Mr. Pitts wanted to talk to her personally. Vargas figured she'd give him that chance soon enough. Riley was dispatched with the other guys, including his brother Curtis, who had suffered his demise at her hands, to escort them back along the tangled web of a route through the bayou. Mr. Pitts had been worried about the Chinese delegation's navigation skills.

As they chatted, Abigail collected and filtered his disclosures. The search was already on for a red and white airboat, helicopter rentals leading to the bayou, satellite imagery centered on the area Riley described as the camp site, airline manifests with Chinese arrivals in New Orleans, and a focus on chemical companies or chemists who might have a lead on the situation.

"Ahh...ma'am?"

"What is it, Bo?"

"You think this trip will help me get full agent status?"

Vargas wanted to respond with a quick 'no way', but she could see the absolute elation the possibility raised in him. "I don't know Bo. It usually takes a bit more training before that happens," she said.

"Jeez...that's the only thing I want. I've been at that house for three years and this is the first time anything has happened." He paused for a moment, perhaps waiting for Vargas to reply. "You think you could help me ma'am? I mean, maybe put in a good word; only if I do well of course."

He was so sincere, she didn't want to crush his dream.

"You have a weapon, Bo?" Vargas asked, without responding directly to his query. The car rumbled past the dead bodies and abandoned car that sat exactly where she had left them a couple of hours earlier, and eventually twisted off onto another dirt road. *Looks like the cleanup team is a little slow tonight.*

"Ahh, you mean like a gun?"

"Yup, that's exactly what I mean." Vargas hoped Abigail wasn't laughing too much. "Abigail, you getting this?" No response. "Abigail?" Vargas removed the transceiver and hit the 'contact' button before replacing it in her ear. "Abigail?" Nothing. She pulled out her iPhone. No signal. She realized they were on their own.

"Bo, you ever shoot a gun?"

"Yes, ma'am. Been hunting since I was ten. That's when my daddy let me start shooting. I tried..."

She interrupted him. "Sweet, all good, but have you ever handled a hand gun?"

"I scored second in my class at the farm," he said.

"Have you ever fired one in the field?"

"Never been in the field, ma'am."

Vargas reached in her bag and pulled out the KAHR P380 pistol.

"It's pretty tiny," she said, reaching over the seat and handing it to him. "But the bullets will kill you just as dead."

"We going to engage the enemy?" he asked.

Engage the enemy? Perfect. Abigail, I wish you were getting this.

"I hope not," Vargas replied, "but I want you to have some protection in case." That was a lie, but no sense in getting him all worked up yet.

"This is almost like I'm a real agent, isn't it?"

"You are a real agent Bo, just not a real field agent."

"I'm almost one now," he stated, more to himself than Vargas.

"Riley." She grabbed his arm by the right elbow, the undamaged one. "This arm looks good." He looked at her, unsure of the next move. "I want you to let me know when we're a mile out. If you screw that up, my first shot will be into your head." She left that hanging. He looked at her. "You copy that?"

Riley nodded.

"Good. Bo, slow down a bit, let's give Riley an opportunity to recognize where we are. His life depends on it."

Bo eased up on the gas and looked back at her. "Yes, ma'am."

It wasn't long before Riley called it. Of course, he wasn't exactly sure, and Vargas figured he probably erred on the side of caution, so she told Bo to keep going for about a quarter mile.

"Okay, stop here, and turn the car around. Park off the road under that tree." She pointed to a large Cyprus. "Motor off, but Bo, stay attached to the car. You understand?"

"Sure do," Bo replied. "But what about you? I mean, heck, I'm ready for some action."

Vargas just looked at him. He understood perfectly.

"Yes, ma'am, I'll be right here." Just as Vargas was beginning to think he wasn't a total donkey, Bo proved her wrong. "But if I hear any fire, I'm heading in with this gun blazing."

Vargas decided not to continue the conversation. She would either have to shoot him or embarrass him, either of which suited her, but she had other things to do. She moved quickly up the side of the road, cognizant of the wet ditches along the way, and certain that she had spotted alligators lurking within. After jogging for about five minutes, she figured she was close to the camp. She double checked her phone for a signal. No cell phone, but there was a faint Wi-Fi signal. Unfortunately, the connection was password protected.

She heard three voices before she saw anything. She moved closer until she could make out the figures. There were four actually, sitting around a makeshift table, a bottle of something in the middle, but no glasses. She figured they were taking swigs, which meant they were relaxed and a little off guard, and perhaps a little inebriated—all of which suited her intentions. The clearing between her and them was too wide for her to get close enough to deliver their deaths by hand, and use of her Maxim 9, even when suppressed, was out. She was still counting on the element of surprise. If Riley was correct, there could be as many as sixteen more guards in the vicinity. She decided to ignore them for now and move laterally to try to get a look inside the building. It was a fair distance around the clearing, and she went slowly to ensure there was no sound to alert them.

She reached the back of the building, but there were no windows or apparent points of entrance. She followed all the way around the structure, but still no luck. That left only the front door. As she was developing a plan, she heard footsteps heading her way.

She hid down behind a small pile of rusted barrels and watched as a solitary figure rounded the corner of the building and stopped, not more than five feet in front of her. The guard unzipped and proceeded to relieve himself, oblivious to her presence. She let him finish, figuring there was no sense getting splashed or something, and then leapt from her spot and cracked him on the head with her pistol. He went limp for a second, but wasn't completely unconscious for long. Vargas quickly sat him against a tree, removed his belt, and tied it around his neck and the tree, fastening it tightly. His hands could not reach around behind the tree. She slapped him a couple of times to bring him back to his senses. She crouched down, held her hand over his mouth, and her ESEE blade next to his left eye.

"I'm heading out on a limb here, but I'm guessing you do not want this blade sunk into your eye, right?"

He didn't answer, perhaps figuring it was a rhetorical question, but Vargas wanted to hear him say it. She loosened her grip a bit.

"Right?" she repeated, bringing the blade tip just a quarter inch from his eyeball.

"Ya, ya right," he replied.

"What's the Wi-Fi password?"

"What?"

"Was that a fucking complicated question?" she whispered, obviously a little agitated. "What is the password to the Wi-Fi? You've got two seconds."

"MickeyMouse. Capital M, capital M, no space."

"Thanks." Vargas punched it into her phone. She launched WhatsApp and sent a message to Abigail, who confirmed reinforcements were thirty minutes out. Vargas responded with 'Can't quite', which she corrected to 'Can't wait'. *God damn spellcheck.*

Vargas looked down at her prisoner. She knew she should just drive her knife up through the bottom of his jaw and eliminate him as a threat, but she didn't. She decided to leave him there and collect him later. She told him of her contemplations. He promised silence in exchange for the latter choice.

"How many inside?"

"There's about eight guys, plus a couple of chemists."

"No Chinese?"

"No, they left some time ago to pick up some broad." He stopped. She knew he had figured that one out.

"What's your name?"

"Carl," he answered without hesitation.

"Okay, Carl, you stay quiet and you live. If you scream any warnings, I'll have to head back this way." She made her point by tapping the knife blade on the top of his head. He understood.

Vargas slipped back to the corner of the building and peered around. There were only three men out front now. She kept her knife in her right, and her left on the Maxim 9 holstered behind her. She took a deep breath and walked out into the clearing. The three men immediately stood and grabbed their weapons.

"Easy guys, Carl needs some help with those empty barrels around the corner."

They looked at one another and then at her. She was moving forward slowly, waiting for one to speak. He would be the leader.

"Who the hell are you?" one blond, but scruffy looking guy finally asked.

She walked up to him, close enough to whisper, and drove her blade up through the bottom of his jaw. The other two other men were stunned. *Amateurs.* She swung her Maxim 9 out and fired two shots into the chest of the second man, farthest from her, and then leapt sideways, delivering a straight kick to the face of guard three, who was much closer. She heard his gurgling sound as she followed up with a straight blow with her open hand to his Adam's apple. All fell silent. She collected her knife, returning it to the sheath around her ankle, and holstered the Maxim 9. It seemed that the silenced shots had not alerted anyone inside the building.

She dug into her goody bag and pulled out the six sticks of plastique gum. She opened them all and pushed them together cautiously into one large ball. *Christ, I hope this works.* Vargas move quickly to the door and pried it open. No one stood guard inside. She moved forward in a semi crouch, down a short corridor. At the end, she could make out a large space with a series of glass windows across the back. Through them, she could see a couple of people in full biohazard clothing. Several men were casually lingering in the room.

She lofted the six-stick ball of plastique like a grenade, and slipped back behind the wall as she waited for it to float into the center of the room. She was not expecting the force of the ensuing explosion. It partially knocked her off her feet, dulling her senses.

She knelt down on one knee to shake on a recovery, and heard the bursts of automatic fire, blasting aimlessly through the thick smoke. She wondered who they were shooting at. She waited for the gunfire to stop. Smoke still shadowed the room, and Vargas crawled along on her belly until she cleared the hallway wall. From her position, she was able to take out two guards with quiet strikes from her gun and noticed at least three more lying on the floor. She wasn't sure how many had been taken out by the explosion, but she figured even those not killed must be slightly disoriented, just like her.

A sudden burst of fire pounded the wall behind her and she felt a ricochet drive into her left buttock. *Shit.* She aimed at where she had seen the muzzle flash and squeeze off three shots. She heard the body drop and a gun hit the floor.

As the smoke was beginning to dissipate, Vargas slid in behind a desk to her right and waited to identify if there were any remaining guards. It was quiet. Eventually, she peaked out from behind the desk, half expecting to attract fire, but nothing came. As she leaned out for a better look, she realized the room was empty, except for the dead bodies littering the concrete. As the smoke cleared, she moved cautiously towards the back laboratory, her buttock pounding in pain. She noticed a stairway leading down and moved along it slowly, crouching at the bottom before looking around the corner.

She heard what sounded like a huge fan at the end of a long corridor and raced down after it, her butt shooting painful darts up her back with each step. She was running, but also limping. As she rounded the end of the corridor, she pushed open a door and found herself standing next to a dock, across the clearing from the house. The airboat was a disappearing spec in the dark.

She sensed his presence before he struck, and ducked just before his knife found her back. She spun as he kicked her hard in the crotch. She managed to grab his leg despite the pain of the impact, as her pistol flew out onto the lawn. He leaned forward in another stab attempt and she wrestled for his knife. They struggled and eventually crashed into the water beside the dock. He was holding her down; air was becoming urgent.

Suddenly, she felt him yanked backwards, losing his grip on her. *What the fuck was that!* She could just make out the screaming face of her attacker as his legs fell victim to a large alligator. Vargas surfaced and grabbed an all important breath. Another 'gator was heading her way; she could just make out his snout along the surface of the water. She reached down and grabbed her ESEE blade, pulling it forward just as the beast arrived. She drove it down through the top of the predator's head and felt the powerful creature spin sideways, ripping the blade from her hand. She swam full force towards the shore, realizing that was her only chance.

She managed to scramble up onto the grass before the gator recovered enough to pursue her, and laid back momentarily to catch her breath. Her butt screamed in pain and she was a little dizzy. Suddenly, the gator was at her feet. She yanked away just in time and rolled sideways, adrenalin once again pushing any pain or disability from her mind. She scrambled up the embracement and glanced back. The gator was not in a mood to chase her on land. She relaxed. A mistake. A body emerged from the building. Obviously, it was someone who had been injured, probably knocked unconscious by the blast, but not killed. He had a gun pointed directly at her head. Her Maxim 9 was on the ground somewhere by the water. Her knife was stuck in an alligator's head. This was it. She heard the shot but didn't feel it. She didn't feel anything. She looked up.

"Bo?"

He was standing there, shaking a little, with the mini P380 pistol still smoking. Her executioner was sprawled lifeless in front of her.

"You okay, Bo?

He looked up at her, a little stunned, a little blank. Then he looked back at the gun in his hand, back at her, and nodded.

At that moment, Vargas heard the distant whirl of a helicopter rotor. She was definitely hoping it was on her side. She rested on the lawn, gathering her breath and her senses. Bo? She realized this kid had just saved her. *Maturing is one thing, but don't tell me I'm getting old!*

Vargas was surprised to see Matt Wagner, the local head of the CIA, all the way out here on a field op. Two of his agents, jumped from the bird with him, leaving the pilot in his seat, ready to depart immediately.

"Hey Matt, what are you doing way out here?"

"Hey back. When the president tells me to look after someone, I swing into hands-on mode," he said.

Vargas smiled. She explained that there was one live bad guy tied to a tree out back, and another cuffed to a car less than a mile down the road.

"The kid will show you," she said, nodding at Bo, who was sitting at the makeshift table in the middle of the clearing. Vargas moved over to him, putting her hand out to get her P380 back. He handed it to her, still somewhat trance-like over the fact that he had actually shot someone.

"I thought I told you to stay with the car," she said, in a mock scolding tone. He looked up at her. She took his face in her hand, leaned forward, and planted a lengthy kiss on his still trembling lips. "Thanks."

An unexpected turn of events for Bo, but he managed not to pass out.

"Does this mean I'm a field agent now?" Bo asked. Vargas just smiled. "Hi Matt," he said to Wagner.

The fact that they were on a first name basis was a little curious.

The next while was a bit of a blur. Vargas collected her Maxim 9 from the shore slope, carefully stepping over her assassin on the way. She cracked off a shot into the brain of the nearly dead alligator, and retrieved her knife as well. The assembled group of agents hit the ground collectively in reaction to the gunfire. She fired another round into the head of the assassin Bo had killed, just to feel better. She looked at the CIA audience, now re-gathering themselves, and winked. *Guess they think I'm crazy. Perfect!*

She was whisked onto the helicopter, enduring the obvious comments from the CIA dudes about her inability to sit on her wounded buttock. She spoke with Abigail through the chopper communication system and felt the lift-off of the bird. She knelt on the floor, her wounded butt up in the air, with her face planted in the seat, where her grimaces could not be seen. At some point, she passed out, either from blood loss, involuntary trauma shut down, or just plain old exhaustion.

"**G**ood morning, Colestah."

She heard the words before she saw the face that delivered them. Her eyes opened but were not yet adjusted to consciousness. She lay on her stomach, her face turned to the left. She felt the rekindling of pain before she finally focused on Clemenson. She was pleasantly surprised that he had come all the way to see her.

"They got away," she said.

"You set them back months," he replied.

She pushed up onto her elbows and suddenly realized that her left forearm was also a pain center. She collapsed back down onto her stomach.

"Easy there," he said. He reached out, ostensibly to clutch her shoulder, but never actually touched her. "You've got a nice sized hole in your, well, in your derriere." *Did he say derriere?* "And the doc says you need some more rest."

She looked at him. She was feeling fully awake and already impatient with the thought of finding the bastards that escaped.

"I can rest enroute to catch up with those dogs," she replied, the look on her face completely without humor.

"It seems our Mr. Pitts has fallen off the face of the earth. Whoever left the camp on Tuesday, made it a clean getaway."

Vargas wasn't sure she heard him correctly. "Tuesday? What day is it?"

"Friday morning. You've been out for more than two days."

"Shit, they could be anywhere."

"We've got full resources on it here. We've got the LA operation surrounded with surveillance, and we've got the China connection closely watched. They'll turn up."

"Look, boss, can we at least get back to Virginia and refocus from there?"

"We're are back, Vargas."

"We're in Virginia?"

"Baltimore, actually."

She knew that meant Johns Hopkins. She also knew they don't usually bring agents there.

"Wow, nothing but the best, right boss?"

"Sibley Memorial was full," Clemenson replied, once again flashing his uncommon sense of humor. "Look, Abigail will be by shortly and will take care of anything needed. The doctor says you can rehab at home for a few days, once he's sure there are no unseen issues, so to speak. By the way, he says the stitching of your arm was first rate. Guess that field doc was alright."

"Shit, I hope he's not pissed about lending me his car."

"Not to worry. Colestah. We took good care of him."

"What about Bo?" she asked.

"Ha!" Clemenson smirked. "You rambled on about him so much that we had to debrief him. Christ, at some point we thought he might be a double agent, if you could believe that." She definitely could not. "Anyway, he told us what his role was, and we ticked off his file. It'll all add up at some point to get him field agent status."

Vargas thought about Bo. He wasn't really ready, but he was so anxious, and so exuberant, and so openly straight forward. "Give it to him now," Vargas said, surprising herself with the request, and careful not to make it too demanding. Clemenson looked at her. "I don't ask for much, boss." She let that hang in the air.

He looked at her, obviously contemplating his response carefully. He smiled. "Done."

She smiled back. "Thanks." She let her head fall back onto the pillow. "It's not that he saved my life, it's more that he recognized the moment to countermand my instructions, and despite his inexperience and complete nervousness, he found the courage to use his weapon." The last part drifted into a whisper as her exhaustion took hold, and she slipped back into unconsciousness.

When she awoke, Abigail was hovering around, arranging some flowers on the bedside table.

"Christ, can you keep it down? I'm trying to sleep here." Vargas smiled.

"Keep it down?" Abigail said." I've been rustling these darn flowers for ten minutes trying to wake you up." They both laughed.

Another day at Johns Hopkins, two days of restless rehab at home, and Vargas was chomping at the bit. She was a little depressed about the lack of a perfect bikini butt, but rationalized it with a carefully thought out response: "Fuck it!"

She spoke to Bo. He was almost incomprehensible as he whirled on about his new appointment to full agent.

"Wow!" Vargas shared in his excitement. "I guess they were really impressed with your swift action out there in the field. Guess it never hurts to save a fellow agent as well."

He was in heaven, the pride rolling off his voice like butter down the side of hot pancakes. She never mentioned her role in his promotion.

Vargas was summoned to Abigail's, not the White House, and sped up in her R8, a pillow from her living room sofa carefully tucked under her still-sensitive cheek. She got there a little early, as was often the case when she had the R8 flying, and Abigail ushered her into the main room of the Den.

Clemenson was there, probably in meetings with her beforehand, and she went through the expected confirmation with him that she was indeed ready to return to the field. They sat and tea was served, though Vargas would have preferred some Belvenie! As the small talk dwindled, she recognized that such small talk always meant they were waiting for someone. A few moments later, there came a knock at the door. Abigail went to answer and Vargas heard male voices before she saw the new arrivals.

"Rogers," she said with a smile and slight jump in her voice, careful not to sound too pleased with seeing him.

"Hey there, Colestah. Heard you've been a pain in the butt recently." He avoided the hug they both wanted to share.

"Oh Rogers, that's so original," she said. He smiled.

The other man was unknown to her.

"Colestah, meet Taranis," said Clemenson.

"Brendan Dunkirk." Vargas held out her hand.

"Vargas Hamilton," he replied, clutching it warmly, without any macho squeeze.

The others in the room were a little surprised that they knew each other, at least by name. No one asked for, and no one offered, an explanation.

"Colestah; medicine woman and fierce warrior," Brendan Dunkirk remarked without any sarcasm.

"Taranis; Celtic god of thunder, I believe. Thunderbolt in one hand and a wheel in the other; something like that." He was definitely impressed.

"Close enough," Brendan replied. He liked her from the start.

"For some unknown reason, I had Celtic mythology as a class back in school. Made no sense at the time, but I'm kind of glad now," she elaborated. She let the words confirm that she had neither ego nor issue with him.

He laughed. "I heard Abigail call you by Colestah last time I was here, and proceeded to look it up." *So, it* was *you in the Dungeon when I came by.* Vargas glanced at Abigail, then at Clemenson, and saw they were smiling. They were seemingly happy that the two agents were hitting it off; fewer complications. Abigail knew it would be hell for her if they didn't get along, if they let their egos clash. They were both serious warriors, full of aggression and self-confidence, but no competition was apparent, and that was exceptional.

Clemenson ran through what they knew so far. Brendan gave a report on the LA findings, and Vargas recounted the NOLA episode, with special attention to the heroics of *Agent Bo*. She sent a careful side glance and smile of appreciation to Clemenson. The fact that Rogers was there meant he was top level cleared, and as much as Vargas liked him, she wasn't sure why he had been invited. Clemenson cleared that up.

"As you've both been informed," he said to Vargas and Brendan, "PT1 is a small and closed operation. It's only been the four of us up until now, but we have reached out to add Rogers here to our team."

Rogers smiled and nodded. Vargas smiled and winked at him.

Clemenson continued. "His specialty is procurement and transportation, both of which seem to be in constant demand. He is also a mechanical whiz. If it's broken, he can fix it, with blades of grass and round stones if necessary."

Rogers smirked and shrugged. Everyone smiled again. *This is turning into a real love fest*, Vargas thought.

Intel had Mr. Pitts somewhere still in the NOLA area. Vargas was to head out to find him. It was time to take down the LA operation as well. Brendan was heading there with Rogers. That was a tough twist for Vargas, as she was hoping Rogers would be taking her to NOLA.

"Better take a look at my R8," Vargas said. "I had some unsolicited visitors, and I think the Intel about my arrival in NOLA might have been gathered from some kind of listening device planted there. I repeated the instructions you gave me, Abigail, when confirming them back to you. That's the only time the plan was available for other ears, unless you have some unwanted ears here. If they were listening, they would have heard it." That made sense.

"We've got constant scanning going on here," Abigail said. "We'll get the car looked at."

"Show me your scanner," Rogers said. "I'll let you know right now."

Abigail showed him one of the scanners. She had a portable MCD-22H All-in-one—perfect for Rogers' purpose. He went outside, asking Vargas to join him, and moved forward to scan the vehicle. Vargas popped the front trunk, if you could call it that. It was about the size of a large carry-on. Rogers easily found the two listening devices located under the front spoiler. He checked the rear and undercarriage as well, but nothing else beeped.

"Sorry guys," he said into the bugs, "we're going to have to shut down now." He dropped them onto the driveway so he could apply his heel to them and ensure their destruction. He picked one up afterwards. "Chinese," he said, and glanced at Vargas. "Interesting."

She nodded. "Your mechanic told me there were some Chinese kids hanging around at Landshark. You'd better take a look at the security there."

The five of them, under the leadership of Clemenson, headed out for dinner. It was, Vargas assumed, some kind of bonding exercise, but Clemenson said it was an opportunity to galvanize the group. *Same shit to me.* It seemed that they all got along, and that was different from his past experiences. His previous PT1 teams had always had some sort of conflict with one another, or lack of a shared history. This was the first time ever that Clemenson had started with a new team, including Rogers, who had come with the highest recommendations. Clemenson was a little annoyed that PT1 had to purchase the Gulfstream V from the CIA, for thirty million, but he didn't really have a budget cap, so those feelings passed quickly. Abigail was the only steady hand, and she had already commented on the cooperative nature of this group. He saw the potential for this group to become something special, more than they already were. They were all getting along and joining forces at the same time.

They moved out in a semi caravan—Abigail with Clemenson, Rogers tucked beside Vargas in the R8, and Brendan following in his V12 Vantage S Austin Martin. Vargas glanced at Brendan in her rear-view mirror. She knew they would have to race these 'babies' at some point in the future.

They were headed to 1789 Restaurant, which was enroute back to the city from Abigail's. She had reserved the Garden Room, where they could enjoy their dinner in a relaxed and private atmosphere.

As discussions turned around their collective futures, and shared support system, Vargas asked Clemenson a question, that brought a little solemnity to the conversation.

"What's the story on the MIA agent still unaccounted for?"

Clemenson looked up at her, taking on a serious tone. "What do you know about that?" he said.

"Just some of my background research on PT1," she said, recognizing the surprise surrounding the info, and not wanting to implicate Abigail unnecessarily.

Clemenson looked at Abby just the same. She shrugged a little. "Carson Wallach, called Honos. An unassuming man with a short balding hairline and vibrant green eyes. Not your typical agent, and really, he was more a CIA man than specifically PT1. He spent significant time in Asia, and we reassigned him to Colombia. We were losing the cocaine battle down there, and felt a fresh face might get some new info moving." Clemenson hesitated, almost as if he was finished with the story.

"What happened, boss," Vargas pushed him.

"After a few months in South America, he came back with some pretty far reaching info about the drug trade. I sent him back to follow up, but he was attacked and stabbed shortly after that. The left side of his chest pretty much ripped open. I had some contact with him after the stabbing, but he fell of the radar. We searched pretty long and hard for him, but couldn't get any closure. His body was never found, so he was assumed dead. That's why he remains as an MIA agent."

Vargas figured there was more to the story, but her questions had been answered, with some candor, and little hesitation. She felt that pursuing it further at this point might damage the mood of the collective evening they were enjoying.

Overall, the night served its purpose well, bringing them

together in some comradery and recognition of the dangerous and important work they were doing. Vargas and Brendan were mutually pleased with each other, neither one feeling competitive, and both respectful of the obvious talents of the other. They would not be there otherwise. Clemenson had made it clear that Vargas was the lead, and Brendan not only took the news well, he actually made a firm statement of acceptance. In the field, she would make the final critical decisions. They managed to chat quite a bit, and clean off the crust of new acquaintances by the time the evening ended.

Clemenson left a little earlier than the rest, and Brendan lived up on Wilmett Rd. in Bethesda, so he took Abigail back to Brookmont. Vargas offered to take Rogers to his hotel, as it wasn't far from her place. It all made sense and they bid their farewells.

Vargas and Rogers detoured enroute to his hotel, and continued their evening for several more hours at her place, cautious of their positions, of course, in respect to her still healing buttock.

Vargas leaned back into her seat, the familiar discomfort of her Maxim 9 in the small of her back. There was no way she was walking into New Orleans again unarmed. Back on United 495, hopefully without any advance notice to thugs, Chinese or otherwise, she relaxed and took stock of the situation.

An extensive search of area chemists found two that had recently left their employment, and had seen significant sums deposited to their bank accounts. Mike Sorenson and Victor Vaygen. The money came from a company called Select Virus Group. Vargas couldn't believe that was its real name.

She was in charge of the next steps, and wanted to wait until she met up with the chemists. Then she would decide whether to either apply significant physical coercion, until they shed some light on Mr. Pitts, which was her preferred method, or just spook them, and let them run to see what hole they scurried into.

Matt Wagner was meeting her, and she had specifically asked for Bo as well. She figured she might as well help him get some field time. She had requested and reviewed his file. His name was actually Bodine LeBlanc, orphaned at twelve, born to an alcoholic Cajun father and heroine addicted mother. It was almost unfathomable that he had been accepted to the farm, and then actually graduated, until

---

his file revealed that his mother's maiden name was indeed Wagner, and she was some distant cousin to Matt Wagner. That had explained both Bo's employment, and his familiarity with Wagner out in the bayou. Anyway, she wanted him to get his feet wet a little more. He had saved her life and, although she didn't consciously articulate it, she somehow felt she could both educate and protect him—if he stayed within earshot.

"How ya doing, ma am?" Bo asked, as he sprung out of the driver's seat and bounced around the vehicle to open the door for her.

Vargas had to smile. "I'm good, Bo. How are you doing?"

"I'm great," he said. He couldn't resist. "I got my field agent status, ma'am!"

"I know Bo, you told me on the phone. Good for you," Vargas said, using the climb into the passenger seat to hide her smile. Bo drove while Wagner barked instructions to his office, from the back seat. Abigail mumbled a little background to Vargas on chemist number one. Thirty-six, married, two kids, eight and five, graduated from Tulane University, specializing in chemical and biomolecular engineering, and until two months earlier, on a fast track to senior management at Grace Corporation, out in Norco, Louisiana. He had walked away from a six-figure income with a growing family to care for and a mortgage weighing him down. He had recently received a deposit from Select Virus Group for two hundred fifty thousand dollars.

They drove out to Destrehan and swung past his residence on Rosedale Dr., hoping to spot some sign of life. Nothing stirred. There was a black GMC Denali in the driveway, and the front window curtains were closed. They circled the block. Vargas knew she would be able to find a way into the house. When they came back around the corner, everything was the same, except the Denali was gone!

"Shit, did they just leave coincidently?" Vargas said. "No way. They saw us and bolted. Bo, step on it, back the way we came in. There was a sign for a highway entrance to the three-ten a few blocks back."

Vargas figured they would head for open road if they were

running. Bo swung the Navigator around in a screeching one-eighty, surprising Vargas and Wagner with the move, and bolted up the residential street.

"There… there!" Vargas pointed as she saw the sign that indicated Interstate 310 to the left. Bo cornered at maximum speed and chased towards the highway entrance.

"Where the hell did you learn to drive like that?" Vargas yelled, letting her voice climb over the physical bounce they were experiencing as they hit several speed bumps.

Wagner echoed her. "Yeah, what the hell was that?"

"I, well I, I used to race all around in Papa's car," he said.

"He never let you drive that thing," Wagner said.

"Ha!" Bo seemed to gain some balls as he sped around another corner and onto the highway ramp. "He couldn't stop me; he was already dead."

He said it so matter-of-factly that no one could argue. Vargas recalled that he had been orphaned around the same age as her, and guessed his driving tutorials came sometime after that.

"Sharp as a bowling ball, kid," said Wagner.

Vargas saw Bo smile as he pounded the Navigator up to full speed on the open highway.

"There it is. Look, on the right." Vargas pointed at the Denali.

"I got it," Bo whispered, bringing the Navigator alongside. Vargas looked over and saw the driver, the chemist, and he was scared. She also saw a woman in the passenger seat, probably his wife, and two kids in the back.

"Shit, he's got the whole team with him," she said. "Matt, give me your ID."

"What?"

"Your ID, come on. If he's running with his family, somebody put the fear of god into him, and if it wasn't us, it must have been them. Matt, you're ID! Christ!"

He pulled his wallet. She grabbed it and flashed it at the chemist, moving her hands repeatedly in a downward sweep, indicating he should slow down.

"Back off, Bo, let him see we're not out to harm him. Get in behind."

Bo slowed and maneuvered the Navigator in behind the Denali, not too close, but close enough that nobody could slip between them. The Denali slowed, and so did they.

"Here's an exit, put on your signal," Vargas told Bo, hoping the Denali would get the message. It did.

The chemist pulled off and drove along for a block or so, pulling into a vacant warehouse parking lot. Bo wheeled in behind him.

"Stay here," Vargas said, as she flipped Wagner his ID. She gently exited the vehicle and pulled out her Maxim 9. She moved behind the Denali, and then peered around the rear towards the driver's seat. The chemist was looking at her through his mirror. She motioned for him to exit, but he shook his head. Vargas re-holstered her gun. She held her hands up and stepped out into full view of the driver, moving slowly towards his door.

"What the fuck is she doing?" Wagner whispered, more to himself than Bo. He pulled his Glock 22 and slid out on the passenger side.

Vargas got all the way to the door and stood nose to nose with the chemist through the glass. She circled her hand, indicating he should lower the window. He did a bit.

"Where you running to, Mike?" she asked in a calm voice, using his first name to endear herself a bit. She kept her hands up so he could see them. Mike looked a little startled that she knew who he was. His wife was in near panic mode in the passenger seat, and one of the kids was crying. "You want to let me know what's going on?"

"Who the hell are you?" he asked. She felt that was a fair question.

"CIA, Mike. Your latest project has been getting a lot of play time with us."

"Look, I had no idea what was going on. I was blending, just blending. No one said anything about a targeting gas."

"Is that what you call it, Mike, a targeting gas?"

"That's what they call it. I just did one part. Jesus, they offered me a lot for just a little work. It was a no-brainer." He was right about that.

"Look Mike, why are you in such a rush. You're risking the safety of your family, scaring your kids. What's that all about?"

"They killed Vaygen. Shot him right in front of me."

"Who shot him, who is Vaygen?" Vargas knew who he was, but wanted to see if Mike did.

"He was working on the isolation formulas. He found the technique and they shot him. Once they get the blending sequence, I'm gone too. These guys are crazy!" Mike was definitely scared.

"Okay, Mike. So where are you heading?"

"I just have to get away. I need to get my family safe."

"I think we're probably the only ones that can do that for you." Vargas maintained her calm and reassuring demeanor.

Mike Sorenson popped the door locks and began to open his. Wagner heard the lock click and swung open the passenger door. He locked his Glock 22 squarely on Mike. The wife screamed and the kids freaked. Mike's hands went up to protect his head.

"Christ, Wagner! Get the fuck out of there," Vargas screamed. "It's all cool." *Christ, what a fucking dummy. Goddamn* CIA. "Close the door."

Wagner closed the door. "Come on, Mike, hop out and get in with us. Wagner will bring your car. Let's get over to CIA headquarters, and we can get you into protective custody until we sort this out."

"Mike, please," his wife pleaded.

Mike opened the door all the way and stepped out. Wagner ushered his wife out the passenger side, and she opened the back door for the kids to pile out. They clung to her like burrs on a hound, carefully watching Wagner and his Glock 22, still being waved around needlessly.

"Good, Mike…" Vargas said. Suddenly, she watched the right side of his head disappear from a single round. *Christ.* She hit the deck immediately.

"Down," she screamed. She rolled under the Denali, trying to triangulate where the shot came from.

She could see Mike's wife and kids lying down on the other side of the Denali. Wagner crouched behind the rear wheel.

"Get Bo," Vargas called. "Abigail, get a chopper in here. I've got a feeling this isn't over."

"On it, Colestah."

Vargas pushed herself backwards, just under the right side of the vehicle, hoping the rear driver side tire would provide additional cover. Suddenly, there was a burst of several shots, raking along the bottom of the rear driver side door, a couple digging into the asphalt in front of her. She knew he had to be elevated. Vargas replayed the terrain in her mind. *Exit ramp, grass slope off the highway abutment; too far for that accurate of a shot; gas station across the street; no second floor, trees behind the gas station; best bet.* The shooter, if he was following them, would have had time to pull into the station and climb up the tree. She shimmied under the vehicle to the far side, signaling Mike's widow to stay calm and motionless. She was screaming her husband's name, but he wasn't answering. Wagner dashed across the gap between the two SUVs, just ahead of a single round from the shooter.

Vargas peeked out carefully from behind the rear passenger tire, aware that if she could see him, he could see her. She went back to the front of the vehicle and tried to yank the mirror off. There was no way it was coming down. She broke the mirror with the butt of her Maxim 9 and located the largest piece before returning to the rear tire. The road traffic was buzzing by like normal. Nobody even knew what was going on.

The next shot hit the Navigator. *Bo?* Vargas looked up and across to the vehicle. She saw Bo's eyes widen a bit and his head tilt in a rather confused look. Then he slumped forward, his head banging into the top of the steering wheel. She let her head fall down and closed her eyes. "Son of a bitch."

Vargas held the mirror out past the tire and tried to scour the tree line on the far side of the road. She spotted some movement. He was descending the tree. He was either heading for them, or heading home. She jumped to her feet and ran full speed out over the sidewalk and across the busy street, barely avoiding several cars. Wagner stood up.

"Where the hell is she going?" he said to himself. He looked in at Bo. He was dead. Clean shot through the left side of his temporal lobe. "Fuck!"

Vargas dashed past the pumps and, with several people watching her antics, continued to the sidewall of the gas station, just as the grey Pontiac pulled out from behind the station. She saw the driver and he saw her. That was all she needed to confirm it was the right person. She stepped out onto the asphalt alleyway and rapidly squeezed off seven shots from her pistol, hitting him squarely in the face at least twice. She jumped sideways as the car sped past with the dead driver still accelerating. The car hit the first two gas pumps, after scattering the bystanders, and knocked the pump caps off. Gas was spewing everywhere, and Vargas was yelling at everyone to clear out. People ran in all directions.

Just when she felt there might not be an explosion, hell paid a visit to the little town. The fireball scorched skyward and the thug's car, along with two others, was engulfed by the flames. She knew more was coming. The second vehicle soon burst into flames, as the recently filled gas tank caught fire, and the third shortly after that. Within minutes, sirens were screaming, police, fire, EMS, and thankfully, one helicopter.

Vargas managed her way back across the street. She saw Wagner, who was huddling with the howling woman and kids—away from the Denali and their dead father.

"Bo?" she asked, even though she knew the answer. Wagner just shook his head. *Fuuuck!* She ran to the chopper. "Get them safe," she screamed at Wagner over the rotor as she climbed aboard.

"Where too?" the pilot asked.

"I don't know," Vargas said. "Just get me out of here." They banked left and soon saw the plume of smoke rising from the chaos.

"Where to, Abigail?" Vargas said.

After a moment, Abigail shot back some co-ordinates. Vargas relayed them to the pilot and they veered right.

"Sorry about, Bo," Abigail said. She knew from the muted conversation following Vargas' question to Wagner that the answer wasn't good. "Since the other chemist is dead, we'd better reconnect with Taranis and see if anything has surfaced in LA. I'll check with Clemenson as well. Look, you'll land at the old house where you were the night the doc stitched you." Vargas appreciated that she didn't call it Bo's place. "Hang in there until I get something to steer us back on course."

"Got it, Abby," Vargas replied. Her thoughts were with Bo and the guilt that was seeping into her skin.

The following afternoon, Wagner rolled up in the Navigator. The window was repaired but Vargas could see the blood stain, wiped away, but still visible.

"Jesus Matt, you didn't have another vehicle?"

Wagner glanced over his shoulder at the stain. "You know the budgets these days." There was a short, uncomfortable pause. "Look, it's rough about Bo, I mean, Christ, he was my goddamn nephew." He waited for Vargas to offer some consolation. She didn't. "The kid never knew what hit him. Funeral is on Monday."

"Let's swing by the mortuary, Matt. I want a last word with him. I won't make it to the funeral."

For some reason, Bo's death hit her hard. Normally, she had little conscience about death—all part of life. She knew her business was beyond dangerous, and she fully expected that one day she would be the one with lead in her head. Yet with Bo, it was different. First of all, he probably shouldn't have been in the CIA, even if he did save her life. She felt a chunk of guilt about dragging him out into the field as well.

She dropped a few words onto his corpse in the mortuary, words to comfort herself, not him, and returned to the Navigator. *Fuck it.*

"I'm driving."

Abigail had tracked two payments from Louisiana State Senator Michael Cartier to Victor Vaygen, the isolation formula chemist. He had graduated from ETH Zurich with an MSc in chemical and bioengineering. He left behind a cushy job with the Louisiana Department of Economic Development, where he was tasked with luring large chemical and research companies, to build or relocate in the state, dangling loaded government incentives and tax exemption arrangements. *And probably pocket loads of cash,* Vargas figured. He left that to work for Select Virus Group. Just before his departure from the government job, two separate transfers of fifty thousand each, from Senator Cartier, had hit his account.

It was time to pay the senator a visit. Getting an appointment was easy; Clemenson pulled all the strings.

"Sorry Matt, I need you to wait here," Vargas said. They cleared the security gate and swung onto the front driveway curve at the senator's mansion. "If he's going to open up at all, it won't be with the local CIA in the room."

Wagner thought about protesting, but he was beginning to know Vargas enough to know that she was decisive, and in charge.

"Okay, boss," he said with a hint of sarcasm. Vargas looked at him like a bad puppy. She reached out and cupped his chin with her hand, tickling it with one finger, and smiling.

"Cute," he said.

She went up to the house, slipping the transceiver into her ear. "Abigail, you there?"

"Right here, where we at."

"Heading in to see Senator Cartier, but I think it might get messy." She was met by the usual secret service characters, but both private contractors this time, who motioned for her to lift her arms to be frisked.

"Not happening," she said. "Whatever weapons I might have are staying with me."

The agents were confused. They had never faced that response before. Vargas wondered where these clowns came from.

"Get the senator and tell him how rude you're being to his guest," she suggested.

That attracted some nasty looks. One agent smiled. "No frisk, no entry."

He moved towards her and raised his right arm to take hold of her. She delivered a closed fist to the underside of his nose, driving him back. He crouched as he held the broken bone. The other agent went for his gun but Vargas had her Maxim 9 pointed at his head before he could un-holster.

"Easy, cowboy," she said. "Keep it in the holster and just lie down." He did as he was told. "You too, Sparky." She motioned to the injured agent. A butler of some sort appeared at the entrance, and looked on with utter shock. He was frozen. "What's your name?" she asked, motioning her gun over in his direction.

He fumbled for his words but managed to say, "Adler."

"Well, Adler, how about you go and get the senator for me?"

"Yes ma'am," he stuttered. He departed in a half run down the hall. She figured he had not run in a long time.

Soon enough, Senator Cartier appeared, surveyed the situation, and looked up at Vargas. He knew anyone sent by Clemenson would be more than capable. "You're making my boys look bad."

"They're capable of that all by themselves," she replied. She decided it was enough with this BS; she knew he was a fraud. "Senator, would you like to entertain me in a private setting, or should we pack a small bag and head to the city?"

It was brash and pushy, but she knew she had Clemenson behind her, and whatever pull he had, which seemed to be extensive.

"Stay calm, young lady. No need to get riled up. Come into the library. I'm sure we will be more comfortable there."

Vargas parked the Maxim 9 behind her and headed towards the senator. "Thank you," she said, stepping over Sparky's outstretched leg.

"Tea or coffee, miss?" Adler offered.

She looked at him for a moment. *Why the hell not?* she thought.

"Aberlour, one rock."

Adler looked at the senator, waiting for confirmation.

"Me too," he said, and turned towards the library.

They sat comfortably in leather arm chairs across from each other.

"Sorry about the boys," Senator Cartier said. "We can't be too careful when living in the public eye."

Vargas smiled, letting the fact that she had easily dispatched them sit in the air. It was a little forewarning for the senator. Adler arrived with the scotch. Vargas was a little disappointed that it was only twelve-year-old. She clinked glasses with the senator and he immediately went into pander mode, moving seamlessly from comments about the weather to remarks about his legacy.

More BS. "Look, Senator," she said, cutting him off and tearing the friendly atmosphere into one of direct aggression. "I'm not CIA and I'm not FBI. What I am is fucking crazy, and I need some answers in the next few minutes or I'm going to start breaking your fingers." The threat tactic usually worked. It certainly set the tone.

She remained calm in her chair, legs crossed and Aberlour being swished around in her left hand. She took a final gulp, downing the remainder, and looked him in the eye.

He was clearly trying to gauge this strange creature. A fine looking woman, complete in every way, who just took out his two best guards, and was now threatening to break his fingers. He rose, ostensibly to contemplate his response, and moved towards his desk.

"What kind of answers?" he said.

She couldn't believe the senator was that predictable. Vargas was on her feet and beside the desk before he was. She opened the top drawer and pulled out his little Smith & Wesson M&P Shield 9mm, popping the seven round cartridge, or candy dish as some referred to it, and tossed it onto the desk. He looked at her. She figured he was thinking that maybe he could just take her physically, and there was no sense in letting him build up his courage. Vargas swooped her right leg forward, catching his legs and forcing him to fall towards her. She stepped sideways, grabbed him under his left shoulder and across his neck to catch him, and spun him around, yanking out his desk chair with her left hand and plopping him into it. She maintained some pressure on his arm, lifting it high over his head in a variation of the half nelson, but also applying pressure with her lower forearm to his windpipe. He started to try to stand, but she kicked his right Achilles' tendon with some force, and he sat back down with a slight yelp.

"Be calm," she said. He struggled a bit. "Be calm, Senator," she repeated, and he relaxed back into his seat. Vargas released him, knowing the control issue was settled, and slid her still slightly sensitive buttock onto the edge of the desk in front of him, so that she was looking down into his face. "Just a few answers and I'll be gone."

"What is it?" he said, obviously conceding her position, and now void of aggressive thoughts.

"Look, Senator, I don't really care about you or your little empire. I'm not here to rain on your parade either. We have a tense national security issue ongoing, and I need some answers."

"I'm a goddamn senator, lady. There's protocol for information gathering."

"New protocol," she said, slamming her hand around his windpipe. His hands came up but her grip was like a vice. "I could squeeze the fucking life out of you right now, Michael, and all you'd have is a headline in tomorrow's paper describing the terrible car accident that stole you from your loving family." She let that sink in for a few seconds. "You following me?" One more squeeze.

He couldn't talk but he nodded. Vargas released him.

"Who's Victor Vaygen?" Vargas was just testing his sincerity.

"Victor who?" Wrong answer. Vargas hooked her leg under his and flipped him backwards, causing the chair to crash down with him in it. She jumped forward and applied the sole of her foot to his throat.

"Wrong answer, Michael. We know you sent him a hundred grand a few months ago. We also know he worked for the government before moving over to Select Virus Group." She played her wild card. "A company you are heavily involved with."

The senator looked up at her, trying to gauge her sincerity, beyond the fact that her boot was on his throat. He found a pure poker face.

"Alright, Christ, let me up," he said finally, pushing her foot away. He clambered to his feet and Vargas lifted the chair to its normal position.

"Sit." He slumped into the chair. Vargas moved forward and stood over him. *So, you **are** mixed up with Select Virus, you little snake.* "Senator, I'm going to make you a one-time offer. This is like winning the lotto." She started to pace back and forth across in front of him. "It's like winning the lotto because you get to avoid twenty to life in, what do they call it, Angola?" Angola, the local nickname for the Louisiana State Penitentiary, probably the worst prison in the country. "And believe me, you would be a main attraction in there. You also get to avoid the humiliation of arrest and prosecution, the demise of your family name, and the complete disillusionment of your children as they disown you."

Vargas knew she was laying it on a little thick. She looked at him and smiled. She put her hands out and shrugged her shoulders to indicate she was waiting for an answer.

He went into self-preservation mode. "Do I get a signed statement of immunity?"

"Nope," she said. "All you get is me out of your face, and a quiet world that knows very little. Once I leave here, it's up to you to change your activity. If local authorities discover what you're up to, it's back to square one."

"I don't get that; I mean, it doesn't really protect me."

"Fuck you," she said, dropping the humoring attitude. "That's the deal. I leave like we never met. You in?"

"Okay, okay. What do you need?"

"Everything."

The good senator spilled it all. He might have left out a few items of particular self-incrimination, but Vargas was content that she had enough info to move forward and crash this little 'target gas' party.

"You get that, Abigail?"

"Every word," she replied.

"What?" the senator asked.

"Just my conscience," Vargas replied, as she walked out the door.

She strode past the two agents at the front door, winked at Sparky and his swollen nose, now stuffed with tissue, and jumped into the driver's seat of the Navigator.

"How long to process and disseminate that, Abby?"

"Almost done." Abigail was good.

"What did you say?" Wagner asked. *Jesus Christ, am I the only one in the world with a secret transceiver?*

Vargas met Rogers at the airport the following morning. He stopped in NOLA enroute from the west coast. The senator's disclosure was extremely revealing, and tied in with some of the findings from Long Beach. It was time to brainstorm a solution to this whole situation.

Brendan was on the plane when she boarded. That brought more disappointment, as Vargas was looking forward to some in-flight service from Rogers. Rogers winked and shrugged, suggesting he felt the same. They were airborne shortly, enroute to Washington, this time heading straight to the White House.

From Landshark they would take separate vehicles.

"Sorry to hear about Bo," Brendan said, seemingly sincere. He knew what it was like to lose a colleague, although he didn't know the details behind Bo's demise.

"Thanks. Good kid."

Brendan grabbed his Austin Martin and Vargas packed Rogers into her R8. They sped out of the airport and onto Dulles Toll Road. Rogers sat up a little stiff and seemed to be getting nervous with the speed they were travelling. Vargas could sense it.

"I never mentioned the speed of your plane, Rogers," she said, smiling at him.

"Eyes on the road, lady," he shot back with his own smile.

B rendan picked up Abigail enroute and Vargas dropped Rogers off at her place. He usually lived on the plane, or some hotel near whatever airport he was sitting in.

"Grab a nice hot shower, stuff yourself, and relax. We'll be back in a couple of hours," Vargas said. She flipped him the key and FOB.

"Think I'll work on some flight plans," he said. "Guess I'll have to book Dulles – NOLA." Vargas hoped so. "Dulles - Long Beach, Long Beach - Beijing, NOLA - Long Beach." He paused. "And a partridge in a pear tree." It was always good to have a sense of humor.

Rogers was not part of this meeting, but Vargas wasn't sure why. Maybe Clemenson just thought he would be fueling and prepping for their next journey, although none of them knew yet what that destination would be.

Vargas pulled the R8 into the usual parking area at the White House. Abby and Brendan had just arrived as well. Vargas led the way inside, using her red card to access the building and nodding at the agents who stood guard. They knew her by now and she said hello. They nodded to her, but extended a more pleasant hello to Abigail.

"Hey, Phil," she said. "Stan's still giving you the best shifts I see."

"Hey there, Abby. I figured she was on your team." He shook his head sideways at Vargas.

Brendan extended a hand, but the guard gave a friendly salute with two fingers to his forehead.

Brendan drew his hand back and returned the small salute. Vargas wasn't surprised Abby knew the guys, she had been coming here for fourteen years.

They went down hallways, through turns and shifts, then through the doors. The president and Clemenson sat in their usual seats. John Brenmar, head of the CIA, was there as well, sitting to the left of the president and two seats down. Vargas, Abigail, and Brendan all sat to the right of the president, three seats down, leaving Brenmar alone across the table. They exchanged pleasantries and everyone got comfortable.

The president spoke first. "Abigail, can you run through what we know so far?" *Shit,* Vargas thought. *Of course she knows the prez too. It's the only time she's offline. I wonder if she also calls him James.*

"Thank you, Mr. President," she said. She stood, removing a group of papers from her bag and sliding copies to everyone attending. Vargas guessed it wasn't the appropriate time for 'James.' "Mr. Pitts remains a mystery, but he'll have to surface eventually. Vargas was able to convince Senator Cartier to provide some hefty information." Vargas hoped she didn't tell them how, before concluding she definitely wouldn't do that.

"I heard she was convincing," Clemenson said, looking straight at Vargas. She shrugged and offered a weak smile. Clemenson smiled back. *Phew.*

"It seems Cartier formed Select Virus Group three years ago, ostensibly to be a front company for disposal of toxic waste and biohazardous material. Mr. Pitts and his partners from China, still unnamed, were having some difficulty getting through the red tape involved for such an endeavor."

"BHR," Vargas added, remembering Clemenson's acronym for bureaucracy, hypocrisy, and red tape.

"Exactly," Abigail said. "And that brought Cartier into the picture. He managed to pave the way and get the facility approved.

Vaygen left the government, at Cartier's suggestion, and took over management. He recruited Sorenson. Of course, Mr. Pitts never had any plans to deal with the toxic waste, and his interest was directed to biohazardous products and their manipulation. Vaygen was very much into the process, and even excited about the developments they were making. Unfortunately for him, once he realized that they were actually planning to use the by-products to kill, he freaked a bit."

"Cartier swears they were both mislead by Pitts," Vargas said, "but I got the gut feeling that he is not quite as innocent as he was making out."

Abigail continued. "Vaygen was basically held captive in the camp. Once he figured out the way to isolate the particular methodology for adhering the toxin to specific DNA, they didn't need him anymore."

"That confirms what Mike Sorenson said as well, before they assassinated him," Vargas said.

"Cartier said there are a couple of new chemists from South America somewhere, but that's vague. One thing for sure, they have replacements for both Vaygen and Sorenson, or they wouldn't have killed them. Cartier also claims the money, the hundred K that he sent Vaygen, was to keep him quite until he completed his work. He said Pitts repaid him. A search of his bank accounts confirms a transfer deposit about a month after the Vaygen payoff. It came from a company in China, through the Industrial & Commercial Bank of China."

"We have a name on the company yet?" Brenmar asked.

"Not yet, sir. Wheels are turning slowly in China on the information sharing program. We're working on it."

"SVG Chemicals (China) Ltd.," Vargas said slowly. She had just realized that the SVG she had seen back in Beijing, when Wancheng was nursing his neck wound, stood for 'Select Virus Group.' "That's the building in Miyun where we were chasing down rats, when Wancheng got shot."

"I'll get onto that," Brenmar said.

Abigail continued. "Cartier claims he wasn't aware of the specifics about the targeting aspects of the gas, says they paid him a bunch to keep quiet, mentioning the risk to his family if he opened up. He claims this Mr. Pitts rolls into town for a few days at a time and sees no one. He has, or more accurately, had, the camp out near Dulac, and rode his airboat out there to collect samples. He was very protective of them, and they were always camouflaged as fire extinguisher bottles—easy to transport, and they could be carried in and out of anywhere without drawing attention."

"Now, Brendan confirmed that there were two separate vehicles, cars actually, with Louisiana plates, at the warehouse on Pier GE in Long Beach—the one that Philip Kennedy lead us to. They may have been courier vehicles. We took the place down two days ago and got nothing really. There was one of the special containers we saw them using though, and we're running though that now. However, no gas, no canisters, and no Pitts."

"Okay," Brendan said. "Looks like we closed down the China run. NOLA's done, and now Long Beach. They have to be hurting. So, where are they?"

"I don't think so," Clemenson said, surprising everyone. "All those facilities were either forward labs, fronts, or temporary storage spots. They have a bigger operation somewhere. Perhaps another China location, or christ, it could be right under our noses. Pitts seems to be the key." Others nodded. "Vargas, you think another chat with Cartier is in order?"

"I think that's a great idea," she replied without hesitation. She knew the info was coming together, but they needed a little more.

The brainstorming session was interrupted by a knock at the door. After a few seconds, one of the Secret Service guards entered and marched up the left side of the table towards the president. He whispered something in his ear. Vargas heard the president ask a few questions, like who and where and when, but she couldn't get the full context, and she wasn't planning to eavesdrop. James leaned over and whispered something to Clemenson. After Clemenson nodded, he leaned back and whispered something to the agent, who left the room, after nodding in understanding. There was a lot of whispering and nodding going on. Vargas looked at Brendan, and he just shrugged.

The president cleared his throat. "It seems one of our other illustrious senators from the fine state of Louisiana is here, and feeling a little frisky about the on goings yesterday at Senator Cartier's place. He's looking to chat about it."

Just as he finished speaking, the door opened, and Senator David Cassian pushed his way into the room. Two security guards were clutching at him, looking forward at the president. He held up his hand to indicate everything was okay, and the guards released the senator. He strode into the room looking steamed up, although he mellowed a bit when he saw the audience.

"Hey John," he said to Brenmar. "I guess it's convenient that you're here too."

"Nice to see you, Dave. How's Emily?"

Senator Cassian turned back as he walked past Brenmar. "She's well, thanks." He looked at Clemenson and waved hello. Clemenson nodded back.

Cassian reached the president. "Sorry to push in here, Mr. President, but I need a moment of your time to discuss some unusual issues back in Louisiana."

"We've just been discussing some things in Louisiana as well, Senator Cassian," he replied. Vargas thought everything was rather formal, and not too friendly.

"Same things I'm talking about?"

"I believe so, Dave, and you can talk freely here." The president smiled, softening the mood. "All the folks in this room are acutely aware of what went on in New Orleans."

The senator looked at the three strangers, whom he assumed were somehow with Brenmar, and turned back to the president. "We can't just walk in to a state senator's house and manhandle him into a deposition, for christ's sake."

"No, you're probably right, Dave. I guess this was a particularly sensitive situation. Perhaps it did get out of hand a bit." Vargas smiled inwardly; he was always the diplomat.

Cassian turned to Brenmar. "Was it your people down there, John?"

"Nope, but the interrogator is sitting in this room." That statement surprised everyone.

Senator Cassian walked slowly back down the table looking at Abigail, Brendan, and Vargas. He stopped across from Brendan. "So, you interviewed Senator Cartier?"

Brendan looked at him, then at Clemenson. "Nope." He pointed his thumb at Vargas. "It was her."

The senator looked at Vargas, then at the president, who nodded. He looked back at Vargas. "What…" he turned back to the president. "What the hell is going on?" He looked back at Vargas, but directed his question to the president. "And who the hell is she?"

Vargas was a little uncomfortable. She didn't like the spotlight, and she didn't react well when people got in her face.

Clemenson knew that. He stood and squared himself to the senator.

"Dave, I have to suggest, with every part of my being, that you distance yourself from Senator Cartier, not to mention Agent Hamilton." He pointed at Vargas. "They will both bring you a headache."

Cassian looked at him. "Is there more to that, Mr. Clemenson?" Vargas guessed he knew Clemenson well, but not well enough to call him Tom.

"That's it, Dave," he replied casually. "Cartier will bring you down the sewer with him if you remain attached. Clear up your affairs with him and build some distance while you can." Clemenson was deadpan. He raised his finger and pointed it straight at the senator. "Don't say I didn't warn you."

The PT1 team was impressed with the tough talk, and that it was to a US senator.

Senator David Cassian started to reply, took a deep breath, looked at the president, Clemenson, and Vargas, and finally stepped swiftly to the door, glancing back once more before leaving.

"Nothing like getting straight to the point, Tom." Brenmar chuckled. He didn't actually like Senator Cassian, or his arrogant tone and assumptions.

"The only asses I have to protect are in this room," Clemenson said. "And that doesn't include mine. The good senator just got the best advice he's ever had." He paused. "And he got it in five minutes, instead of after an hour's worth of useless chit chat."

"Might be tough swinging his vote on the pipeline issue," the president smirked.

"I don't know," Clemenson said, "I think he's ass deep with Cartier, and will be building up some brownie points with you before it's over." Brenmar smiled, Clemenson smiled, James smiled. *What the hell*, Vargas thought. *Let's all smile.*

When everyone settled down, Abigail ran through the info in her handout.

Clemenson got serious. "Vargas, go back to NOLA this afternoon. I don't care what time; I'll let Cartier know you're coming. We need a bigger scoop on China, and whatever the South American connection is. You can corner him with an offer of immunity this time." He looked at the president.

"It's your show, Tom," he said. "But remember that he's an elected official, and one thing I don't want is a press mess, churning up the sacred earth of the electorate." *Very poetic*, thought Vargas, *but I can quell that.*

"Not to worry, Mr. President," Vargas said. "I'll keep it very much under the radar this time. I think the senator is already loose enough from our visit yesterday to jump at the immunity offer."

"Okay, Vargas, keep that in the back of your mind."

"Don't shoot him in the leg," Clemenson added. They all chuckled again. Vargas peeked at Abigail. *So Clemenson does know some of my interrogation techniques!* Abby shook her head slightly to indicate he didn't find out from her.

Clemenson slid a small envelope towards Vargas. "This is a statement of immunity, basically confirming Cartier was not privy to the illegal aspect of the whole scenario, and that he co-operated fully with the investigation."

Vargas picked up the envelope, nodding to Clemenson without comment. She realized he had her return visit planned before this meeting. Always be prepared.

"Brendan," Clemenson said, "you're off with Rogers to LA." *Shit, another missed flight with Rogers.* "I want that place covered in minute detail. See if you can dig up any manifests for shipments originating there, either chemicals or any of these special containers. Abigail, get that investigation going immediately. Maybe you'll have something before they get there."

Brendan nodded. Abigail gave a thumbs up as he continued. "Let Rogers in all the way. He can analyze those containers, and hopefully get some insight on their manufacturing process or location, or whatever."

"Will do, boss," Brendan replied.

"Look folks," said Brenmar, "I understand that this is running through your hands right now, and I'm all good with that—heaven knows you've demonstrated your perspicacity." Vargas considered that a robust word for a CIA dude. "But remember that there is a full support team out there. All you have to do is buzz me and I'll put the resources at your disposal."

"Thanks, John," Clemenson answered for them. "They know they're supported by the best." Vargas loved it. After all the tough talk, he had to play politics a bit. "Okay, let's roll, folks."

Vargas looked at Brenmar. "I can use Wagner again if he's available, sir." She buttered him up with the 'sir' business. She didn't like Brenmar; there was something insincere about him.

"Done. Same time tonight?" he asked. Vargas nodded.

"Listen," the president said as everyone rose to leave. "Get this closed off, please. This gas could cause a real panic, not only here at home, but globally. The results could be devastating, even if it's never released."

"And I need those handouts back," Abigail added. She stood at the door like a professor collecting exams.

B rendan collected Rogers from Vargas' place and brought him out to Dulles for their flight to Long Beach. Vargas went straight to the airport from the White House. Rogers was wheels-up with Brendan before he had a chance to thank her.

United 495. The stewardess said hello and welcomed her back. She ate the same flat iron steak with grilled broccolini, drank the same Reliz Creek Pinot Noir 2011, switched up the music to Dylan's 'Before The Flood' live concert, letting, 'It Ain't Me, Babe' run into 'Ballad of a Thin Man,' and relaxed into a Senator Cartier dialogue projection. *You know something's happening here, but you don't know what it is, do you, Mister C?* she sang along with the song internally, substituting Cartier's initial, for Dylan's 'Mister Jones'.

Wagner rolled up, Abigail was connected, and they were underway. Vargas thanked Wagner for his help. He had always been a great chauffeur, and would no doubt be a good back up if needed. She explained again that it was a private meeting with state Senator Cartier. She wondered what kind of reception she would get.

They pulled up around the semi-circle driveway a little before eight PM, and Vargas hopped out on the passenger side. Sparky and Cowboy were there as usual, but they parted like the Red Sea and let her march up to the door. Adler opened without her knocking and spread the door wide to indicate she should enter.

"Aberlour, ma'am?"

"Double, one rock."

"Yes ma'am." He led her back to the library.

Senator Cartier was sitting at his desk. The Smith & Wesson M&P Shield 9mm lay on top of it, in front of him, with the seven round candy dish removed and lying beside it. Vargas looked at it.

"Just trying to avoid any sense of disingenuousness." He smiled. Definitely a creep.

Vargas picked up the gun and clip before sitting in the armchair across from the desk. She loaded the cartridge and pointed the gun at him. The senator looked on with a little trepidation. She liked his concern, but had no intention of shooting the little weasel. She handed the gun to him handle first.

"Put it away. If you ever bring it out again, be ready to use it."

Her left hand fingered the handle of her Maxim 9 behind her back, just in case. The senator took the gun carefully with three fingers, opened the drawer, and placed it inside, before sliding the drawer shut slowly.

"If you answer my questions, I'll be on my way. No need for any other BS. Just don't try to dance me around. I'll definitely get upset. I could be home taking a sauna and sipping better scotch," she said.

Right on que, Adler walked in with the twelve-year-old Aberlour, two glasses, doubles.

"Anything else, sir?"

"That's all, Adler. Close the door, please," Cartier said.

As the door clicked shut, Vargas leaned forward and looked the senator straight in the eyes. She could see the concern there.

"You're in a bag of shit, senator. I have a shovel in my pocket from the president." She tapped her left breast, drawing his eyes there. She snapped her fingers to regain his attention. "Your problem is that I am the one who decides whether or not you get it."

He looked at her, up and down, nodded, and whispered, "I guess you're holding all the cards, Ms. Hamilton." He still had a little smirk, which Vargas didn't like.

"I have no plans to repeat yesterday's joke. I have no plans to ask if you're sure it's the right answer, or if that's all you know about it. Nope. Today, you are fucked if you don't come clean, and I mean right to the bone. If Pitts doesn't nail you, the local authorities will. If they don't get you, the feds will have your ass for all kinds of environmental irregularities. You getting the picture?" The senator nodded. "And I have your pardon, your immunity, your new start, right here in my breast," she said, patting it again for effect. She gently squeezed her breast. "Your ticket to survival, just like your momma had when you entered this world."

"Shit," the senator said. "That's a little dramatic, even for you." He was right, but it was fun. "Let's get this over with. I'll give you what I have. Just make sure that paper's signed."

"Let's start with China," Vargas said.

"China?"

Vargas put her finger to her lips. "Senator, do not fuck with me." She leaned in more, pointing two fingers at his head. "I leave this room with everything, or you don't leave this room alive." She clicked her thumb like a pistol shot. No smile. No smile from the senator either.

"You're crazy," he said.

"Shit, are we going there again?"

"Okay, Christ, China…." Cartier confirmed that the backers of the whole project were Chinese, but definitely not the Chinese government. They were the Sun Yee On Triad, which was the largest in the world, with more than 50,000 members. Vargas knew they were into gambling, loansharking, extortion, human trafficking, and many other activities, both legal and illegal. The Chinese, their head honcho unknown to Cartier, got wind of Pitts' plans to expand the use and scope of the toxin to include direct individual targeting. They were not against it, as they also realized the immense potential, but the trust level was somewhat diminished by the lack of revelation on Pitts' part, necessitating the Chinese tough guys, or more specifically watch dogs, to be on site at the camp around the clock. Except, of course, when they were hijacking female secret agents.

They targeted Vargas because of the damage she did in China. It had nothing to do with the Louisiana camp. Vargas looked at Cartier. *Such a snake!* She realized he knew about the plan to grab her. Pitts had indicated he wanted her alive, feeling he might be able to turn her with cash, or other, more painful incentives, but the Chinese just wanted her dead. Vargas guessed that might have been the conflict in the car between the four Chinese thugs.

"Why would the Triad want to back a targeting gas. What's the upside for them?" Vargas asked. She believed him, but didn't feel that was the real story behind their involvement.

"I don't know the details. Jesus, they don't consult me. I mean, I never met anyone from that side."

"Fair enough senator, but you must have gathered some opinion on what was going on." Vargas was getting her nasty look going again.

"Rumor has it," Cartier explained, "that the Triad formed some kind of connection with the FARC in Colombia." Vargas spread out her hands, waiting for a more detailed clarification. "Look, I don't know any details, I think there something about using the containers to move Colombian cocaine into China as well. That might be the Triads main interest. I just don't know."

There's Colombia again, Vargas noted. She nodded, indicating some understanding. She knew the drug was gaining a large audience among the nouveau riche youth and social elite in China.

"It's probably a double win for them. They get a weapon to assassinate …whoever it is they assassinate…and they get a fairly safe way to bring their product into the country."

"Interesting." Vargas said. She realized those travel containers might be in line to facilitate both tasks. "Where do I find Pitts?" she asked.

"Are you kidding. That guy scares the shit out of me. I haven't seen him in months…and I don't want to.

"How does he reach you?"

"He calls when there's a reason, but I don't know where he is."

Cartier reached into the left hand drawer. Vargas reached for her gun. He held up a cell phone; a burner no doubt. He was scared. Maybe even more scared that he was of Vargas, or the criminal charges being dangled over his head.

"You'll let me know if you hear from him, won't you?"

He nodded, looking up at her. "Sure."

"Okay, back to China…"

He gave Vargas a whole new encyclopedia of information. She was pretty sure this was it. The only area he was vague on was South America, specifically Colombia, but she figured that was probably a need-to-know area, and he probably didn't need to know.

They talked for two hours. Cartier blabbered endlessly, once he got over the sense of betrayal towards his previous partners in crime. Cartier confirmed that they had a manufacturing plant in China, but he didn't know where. Vargas had given him the death look when he said that, and she believed him once he was ready to die before answering. It wouldn't be that hard to trace SVG Chemicals or their subsidiaries. Wancheng would be on that, no doubt—hopefully with his neck back in one piece.

Apparently, Pitts saw the potential for the gas in alternative environments, both as a weapon and as a pesticide, herbicide, or whatever. The potential uses were staggering: Isolating the DNA of the malaria mosquito, for example, or eliminating various invasive insects, animal culling… it was endless. Vargas pressed for more details on Pitts. How did he get to Dulac, Louisiana? Where did he go from there? Cartier thought Pitts had his own jet, and must have taken off from Houma-Terrebonne Airport. He could drive up there, or even get a chopper from the Union Dulac Heliport. Abigail was tracking flights and filings for every possibility. Where the hell did he go when he left Dulac?

Now Pitts had the isolating agent, and the methodology for blending the toxin; he was almost there. What he didn't have was the DNA samples from some key, predetermined targets. The cow tests were a great success. They had not only targeted cattle in general, but a specific species of cattle, with one hundred percent success. The Mongolian cattle lay dead in heaps, while the Chinese Black Pied rambled among the grassy fields, littered with their dead cousins.

They had also tested the transportability of the toxin, maintaining the specific integrity of the product over distance and time—hence the tests in North Africa. They served the dual purpose of impressing the local terrorists, and hopefully, from Pitts' point of view, opening up a new customer base. The new transport container design was an offshoot benefit that rose from the R&D to develop a reliable and secure delivery system for the toxin. It had some significant potential of its own, not just as a criminal vehicle, such as smuggling terrorists or cocaine, or human trafficking movements, but for commercial and industrial uses as well.

At this point, Cartier was hoping the CIA, actually PT1, would get Pitts before Pitts got him. Vargas, on the other hand, was hoping to get Pitts right *after* he got Cartier! "Got that, Abby?" Vargas said, once she felt they were finished. The senator wanted to talk more, but Vargas knew he was just rehashing old news.

"The whole thing," Abigail confirmed.

Vargas got up to leave.

"Hey, my papers," he said, jumping from his seat.

"Oh ya," Vargas said, reaching into her breast pocket. She pulled out a slightly crumpled envelope, lifted it to her nose, and sniffed it. She threw it onto the desk. "Smells pretty sweet for a shit shovel," she said.

Wagner dropped Vargas at the Omni Royal Orleans Hotel around ten-thirty, after trying fruitlessly to get her to join him for dinner. She was tired, had eaten on the plane, and preferred a quiet snack by herself tonight.

She checked in and went up to her suite. It was a nice room with a long couch and dining table in the living area, and a separate bedroom with a fair sized bathroom. She ordered braised kurobuta pork belly, with bacon wilted frissee, port wine-pecan syrup, and a couple of cans of Woodchuck Hard Cider from the Rib Room, requesting delivery to her room at eleven-forty-five. She then shed her clothing and stepped into a steaming hot shower, washing away the dirt, dust, and sweat of the day, along with the creepiness of Cartier.

As she munched her pork belly, she booked her flight online: United 6271 at twelve-twenty the next afternoon. Perfect timing. It let her sleep in, and still got her to Dulles by three-thirty. She didn't want to wake Abigail for secretarial duties. *I'm definitely maturing.*

Her meeting with Rogers, Brendan, and Abigail was set for Abigail's place at six that evening. Clemenson hadn't confirmed. Rogers and Brendan were arriving around four-thirty. She would take a cab to the airport for her flight. Poor Wagner had spent the whole evening as her driver, and she didn't want to abuse their relationship.

As she was drifting off, she received a text from Abigail:

> Hope this doesn't wake you.
> Pitts flights are from Houma to Cancun.
> Cancun to Aruba.
> Aruba to Cali Colombia…
> That's why no red flags – interesting – chat tomorrow.
> You need a flight home?

Vargas respond with two words: All fixed. She laid back with this new information swirling in her mind. *Abigail is good. Good thing I didn't wake her, ha ha! Easy to transport those toxic gas cylinders, since they look like fire extinguishers. Just prop them up, out in the open on your jet, and away you go! Pitts has his deal with the Chinese, but he's also somehow based in Colombia. The Chinese are getting cocaine, obviously through Pitts. Is he an American or Colombian? How can he get in and out of those spots if he's not American? Interesting chat indeed. I need to have one with him soon.*

▶ ▶ ▶

The R8 powered out into the damp Washington afternoon, oblivious to speed limits, and danced among the building traffic. She cooled it a bit, deciding that going out in a flaming car accident seemed a little crazy after all the dangers she'd survived; but then she changed her mind and revved up. *Fuck it!* She swung by her place to change clothes. Emma was there sparkling things up. *Every Tuesday and Friday*, Vargas reminded herself.

"Oh, you're back already, Ms. Hamilton."

"I guess you're Emma," Vargas said.

"Yes, I am, Ms. Hamilton. It's nice to finally meet you."

"Just for a quick change and a little travel bag, Emma. Heading out again right away."

"Don't you want to eat?" She didn't wait for an answer. "I can have something ready in a jiffy."

"No thanks. No time, really. By the way, I really enjoyed that lobster plate you made for me; it was a perfect hunger quencher."

"Well, let me help you get packed."

Emma gathered the few clothes Vargas flung from the closet and folded them with a veteran's hands. Vargas pulled out four ammo clips for her Maxim 9 and handed them to Emma, trying to gauge her response. There was none. She handled them just like another pair of socks. Not your ordinary cleaning lady.

"You're running low on those. I'll make sure to restock when I come by next Tuesday," she added matter-of-factly. "That gentleman who was here on Wednesday left a small note on your pillow, my dear." She mentioned it casually.

Vargas looked at her, unsure how she knew Rogers had been there, but assuming he left some wet towels or similar.

"Oh ya?" She walked over and picked up the small folded sheet on top of her pillow:

'Thanks for the hospitality, C. I look forward to providing personal in-flight service again in the near future.' There was no signature or name.

She wondered if Emma had read it. Of course, she had, and of course she knew exactly what it meant. Big deal. She crumpled it up and went to toss it in the waste basket.

"Here," Emma said. "Give it to me."

C lemenson was at Abigail's when Vargas arrived, even though she was ten minutes early. As she was walking through the door, she heard the Austin Martin screaming up the street behind her. Rogers climbed out with Brendan. Right on time.

Abigail had a full report package on the Vargas – Cartier dialogue, as well as the follow up from Long Beach. The west coast warehouse had not revealed much. It was clear that they had closed up and run before PT1 got there, probably scared off after the Louisiana compound confrontation with Vargas. Brendan had managed to get a license plate number off a grainy parking lot cam, and track it down to one James Fabulous, living at 215A Market St. in Raceland, LA. The local CIA team had collected Mr. Fabulous and shipped him up to Washington for some delicate interrogation. They were currently holding him at the airport, pending further instructions.

Cartier's disclosures about the Sun Yee On Triad, and their connection with FARC, was important news. Abigail had already informed the Guoanbu, and they most likely had Wancheng active on the matter. Vargas knew he was probably better at half-speed than most in perfect shape. Even more intriguing was the connection between Pitts and Colombia.

"Vargas, you're with Rogers enroute to Cali, in beautiful

Colombia," Abigail said. "You'll have to fly the Gulfstream V into Panama City and go commercial from there. We don't want the locals to see you coming." Vargas nodded. She was finally getting a flight with Rogers! "Fortunately, we had Pitts' tail numbers. From that starting point, we were able to track his movements, and eventually, what we believe to be his local residence.

"I booked you into the AcquaSanta Loft Hotel. Same suite, but with two bedrooms." Vargas appreciated that, even though Abigail knew they would only use one bedroom. "Seems our local assets already had him under soft surveillance for his potential roll with the local drug cartels. They indicated he has a place out in Ciudad Jardin. It's not far from the hotel. I have some original blueprints for the house scanned to my computer, so once you're inside I can help if needed, as long as he hasn't redecorated."

"We still have local assets there?" Vargas asked.

"Brenmar has someone everywhere," Clemenson said. "They follow every private jet that bounces in and out of Cali. It just seems that our Mr. Pitts only files a flight plan from Cali to Aruba and back, which makes him just another rich Colombian playboy. It wasn't until we tagged his plane number that we started to get some decent intel."

"Well, that's good," Rogers said. Vargas was glad to see him feeling like a part of the team. "At least we have a starting point."

Clemenson nodded. "The Colombian secret police, DAS, also follows every private jet in and out, which would indicate that Pitts either knows them, or is paying them something to ignore his travels."

"It's actually called the DNI now, boss," Vargas said. "They changed names back in 2011."

Clemenson scowled a bit, never appreciating a correction. "Fair enough," he said. "The DNI is also why we want you to park the plane in Panama and go commercial. Low profile will suit the situation better. Abigail, can you lay the rest of it out for everyone?"

Clemenson sat down in one of the easy chairs that dressed the walls of Abigail's living room and reception area. It reminded Vargas of their first meeting, complete with the stoic look on his face that said, 'I know everything that you *will* know, and everything that you *don't* know, so yeah, I am superior to you'. He was a smug bastard sometimes, but he was okay.

Abigail laid it out. "Taranis, you're off to China." She glanced at Vargas. "Colestah, a quick call to Wancheng to provide an intro will no doubt be useful to Taranis."

"Sure thing, Abby," Vargas replied. She looked at Brendan, who pursed his lips and nodded in thanks. She didn't want to ask how Wancheng was doing; it seemed a little too personal at this point.

"Wancheng will take the lead since it's his country. Our mission there is to search and secure any facility that has production or storage capacity. We don't want this toxin released or moved out. We are not there to battle the drug running arrangement that may be involved; not our scope. Though Wancheng might be focused on that as well, PT1 needs to be in toxin mode only."

"Brendan, are you clear on that?" Clemenson asked.

"Yes boss," Brendan replied.

Abigail continued. "If you can secure the toxin, especially the formulas, try to bring them home. We don't want the Chinese to have them." She paused and looked at Clemenson. "Same for you, Colestah. Anything you can bring back will be useful here at home. We don't want a foreign power to have this potential weapon."

Vargas looked at Abigail. She didn't sound too convincing, which was definitely out of character for her, especially after she just spoke to the president like he was a high school senior. Abigail's glance at Clemenson further revealed her discomfort. Clemenson sensed it too.

"Look folks, this is one serious weapon, with tremendous potential for both military and commercial uses. Of course, we want it back in the US, and not in the hands of one of our enemies."

Vargas glanced at Brendan. He was looking at her. It was likely one or both of them would have the toxin, and perhaps the formula, in their hands; that they would be the couriers of this weapon. It was also clear to both of them that they had doubts about the future of this gas.

Abigail turned to Vargas. "Colestah, you and Rogers have to find a way in to Pitts. Our intel says he's pretty well guarded and always cautious about his movements. The unknown factor is whether he has the local secret police spooks on his side or not."

"Do what you need to do, Colestah." Clemenson switched to code names too. *Funny guy.* "We have to put an end to this toxin, now."

"Consider it done," Vargas responded. She stared at Clemenson. He didn't waver. She got it—Okay, whatever it takes. "You need Pitts, or just the formula?"

"The formula," Clemenson replied. Everyone was clear. "And you can have Mr. Fabulous on the ride down with you, a sort of in-flight interrogation project. He's at Dulles now, at the police station on Autopilot Drive. I'll have them tuck him in of the Gulfstream."

Vargas was not happy to hear that. She had some more interesting inflight interrogation in mind.

"Sorry if that spoils the trip," Clemenson added, as though he knew exactly what she was thinking. Christ, she hoped he didn't know about Rogers. *Emma, you didn't?!*

Abigail smiled a little.

"Should be an eventful flight, boss," Vargas replied. She smiled.

Clemenson wasn't sure if she was just happy with the opportunity to interrogate another scumbag, or couldn't hold back her delight at hatching some mischievous plan. It didn't matter.

Clemenson stood and headed towards the exit, clearly ending the meeting, or at least his participation in it. He paused after opening the heavy steel door and turned back towards the room. All eyes were on him.

"I always try to keep an even keel when we have a field op running.'" He paused. "But this whole deal has me a little concerned." Vargas translated that in her mind to *really freaked out.* "You folks better get this closed off quickly, or we might see flashes of that Armageddon we've all read about." It was clear just how serious and concerned he was. He turned and closed the door behind him.

"Wow," Abigail said. Everyone looked at her. "I've never seen him look so…" She paused, looking for the right word.

"Afraid?" Vargas said.

"Exactly," Abigail replied.

The ringing silence left the four of them with their own thoughts for a moment, but they were all thinking the same thing: Secure the toxin and formula.

Vargas spoke first. "Abigail, get me Wancheng if you can." She looked at Brendan again, confirming that she was going to make the intro. She turned back to Abigail and smiled. "Please." Abigail smiled back.

"Rogers, get a flight plan filed for Panama City, wheels up ASAP." She paused again. "Please." Rogers smiled.

"Abigail, you going to be connected with me or Taranis?" Vargas figured the party was over, so she might as well switch to code names. Abigail responded by pointing her two index fingers at her two ears, indicating she would have both on at the same time. Vargas shook her head, still with a little amazement, and gave her two thumbs up.

"But I can only speak with you one at a time. Taranis, you're on United 807 out of Dulles tomorrow at 12:35, straight to Beijing," Abby said. He nodded.

Abigail shifted her attention to finding a connection with Wancheng. Rogers was on hold, waiting for the confirmation of his flight plan. Vargas looked at Brendan.

"This is some seriously screwed up product," she said. "Let's get it closed off."

"I'll clean out in China," he replied. There was a serious look on his face that she hadn't seen before. "It would be a shame if that formula was lost along the way as well."

Vargas looked at him, trying to read that. "Sure would," she replied, with a hint of a smile.

The conversation with Wancheng was short, sharp, and full of sarcasm. Exactly what Vargas expected. She liked the man more than she wanted to admit. He had already been briefed on Taranis' arrival and was eager to assist, and for assistance.

"I'll treat him like I would you," he told Vargas.

"Well, I hope he doesn't treat you, like I would!" She laughed. "How's your neck?"

"Perfect, like new. I just can't turn it to the right."

"That wouldn't matter if you were a stock car driver," Vargas said. "Vroom, vroom."

After ensuring everyone was on the same page, they bid goodbye with a shared smile, a little chat about Vargas needing to collect her laundry, and Wancheng needing to use his neck to support his head, rather than absorb enemy fire.

▶ ▶ ▶

James Fabulous. An unwanted passenger in line for an unpleasant interrogation. What a piece of work he was. Several stints in prison; everything from B&E as a youth, to armed robbery, sexual assault and a pending child pornography case. Not a pleasant individual. Vargas had no sympathy for him.

He gave Vargas the once over as she climbed aboard, figuring her for the flight attendant. She knew he'd figure it out in due course. She smiled, thinking of how she would extract info from this slimeball. He smiled back, like he was on a flight to Disneyland, the fantasy shattered only by the fact that his hands were cuffed behind his back. He was propped up in one of the rotating armchairs in the lounge area of the plane, seatbelt secure, holding him in place.

Rogers slipped into the cockpit and swung the door closed. Vargas sat down in a seat across the aisle from Fabulous and was about to buckle herself up, but she definitely did not like his smile. She decided to set the tone from the start. With that in mind, she moved forward to the clothes closet near the entrance of the plane and opened it, pulling the plastic cover down and away from one of the dry cleaned uniforms. She went over to Mr. Fabulous and spread the plastic around on the floor, lifting his feet gently so she could slide it under.

"My shoes aren't muddy," he said with a little laugh.

Vargas stood up and smiled at him without saying a word. She went back to her seat and picked up a ballpoint pen. She stepped back across the aisle, standing in front of her travelling companion. He smiled. She smiled. She then reached back and plunged the pen into the upper thigh of his right leg. He howled, kicking out at her. Vargas dodged the flailing leg, returned to her seat, and buckled up without saying a word. She had made her point.

Rogers bolted in, scanned the situation, and shook his head, half in wonderment, half in admiration.

"No guns," he said, waving a finger at Vargas. That also let Mr. Fabulous know that there would be no help from his side.

Vargas glanced over at Fabulous, his face a little contorted with the pain and the rather unusual sight of a pen sticking out of his leg. The blood was dripping down onto the plastic floor covering. She saw no reason to soil the nice beige carpet. She looked back at Rogers.

"Oh, I'm sure that won't be necessary," she replied, as though she was discounting the need for an additional pillow. She winked. Rogers shook his head again and slipped back into the cockpit.

Fabulous twisted some more, mistakenly thinking his movements might somehow dislodge the pen. He offered a few choice words, mostly referring to Vargas, inferring she had been intimate with somebody's mother. He was not helping his cause.

"Calm down, Mr. Fabulous," Vargas said in a sweet monotone. "The seat belt sign is still on."

"Fuck you," he replied.

"Tsk, tsk," said Vargas, leaning back. She popped her earphones in, letting Dylan's 'Journey Through Dark Heat' gently come to full volume, and closed her eyes for the takeoff.

She looked up a few minutes later. "Sooo," she said, leaning over Fabulous. "Where did Mr. Pitts take all the Long Beach product?"

Fabulous looked back at her. "What?"

Why do all these guys have to start our conversation with that same stupid opening. Vargas took off her shoe, glanced at it for a moment, and then used it to hammer the pen another half-inch into his thigh. He kicked out with the pain, catching her leg and nearly sending her to the ground. She caught herself on his shoulder for balance as he screamed.

"Again, where did Mr. Pitts take the Long Beach product?"

"Look, all I did was deliver some canis…" Before he could finish his sentence, she swatted at the pen again, quickly catching it before Fabulous could move aside. It didn't drive too much deeper, but it had to hurt like hell. He yanked his leg again, but Vargas was well on the side this time.

"And don't forget," she said calmly, "you have two legs." He looked up at her, her smile frozen, eyes steady.

"Okay, okay, just pull that thing out!" He looked at her again, like a puppy full of expectation. Vargas reached over towards the pen calmly, watching a look of relief crossing his face, and then slammed her shoe onto it again. This time the pen went all the way in, bouncing sideways off his thigh bone as it lodged deep into his muscle tissue. He howled again. She waited for it to subside.

"First you give me info, then I remove the pen." He was hers. He began to talk, but Vargas held her finger up to her lips.

"Hang on a sec," she said, as though their situation was a naturally social one. Vargas went to the rear of the jet and grabbed the sat-phone, quickly connecting with Abigail. She explained the situation and propped the phone up on the table in front of Fabulous. The data flowed out of him like a seventies telex tape. He told them everything he knew, and even a few things he didn't know.

"The pen, the pen," he screeched a little, after what he thought was full disclosure. Vargas yanked the pen out, eliciting another soft howl.

She picked up the phone. "You get all that, Abby?"

"How'd you get all that out of him?" Abigail asked. Before Vargas could reply she said, "Never mind! I got everything, but what was that last part, something about a pen?"

"Oh, that! It's nothing, just something between me and Fabulous here." Vargas looked at him. "He definitely would have preferred a different travelling companion." She winked and returned to Abby. "I'll connect once we hit Colombia."

"Okay, and by the way, I left some of that explosive fun-gum in your purse."

"Thank you, Abby," Vargas replied playfully. She clicked the phone off.

Blood was flowing freely from the wounded leg. Vargas moved to the galley and reached underneath the sink, pulling out the bottle of twenty-one-year-old Belvenie, Port Wood Finish of course, along with the roll of duct tape Rogers kept for 'repairs'. After chipping out a piece of ice, she poured a nice long scotch and took a sip. *Now that's nice*, she thought. Then she took the tape and wrapped it tightly around Fabulous' leg several times, ending the blood drip, before putting one last large strip across his mouth. She needed a nap.

Vargas carried her glass and the bottle of Belvenie to the back cabin, and laid back onto the bed. Fabulous mumbled his complaints for a few moments but was soon silent. She was anticipating the engagement of the autopilot and the corresponding visit it would afford Rogers. He didn't disappoint.

"We have another three hours to go." He smiled as he entered the tiny room and slid the door shut behind him. She smiled back. "What did our friend chat about?" he asked.

"I'll tell you after," she said coyly. "After *you* interrogate *me*."

Yup, Rogers has some pretty awesome in-flight service. They shared another drink after he returned to grab some ice and check on Mr. Fabulous. He was not doing well.

"Did you give him some water?" Vargas asked.

"No, no I didn't, but I probably should have."

"After," Vargas replied, snuggling back into his arms.

"So, what's the scoop?"

"Oh ya, Fabulous. Interesting thing he mentioned, the gas can be destroyed by just releasing it into the atmosphere. As long as it hasn't been primed with any DNA sample, it is completely harmless. Even if it has been primed, and the particular DNA target is more than a couple of miles away, it dissipates without harm."

"That can make it a lot easier to deal with."

"Abigail will let Taranis and Wancheng know that," she said. "It might alleviate any concerns they have over destroying the gas." She paused for a bit, but Rogers said nothing. "As a matter of fact, the gas itself is a common delivery compound. Fabulous said it's only the targeting formula and method that makes it dangerous."

"And who has that?"

"He says only Pitts, as far as he knows, but said he heard a lot of chatter about the Chinese and their capabilities. He figures they wouldn't be making such a large investment unless they had some access to the formula. That sort of made sense."

"Ya, it does sound logical."

"That's why I stopped stabbing our friend. He seemed to be offering his view of reality."

Rogers looked at her, recognizing how dangerous she was. She was staring up at the ceiling. Vargas went on. "Apparently, Pitts is very connected in Colombia. Mr. F. says he has the authorities on the payroll, and he also has a relationship with FARC."

"Playing both sides of the field, I guess," Rogers said.

"Mmmm…that can always be dangerous." She let that thought drift, along with the two of them, into semi-consciousness.

Two hours later, Vargas woke. The bed was bare, as usual. She walked back up to check on Fabulous. He was sweating and sucking air through his nostrils. She saw the water bottle on the table in front of him, confirming Rogers had given him a drink, and then replaced the tape.

She held his face in her hands and brought his eyes into a close focus. "I will remove that tape if you promise to be absolutely quiet." He nodded. "You have to understand," she continued, "not one single word. No bathroom request, no wondering about the future, no emotional pleadings. Are we clear?" She continued to hold his head. He nodded again.

Vargas grabbed the corner of the tape and ripped it off his mouth. He winced a bit, but the quick intake of air confirmed he was appreciative. He looked at the water bottle and shook his head towards it. She acquiesced, bringing it to his lips and emptying the balance as quickly as he could swallow.

Vargas moved up and into the cockpit. "Hey there."

"Nice nap?"

"Absolutely," she replied.

"We're almost there," Rogers said, as he pushed the two black throttle handles forward, disengaging the autopilot and initiating their descent.

Vargas went back to her seat. She wondered what they were going to do with Fabulous, but there really was no option—he had to go. Vargas tore another piece of duct tape off and moved toward Fabulous. He gave her a 'Oh-no-please-don't' look as she pressed it over his mouth once again, forcing him to try to breathe through a nose partially blocked by the residue of his ordeal.

Vargas picked up her Belvenie and took a sip. She stood beside Fabulous, reached over with her left hand, holding his head tightly against her hip. She used her right thumb and index finger to pinched his nostrils shut, pressing her palm into his face to hold it as steady as possible. It took him a moment to realize that she was serious. He struggled to shift his head away and open the breathing passage, but to no avail. Her left hand held his face firmly, and her clenched fingers swayed with his movements, maintaining pressure on his nostrils. It only took a couple of minutes.

ouchdown bumped along at 00:30, too late for any domestic flight to Cali. Rogers hopped out of the cockpit once they came to a full stop. He looked at Fabulous, now slouched in his chair, still taped and buckled in. Then he looked at Vargas. He said nothing. Vargas figured he had to know there was no choice. He was a vile human being as it was, and they couldn't just leave him sitting on the plane in Panama, while they wandered off to Colombia.

Vargas had transferred the explosive gum from her purse to her sock, figuring it was probably a safer spot. She linked with Abigail again.

"Hey Abby, two little issues. First, we need a hotel for tonight, something close to the Panama airport, and please get us the first flight out in the morning."

"No problem," Abigail replied. "Anything else?"

"It was a fairly long trip and we managed to accumulate some garbage, as you probably know. As a matter of fact, it is fabulous garbage."

There was momentary silence, which was out of character for Abigail. "Okay, I'll get someone over there to clean it up."

"Did you just hesitate, Abby?" Vargas wondered if the news of Fabulous' retirement had rattled her a bit. She let a smile creep onto her face.

"Ya sorry," Abigail responded. "I was just waiting for the hotel confirmation to pop up. You're confirmed at the Sheraton Panama Hotel and Convention Center. It's only fifteen minutes from the terminal. Unfortunately, there was only one room available, but it is a suite, so there's a couch someone can use."

"Perfect," Vargas said. "I should have known better!"

"Bye bye." Abigail signed off.

Vargas liked Abby's anticipation. It was a rare to find her unprepared.

The private jet terminal at Tocumen International Airport in Panama City was beautiful. Brand new and full of luxury services. The problem was, however, no guns, and certainly no bodies, were allowed off the plane. Rogers was clear in his warning. No worries. Vargas pulled out her iPhone and punched in the number she had tucked away in her memory cabinet.

"Brenmar." The CIA director answered after two rings. That was impressive considering it was one o'clock in the morning in Panama City, and 02:00 in Virginia.

"Colestah," Vargas replied, keeping the cloak-and-dagger dialogue going.

"What do you need?" he asked without emotion. There was no small talk going on here.

"At our hotel in Cali, AcquaSanta Lofts—a Maxim 9. Silencerco has an integrally suppressed one and," she looked at Rogers. He was unsure at first what she was asking. Vargas used her fingers to form a pistol, cocking her thumb a couple of times, and then spreading her hands and shrugging her shoulders to reinforce the question.

"Oh," Rogers stuttered for a second. "Glock 19 I guess."

"And a Glock 19, also with a silencer," Vargas said. "Oh, and two night-vision headsets as well." She waited for a moment. "Please."

"Shouldn't be a problem. There on arrival," Brenmar replied, ignoring her request for a hotel delivery.

"Thank you, sir," Vargas said, only half sarcastically, closing the line before he could comment back. Brenmar seemed like such a little man for such a big job.

The terminal services included a shuttle over to the Sheraton Panama Hotel and Convention Center. It was the closest decent hotel to the main international terminal, and more than comfortable. Somewhere during the early morning hours, a text came in from Abigail.

> Copa Air 677 at 15:38
> Cali informed – meet Daniel
> Buenas nochas

Vargas set her alarm for 09:00, clicked the screen off, and sank back into the arms of Rogers. *Thank you, Abby. I know there's an earlier flight.* They were exhausted and soon asleep.

▶ ▶ ▶

Daniel was like a cartoon character. He had a huge American-made van, bright yellow, and probably twenty years old. Quite different from the hoard of mini yellow Honda and Kia cabs that congested the streets of Cali. He chatted the entire time, playing the role of dimwit taxi driver, honking and waving at various other cabs as he slipped in and out of traffic. A few stop-and-go situations, some speeding down Autopista Sur, an hour of unbearable chatter, and the Aqua Santa Lofts sat calmly in front of them. When he pulled up, Daniel turned to face Vargas and Rogers. His voice suddenly turned to perfect English, educated, a serious undercover operative.

"The guns and night vision gear are in a small bag just beside your luggage. I'll be back here at midnight. Get some rest. We'll be up all night." He looked straight at Vargas. "My instructions are to follow you without question, and you can count on that. However, I am very familiar with both the terrain, the target residence, and the local crowd. I hope you'll let me guide you."

Vargas was more than a little surprised by his sudden and complete metamorphosis. She looked at Daniel and smiled a little, nodding her head in recognition of his cover act.

"I'll trust you, until I don't. Get me to where I need to be and I'll take care of it from there." She made a point to hold his gaze. As usual, not too macho, but unmistakably in charge.

"Deal," he said. He spun around and hopped out of the car.

Rogers took it all in, a little bit unsure of his own role. He had been with the agency for a long time, but was not really a field agent.

Daniel arrived promptly at midnight, complete with gloves, black clothing, head to toe, and some light body armor visible under his T-shirt. Vargas guessed he was pumped about the evening's work, and looked like he planned on participating full throttle.

"Hope you don't mind if I come all the way in with you folks. I'm pretty sure the place is crawling with Pitts' army." He looked Vargas up and down.

"Body armor?" she asked.

"Always thought of it as useful in a gun battle," Daniel replied, only half joking.

Vargas gave a sideways turn of her head, almost in admonition.

"You have field experience?"

Daniel responded with one word, finally looking Vargas in the eye. "Significant."

"Good," Vargas replied, "because he doesn't." She pointed to Rogers. Daniel looked over at him. Rogers shrugged with a bit of a smile. Vargas looked at Rogers but spoke to Daniel. "Your number one task is to make sure he comes home tonight. I like him." Vargas winked at Rogers and turned back to Daniel. He smiled and nodded.

Daniel handed Vargas a small magnetic tracker. It was no bigger than the tip of a ballpoint pen.

"Stick this somewhere metallic and we'll be able to track you at all times."

Vargas was in her cat-suit as well: Haider Ackerman lace-up leggings, a Hannie Sleeveless Peblum top, and Giuseppe Zanotti Black

Suede May London Zip high tops, with several sticks of Abigail's gum tucked down the side, all covering the usual lace underwear. Definitely ready for battle.

The drive over to Pitts' compound wasn't too long, and Daniel parked a half-mile away in a small wooded area off the main road. He had cased the place several times before.

"Look, I've had eyes on Pitts for a while, based on his links to the drug trade. This is a great spot to leave the car unnoticed and get down close to his fence," Daniel said.

"Have you been inside the grounds before?" Vargas asked.

"Nope. Never could get close enough, but I was able to get blue prints to the place from the original builder's submission to the city. That's assuming Pitts hasn't done any renovations."

It was the same thing Abby suggested.

"He has probably changed some things around," Vargas said.

Daniel just shrugged in agreement. They grabbed their hardware, including the night-vision headgear. Daniel had his own as well. It seemed he knew he was joining them. Vargas put on her support belt and wrapped a thigh holster around her right leg before jamming her integrally suppressed Maxim 9 into it. She then parked several clips into the back of the belt and slipped her top over them. Rogers looked on, unsure if he should admire her, or remind himself not to piss her off. She looked at him.

"Gear on," she said. "Not to be confused with gear up." She smiled. "Be careful, stay with Daniel."

Vargas surreptitiously slipped the tracking chip under the barrel of Rogers' gun. She feared that he was the only person that might need tracking.

They shimmied down a small embankment and jogged down what seemed like a long dried-up river bed. No doubt a gift from global warming. They covertly moved past several other residences, and came to an abrupt halt when Daniel raised his left arm.

He looked back at Vargas. "Next one. There are guards up on the fence for sure. Always are."

Vargas scanned the area.

"Wait here," she said, and motioned the other two to crouch down. She moved sideways up the embankment and into the yard of Pitts' neighbor. She scanned the back of the house, seeking a way up to the roof. *Are you kidding me?* Among several yard maintenance items tucked against the high fence separating the two properties, was a ladder. It would do perfectly.

Vargas uncoupled the garden hose from its spout, coiling it over her shoulder and arm. She laid the ladder quietly against the back wall of the neighbor's house, and climbed onto the roof with the hose in tow. From there she had a decent view of Pitts' yard. Two guards at the back fence, as Daniel mentioned, two more in the front that she could see, and one at the back door. She could only see his lower legs, but that was good enough.

Vargas silently pulled the ladder up onto the roof. She tied the hose to the top rung, stood the ladder upright, and slowly laid it out and across the divide between the two residences, using her foot as a stopper and the hose as a guideline. It barely reached, and laying it flat without a crash onto the opposite roof was no easy task.

It finally arrived with a slight bump, and she saw the back door guard move towards the sound. She huddled quietly. She couldn't afford to lose the element of surprise. The guard peeked around the corner, but never looked up. *Where do they get these guys?* He slowly moved back to his post. Vargas walked across the ladder cautiously, keeping any noise to a minimum. She felt like a duck in a shooting gallery.

Once across, she moved over to the area above the back door. She wasn't sure how many guards might be below her, but she was going to find out. She leaned over a bit to see the ground and identify a landing spot. Standing backwards, she grabbed her pistol, glanced over her shoulder to confirm her landing spot, and leaped off. She discharged two rounds into the shocked back door guard as she flew by. She hit the ground and rolled to a stop. He hit the ground and did not roll anywhere. Fortunately, no one else was on the back porch.

Vargas moved silently towards the back of the grounds in a semi sprint, and dispatched the two guards with ease. As she went by their motionless bodies she plugged two more in each of them, just to be sure. There was no sense having some wounded combatant regain consciousness and start firing. She opened the rear gate, pushed a new clip into her Maxim 9, and looked outside to spot Daniel and Rogers. No sign. She gave a small whistle and they appeared.

Daniel looked at the two bodies, then up at Vargas.

"How'd you do that?"

Vargas looked at him. "It's easy, just form a circle with your lips and blow." She repeated her soft whistle and winked.

"Very funny," Daniel replied. Rogers chuckled.

"Christ, that's what I do. Why do think I'm here?" she whispered. "Let's move."

The rear entrance to the house was well lit. Vargas directed Daniel and Rogers to the right side with a hand motion, and then held her finger to her lips, reminding them to do so stealthily.

"There's at least two out front," she whispered. Daniel gave a quick thumbs-up and tapped Rogers on the shoulder, indicating he should follow him.

Vargas slid up to the back door, keeping low enough to be beneath the line of sight from the window. She raised her head to peek inside, spotted the automatic weapon pointed right at her, and hit the ground, rolling backwards off the porch.

The first burst smashed through the window, the second through the door. That was the end of the element of surprise. Another burst cut through the bottom of the door and dug holes into the porch, not to mention the indignity they did to the corpse of the outdoor guard. The weatherproof stain was taking a real beating.

Vargas looked up, waiting for the guard and perhaps his team-mates to come busting through the badly damaged door. She heard the popping sound of a single suppressed gunshot off to her right, and saw the guard tumble through the door and fall flat, joining the previously cancelled outdoor guard. The bodies were piling up.

Fortunately, all of them belonged to Pitts.

Vargas leaped up and grabbed the dead guard's automatic weapon, an HK21. She wasn't surprised he had reacted slowly; the thing weighed a ton. She dropped it back onto the ground and moved on through the door, looking to her right to see Rogers at the side window, pointing at the tip of his Glock, obviously taking credit for the last kill. He was being a smart ass. Daniel peeked through the side window as well.

She motioned for them to continue along the outside of the house. They moved out of sight, as she took note of her surroundings. She knew everyone was aware that they were there, and they would have to make this happen fast if they were going to get the gas. She was in a breakfast room. She could see the kitchen through a door to her left, but the door in front of her was closed. It was on swinging hinges and opened to the right, so she pumped three shots into the wall to the left of the door, about six inches apart and three and a half feet up. She calculated that if he were crouching, he'd get it in the head, standing in the gut. She wasn't wrong. She heard the thump of his body hitting the ground.

She took one of the dinette chairs and slid it along the floor, pushing the door open slightly. No return fire. She left the chair there, keeping the door slightly ajar, and then moved quickly to the kitchen. Through the passage, she crawled along the floor silently and peeked around the corner of the kitchen door from her prone position. She spotted at least six soldiers from Pitts' army, hunkered down and waiting for her to push the swinging door from the breakfast room all the way open. That was a mistake. She was slightly to their left, and they were unaware of her position.

Several shots rang out from somewhere on the other side of the house. No doubt it was Daniel and Rogers in action. The men waiting for Vargas shifted and glanced that way. Vargas pushed forward and let her Maxim do its work. One, two, three before anyone knew what was happening. A fourth went down hiding for cover behind a couch. It was a stupid choice. The couch was a nice place for an afternoon nap, but it couldn't stop a slingshot.

The two remaining guards returned fire as Vargas scrambled to get behind the kitchen island. Unfortunately, that wasn't the best protection either, as several rounds burst through both sides of the unit, scattering glass and cutlery everywhere. Another roll and she was back in the breakfast room. She moved quickly to the swinging door and pushed it open, crouching down low, catching the bad guys by surprise, as she once again came at them from a different angle. She cancelled one immediately, smirking at the surprised look on his face. He had to be a dummy; what did he think was going to happen?

The last guard dropped off a couple of shots in her direction as she recoiled back into the breakfast room, before she once again heard the unmistakable pop of Rogers' Glock, and saw the last identified enemy tumble down, lifeless.

Vargas got up and looked at Rogers, tilting her head in thanks.

"You're bleeding," he noted casually.

Vargas looked at her arm. A trickle of blood was rolling down towards her wrist.

"Not hit. Has to be a piece of glass on the ricochet or something." She grabbed a paper towel and wiped it away. "See, just a nick." She didn't want to stain her Hannie top. She fired another shot into the guard Rogers had hit. "Precaution," she said, looking at him with a little smile, as she reloaded. She looked at Daniel. "Abby, you there?"

"Are you hurt, Colestah?"

"I'm fine. Scan those blueprints and tell me where we're going."

Daniel jumped in before Abigail could reply. "Basement stairs are to the left. Whatever Pitts has going on, it's probably down there somewhere."

Vargas looked at Daniel a little more seriously. "I thought you were going to keep Rogers behind you," she said.

Rogers replied for him. "He was busy taking out the other three macho-men."

She looked back at Daniel. "You lead the way."

Daniel smiled and pushed forward in front of them. He pried

open the door to the stairway and peeked cautiously inside. Nothing there. He moved through the door and began descending the stairs as Vargas looked down after him. At the bottom, he signaled with a thumbs up and Vargas waved Rogers through the door as well.

Halfway down the stairs, shots rang out and Daniel slumped forward. Vargas and Rogers were in no-man's land! Should they go back upstairs or straight down? Vargas was calculating both scenarios simultaneously. Back up left them nowhere, *and Daniel dies for nothing*; straight down and they'd probably be hitting a full force attack, with little likelihood of survival. She heard Abigail's voice call her name. As she pondered the possibilities, an unusually sweet odor permeated the air. Vargas sniffed and then looked at Rogers. *Shit, halothane gas.* It was her last thought before blacking out.

V argas gradually regained her senses. She felt cold, and sus-
pected it was a side effect from the gas. The soft daylight creeping into the room told her it was morning. Blurry images focused into
important looking people in lab coats, straps holding her arms and
legs tightly to a post, and, most unpleasantly, the piercing blue eyes
of Mr. Pitts, only a foot away from her face. He smiled, holding up a
piece of used paper towel, Vargas' dried blood dimpling the material.

"With this, I will demonstrate the accuracy and certainty of our
little gas toxin," he said with a wry smile. He tore a small piece of
blood stained material off the towel and soaked it onto a small pre-
moistened microscope slide. "Clara," he called, holding the slide out
behind him, without turning his eyes away from Vargas. A young
lady scurried over and carefully took the slide.

"Don't tell me she's got the mixing formula," Vargas asked, fishing
for clues about the mixing process.

Pitts pointed to his head, indicating the formula was buried in
his mind. "Me and Mr. Ma," he said. That was a name she hadn't
heard, but if he was real, it was a great piece of intelligence, garnered
through a cheap conversation. She reflected that all she had to do,
was kill Pitts and Ma.

Pitts kept his eyes focused. He raised his left hand and winced a bit as he took hold of her face between his thumb and fingers, holding it steady.

"You have been a significant PIA, my dear. It's time for you to find that which you seek." He let go of her.

"You having some shoulder problems?" she asked. She remembered his wince when moving his left hand.

He used his left hand to pull his shirt aside, revealing the top portion of his upper left torso. "Old battle scars," he said.

Vargas recognized the zig-zag of knife wounds. She remembered Clemenson's description of his MIA agent. 'An unassuming man with a short balding hairline and vibrant green eyes'. Fit Pitts perfectly, except for his blue eyes.

"You're wearing contacts." She looked him in the eye. "Honos?" It was a bit of a shot in the dark, but his facial reaction revealed it all. She was a little bit smug in her realization that this was indeed Carson Wallach, the MIA PT1 agent, long thought dead. *Blue contacts covering green eyes,* she thought. *Hell, I used to do the opposite when I was a teenager.*

"Well done," he replied, truly impressed with her perception, "but too late."

"Why the betrayal, Carson?" she asked, dropping the code name.

"This scar didn't come from some Colombian rebel, or even a loyal soldier," he said. "It was a gift from the CIA."

Vargas was surprised. "No way."

"Seems the CIA had, or should I say has, most of the drug trade here running under their auspices." He paused, letting the thought sink in. "They ensured the quality, built the mule lines into the US, and took their 15% off the top. That's probably around fifty million bucks annually, Ms. Hamilton. Incentive enough. I don't know where the cash goes to, but I'm guessing the pockets of some fairly high ranking officials."

"So, you found out about it and they sent a hit team?"

"Oh no, that was later, young lady. I brought the info home with me. Your buddy Clemenson told me to keep it quiet. He said he

wanted more proof and sent me back down to Colombia to get it."
He waited again, letting the story gain momentum in the silence.
"*Then* the assassins came. They botched it and I survived, thanks
to the FARC, who saved my life. They knew who I was, but they
somehow respected the idea that I had revealed the CIA's true role
down here. They hate the CIA. Not because they hinder their efforts,
but because they take too much profit! Leaves them a little shaky in
the funds department."

Vargas looked on as the story unraveled. "Why not get back to
Clemenson now?" she asked.

"You are naive for such a senior agent. You think Clemenson
doesn't know all this already? Don't you realize *he* was the one who
sent the hit team? I would even guess that he's one of those high
ranking officials with deep pockets."

Vargas tried to digest this while maintaining a poker face.

Pitts' face slid into a mischievous smile. "Now, we're running
the distribution without the CIA. That means a lot more cash to
go around. I'm sort of the hero in all this, loved by the Colombian
government and the FARC. I make sure they both get their handout.
As a matter of fact, I've got them sitting down at the negotiating table
right now. If they settled their differences, the whole process would
be a lot easier—and more profitable for everyone. I'm sure the news
of their truce will be hailed as a victory for peace and reconciliation,
but it's really just a business deal in the distribution process." Pitts'
smile widened at the irony of the possibility. "But you will not be
around to read about it, Ms. Hamilton."

"Call me Vargas, please. Ms. Hamilton makes me feel a little
aged," Vargas said, trying to casually hide the raging confusion his
revelations had delivered. Could Clemenson really be involved? He
was so…official. The CIA? Brenmar? The president?

Pitts spun away and stormed across the room, to where his lab
tech was busily administering something to the microscope slide
containing Vargas' blood.

It wasn't easy to leave Vargas with a dropped jaw, but Pitts had.

There has to be some explanation, she thought, trying to piece together everything she knew about Clemenson and their relationship so far. She realized it wasn't much. He was always silent, a sideline pacer, never committed, always ambiguous.

"You get that, Abigail?" she whispered, as loudly as she dared. There was no response. The earpiece was definitely gone, though it felt like it was still there. *Christ, it's not like I lost a limb, but I'm having phantom pain over the earpiece.* This CIA, Clemenson, drug smuggling scenario would definitely require more investigation. Two pressing questions remained, however. How would she get out of there, and more importantly, where the hell was Rogers?

Both questions were answered in short order as a blast of rapid fire burst across the lab. Vargas jumped at the sudden noise, as much as she could muster in her current tied position, and then recoiled as several rounds banged around above her head. Lab techs and security personnel dashed left and right. Pitts dissolved into the back of the lab somewhere, and Vargas saw Clara, the tech with her DNA in hand, running to the exit, and then falling sideways from a ricochet that caught her through the top of her right eye. *Ouch, that's gotta hurt. Can I have my DNA back now?*

As Vargas spun slightly, as allowed by her bindings, she saw two things of interest. First, Daniel was leaning against the entrance to the lab with an HK21 automatic rifle, apparently not as dead as she thought. Several additional backup agents were helping to overwhelm the lab security. Then she saw Rogers, up beyond the DNA mixing terminal. He was secured to a long stainless table, reminding her of a poor creature in a testing lab. He was struggling to escape his own straps, without success.

The fire fight lasted only a few moments. Daniel's surprise attack had secured the room, leaving any enemy survivors on the run through the back of the lab. The reinforcements continued to pursue them out through a rear door, which must have exited into the back yard, or perhaps the dried riverbed.

Daniel moved forward to free Vargas. His left cheek was a mess, clearly the result of a bullet from his initial confrontation with Pitts' men at the foot of the stairs. The blood was already beginning to coagulate around what would certainly be a lasting scar. His shirt was also tattered in a couple of spots, revealing the chinks in his body armor where two bullets had impacted. *Okay, so I was wrong about the body armor.*

"Looks like you were wrong about the body armor," Daniel said as he snatched the straps off her arms. *Smart ass.*

"I don't know, you might have been more cautious if you weren't wearing it," she said, smiling at her inability to admit the truth.

Daniel looked at her and dipped a slight nod of his head. "Ya, that must be it," he said, also smiling at her inability to admit the truth.

She moved to free her legs.

"Get Rogers," she barked, nodding in his direction.

Daniel moved that way and freed him from his bindings. They both moved back towards Vargas.

"Where did the reinforcements come from?" Vargas asked.

"My colleagues. Seems they got an emergency call from some lady named Abigail. You know her?"

"Ya, we've met," Vargas said. She guessed Abby must have heard the drama of the situation, before the earpiece was lost.

Daniel started to move towards the rear of the lab, following the other agents in pursuit of the fleeing villains.

"Forget them," Vargas shouted, bringing him to a sudden stop. "We need to secure this gas."

Rogers was still rubbing his wrists where the straps had held him down. "Did they load it with your DNA?" he asked.

She looked at him, surprised he was aware of that possibility.

"I heard that lab tech telling her co-worker," he said. "It seems they may have completed it before the bullets started flying."

"Did you hear my discussion with Pitts?" Vargas asked, hoping he had not.

"No, not a word, you were too far away. What did he say?"

"Usual bravados," Vargas said. She needed to get a lot more info on this whole assassination and drug cartel thing, before anyone else pieced it together.

She thought for a moment. "Doesn't matter; the gas has to be dumped. Help me get these canisters upstairs and outside."

"We don't know if this will affect you," Rogers said. "For that matter, we don't even know if anyone else has been targeted. We can't just release the gas in such a populated area."

Rogers was right. Vargas would be willing to risk her own safety, but not the possibility that they had already matched the DNA of someone, or even something, else. She could see the headlines now: *'All Cali Citizens with Red Hair Die Suddenly,'* or *'All Short Tail Hawks Fall from the Sky.'*

"Daniel, get us a chopper. Rogers, help me carry these canisters upstairs."

It was clear which canisters contained the gas; they were marked with a large 'DNA GAS' on their side. How convenient. Rogers and Vargas hoisted them one by one, lugging them up through the basement to the back yard as Daniel contacted his office and arranged the bird. Eight full canisters— enough to take out an entire city.

Several members of the CIA posse returned from their pursuit of Pitts and his team, coming back into the house through the rear exit. They had captured a few lab techs and thugs, but no Pitts. Daniel put out a full APB on him, mobilizing every resource he could command, but Vargas knew it was futile, without support from the local police. Pitts was probably already far away via some unknown vehicle, or safely in the hands of the local FARC underground. Either way, no one was catching him today.

As she climbed the stairs one last time, it occurred to her that Pitts had always transported the gas in dummy fire extinguishers. She had seen one hanging on the wall in the lab and returned to get it. "Search the house and the garage," she called to Rogers and Daniel. "Any extinguishers have to come with us as well." They found four more.

The helicopter arrived and Vargas let the CIA locals do the

loading. She looked at Daniel.

"Get this somewhere remote and dump the gas. I'm heading back to the hotel to get in touch with the US."

"They can dump it. I'll get you back."

"No," Vargas replied. "I need someone I trust to make sure this is all gone." She pointed at the chopper, ready to lift off. "I will take your keys though." She smiled. Daniel tossed them over.

"Thanks," she said, looking at him and forming a small kiss with her lips. "And thanks for these keys as well." Daniel nodded back, recognizing the kiss was for his survival, and subsequent rescue, not the keys.

Vargas started to leave, but turned back. "One more thing," she said to Daniel. "We need all the info you can extract from those captured soldiers. Anything and everything about this operation. You know how to get information, don't you?"

Daniel smiled. "No one is better at it than me. I'll let you know." He climbed aboard the chopper.

"Thanks. We'll leave the balance of the ammo with the concierge, the guns and gear are long gone with Pitts," she called out, a little louder to clear the whir of the helicopter blades.

She waved goodbye. Daniel had proven to be much more than just a taxi driver with a gun. Rogers gave a short salute to Daniel as well, but didn't say anything. He thought about Daniel's last statement. He wasn't sure he agreed, preferring not to bet against Vargas and her information extraction processes.

Once the chopper lifted off, Vargas when back down into the lab. "Everybody out, now," she screamed. The few remaining agents hustled upstairs and outside.

Rogers followed her into the lab, curious about what she was doing, but patient enough not to ask. She reached into her Giuseppe Zanotti Black Suede May London Zip high tops, and pulled out several sticks of the explosive gum. She folded the white and green portions together and placed them strategically beside anything that looked like it might be essential to the lab's function. Rogers still said nothing. Vargas kept one final piece as the detonator and moved back towards the stairway.

"Get in the stairwell," she told Rogers. "It's going to get loud."

She folded the last piece together, rolled it carefully into a ball, and tossed it through the lab door. Vargas dashed back to the stairway as the ball took flight, and dove inside for shelter. The first explosion shook the walls. Several additional explosions followed immediately as the initial impact set off the other charges. She looked up at Rogers and smiled.

"Cute," he said, realizing she'd had the explosives in her shoe the whole time.

By the time they got out into the back yard, they could hear the sound of sirens. They guessed it was reasonable to assume that the gunfire and explosions would inspired some 123 calls from the neighbors. That was their 911 equivalent.

They moved quickly through the back yard, past the two dead bodies still guarding the back entrance, and dropped down into the ravine. Vargas looked back and saw the ladder still traversing the two houses. They were long gone by the time the local police made their entrance.

Back at the hotel, Vargas got Abigail on the phone. She gave her a quick synopsis of what transpired, keeping it brief and general because the line was not secure. The gas was secured and being disposed of. Unfortunately, Pitts was gone. She relayed the fact that Pitts and one Mr. Ma, were the only people that knew the formula coding.

"Get that name to Taranis ASAP, Abby. He needs the gas destroyed and Mr. Ma under wraps."

Vargas also mentioned that Daniel was a great asset. She wasn't sure if saying so had any value to him, but she wanted to tell someone. Vargas didn't mention anything about Pitts being Honos, or Clemenson, and the story Pitts had told about her boss' involvement in the assassination attempt. She had to plan that dissemination a little more carefully. Besides, she wanted to see Clemenson's face when she finally revealed the details.

"And thanks for the cavalry, Abigail. Oh ya, and the gum."

▶ ▶ ▶

They returned to Panama City on Flight Copa 614 at 15:24. They shared scotches and a promise to get dinner somewhere decent, before heading back to Washington.

Once back on the ground at Tocumen Airport, Vargas used her iPhone to contact Brenmar again.

"Brenmar." He answered after two rings.

"Colestah," Vargas said. Brenmar said nothing, waiting for her to continue. "Decent success, with huge thanks to Daniel down there. Hell of a guy. Really came through." She didn't want to put too much sugar on it, but also wanted Brenmar to know the man was an asset. Her praise had to filter down at some point.

"They're in the process of destroying the local gas. I'd greatly appreciate a confirmation once that's done." She paused. "If that's not being pushy."

"I'll let you know. Where's the equipment?" he asked. *That's his first concern?* "Except for the weapons and night vision equipment, everything's in a bag with the concierge. Being held for Daniel."

"What else is there? Where are the weapons?"

"Well," Vargas said slowly, controlling her building anger, "I believe they were taken by the men who gassed us and tried to assassinate us with our own DNA."

Brenmar fell silent. Vargas guessed he was probably trying to decide whether to dock her pay or call her incompetent. Finally, he responded. "Anything else."

"That's it, thank you … sir." Once again, she disconnected before he could.

United Flight 807 touched down at Beijing Capital Airport just after 15:00, local time. A little late, but not too bad. After taxiing up to Terminal 3, Brendan popped Abigail into his ear, deplaned, and was immediately met by a rather striking young Asian lady.

She held no sign or other visual communication, but she did say, "Welcome to Beijing, Taranis. Wancheng is down in Tianjin. He regrets not being her to meet you personally, and asked me to convey his appreciation for your assistance. I hope that I will suffice as a surrogate."

Brendan looked at her. He wondered how long she spent memorizing that little speech.

"I could not imagine anyone I would rather have greet me than you," Brendan replied, pouring it on thicker than necessary, but also testing her stature in the Guoanbu hierarchy. If she smiled demurely, she was just a messenger; if she clawed back with her own remark, innuendo or not, she was probably a field agent.

"You have no idea how accurate that is," she replied, winking. "You've been spoiled by Colestah and her brazen antics in the field. You'll find my techniques more subtle, but also more effective."

Brendan was shocked. This was no messenger. Even though Wancheng had evidently brought her up to speed on Vargas, dropping her code name, and clearly demonstrating her awareness that Brendan and Vargas worked together was one thing; reflecting on the personality of Vargas' work ethic was another thing all together. Still, he did not want to appear surprised or off guard.

"Well then, if you can provide me with a name to call you, I can ask you to get us underway," he responded.

"Fu Hao," she said. She then spun and marched off toward the baggage claim area, waving her hand to indicate he should follow her. Their pathway bypassed the official customs hall and brought them through several doors and passageways until they walked onto a helideck. A CAIC Z-10 sat patiently for them. It was a dangerous looking attack helicopter, with a top speed of nearly 200 MPH. A favorite toy of the Chinese military.

Abigail chattered in his ear, scooping Brendan on the significance of her name.

"Fu Hao was a general, and the emperor's wife, back in the thirteenth century. Her legacy was that she recruited soldiers with her charm, and then led them into battle, which usually meant death, with her sword. Sounds appropriate." She laughed, which was less comforting to Brendan than she planned.

Brendan turned to Fu Hao as they navigated the maze. "Pretty famous, if not ominous name, Fu Hao. Are you a general as well?" Brendan thought that would give him the upper hand in the coy little game they were playing.

"Ah, Abigail is already with us, I see," she replied, without turning or changing pace.

"She's definitely informed," Abby whispered in his ear. "Better not underestimate her." There was no chance of that.

"We should be in Tianjin in less than an hour," Fu Hao said as they boarded. Brendan climbed into the gunner seat, behind the pilot, and watched as Fu Hao went around the bird to climb in. She turned to look at him as she pulled herself into the segregated pilot seat, a little smile dancing on her lips, enjoying the surprise in his eyes.

"Don't forget your seatbelt," he deadpanned to her, visualizing the smile on her now hidden face.

Fu Hao swept in low over Bohai Bay as she approached their landing site; a dusty yard in the thick of the chemical storage tank clusters. Tianjin was the site of a deadly chemical explosion a few years back, killing more than a hundred souls. It was a perfect hiding place for a small chemical company to lose itself, swallowed by the giant chemical tank farms.

They were met after landing by three men. No introductions were given. Fu Hao spoke with one of them. The man was tall and rather rugged looking. He listened to her for a while and then seemed to take a harsh tone. Brendan recognized him as Wancheng. Fu Hao turned abruptly towards Brendan.

"Hope you enjoyed the ride. I'll see you later." She didn't sound happy.

"Nothing changes my opinion on who I would like to greet me," he said as she walked past him. "Whenever I visit China." He hoped to keep her friendly, despite her obvious annoyance.

Without looking back, she waved goodbye with a single swipe of her hand and climbed back into the Z-10. It did not kick back to full power, however, and sat idle while Brendan moved to meet the man who had apparently angered her.

"You get anything, Abby?" he whispered, hoping for a little insight.

"I believe the gentleman speaking with her is Wancheng."

"Yes, I recognize him."

"I couldn't get the whole conversation, but it seems she wants to be part of the action and he told her to sit tight with the chopper."

"Wancheng," he said, extending his hand. Brendan stepped closer to the man apparently in charge. He had some sort of brace on his neck and a wide scarf-like wrapping around it.

"Taranis," he replied. They shook hands.

"Thanks for joining us. If Colestah vouches for you, and if you're anything like her, I have no doubt you'll be a great asset."

"No one's like her," Brendan replied with a smile.

"Fair enough."

"What do we have here?" Brendan switched to serious mode. "Any lead on the gas facility?"

"We've identified the building they're in, and the production point. What we are unsure of, is whether any of the toxin has been... what shall we call it, activated?"

"Let's go find out," Brendan said.

"There is significant concern about our proximity to such a large civilian population. We want to isolate the gas, get control of the entire inventory, and hopefully identify the production process. I'm sure the powers that be, would be most interested"

Wancheng's poker face tweaked slightly, and Brendan picked up on the nuance. He meant the Chinese government wants the formula for their own use.

"I believe your participation in this tactical action will legitimize the process," Wancheng continued. "By providing some appearance of transparency; regardless of the outcome."

Brendan translated to himself once again. *You want to destroy the formula if possible so the government can't get it; and maybe I can help. I hear ya.*

Brendan had to deliver a reply that would confirm to Wancheng that he understood. "I hope I don't screw anything up," he said with a wink.

Wancheng looked at him for a moment, assessing whether he actually understood the conversation between the lines. Brendan's stoic demeanor confirmed it.

"Colestah is taking out the Cali operation as we speak. We'd better move before they get wind of it and shut down," Brendan said.

Wancheng agreed. They had staged themselves far enough away that the gas guys would not spot them, or suspect the helicopter when it arrived among the multitude of chemical tanks. He called to the other two agents with him, speaking in Chinese. His hand motions indicated they were to flank the target building entrance, which sat about four hundred feet ahead.

"He's sending them to the perimeters, Taranis. Guess that means you two are heading down the middle," Abigail whispered in his ear.

"The main entrance isn't that well guarded," Wancheng said, "but we're not sure about the interior compound."

"Hang on," Brendan said. "Abigail, any chance we can get a satellite shot of the compound? We need some intel on the activity inside."

"Let me check it out," she replied.

"Good idea," Wancheng said. "We have the entire USA covered by satellites, but not China." He chuckled.

"Same for us, all of China, but not Idaho," Brendan replied, also smiling at the absurdity.

After a couple of minutes, Abigail came back. "Nothing for at least an hour," she said.

Brendan informed Wancheng.

"Perfect," he replied. "We want darkness to settle in a bit anyway."

"Let me know once you know, Abby."

Wancheng instructed his men to hunker down and wait for instructions. Brendan thought about Fu Hao, her chopper some distance away, sitting at low idle. He didn't imagine she even possessed such a gear!

The sun began setting, the satellite swung overhead, and Abigail jumped to life. "You there, Taranis?"

"Yup, go ahead," he replied immediately, even though her voice had jerked him from a creeping sleepiness, fueled by jet lag.

"Numerous vehicles and several people on the inside. It's a little dark, but I can make out about eight or ten individuals, although they are entering and leaving one of the three buildings facing the yard, so there could be more. Some of them are definitely armed. There are also two helicopters in the yard; one of them is already running."

Brendan relayed the info to Wancheng, who decided to move right away. The fact that one of the birds was already warming up meant there might be an imminent departure. He spoke to Fu Hao.

"Nothing leaves the yard," Abigail translated to Brendan.

The support agents moved in on the sides and Brendan accompanied Wancheng straight towards the front doors. The element of surprise allowed them to easily dispatch the front guards and get access to the door. Wancheng pulled it open slightly and Brendan peered inside. Nothing visible. They moved forward, joined now by the other two agents.

Halfway down the main corridor they heard the footsteps of several men approaching. There was little cover around them. Wancheng motioned everyone to hit the ground. Just in time. A column of at least twenty men turned the corner. By the time they realized there were intruders, the popping of silenced automatic fire echoed down the hall. Several combatants fell, though a group retreated back around the far corner.

Wancheng realized they would be sitting ducks once the locals regained their senses, so he launched a stun grenade down the hall and waved the four of them back away from the charge. The grenade stunned the guards, and Wancheng led the charge down the hall. He dove headfirst just before the end of the corridor, sliding past the corner and spreading fire in a soft arc towards where the enemy might be. Brendan was right behind him, collapsing to one knee and peeking around the corner, seeking more specific targets. There were none! The enemy had apparently fled the initial contact, all the way back and outside the building.

They regrouped, reloaded, and moved towards the small door at the end of the second corridor. Wancheng didn't know what exactly lay on the other side, but he knew it wasn't friendly. He pulled his radio close and barked some instructions into it. The only words Brendan understood were Fu Hao. Abigail loosely translated the balance once again.

"Guess she's going to clear out the other side of the door." Wancheng motioned everyone back down the hall and around the corner.

Surprise was a lost ally at this point, and the only other play was full power. A quiet calm enveloped the area. Brendan could make out the whir of chopper blades outside, presumably the one Abigail had referred to. He looked at Wancheng, who held three fingers up. He folded one down, then the second, and finally the third, in a quiet countdown. The yard erupted with the impact of Fu Hao's strike. The door blew inward. The yard was awash in a fireball and the accompanying dust storm.

Wancheng pushed forward, staying low to the ground. Shots screamed though the doorway, and one of the support agents went down immediately. Brendan felt the burn in his left arm. He fell forward onto the floor, and glanced down at his torn shirt and seeping blood. It appeared to be just a flesh wound. He looked at Wancheng and shook his head forward, indicating he was ready to go.

A burst of high caliber machine gun fire cleared away several assailants, and another rocket brought sudden death to the idling helicopter in the yard. As they cleared the doorway, Brendan looked up and saw the Z-10 hovering motionless above them. Fu Hao was looking down through the bulletproof window screen, and he caught her eye. It was a little dark out, but the flames of the burning chopper illuminated her face. She waved, calm and casual, as if greeting a friend for a quick pint after work. Brendan moved forward and sought some cover. He was sure she had started to laugh as he glanced away. He remembered her remark about being more subtle than Vargas!

Suddenly the Z-10 spun on the spot and tilted. Once again, the high caliber burst found its target, and several of the enemy fell to the spray. Brendan, Wancheng, and the other agent spread out along the buildings, exchanging fire with the few remaining guards. Fu Hao's next burst took out the other helicopter in the yard. It went with a large crashing explosion, full fuel tanks releasing into the air. The explosion stunned everyone.

Brendan looked at Wancheng, who was at least fifty feet away, along the wall to his left. Wancheng just shook his head in mock disbelief at the fun Fu Hao was having. She now had her sights on the other vehicles in the yard: Two small trucks and a couple of cars. She hovered in a stationary position but rotated the bird, taking them out one by one, just like in another video game.

Several men escaped from the courtyard and raced out onto the street beyond. Wancheng looked up at Fu Hao, who was now no more than a hundred feet off the ground, and pointed repeatedly towards the fleeing guards. She nodded and lifted off after them. Brendan couldn't see her beyond the wall, but her short, targeted bursts could be heard, and he felt little doubt that the escaped guards would not be making it home for dinner.

Wancheng made eye contact with Brendan. He used two fingers to touch his eyes and then point at the building in front of Brendan, indicating that he wanted him to search inside. He pointed again at himself, and then at the building behind him, indicating where he was heading.

Brendan entered cautiously, expecting enemy combatants to be dug in at some point. They weren't. On the third floor, the top, he found two men cowering under a counter ledge. They were obviously not soldiers. They beseeched him for something in wailing Chinese, that Brendan assumed was a call for mercy.

"They're begging for their lives," Abigail said, coming to life once again in his ear. "Something about grandchildren and being forced to work here."

Brendan motioned them up and forward, out to the hall, down the stairs, and through the door. Wancheng appeared about the same time and moved towards Brendan. He spoke to his other agent, who immediately returned to the entrance.

"He's going to greet the local cops." As Abigail said this, Brendan heard the wail of several sirens, still some ways off.

Fu Hao's Z-10 suddenly zoomed back over the outside wall, bringing fresh noise and dust to the yard. Wancheng covered his eyes as she set it down carefully between the burning carcasses of her mechanical prey, and hopped out. Wancheng walked up to her and appeared to be admonishing her, perhaps for being crazy and reckless, but Brendan couldn't hear. She listened to him, then gave him a thumbs up and walked towards Brendan, with a big smile and little wink lighting up her face. Brendan glanced at Wancheng. He shrugged in mock surrender.

The two captured lab techs were led into a separate room and placed in a corner, where they cowered together, still mumbling their pleas. Fu Hao strolled into the room and moved past Brendan, turning slightly and walking sideways for a moment.

"My favorite part." She winked again. "The interrogation."

Brendan drew his weapon as she approached the men and spoke to them in Chinese. Abigail translated roughly for Brendan.

"May I please have your name," she asked, overly polite.

The man stuttered out that he was Mr. Chua. Fu Hao moved towards him slowly and removed a long, thin dagger from somewhere in the folds of her chopper suit. Brendan hadn't noticed it earlier. It reminded him of the ESEE knife he noticed back at Abigail's, attached to Vargas' right ankle. Fu Hao lifted the blade close to the left eye of Mr. Chua and spoke again in a polite voice.

Abigail translated. "You have lovely eyes. I would like to have one of them. Not both, I'm not greedy, but one would be an awesome toy for my cat." Once again, Brendan reflected on her statement that she considered herself more subtle than Vargas.

Mr. Chua retreated as much as the counter behind him would allow and wailed.

"I'll tell you anything," was the translated version, although he seemed to have said much more than that.

As if Abigail sensed Brendan's thoughts, she added, "I'm paraphrasing."

As Fu Hao leaned in further to Mr. Chua, the other prisoner, probably panicked by a highly elevated sense of mortality, and unexpected rush of adrenalin, dashed up and snatched the sidearm from her belt holster, wrapping his arm around her throat and putting the gun against her head. He screamed something in Chinese, which required no translation. Brendan was surprised at how amateur that was on Fu Hao's part.

Without hesitation, Brendan raised his hand and fired a round into the man's forehead, zinging less than an inch from Fu Hao's right earlobe. When the assailant relaxed his grip, Fu Hao spun around, ready to strike with her knife, but soon realized Brendan had completely neutralized her attacker. She looked at Brendan, tilting her head as if to say 'not bad.' Brendan winked. She also knew it was an amateur mistake on her part.

Fu Hao returned her attention to Mr. Chua, who was now ready to provide every detail he knew, about any subject he had ever encountered. Brendan smiled at the thought of letting Vargas know that you can extract information without actually changing the composition of a person's body first—just by shooting his colleague in the head. He wasn't aware that Vargas was quite fluent in that particular technique!

Mr. Chua revealed the location of the gas stockpile, and the fact that it had not been targeted. There were numerous canisters, but no large tanks of any kind. Production facilities were just about ready to come on line in the building to their left, but all current gas was being prepared stateside. He confirmed it was completely innocuous and safe to release.

Wancheng called in reinforcements to police the area and remove his fallen comrade, and the deceased enemy combatants. Each captured bad guy would be vetted for upstream and downstream connections. They were accompanied by technicians mandated to dismantle the facility, hopefully with some revelation of the production process. They would destroy the lab and dispose of the gas, or at least most of it. Brendan felt certain that a sample or two would be secured by the authorities for future analysis.

As the evening drew late, Wancheng instructed Fu Hao to take Mr. Chua via helicopter to their local HQ for holding and processing. Wancheng would take care of Brendan. Fu Hao definitely looked a little disappointed. She responded to Wancheng, out of earshot from Brendan. After a few shrugs and waves, Wancheng shook his head again and presented the reformed plan.

"Seems she wants to take care of you personally, whatever that means," he said.

Abigail could hear him now and remained silent. They knew what that meant.

"Once we get your arm stitched up, she will fly you back to Beijing and make sure you get some rest, before a flight home tomorrow. She has a good point; the drive back is over two hours." It was Wancheng's turn to wink. *Shit, everybody winks here,* Brendan thought.

Abigail's voice suddenly turned serious. "Taranis, I just spoke to Vargas. She was in some difficulty down in Colombia."

"Is she okay," Brendan asked. Wancheng and Fu Hao looked up at the sudden anxiousness in his voice. They couldn't hear Abigail, but they knew he referred to Vargas.

"Yup, everything seems okay now, but it was a rough for few hours. Anyway, she says you need to secure a Mr. Ma. It seems he is one of only two people that know the gas formula. He has it memorized, so try to get him alive."

"Okay, noted." He was relieved that Vargas wasn't hurt.

Brendan turned to Fu Hao and Wancheng. "It seems a certain Mr. Ma is the key man here in China. He is one of only two people that know the formula; he's the one we need to find."

Wancheng looked at Mr. Chua. Fu Hao jumped in first.

"Do you know someone named Mr. Ma?" she asked. She pulled the skin below her eye to stretch out her eyeball and remind him of the consequences for withholding information.

He responded and Abigail translated. "I know him." Mr. Chua looked at Brendan and nodded. "He just shot him in the head."

Brendan looked at Fu Hao. "You mean, the man who grabbed your gun was Mr. Ma?"

"It would seem so," said Fu Hao. They all looked at one another, disappointed and a little discouraged.

"Oh my," said Abigail.

Enroute to Beijing, though it was nearly midnight, Fu Hoa radioed in various arrangements, all of which Abigail loosely translated to Brendan. She arranged for a premier suite at the China World Summit Wing Hotel, with direct landing coordinates for the hotel heliport on the roof. After admonishing the hotel staff for suggesting the restaurant was closed, she ordered room service for two from the menu at Grill 79, including ravioli fois gras, and of course, a bottle of 2012 COFCO Great Wall Centenary Old Vine; and, for some unknown reason, a roll of saran wrap.

"Looks like the night isn't over yet," Abigail said, with only the slimmest hint of sarcasm.

"Good night, Abby, you've been awesome. Thanks for staying with me throughout. I've got it from here."

"Sweet dreams," she replied. "And, by the way, you're booked on United 808 at 18:00 tomorrow. You're in global first class with a nice lie flat bed, so you can catch up on sleep then. Arrival at Dulles is 19:50, so plug back in with me once you arrive, just in case there's anything urgent."

Brendan thanked her and disconnected.

After landing on the hotel rooftop, sitting atop the highest building in Beijing, the China World Trade Center Tower Three, they were escorted to their room by a staid, rather rotund butler. Once inside, Fu Hao used the saran wrap to cover the bandage on Brendan's upper arm, more or less water proofing it. Then they both moved to the bathroom to wash away the long day, and enjoyed a soothing hot downpour in the rainforest shower, before a short stay in the soaking tub. Fu Hao provided ample preview to what she had planned for the balance of the night.

By the time the ravioli was gulped down, aided by the wine, which was indeed a decent vintage, she had Brendan spinning in the oversized king bed that dominated the premier suite bedroom. Fu Hao was like the CAIC Z-10 she buzzed around in. When they were done, or more accurately, when she was finished devouring him, Brendan felt like one of the burned-out helicopters in the storage yard back in Bohai Bay.

They slept much of the next day, in between Fu Hao's attacks, and a quick change of dressing. They parlayed back and forth in a banter that was unique to those who shared their kind of life—one that embraced great risk without hesitation. Fu Hao whisked him to the airport in her Z-10 and through security with ease. Their last goodbye was filled with some sarcasm, much appreciation, and of course, a wink or two.

Vargas and Rogers arrived in Panama at 17:00 and showered at the hotel. They reserved at Donde Jose for the 7:00 PM seating. After two hours of culinary delight, much wine and wind-down, they caught a taxi back to the Sheraton. The night closed with a furious release of the tension, accumulated over the past two days, before settling into a soft and relaxing embrace that delivered a deep and lasting sleep.

In the morning, they found the time, energy, and desire to renew the previous evenings pleasure, before heading to the Gulfstream V for the return flight. They arrived in Washington mid-afternoon, and Abigail confirmed a meeting with Clemenson at the White House at 15:00 the following day. She was to bring Rogers as well.

"That's a little late for Clemenson," Vargas remarked.

"Taranis is rolling in late tonight. He had quite a whirlwind trip. I guess he's giving him a couple of extra hours for jet-lag adjustments."

"Sound reasonable," Vargas replied. Such consideration for others was also out of character for Clemenson. "How'd he make out over there?"

"Mostly good. The gas is gone. We'll get a full debrief later."

Vargas recognized that Abigail was not telling a complete story. Something must have gone wrong there too.

Rogers stayed over with Vargas that evening. So much for never even having two in her four-person bed. There was no sense making him sleep on the plane, but Vargas was distracted. She was measuring how to handle Carson Wallach's entire disclosure about Clemenson and the CIA. She would have to be cautious about how she introduced the subject.

► ► ►

They swept into the White House entrance at 14:47 in the R8. It was Rogers' first trip to the president's residence, and he was more than impressed by the familiarity Vargas had with the security. He was even more interested in the swipe card she used to open the gate, but said nothing. The security detail was expecting him though, and there was no issue in moving up and into the building. Rogers received a metal detector scan. No red card meant no screening skip. They marched down the usual hallways and turns, before they were asked to wait just outside the situation room. A few minutes later, Brendan arrived. They exchanged mutual relief that all were okay, but did not discuss anything about their missions; the hallway was not the place.

A few minutes passed before a security guard led them into the room and closed the door behind them. No one else was there. Another few minutes passed, and Abigail came in through the same entrance.

"Where is everyone?" she said, to no one in particular.

"No idea," Vargas said. "I thought they'd be with you."

Brendan shrugged, indicating he was also unaware of where the others might be. Rogers only expected Clemenson, although having the meeting at the White House indicated there was the possibly that others might participate.

They remained standing, waiting to see who else was joining them. A short while later, a different door opened, one that was concealed within the architecture of the back wall, behind where the president usually sat. In walked John Brenmar and General O'Keefe, the NSA director, followed by the president, and finally Clemenson, with a middle-aged lady right behind him. She was quite tall and well dressed in full business-battle attire. She neither smiled nor glanced around, walking in as though she was walking alone. Vargas didn't recognize her, and looked to Abby for some enlightenment. Abigail caught her glance, and her curiosity, but frowned a bit and shrugged, indicating she was not familiar with the lady. The only person missing from previous meetings was General Danforth.

Clemenson usually sat to the right of the president, but today he sat to his immediate left, and the right hand chair was occupied by the woman. Once all the dignitaries sat down, the members of PT1 followed suit, selecting three seats along the back wall, while Abigail sat opposite them. Clemenson introduced Rogers, O'Keefe, and Brenmar, but the mysterious middle-aged lady was never mentioned. Vargas thought they seemed like one big happy family—with a few skeletons in the closet, of course.

"Everybody's read Abigail's report, I assume," Clemenson began.

"Not yet, boss," Vargas said, looking at Abigail.

"Sorry, boss, the team hasn't received it yet. I haven't met up with them." Vargas thought about that. She knew it wasn't in error that they didn't received a copy; something she would bring up again later.

Clemenson didn't miss a beat. "I guess they know what went down, they were there." He chuckled a bit at his own remark, but Vargas was not feeling the humor.

"Actually, boss, Taranis and I have not discussed the mission, so we're a little bit in the dark about what transpired in each location."

Clemenson looked at Abigail, expressing some surprise, but it was fabricated. "Abigail, please provide them each a copy."

Abigail slid three copies across to Vargas, Rogers, and Brendan. Vargas scanned the report quickly. It was only twelve pages long and her photographic memory had no difficulty in registering everything pertinent. *Brendan killed Mr. Ma. Shit!* She flipped the report closed.

Rogers and Brendan looked at her. They were still speed-reading.

"Bottom line here is the gas has been destroyed, but the owner of the formula, at least one of them," Clemenson glanced at Brendan, "is still on the loose."

He paused but no one interjected. Brendan kept his head slightly bowed. The report didn't provide all the details surrounding his decision to put a bullet in the head of Mr. Ma, and he wasn't about to highlight the fact by offering any additional info.

"Now we need Pitts, and we need him alive. If Vargas' intel is correct, he's the only remaining person who knows the formula, and we need it intact." *If my intel is correct?* "We also need to find him fast, before he can manufacture any more gas." Again, as with Brenmar earlier, Vargas was surprised there was nothing about PT1, the risks they took, the success they had … and poor Daniel's face.

Vargas knew something was preoccupying Clemenson. Something was worrying him. Was it the possibility that Pitts' would make more gas, or that the formula would be lost, and with it, the opportunity for the government to possess the weapon? Or was it more personally dramatic, that Pitts was actually Wallach. She was holding on to that little tidbit until a more appropriate time.

Clemenson looked at Vargas. She knew he was expecting her to comment.

"Okay, we know Pitts is in Colombia. We know his plane, so first thing is to make sure it doesn't leave the ground. Let's get his picture and info to all points of exit from the country. Even if he has friends at the airports, if we make a loud enough noise about it, they might hesitate to help him depart. If we can keep him in Colombia, we will narrow the search area."

"Jesus, that's a big search area," said Brenmar. "How are you going to find him? He's a grain of sand on the beach."

"I'm guessing that they took our weapons. The lovely pistols and night vision gear you provided, Mr. Brenmar."

"Ya, thanks for the reminder," he replied.

"Daniel might have garnished some intel from the lab folks we captured during the op. Besides, I placed a small tracking device on the pistol Rogers had." Rogers looked at her with some surprise. "It doesn't have a wide range, but we have to start in Cali and sweep for it. It's still a needle in a haystack, but maybe not a grain of sand on the beach."

"That's great, Colestah," Abigail said. "At least we have a starting point. We can get the local authorities on it as well."

"I think we'd better keep this little detail in house, Abby. The locals are questionable at best, in terms of their loyalty and commitment. If news of this tracker gets out, it's a lost cause."

"Agreed," Clemenson added. "Let's get everyone back to Cali ASAP and see what we can come up with."

"We can get Daniel started right away," Vargas added. "He's good, and loyal."

"Yes, he's our man down there," said Brenmar. "Excellent operative." *Jerk, like you get the credit now for his courage.*

"One more thing though," Vargas said. "The window is only another two to three days. After that, the tracker will die out."

"Jesus! Okay, John, get your guy on it right away. PT1 will have wheels up this evening. Straight to Cali this time, we'll clear it locally."

"What's the frequency?" Brenmar asked.

"Daniel has it," Vargas replied. "It was his tracker."

"Okay, let's roll," Clemenson said. "We can continue updates on the fly, through Abigail."

Vargas stood up to go. She liked being in the field much more than being in a chat room.

The president stood up. "Vargas, can you stay behind for a minute please." It wasn't a question.

Everyone cleared the room except Vargas, Clemenson, the president, and the mysterious lady to his right. Brenmar and the general left through the back door, and the PT1 team headed out the way they entered.

As they were leaving, Vargas dictated a few instructions. "Let's gather at Abigail's to run through our plan. Everyone pick up some

clothes, and we'll meet there at..." Vargas looked at her Rolex, "19:00."
They nodded. "Rogers, get us a flight plan." He nodded again.

Once the room was clear, the president asked Vargas to come
closer and sit down again.

"Vargas," he started, looking at her, wearing a very presidential
face. She figured that was the face that wins elections. She waited for
him to spit it out. "We want that formula. It has enormous potential.
Imagine the uses we could develop from it: Advances in medicine,
agriculture, who knows what else." *How about war, terrorism, murder.*
"I need you to take every precaution in the acquisition of Mr. Pitts.
Let's make sure he comes back in once piece."

Vargas nodded. "I'll do my best, Mr. President."

"That's always been enough," Clemenson said.

"One thing though," Vargas said. "Tell me where I stand if it
comes down to kill him or lose him."

The president said nothing. Clemenson said nothing. The
mystery lady never twitched a muscle or blinked an eye.

"Got it," Vargas said. *They want him back alive, but they should
have said kill him! This doesn't feel right, and who the hell is that lady?*

Vargas took K St. and Pennsylvania Avenue to get home, despite
the heavy rush hour traffic. She gathered her usual travel bag, including guns, knives, clips, and of course, lace bras. She also packed some
stealth clothing, anticipating a silent raid on Pitts' castle.

She reflected on the situation, trying to put the puzzle together.
Clemenson was involved with drugs? She couldn't get that around
her brain. Brenmar though, that was easy. But why would Pitts
mention Clemenson? And if Clemenson was still under the CIA
umbrella at the time, why didn't he know about this huge drug conspiracy theory?

She headed out in plenty of time, not feeling anxious or rushed
about getting to Abby's, but still accelerating beyond the norm. That
was just the way she drove the R8. Their departure time was set, so
she had nothing to worry about. Even so, it took her less than fifteen
minutes. She used the time, aside from navigating between angry

drivers, to reflect on the past two days. *Pitts laid out an incredible, yet somehow plausible, conspiracy. Clemenson begins acting strange, the president asks me to get Pitts alive, Abigail withholds information, and Brendan kills Mr. Ma, the only other formula holder. I have to figure out who's on the team and who's not!*

The team was reviewing the field ops when Vargas arrived. Brendan was just inquiring how Rogers had the foresight to put a tracker on his weapon. As Vargas walked in, he flipped his thumb at her like a hitchhiker. Brendan smiled.

"Rogers," she said, tossing her R8 keys to him. "Get the Gulfstream ready, and make sure the route is cleared. We'll be there right behind you."

Rogers was surprised but said nothing. It was like he was being excused, almost dismissed. The reality was, he was the only one Vargas was feeling one hundred percent about, and he didn't really need to know the mission details anyway. Abigail and Brendan were a little surprised as well, but stifled any desire to comment.

"I'm on it, boss," Rogers said, heading towards the door.

"Rogers," Vargas called, realizing how her instructions might have been perceived as a dismissal. "We just can't afford any screw-ups. The plane has to be fueled and prepped. We'll finalize the mission details once airborne; you're in all the way."

Rogers looked at her. It was clear that she was apologizing for the way she dismissed him, and he had to make it smooth as well.

"Thanks, Vargas, I never doubted it. She'll be ready and waiting."

"What's the flight time to Cali?"

"I figure about eight hours, maybe nine."

"Okay, let's take off at twenty-one hundred; that'll get us in at sun up, more or less, and afford us a little sleep time," Vargas said.

Once Rogers closed the door, Vargas looked at Abigail, then at Brendan, then back at Abigail.

"We're chasing important shit, in crazy circumstances, against ridiculous odds." She paused. They carried no reaction. "I need to know one thing from each of you, and we need to make one decision together."

"What's up?" Brendan said.

Abigail raised her eyebrows.

"Abby, why didn't you disseminate the report before we went to the White House?" Vargas dropped the bomb without preamble. Abby's answer would reveal a lot. Vargas would know if there was any bullshit going on. Brendan was shocked at the question.

"Clemenson told me not to," she replied, without a moment's hesitation, and without a hint of emotion or regret. That reflected well on Abigail.

Vargas turned to Brendan. "Did you assassinate Mr. Ma for Clemenson to ensure the Chinese would not get the formula?"

The only sign that Brendan even heard her was a slight pursing of his lips.

"The short answer is that I probably did." He paused. "But not under any instructions. When I shot him, I had no idea who he was. He was about to put a bullet in Fu Hao, who by the way, is the watered-down Chinese version of Colestah."

Abigail jumped in. "I was along for that ride Vargas. Brendan was in shock when he found out who the guy was."

Vargas was glad she cleared that up. Now it was time to stop being an asshole.

"They want Pitts alive, at all costs," she said. "They want him for the formula. They calculate there is a huge upside to owning it, and I don't mean for the eradication of Mountain Pine Beetles." Brendan and Abigail looked at each other. Vargas continued. "From my point of view, we need to get Pitts soon."

"You want to go against orders?" Brendan asked.

"I want to do what we need to do to end this threat; forever. There's other stuff too, but I can't get into it all right now. I just needed to know that you are both with me on PT1."

"I told you from day one, Vargas. I'm on your side."

"Thank you, Abby."

"There's no doubt, Vargas. How the hell are we going to handle the next crisis if we're not together on this one?" He smiled at his commitment of loyalty, without actually saying it.

"Let's roll, Brendan. Abby, we'll connect once airborne and get a little more detailed." Abby nodded. "Meanwhile, find out everything you can on Carson Wallach, particularly after he went missing."

Abigail was definitely caught off guard by that request. "You think he had some play in this?"

"You mean 'has,'" Vargas said, shooting her a serious glance. "I don't know everything yet, but gather what you can without letting anyone else know, including Clemenson." That hung in the air. It was a break in the trust factor so imperative to PT1 and the missions.

"I'll see what I can dig up, but at some point soon, you're going to have to share a little bit of detail."

"I will, Abby, just let me make sure I'm right before I get anyone else involved."

They climbed into the Austin Martin. Brendan drove.

"There's some funny shit happening right now, Brendan. The fact that we didn't get the report before the meeting, the death of Mr. Ma, and some funny things I discovered in Colombia all add up to somebody not being honest. I knew what answer you and Abby would give to my questions, I just wanted to see how you answered. I apologize for doubting things. I've only apologized a few other times in my life."

"No need, Vargas. If Clemenson had told me to take Ma out, I would have without hesitation, and informed you of that. Fact was, when I did cancel him, we'd never even heard of Mr. Ma."

"I know that now." She trusted Brendan too.

"You let me know what's really going on—when you're ready," he said. "But don't question our loyalty too much, while you're the one hiding things from us." He had a valid point.

"How did you like Wancheng?" Vargas asked, after a short pause to confirm she understood his message.

"Definitely not what I expected. Sharp guy, and a strong leader."

"How's your arm?"

"Just a scratch. All good."

"I noticed from the report that you met some of his team." Brendan didn't respond. "How was the Chinese version of Colestah," she asked, with a little innuendo sprinkled in.

"We'll need a longer conversation to relate all of that." Brendan laughed. Vargas did too. Nope, those Chinese folks were definitely not what they expected.

O nce airborne, Vargas waited for autopilot altitude, and then asked Rogers to join her and Brendan for some brainstorming. She sat in one of the armchairs, and Brendan in the one across the aisle—the same one Mr. Fabulous had enjoyed so much. She was glad chairs couldn't talk. After Rogers made a pit stop in the boy's room, he slid into the seat across from Vargas.

"We've got about six hours before touchdown. I grabbed some groceries on the way to the airport so there's food in the fridge, in case you're hungry," Rogers said.

"Thanks. Some food and sleep are probably in order. Tomorrow could be a long day," Vargas said. She tapped the sat-phone and got Abigail on the speaker.

"We're on an unsecured line, so let's be cautious about how we phrase things," Abigail said, even before the 'hello' that followed it.

"Noted. What can you tell me about Honos?" Vargas asked, switching to the code name for Wallace.

Abby laid a few things out.

"First, I knew him fairly well. He was always polite and considerate, but a loner, and much more secretive about his activities than the current team. He seldom plugged in. His last mission was also a return to Colombia, after a short visit back to Washington. That was almost four years ago. We continued to look for him for almost two months with daily patrols, much official pressure, and unofficial interrogation. Of course, he was undercover, so he did not officially belong to any agency. The official search was for a tourist, not an operative, but the local authorities knew we wouldn't put that much energy into the search for a mere citizen."

"What was he supposed to be doing down there? I mean, were there progress reports, any kind of debriefing up in Washington?" Vargas asked. "Jeez, you have every move we make logged and tagged; surely there was some reporting done."

"Like I said, he was much more secretive about his missions. His debriefing was done through CIA channels, not me. It changed after him. He and his missions were actually the catalyst for moving PT1 out of CIA oversight."

"Did Clemenson change it, or was he being blamed for the missing agent?" Vargas was peeling back some of the layers to this rotten onion.

"As I recall," Abby went on, "Clemenson was quite animated about the situation, and at odds with Brenmar about how everything was handled."

"How what was handled, Wallach's disappearance or how his missions were reported?" Vargas asked.

"Both, I guess. As I recall, Clemenson was upset with Brenmar. I don't know if it was the mission, the reporting, or whatever, but he definitely took a stand."

"Come on, Abby, you have your finger on the pulse. What's the story? I have reasons for asking, and I will tell you about them, but I need you to be straight with me right now." Vargas' tone was rising and Abby could feel it.

"Look," Abby replied. "I'm not supposed to share info on what transpires in private meetings, and I can't give you word for word transcripts." She hesitated.

Vargas waited, sensing Abby was challenging herself. All concern about the unsecure line was long gone. She quietly hoped no one was getting an earful.

"What happened, Abby?"

"Clemenson took a stand against Brenmar. He told the president that he was either independent of the CIA, or he was resigning. He wanted PT1 outside the auspices of the agency." Abby let that hang in the air for a minute. "Brenmar was upset at the time. The president supported Clemenson, and PT1 became an independent entity."

"Let me guess," Vargas added, "Brenmar was instructed to provide full co-operation, which explains why he is such a dick towards us."

"More than that, Vargas. Brenmar was clearly informed that his status was below that of Clemenson. Clemenson was the top security official in the country. The president gave him a ringing endorsement. I don't think Brenmar, or the CIA, welcomed that fact with any zeal."

"Wow," Vargas said. "I can see why Brenmar might have a bit of a grudge. I guess he's hoping for PT1 to be a failure. That might explain some of the things I found out down in Colombia."

Rogers sat stoically, saying nothing, and hiding the surprise he was feeling. A short time ago, he was just a pilot and provider, albeit on a national security level. Now, he realized he was in the thick of the very structure of that national security. This little team of agents were just pawns in some much larger game. He wasn't sure he was comfortable with that.

Brendan was less pensive. He wanted to know what was going on, what Vargas knew. "Time to get us up to speed, Vargas. Abby's gone past protocol in sharing that history with us. Time to let us know why you're asking her to do so."

He was right. Vargas knew that. Putting Abby on the spot without reason was presumptive on her part. But the way Abby responded, without real hesitation or question about the integrity of Vargas' intentions, meant she was beyond reproach, as far as she was concerned. As a matter of fact, Vargas realized that she had no option but to trust the team completely.

"Here's the thick of it," she said. "Wallach is alive and well, living a life of luxury and crime in the heartland of Colombia. He makes frequent visits to the US and enjoys the tacit support of both the Colombian forces and the FARC. Quite a set up."

"How do you know?" Abby asked.

"I met him," Vargas said. "So did Rogers."

"What?" Rogers said.

"Mr. Wallach had you strapped to a table in his lab."

It took a moment for this to sit with everyone.

Rogers spoke first. "Pitts?"

"Absolutely," Vargas replied, letting the others absorb the news.

"You mean Pitts and Wallach are one in the same?" Brendan asked.

"Same person," Vargas confirmed.

Abby's first question was quite revealing to Vargas. "Does Clemenson know?"

Of course, if Clemenson knew, his integrity with the team would be in shambles.

"I don't know," Vargas said. "That's why I'm walking on egg shells with all this. Abby, I can't tell you how to react to this news, but I would ask you to say nothing for the moment. Wait until we get the whole story before we start questioning anyone, including Clemenson." She hesitated. "And maybe even the president!"

"How did you find this out?" Brendan asked.

"When Pitts was questioning me, or rather threatening me, I noticed how he winced whenever he used his left arm. It made me think of the bio on Wallach, and the fact that he had...how did Clemenson put it; had 'the left side of his chest ripped open'. Then I thought about Wallach's description and realized it matched Pitts exactly. I really took a shot in the dark, but I was a little desperate to make some conversation, and hopefully delay the DNA gas that was being prepped for me. Anyway, I called him Honos, and his eyes told me the rest."

"That's crazy," Brendan said, not in disbelief, but in realization.

"Oh, that's not all," Vargas continued. She couldn't see Abby, but she knew her mouth was hanging a bit. "Pitts, or Wallach, claims that the assassination attempt on his life was ordered by Clemenson." She waited for that to sink in.

Brendan looked stunned.

"That's unbelievable," Abby said, still shocked at the fact that Wallach was alive. "Why?"

"Here's the real part. Wallach claims he uncovered a drug connection between the CIA and the FARC. He claims the CIA was paving the road for the FARC to get their drugs into the US, in exchange for a cut of the profits. Big dollars."

"No way," Brendan said.

"You believed that?" Abby asked.

"He ran through it with an awful lot of sincerity, though not much detail. He said the CIA was able to control the flow, that the drugs were going to hit the streets anyway, and this was their way of ensuring quality and integrity of the product." She smirked. "They wouldn't want anyone to die from bad coke." Vargas waited for everyone to absorb that, then dropped the punch line. "That's the good news folks, the bad news in that the FARC was kicking back a portion of the profits, and the cash was divvied up among top US government folks, including Clemenson—according to Wallach."

That had the same effect on the team as it did on Vargas when she heard it. They protested a bit, but fell silent eventually.

"Wallach said he came back to Washington with information about the CIA–FARC partnership. He says Clemenson sent him back to Cali to gather more info, and shortly after that came the assassination attempt. He said Clemenson was the only one he told." She let that set in. "Is that true, Abby? Did you have any knowledge of these allegations?"

"Not a peep," Abby said immediately. "I remember his return from Colombia that time. Usually we have a debriefing, but he was only here a short time, less than a day, and he was gone again. Like I said, he seldom connected with me, and I didn't think anything of it at the time, but now everything makes sense." She paused. "I remember that Clemenson took Wallach for a meeting with the president. I was not invited, which I found a little strange at the time, but just figured it was something less important—nothing like this. I even remember Clemenson making some derogatory remark about Brenmar the next time I spoke to him, which was a little out of character."

"I wonder if he was upset that Wallach had figured things out."

Rogers had been completely silent throughout the discussion, but he jumped in at this point.

"I don't know much about Clemenson, Brenmar, and the rest of the leadership, but I know this: To control and manipulate the inflow of coke from Colombia takes more than a few people. We're talking about a major operation involving hundreds, if not thousands, of people."

Everyone reflected on that for a moment. It was obviously true.

"Now you understand my dilemma in revealing all this," Vargas said. "I think for the time being, we'd better keep this between the four of us. We still have a mission to fulfill. We can try to figure this out later."

"Agreed," Abigail said. Rogers and Brendan nodded as well.

"Abby, I know this will be difficult, especially if you are in contact with Clemenson, but we need to get this mission accomplished before we confront him."

"Yup, don't worry. Just get that fucker, Pitts!"

"Abby!'" Vargas feigned shock at her language.

"Sorry," she said, returning to her sweet self. "Good luck."

A little food, a little rest, and Rogers glided gently onto the runway at Alfonso Bonilla Aragón International Airport, beginning his reverse thrust. Vargas sat in her usual chair. She reached down to check her ESEE Strike Knife and then her Maxim 9. She wasn't sure if the local police authorities were aware of their arrival, or how they might react to her armaments. She glanced at Brendan, who responded with a gentle shrug, indicating he understood the dilemma. He tapped his trusted Glock through his jacket.

Vargas peered out the window at the rising sun. She got up, stabilizing herself against the rapid deceleration, and headed towards the cockpit.

Suddenly, a burst of automatic fire echoed from somewhere outside. Vargas didn't realize they were the target, until two rounds smashed through the port side window and support frame, narrowly missing her and Brendan. They both hit the floor. After a quick glance at one another, Vargas began to crawl towards the cockpit. She could feel the full-throttle thrust returning to the Rolls Royce BR710A1-10 engines.

She reached up and pulled the cockpit door open, lifting herself to a crouching position, getting a view of the full panorama outside. Rogers was fully intense on his task of getting airborne. More automatic fire sounded outside, but no other rounds came through the cabin.

Vargas raised up slightly to peer through the windshield. She saw the dirt at the end of the runway approaching at what seemed like an unavoidable pace. The cluster of agricultural fields beyond that loomed equally dangerous. She held her gaze at the onrushing field and said nothing. She figured Rogers got the idea; no point reminding him that he needed to get this bird off the ground!

The runway blurred out of sight. Vargas tensed in anticipation of their impact, but that did not happen. The plane left the ground at the exact moment the runway ended, and began a gentle climb skywards. The road immediately after the dirt field at the end of the runway was only a few meters below them, and they rumbled over the top of several cars. More automatic fire could be heard, but they were clear of the airport.

"What the fuck was that?" Vargas shouted.

Rogers looked at her. For the first time, she noticed the blood oozing out of his left shoulder. He winced.

"Unwelcoming committee, I guess."

"You're hit!"

Rogers lifted his arm. "No bones." After a little hesitation, he said, "Thank god for ten thousand feet of runway."

An alarm began sounding and their attention was drawn to the control panel. Then another.

"What's going on?" Vargas asked, trying to remain calm.

"Looks like they hit a fuel tank—make that both of them," Rogers replied, equally calm, despite the flesh wound in his shoulder. The obviously damaged fuel tanks, and several thousand feet of air between them and the ground, made for enough drama on its own.

"Figure it out," Vargas said. She turned back to the cabin to check on Brendan. She would only be in the way in the cockpit.

Rogers veered left. He knew there was an airport in Buenaventura, but he wasn't sure if they could get there before the fuel was exhausted. It was just habit from his training and experience, to know where the next closest airport was.

Vargas looked at Brendan. He was standing with hands on the fuselage wall for support. The pressure howled through the bullet holes, but they weren't high enough to lose oxygen…yet.

"Get Abby on the line, and get her to put us in touch with Daniel."

"On it. How's it look up there?" Brendan asked.

"Shit show," Vargas replied.

They both felt the plane turn sharply to the left, throwing them sideways. They looked at one another again, reaffirming their blind faith in Rogers.

"Rogers is on it," Vargas said. She turned back to the cockpit. "Just get me Daniel."

Vargas grabbed a towel from the galley and returned to the cockpit. She pushed it under Rogers' shirt, applying some pressure to the wound. She tucked it under the hold of his seatbelt strap before squeezing into the co-pilot seat.

"Plan?"

"Heading to Buenaventura. There's an airfield there," he paused. "Hopefully without another welcoming committee. We have to stay low; there's no pressurization."

"Ya, I can see that," Vargas said. "How's your arm? You have a first-aid kit?"

"There's a full medical kit above the galley, but let's get on the ground first, then you can tell me how my arm is." He intended to add a little levity.

That makes sense. His arm would be the least of his problems if they crashed into some jagged, woodsy terrain.

Brendan pushed his head through the cockpit door, sat-phone in hand.

"Daniel's coming on."

Vargas took the receiver. "Hello," she said. No reply. "Daniel, you there?"

Abby responded. "Just a sec, I'm patching him through."

"Colestah, is that you?" Daniel's voice was reassuring.

"Yes."

"Welcome back to Colombia, beautiful."

"Apparently not, Daniel. We landed in Cali and got racked by automatic weapon fire. Someone knew we were coming. You know anything about that?"

"Not me," Daniel replied. "Mierda! Is everyone okay?"

"We're hanging in," Vargas replied, "but we're in rough shape. We're leaking fuel and smoking a bit. Looks like we're going to ty for Buenaventura."

"Good idea," Daniel said. "We're not far from there. I think our man Pitts is in the area. His lab guys were quite co-operative. They told us he had a little get-a-way up here. We got a ping on the transceiver."

"You want to meet us at the airport?" Vargas asked.

"Eduardo will meet you, wait for him. It will take him a half-hour to get there. He has a funny scarf-hat, you'll know it when you see it. He's driving a grey Rav 4. I'm chasing this down. I'll try to have a position on our guy by the time you get here."

Vargas recognized how important Daniel had been to the entire Colombian mission. "Thanks, see you soon." *I hope.* Vargas turned to Rogers. "What's the good word, Mr. Pilot?"

He looked at her and smiled. "Just another day in the happy-go-lucky world of Vargas Hamilton," he said. They laughed a bit.

"Just get us another day, if you don't mind," Brendan said from the doorway.

Fortunately, Gerardo Tobar Lopez airport was well south of the city, so there were no civilian issues. With a stream of black smoke announcing their arrival and a collective but quiet sigh of relief, Rogers touched down on the 4000 foot runway. He even had room to spare. He navigated a one-eighty and taxied back down the runway, turning left towards the terminal building, and turning left again into one of six plane parking spots. The door opened towards the runway, not the terminal. Vargas and Brendan punched it open, braced for an attack. Nothing happened.

The two of them deplaned. The plane was still smoking a bit, but with the fuel almost completely depleted, there didn't seem to be much risk of an explosion. They could see the approaching police vehicle from under the fuselage. Vargas was leery of the officer inside, and watched carefully as he rounded the tail, stopped a few feet away from them, and put the car into park. He got out, quizzing them in Spanish before he even cleared the vehicle doorway. Vargas felt her hand inching towards the Maxim 9 tucked in her lower back. No emergency vehicles, no perceived panic. Everything was a little too calm.

Rogers appeared on the top step and barked back in Spanish. The officer looked at him, and more questions and answers followed. Rogers seemed to be trying to convince the man that they had no choice but to land due to mechanical problems. The officer wasn't buying it.

He leaned his head sideways and communicated something into his radio. An answer came back. Vargas couldn't make out the conversation, but she heard him mention Cali, and begin to draw his pistol. That was enough. Vargas drew first and held her Maxim straight at his forehead, as she moved rapidly towards him. She didn't know if he was part of the assassination team, or just a local cop. His radio didn't have the range to reach Cali, so he must have received some local, second hand news. She figured the word had spread about their escape, and he probably just heard about it.

He froze as she moved in on him. She disarmed him and used his cuffs to secure his hands behind his back. She wasn't sure if anyone from the terminal tower had seen them, as both the plane and the car were blocking any clear line of sight.

She quickly ushered the officer towards his car. Brendan joined her, and they placed him in the front seat, his hat on his head, like he was out for a Sunday drive. Brendan slipped in behind the wheel, and Rogers got in behind him. Vargas opened the door behind their unwilling passenger, but hesitated. She glanced at Rogers, then at his arm, and the blood-soaked towel he was clutching.

"I'll get a needle and thread," Vargas said. She turned and dashed back towards the plane to collect the medical kit and the bottle of scotch.

"Give me a few minutes for this surgery, Bren, then drive normal," Vargas said, as she entered the vehicle. "If they saw what happened, they'll be waiting for us. If not, we want it to look like everything's routine, aside from the smoking plane, of course. You know, just another private jet with a little smoke pouring out of it."

Brendan shifted his head around, glancing at the officer, and watched Vargas go to work. She reached up and pulled back Rogers' shirt, then lifted the towel and saw the ugly flesh wound for the first time.

"Cute," she said, shaking her head and looking up at Rogers. He was grimacing a bit as the adrenalin of the landing wore off, and the pain in his arm began to surface. The bullet had gone straight through the fleshy portion of his upper arm. It was ugly and bloody, but otherwise manageable. Vargas handed him the bottle of scotch.

"Take a nice long swig," she said. He did. Vargas did as well.

She flipped the kit open and found the nitro-pak tactical suture kit. Perfect. She had planned to dump some of that twenty-one-year-old scotch on the wound as a disinfectant, but the kit had antiseptic pads and a skin-tac wipe. She cleaned up a bit before grabbing the pre-strung, 3.0 nylon suture, and pinched the wound shut. She quickly installed four ragged stitches on the back-entry point, six more at the exit point, which was a little messier, and all together, pulled the flapping muscle into some sort of structure.

Rogers was in significant discomfort, but more scotch seemed to help him stay steady, even if much of it flowed down the sides of his mouth, as he gasped for air through his clenched teeth. Vargas used a couple of closure strips to reinforce her needlework, then applied the skin-tac wipe, and wrapped the wound with a four-inch gauze from the kit. His bloody shirt, which she had ripped away, dangled around his body. She pinched his left nipple playfully, eliciting the usual head shaking from Rogers. The whole process took just a few of minutes.

"There we go," she said in a cheery voice, patting Rogers on the head.

He took another swig of the scotch and handed her the bottle. She also took another generous gulp. Brendan eased into a parking spot across from the tower building.

There were several taxi drivers standing around outside their cars, a little curious about their smoky arrival, but there was no sign of additional police.

"Rogers, can you kindly remind our passenger that his silence will result in a nice quiet evening at home tonight, while any rambunctious behavior will leave him gagged in the trunk, possibly injured," Vargas said.

Rogers relayed her comments in Spanish, flipping his thumb towards Vargas, and the driver nodded vigorously. They both accepted that as his acquiescence.

Vargas slid out the back door as Brendan opened his. No authorities were sight.

"Rogers, stay low. Brendan, I'm going to peek inside. Stay here and pretend you're having a chat with our colleague. Keep your eyes open for a grey Rav 4. Honk if you see it."

Vargas tucked the Maxim 9 behind her and flipped her shirt over it. She smiled at the taxi drivers as she walked past and, of course, they clucked and winked at her. *Assholes.* She recognized they were playing an animated card game called Toruro, something she had seen many times in between the chess and checkers in Washington Square, back in New York. Inside were a couple of cleaning personnel and someone looking official, but wearing an 'Avis Car Rentals' badge. She guessed they were not expecting a regular flight any time soon. She looked at the arrivals board. It was completely empty.

Vargas moved back outside, just as the Rav 4 sped into the parking lot. It pulled up a few spots away from their police vehicle. A funny looking guy popped out and walked towards her. He had a flowing bandana around his head that looked a little like a blonde wig.

"Colestah," he said. He lifted his head to indicate he was talking to her, even though there wasn't another soul there.

Vargas noticed that Brendan had his window down, and his pistol pulled and ready. She held her hand out slightly, glancing at him and indicating everything was all right. "Eduardo," she replied.

The man's face lit up. He moved forward a little more quickly and extended his hand. Vargas accepted it. He shook her hand vigorously, bringing his other hand into the greeting as well. *Christ, I think he's applying for a job!* Vargas smiled.

"Your plane is burning."

"We noticed … that's why we got off." Unfortunately, her sarcasm was lost on him. She turned and moved towards the Rav 4, waving at Brendan to join her. "Let's go."

Brendan got out and jumped around the vehicle to make sure Rogers was okay to move. He was in some pain, but fully mobile. Rogers grabbed the suture kit as Brendan assisted him to make the vehicle transfer.

"Mierda," Eduardo said as he saw the bloody mess of Rogers' upper body. "He is okay, yes?"

"No worries," Vargas replied, loud enough for Rogers to hear. "It's an old wound."

She turned and smiled at Rogers, who gave a little thumb up. "You have an extra shirt?" she asked Eduardo.

He raced to the back of his SUV and opened the hatch. He pulled out a light hunting jacket, camouflage pattern, with a zipped front. He held it up, waiting for a confirmation that it would suffice.

"Perfect," Rogers said. He moved to the Rav 4 and tossed the kit into the back, before removing his torn and bloody shirt.

"What about our local official over there." Vargas asked Eduardo.

He went back to the squad car, reached in behind, and clobbered the officer with the butt of a pistol. He tipped the unconscious police office down onto the front seat, cautiously checking out the taxi drivers to see if anyone was watching. They were busy with cards. It would be a little while before anyone found him, and PT1 would be long gone by then.

Eduardo sped them down some rough roads, keeping up an endless chatter about working for the Americans, helping Daniel, being trusted to collect the famous Colestah, not to mention his wife and three children back home, his favorite TV shows, and everything else he could jam into their half hour ride. He stopped only for the occasional breath and a sip of his Cola. Vargas nodded every few minutes, just to let him know how interested she was in his babble. He was definitely more entertaining than a local radio station.

"Daniel is just ahead," Eduardo said, pointing up the road towards nothing in particular.

"How far?" Vargas asked.

"Not far, maybe two minutes."

"Stop here," Vargas said. Eduardo looked at her but didn't react. "Stop," she said again, this time a little more animated. He did.

She wasn't sure why she had concerns about their safety, but her intuition was usually right. She looked back at Brendan from her shotgun seat. "Taranis," she said, switching to Brendan's code name for Eduardo's benefit, "follow us in on foot from here. I have a funny feeling about this."

"What?" Eduardo asked. "No problem, everything is okay."

Brendan climbed out of the car and looked at Vargas. "See you in a bit."

"Okay, let's go," she told Eduardo. He still looked confused. "Muevelo!"

Eduardo continued up the road a few hundred yards, and then pointed when a small cabin came into sight.

"There," he said. "See? Everything is good."

"Slow down," Vargas said. She opened her door. Eduardo began braking. "Don't stop, just slow down a bit. Rogers, stay alert, I'll follow in from here." She tumbled out of the moving vehicle, pushing the door shut behind her.

Eduardo was confused, but kept moving.

"Loco lady," he said under his breath. They were his last words.

As they neared the cabin, several shots hit the Rav 4. Eduardo was gone in an instant. Rogers hunkered down in the back seat and managed to get his door open. He rolled out of the vehicle as it began to speed up, Eduardo's dead foot still resting on the accelerator. Rogers continued rolling off the side of the road into the drainage ditch, as gunfire bounced around him. He did his best to insulate his arm during his tumble, but it was the source of significant pain. He wasn't sure if the sutures had ripped. He wasn't happy that everyone seemed to be shooting a him. In fact, he was a little angry about all the attention.

Vargas saw Rogers roll into the ditch and hoped he wasn't hit. She wasn't sure if the people in the cabin knew she was there or not. Her sixth sense had warned her of the potential for danger, fueled by the fact that they had received such a cold reception in Cali. Somebody knew their plans in advance, and that wasn't good. Whoever was gathering information on them would have to be figured out later. Right now, the cabin needed some cleaning up.

Vargas knew Brendan was roughly two hundred yards behind her, and the sound of gunfire would have him fully alert. She pulled herself forward by her elbows until she got a clear view of the cabin. No one in sight.

The Rav 4 missed the next curve and rolled into the ditch beside the cabin. She guessed Eduardo was not making it home tonight.

Vargas continued until she came to the end of her cover. There was a clearing to the cabin of about thirty yards. Too far to dash across without being seen. Just as she churned around the possibilities, she heard a couple of shots from inside. The cabin door burst open and someone came stumbling out, his hands behind his back. Daniel! There were a couple more shots as he dove, or perhaps stumbled, onto the ground just beyond the door.

A man appeared in the cabin doorway, pointing his gun at Daniel. Vargas reacted immediately, squeezing off two rounds and catching the unsuspecting man with both. He went down, certainly surprised at his fate, and Daniel scrambled to get farther away from the building. Vargas sent another few rounds towards the doorway to inhibit any others from getting a shot at him. She heard the glass of a window being shattered, and redirected her cover fire towards it.

Daniel managed to make it to the ditch, rolling sideways and landing not more than a few yards from the Rav 4. Rogers hustled up the ditch towards him. Their reunion was unexpectedly forced. Rogers was now bleeding from his bandaged wound, and Daniel waiving his tied hands at his left leg, which was obviously housing at least one bullet.

"Welcome back to Colombia," he managed to say, smiling at Rogers.

"Such a lovely place," Rogers replied. He started cutting the ties holding Daniel's hands behind him. "What the hell is going on?"

"They're looking for Pitts. They caught us off guard and took down Jose and Mario."

Rogers was finally able to cut the nylon ties using the plane's keys. He lifted his head towards the toppled Rav 4.

"They got Eduardo as well."

Daniel looked back at the vehicle. "Nice guy," he said. "Nice family too." He looked at Rogers more closely. "You been drinking?" He waved his hand across his nose to emphasize his point.

"Just enjoying a quiet, afternoon scotch," Rogers replied.

Daniel shrugged, not really getting the humor of it.

Meanwhile, Vargas was rolling sideways, maintaining cover and trying to get out of the path off incoming fire. She got close to the edge of the road and then jumped up and dashed towards the ditch, diving in just as several rounds kicked up dust beside her. She moved forward under her new cover and soon reached Rogers and Daniel.

"Pitts?" she asked Daniel, noticing the still healing wound, across his check.

"Nope. He bolted when these clowns showed up," he replied. "There were seven hombres, I mistakenly took them for good guys. Well, there were seven, but I managed to get one, and you got another."

"What were they planning? Why did Pitts take off? Aren't they his guys?" Vargas had a lot of questions.

"His guys?" Daniel responded. "Hell, these are local thugs. They were chasing Pitts as well, I believe they want to kill him."

"Are they FARC?" Vargas asked.

"Nope. I recognized one guy. We used him and some others a few times when we needed some local muscle. If I had to guess, I'd say they were on loan to the CIA."

That's fucked up. CIA thugs, wow! Vargas slid another clip into her Maxim 9. She peeked up and sent a few rounds towards the cabin. Fire was returned and she slid back into the ditch.

"No way to get in there," Daniel said. "Too many of them, and they're armed to the teeth."

"But they don't have a secret weapon," Vargas replied, once again clicking off a couple of rounds towards the structure.

"Secret weapon?"

"Taranis, of course," Vargas said.

Vargas continued down the ditch until she reached the toppled Rav 4. She stuck her head inside the window and located Eduardo's Coke bottle. After ripping off a bit of his shirt, she moved back to the rear of the vehicle and used her knife to pierce the fuel tank at its lowest point. Gas began trickling out and she captured what she needed in the bottle. The cloth from his shirt was then tucked into the bottle opening. She tipped the bottle to let some fuel soak the rag slightly, and then slipped her Abigail earpiece on.

"Abby, you there?"

"Hi there. I was wondering where you were."

"Is Brendan on?"

"Absolutely, we've just been chatting, trying to figure out what's going on."

"Tell him to get close to the north side of the cabin and wait for my fireworks. Let me know when he's there."

"Okay, will do," Abigail replied. There were never any questions from her, just action.

"He should be able to get right up to the back of the cabin. Their attention is all directed my way."

"Roger that," Abby replied.

Vargas waited a few minutes, firing the occasional shot to keep their focus on her. Rogers and Daniel had joined her at the Rav 4. Daniel managed to pull the rear door of the SUV open and several things came tumbling out, including several rifles, the medical kit, and a box of flares.

"Christ, why didn't you say so?" Vargas smiled at him.

"I usually wait until someone asks," Daniel replied, smiling back.

"Get a flare ready," Vargas said as she waited for Abby to return to her. "Grab a rifle, Rogers. All hell is about to break loose."

"He's in place," Abigail chirped.

"Thanks, Abby. Tell him to be ready. When we light the place up, he can move in from behind." She held her Coke bottle Molotov cocktail towards Rogers. He looked at her. "Got a light?"

Rogers got it. He reached into his pocket and produced his gold Dupont.

As he reached to ignite the rag, Vargas reminded him, "Spin sideways."

Rogers laughed as the flame burst into life.

"Daniel, follow this with a flare. Rogers, as soon as this hits the cabin, open fire with that rifle...if you can hold it," she added, thinking of his wound.

Vargas reached back and threw the missile with all her might. It sailed through the air and landed a few feet short of the cabin, just on the front edge of the porch. It didn't matter. The purpose, to draw all attention to the front entrance, was accomplished. Daniel fired a flare directly through the front door and Rogers began some rapid fire, accompanied by a spray of bullets from her Maxim 9.

Return fire was received, but only temporarily. Vargas heard the pop of Brendan's Glock 19. Several rounds, in fact. Then there was silence. A minute passed.

"There's fresh coffee in here," Brendan called, bringing a smile to everyone's face.

They gathered inside the cabin. Vargas didn't notice Daniel was hobbling up the rear, with a bullet still buried in his leg.

Once inside, she relayed to Brendan what Daniel had told her about Pitts.

"That fits in with the scenario in Cali," Vargas said. "Probably a CIA hit team at the airport, or at least a CIA sub-contract." Vargas looked at Brendan, then Rogers. "It's not good when the fox is already in the henhouse!"

Daniel didn't understand the comment, but he reiterated his previous remarks.

"Pitts took off when he saw these men arriving, that much is for sure." He pointed at the dead bodies strewn across the floor, courtesy of Brendan and his Glock. "I believe they want Pitts dead, or maybe alive, I'm not sure, but don't worry." Daniel took out a small receiver, flicked it on, and waited for a second. "He's right... there," he said, pointing at the screen with a blinking red light.

"Where the hell is that?" Vargas said.

Daniel turned slightly, focusing on the direction, and then raised his arm, pointing directly at the rear wall of the cabin and the stunning Blue Marlin that sat staring from its mounted perch.

"That way," he said, smiling. "Can't be more than about a mile away, maybe less. It's dense out there. The range is two miles, but he must be waiting to see how this scenario plays out."

"Let's move," Vargas said. She headed towards the door.

"Not me," Daniel said softly.

Vargas turned, and for the first time realized that Daniel had been hit. "Shit, why didn't you say something?" She knelt to take a look at the wound.

"Like I said, I usually wait until someone asks," he replied. *Ever the smartass.* Vargas smiled.

"Rogers, I guess it's the blind leading the blind here. Take care of him as best you can. The medical kit is in the ditch behind the Rav 4. Taranis and I will go after Pitts."

Daniel handed her the receiver. "Just follow the flashing light. It's directional, but won't tell you how close you are. Be careful, alert. Even though the range is about two miles, he could be anywhere from around the corner to all the way out."

"Got it," Vargas said. She headed out with Brendan. Before exiting, she turned back to the two men. "Stop the bleeding, Rogers. Oh, and if you have time, try to get that fuel leak stopped and the Rav 4 upright." She smiled at the ridiculousness of her request.

The two men looked at her. Rogers just waved goodbye.

"This whole scenario is beyond crazy," Abigail whispered to Vargas.

Vargas touched her ear and felt for the earpiece.

"That's an understatement. We're signing off for a bit. We'll reconnect soon." Vargas signaled for Brendan to do the same. Once he closed out, she said, "Look, I don't know how it will go down with Pitts, but we need to be sure we're on the same page before everything goes over the airwaves. If that was a CIA operation in Cali, and if these dudes are also working for them, we need to be real sure who we can trust."

"No problem," Brendan replied. "I couldn't agree more. First, let's get Pitts.

They followed the dirt road a little further. Eventually it became a travelled path before finally disappearing altogether. Brendan saw the broken twigs and pointed. Vargas did not like traipsing through the woods. Trees, bugs, and excessive sweat were not really her style. She reminded herself to remember the mission. That was paramount.

They soon realized, from the two distinct parallel paths, that it was Pitts and one other guy. Vargas kept the red blip in front of them, without knowing exactly how far ahead they were. Somewhere between two hundred feet and two miles. The forest was thickening now and Vargas could hear the sea, or perhaps a river. The rush of water was unmistakable. They were gradually climbing upward and the route steepened considerably.

"Christ, we could use a chopper about now," she muttered.

"Wouldn't do much good in this terrain," Brendan said.

"I know," Vargas responded. "But it eases my weary legs to think about the possibility."

Brendan smiled. "Hold it," he suddenly whispered, holding his hand up like a crossing guard.

"What is it?"

"I heard something. Hang on."

They listened intently. There it was, another unmistakable sound. Feet crunching branches. Vargas motioned for Brendan to spread out, and they continued forward cautiously. A few minutes went by. Suddenly, Pitts bolted from behind a downed stump and raced towards the deeper forest. A second man pointed his pistol at Vargas and squeezed off a round, just as she dove back towards the cover of a tree. A second bullet hit the bark next to her head as she crouched down.

She heard the now familiar pop of Brendan's Glock, and the thud of a body hitting the ground. Vargas was glad he was on her side!

"What are you waiting for?" Brendan called.

"I was waiting for you to get him, that's why I lured him out into the open." They both chuckled.

A sudden crash of branches and pounding steps indicated Pitts was taking off. Vargas took off after him, Brendan right with her. The branches whipped their skin, and the uneven ground made running both difficult and dangerous. Vargas turned a corner and slammed on her brakes. Ahead was a significant cliff, with water raging some two hundred feet below. Brendan pulled up behind her.

"Don't think he went that way," he said.

They continued along the edge of the cliff, following the red blip. Brendan spotted him first. He was struggling to climb a small embankment and slid back towards them. They closed quickly.

As Pitts finally hurdled the embankment, he caught his foot on a downed branch and lunged forward. His momentum forced a somersault and he bumped up, almost standing, before he tumbled near the edge of the cliff. He clawed back for any type of anchor to prevent him from falling, and caught the root of a tree. He held on precariously with his left hand, his damaged side, dangling close to a lengthy fall. He managed to pull himself up and back onto the path, once again taking flight. His tumble took up precious time, with Vargas and Brendan closing fast.

Vargas ran full speed along the path, also dangerously close to the edge, now only a few steps behind Pitts. He drew his pistol and turned to fire once, but it was impossible to aim backwards while running through a forest. Vargas dove forward when she saw his pistol swing back again, easily avoiding the bullet that buzzed over her head, as she went to the ground in a somersault. Brendan was another ten yards behind her, trying to keep up.

Pitts was swinging his arms to push the branches aside as he sped down the path, but many still struck him as he ran, raking his face and body. Vargas held her arms up too, like a boxer defending herself. She let the branches bounce off her, dipping and weaving in and out to avoid the larger ones. Pitts turned and fired again, but the bullet flew off into the trees. Vargas was closing.

Turning to fire left Pitts unaware of the ground in front of him, and he caught the edge of another root. He flew sideways, his gun danced out over the edge of the cliff, and his body followed. He reached desperately with his hands, and once again managed to grab hold of a last dangling vine. He clung to the plant, wrapping it around his left wrist while grabbing on with his right hand. Vargas arrived and looked down at him. She smiled, panting loudly, and glad the chase was over.

"Tough route for a nature hike." He didn't laugh. He didn't even smile.

"Get me up," Pitts demanded, as though he was somehow in charge. "Get me up. You need me, Vargas. I am the only one with the formula."

Brendan came up behind Vargas. "Let's get him up," he said.

Vargas took off her belt, looped the buckle, and slid her hand through the loop, ensuring it wouldn't accidently slip. She tossed the loose end to Pitts.

"Grab it," she said. "We'll pull you up." Brendan reached in and held Vargas around the waist. She reached sideways and grabbed a sturdy shrub for some additional support.

Pitts grabbed the belt with his right hand, wrapping it tightly by swinging his hand in a circular motion around it. He gradually let go of the vine circling his left hand, transferring both of his hands to the belt Vargas was anchoring. Vargas, with Brendan's assistance, began to pull him up. He placed two feet on the side wall and was about to make a final lunge up, when Vargas released her grip slightly. Pitts swung back out a little, his feet on the cliff edge, and both his hands clinging to the belt. He was about thirty-five degrees out, completely at her mercy.

"What the fuck are you doing, lady?" Pitts bellowed. Vargas waited until he calmed down.

"I'm interrogating you. Consider this truth or dare, or should I say, truth or death. I have a few questions, and if you give me the right answers, we will yank you up to a nice rosy future. If your answers are crap, I'll release you and let gravity be the executioner."

Pitts was not amused. "Get me the fuck up and I'll answer anything!"

Vargas let the belt slip a little more, Brendan still providing anchoring support around her waist.

"Answers first," she said, still calm and collected. "There are a few things we need to talk about before I can help you up."

"What?" Pitts said.

"I want to know the whole story about the cocaine being run into the US," Vargas said. "And make it the Reader's Digest version, my hand is getting sore."

"Christ, everybody knows about that."

Vargas was not amused. The belt slipped again.

"Not much left here, Pitts. Cut the BS and tell me how it works. Who's running that show? What's Clemenson's role."

"Clemenson?" Pitts seemed genuinely surprised. Then he chuckled. "Jesus, Clemenson doesn't know shit. He's the cleanest boy scout in the whole country."

Vargas was confused. "Back in your lab you told me Clemenson ordered the hit on you. You indicated he was running the show."

"Ya, ya. Originally, I figured he was the one who sent the dirty team after me, but once I discovered the whole scenario, I realized he was just another dummy on a high horse. The story in my lab, well, that was for your benefit. Just thought I'd throw a wrench onto the information trail. I figured you feeling betrayed might make your demise a little extra painful."

That did not amuse Vargas. She glanced at Brendan. His eyebrows went up.

"Who's running the show, Pitts?" Vargas repeated her question, allowing the belt to slip to its maximum extension.

"Brenmar runs it. Christ, everyone knows Brenmar is the man. Look, I've got everything on a stick—names, places, points of entry, payouts, the whole shit pile. Get me up and I'll give it to you."

Vargas looked at him again. "Where is this stick?"

"Pull me up first."

"Fuck that," Vargas replied. "My hand is so tired, I'm not sure I can hold out long enough to hear the story. Tell me where the stick is and I'll bring you up."

"Okay, okay. It's in my lab back in Cali."

"What, the one we burned to the ground?"

"It's there. There's a safe under the stairs. Solid steel, it wouldn't be damaged by fire," Pitts said. "Now get me up, for christ's sake."

"Combination, please," Vargas said.

"Seven, twenty, ten," Pitts said. "The date of Colombia's Independence Day."

"How appropriate," Vargas replied. "How about the gas?"

"Pull me up!"

"Location of the remaining gas?"

"There is no more god damn gas. You bastards have destroyed everything." He looked up at Vargas with some serious hatred in his eyes.

"Sorry Pitts, we were only doing our job."

"Okay!" Pitts looked down at his precarious footing. "Okay? Let's go now. Besides, I'm the only one with the formula. Do you have any idea how valuable that is to the US Government?"

"Yup," Vargas replied, beginning to pull him upwards. "It will probably get you immunity. Provide the government with a weapon of leverage to control the world, and set back human relations a hundred years. Quite the weapon."

Pitts looked up at her. Vargas had a moment of clarity. Then Pitts had his own, and started to panic as he realized the situation. It was too late for him.

Vargas released her grip, watching him stagger on the edge, trying to gain his balance. She locked eyes with him, and then kicked out, striking him on the right leg and knocking him off the edge. It was a long way down, but he didn't scream. After a few seconds, she heard the distant crunch of his body striking the ground.

She turned slowly and looked at Brendan. She couldn't read his demeanor immediately. He looked over the cliff, then back at her.

"Shit, that was a rough ride," he said, flicking his head sideways towards the cliff and raising his eyebrows.

"I don't know," said Vargas. "The ride seemed pretty smooth, but the landing was a bit harsh"

"There goes the formula," Brendan said.

"And what do you think about that?"

"I saw you trying to help him up, trying to keep him safe, so we could get the formula back to Clemenson," Brendan said. "It's too bad he slipped and fell before you could complete the rescue."

Vargas looked at him, gauging the sincerity of his comment. It was real.

"Not to mention I lost a nice belt."

Back at the cabin, they found Rogers and Daniel resting comfortably. As they walked in, Daniel grabbed a pistol, unsure of who it was.

"Where's Pitts?" he asked.

"Didn't make it," Vargas replied. She looked at Rogers, wanting to see his reaction. "Thank god," Rogers said. "He was a bloody menace to this world."

That was more or less the reaction she was hoping for. Rogers was definitely in her good books.

"Wait until you hear Daniel's story, Colestah," Rogers said.

"What's up?" she replied.

Daniel started his tale. "I was chatting with Rogers about Cali, and suddenly it hit me."

"What hit you?"

"Brenmar."

Vargas didn't understand. She looked at Rogers, who pointed at Daniel.

"I told him yesterday that we had located Pitts. He said he wanted any news on Pitts to come straight to him, and only him. We figured Pitts was in this area, and requested reinforcements from Brenmar. When you called me, I assumed *you* people were those reinforcements. After Eduardo left to get you, five guys arrived. I guessed they were more local reinforcements. Pitts bolted right away with some other guy. He must have known something was up"

"Ya, we met his buddy too. You didn't mention him before we left," Brendan said.

"Sorry about that," Daniel said, a little sheepishly. "Anyway, we thought these guys were some additional local reinforcements, sent by Brenmar, but they quickly disarmed us, killing Jose and Mario. They were questioning me about your ETA when you got here."

"That means they knew we were coming," Rogers said.

"If Brenmar knew you had Pitts, why didn't he tell us?" Vargas asked.

"Guess that explains the reception in Cali," Brendan said. "I expect it was orchestrated by Brenmar."

Suddenly, it all became clear. Brenmar was the culprit. He had sent the welcoming committee and the extraction team, but Pitts must have known that too.

Vargas sat down. "This wasn't an extraction team, it was a hit team." She had to let this all settle in, to formulate some plan of action. "We can't just walk into the White House and accuse Brenmar of being a drug trafficking, murdering traitor. We need to get that stick!"

"What stick?" asked Rogers.

"Apparently, there's a memory stick with details about the drug trade," Vargas said. "And we need to get it. Daniel, we need a ride back to Cali."

Daniel's man arrived almost three hours later, and then it was two and a half hours back to Cali. It was getting dark by the time they arrived, and Vargas asked Daniel to drop his man off on the way. She didn't want anyone else being aware of what they were doing.

The house that had held the lab was now rubble. They parked down the street and Brendan joined Vargas as they headed in. Rogers and Daniel waited by the vehicle, both still nursing their wounds.

They had little trouble locating the stairs, but digging down to get underneath them was a different story. It took some effort, and they were both soaked and filthy by the time they touched the blackened steel shell. Somewhere in the middle of it all, Rogers had come to check on them, with a couple of bottles of water in tow.

Vargas found the dial and twisted in the combination. The safe cracked open. Inside were several items, including a healthy stack of American money. Vargas found the stick, tucked it into her bra, wishing she still had the secret pocket in the rear of her belt, and pushed all the other documents down inside her front waistband. She handed Brendan the cash. He removed his jacket and wrapped up the notes, perhaps fifty bundles of ten thousand dollars each.

Now all they needed was a plane to get the hell out of there. Daniel got them to the airport and Rogers took care of the rest. A beautiful little Lear jet 45XR sat on the runway, probably prepped for an early morning business trip. Rogers calculated it was nearly four AM, and there was no sense making it wait any longer. He went on board, after Vargas dismantled the mechanic who was sitting with his warm coffee and a copy of Noticias De Cali. Rogers eyed the cockpit. It was perfect.

He leaned out the door. "Let's roll, folks."

Vargas turned to Daniel. "That plane in Buenaventura has to be destroyed. No trace."

"That's an easy one, Colestah. Consider it done."

"Make sure Eduardo's family gets a nice chunk of cash too, and your other colleagues."

Daniel raised his eyebrows. "Cash? Unfortunately, there's not much dinero floating around here."

Vargas asked Brendan for his jacket, removed one pack of ten thousand, and gave the jacket to Daniel.

"There's a decent amount in here, take care of Mrs. Eduardo, and then you'd better get going somewhere safe for a while. I know Brenmar is your boss Daniel, but something funny is going on. I'd appreciate it if you fall off the radar for a while. I'll find you when the coast is clear."

Daniel smiled. "Don't worry about me, Colestah. You know I'm invincible. I'll wait to hear from you" He smiled.

Vargas smiled back, then scampered onto the plane behind Brendan.

"Abby, you there?" Vargas asked as she plugged in.

"I'm here. That was a long break. What's up?"

"We're headed to…" Vargas trailed off and looked at Rogers.

"Key West is our best bet," he offered.

"Key West, we'll be there in about…"

"About six hours," Rogers said. "That's about all we have fuel for. We're in N939HB."

"Six hours Abby; N939HB. We need the local authorities to know we're coming and who we are. We also need transport up to Washington from there, ASAP."

"Consider it done," she replied.

"Do *not* tell the CIA. We have some concerns about the integrity of that information chain."

"Understood."

Rogers hit the guarded start buttons and the engines kicked into life. He checked the radar for any other traffic and found there was nothing. As they taxied onto the runway, there was some immediate chatter from the tower. Rogers responded in Spanish, indicating it was an emergency medical flight. He said the owner of the plane was gravely ill, and they were heading to Bogota. The tower argued about flight plan filing details, but the plane was airborne before the discussion could get too far. Once up, Rogers keep the plane low and pointed straight north.

Vargas rifled through the various compartments on the plane and found an expensive little Hornback crocodile-skin portefeuille in one of the cupboards. She figured it was worth at least a grand, and made a nice little carrying case. She slid the various documents from Pitts' safe into it.

Almost an hour into the flight, Rogers climbed up to twenty-seven thousand feet. Panama picked him up. He radioed local authorities, figuring to bluff through the fact that a flight plan had not been filed, but he was informed that he had already received clearance in to Key West. Once again, Rogers recognized the value of having Abby on the team.

With autopilot engaged through the Glareshield control panel, he went back into the cabin. Vargas and Brendan were both sound asleep in their chairs. He saw no point in waking them. Rogers rummaged through the galley and found a bottle of Chivas. Not his favorite, but more than suitable for the occasion. More importantly, he also located a few bottles of Five-Hour Energy. They were just what he needed.

Rogers touched down at Key West International Airport, rested and bushy-tailed agents in tow. Everyone was a little dirty and disheveled, but the Five-Hour Energy was doing its job for him. Welcome to the Conch Republic. Rogers followed the airport security vehicle that met them at the end of the runway, and eased to a stop just outside the Monroe County Fire Station. A minivan pulled up outside, and two rather burly gentlemen waited as they deplaned.

"Ms. Hamilton," one said.

Vargas looked at Brendan, then at Rogers, before replying. "In the flesh."

"If you folks climb aboard, we'll get you to your next flight."

Vargas didn't like the looks of the situation. They were far too much like CIA goons, and her trust level of the CIA was at an all-time low.

"Sure, thanks, just let me grab my bag. I left it on board." Vargas climbed back onto the Lear jet and plugged in. "Abby, you there?"

"Right here, Colestah. What the heck is going on?"

"What do you mean?"

"Clemenson's been all over me this morning. He says Brenmar is freakin' out about whatever it was that you did down in Colombia. He wants you in here ASAP."

Vargas pondered her comment. That issue could wait. "Did you send a CIA greeting team, Abby?"

"What? CIA? I never talk to them. You're booked on American 4460 at 11:55, into Reagan National. Gets you here around 14:40-."

"Okay, thanks Abby. Let's see, ten-thirty now… Shouldn't be a problem"

Vargas climbed back down the stairs. She knew this was definitely a hostile meet and greet.

"Let's go, gentlemen," she said. She climbed into the minivan, sitting directly behind the driver's seat. Brendan and Rogers slipped in behind her onto the back bench, and thug number two sat beside her.

"Where to, boys?" she asked.

"We're heading over to the private terminal. There's a plane waiting there." Bullshit.

They drove past the main FBO hanger and headed for several smaller ones out along the inner runway. As they turned to enter the hangar, Vargas brought her right elbow up and out in a rapid motion that caught thug number two, sitting beside her, completely by surprise. The blow was delivered just under the tip of his nose, driving the entire breathing apparatus back into his face. Her left hand pulled the Maxim 9 from her rear waistband and slammed it into the side of the driver's head, leaving him unconscious behind the wheel. Her first thought was about the integrity of the weapon's grip, and hoped it wasn't damaged. She transferred the gun to her right hand, glancing at the still intact grip, and whacked the broken nose with it as well, ensuring he was out of commission.

The vehicle continued towards the hangar entrance. Vargas tossed the pistol on the seat beneath her and reached over, turning the wheel, while pulling the driver's leg off the accelerator. Brendan and Rogers, not completely sure of what was happening, were content to let it play out. Vargas climbed over the seat and took control of the vehicle from the passenger side. She drove back near the Lear jet and stopped by the stairs.

"The CIA gets an 'A' for effort," Brendan said.

Vargas smiled back. "Thanks for the assist," she said sarcastically.

"I don't think you need me involved until there are at least five combatants, maybe six."

"Let's get these two bozos onto the plane." They carried one from the front, while Rogers flipped the other over his shoulder and carried him up solo.

"Make sure they're tied down. We don't want any reports going back to Brenmar just yet," Vargas said.

"You figure they're his men?" Rogers asked.

"They aren't ours, so either they're CIA, or under their employ. Either way, I don't think their plans for us included a safe flight into DC." They looked at one another. "Abby has us booked on American at noon. Unfortunately, it's into Reagan National. We need these guys incognito for about three hours."

Rogers and Brendan secured them tightly to the rear seats. Quite a bit of blood was streaming from thug two's nose, but at least he wasn't dead.

Once they were back down in the van, Vargas holstered her Maxim 9 and drove over to the main entrance, using her red card to access the arrivals hall without wandering through the customs checkpoint.

The agent at American Airlines looked them over. They were a ragged and dirty group. Vargas starred her down. After all, they were in first class, even though it was only an Embraer RJ-175. Vargas used her card again, pushing them and their weapons through two separate security entrances without confrontation.

"Abby?"

"Right here."

"We had a little welcoming committee, an unfriendly one."

"Is everything okay?"

"They're resting comfortably on the Lear jet. Better let someone know that, but only around six thirty."

"Will do," she replied.

"I'm going to swing by my place for a quick shower before heading in. We are a real mess right now."

"Okay, Vargas. I'll tell Clemenson around, what, six o'clock?"

"Better make it eight. We need to get cleaned up first."

"Okay, sounds good. See you then."

Vargas disconnected. She looked at Rogers and Brendan, and laughed.

"You guys look like shit!"

They looked at one another, also laughing a bit.

"That's okay, Vargas, you look good enough for all of us," said Brendan. Everyone smiled.

She looked at him. "When we get to DC, can you take Rogers to clean up?" Brendan nodded. "I believe he lost everything on the Gulfstream V. Hopefully you have some clothes he can wear. I'll head to my place, and meet you guys at Abby's at eight."

"Sure thing. He'll have to squeeze into my things, but we'll make it work."

Vargas flipped a thumb towards Rogers. "I'll get a cab home, it's not far. If you're going out to Dulles to collect the Austin Martin, maybe our pilot here can fly my R8 back with him. He's got the keys anyway."

"No worries," Brendan replied. "I guess he's qualified."

► ► ►

When Vargas arrived home, she tossed her Maxim onto the couch and kicked off her clothes, piece by piece, as she walked through her penthouse towards the shower, leaving a trail behind her. The stick from Pitt's safe landed squarely on the bed.

She wasn't sure how hot she could withstand the water, but she was going to find out. She scrubbed out the remnants of Colombia, and triple shampooed. *Christ, I am in serious need of a mani-pedi.* After a little soap, hot water, steam, and cream, Vargas wrapped herself in a towel, threw another over her wet hair, and went into her bedroom. She pushed her laptop open and grabbed the memory stick. She plugged it into the USB port and clicked the file icon that popped up. She didn't have a chance to read it.

She saw the unmistakable flicker of infrared and dove behind her bed, just before a suppressed burst of gunfire exploded through her bedroom window, killing one of her down filled pillows. She guessed it wasn't the best thing for the levitated draperies either. Her Maxim 9 was on the couch back in the living room and well out of reach. Her knife was in her boot somewhere near the entrance.

She could hear the gunman pushing through the broken glass window. *I am so fucked!* Vargas rolled towards the bedroom entrance, hoping to make a dash for cover, but there was no chance. The gunman, complete with full mask and ninja attire, stood over her. *Really? That's how you dressed to hunt me down?* Her towel was gone and Vargas laid back, her body glistening in the soft light of the bedside lamp. He looked at her, enjoying the view, and pointed his rifle. A single shot rang out.

Vargas spun around as her attacker crumpled to the floor, most of the back of his head now decorating the wall above her bed. Emma stood in the doorway, the Maxim 9 held deftly in a double grip. Vargas was shocked.

"I forgot my house keys after I cleaned up today. I'm so mad, I had to drive all the way back here to get them. Come on, dear, you'll catch cold if we don't get some clothes on you."

Emma said it as if she had just picked up a pair of dirty socks. Now, she was definitely more than just a cleaning lady. Vargas regained her wits, grabbed her earpiece, and plugged in.

"Abby?"

"Right here."

"Someone just tried to take me out in my home!"

"My god, what's going on?"

"I don't know, but I'm going to find out. Look, get to Brendan, tell him to keep his eyes open. They're probably gunning for him too."

"Right away."

"And Abby, I don't know if our communication is compromised, but we have to assume so. Change the meet to the Jack Rose Saloon, eight thirty."

"I'll let Brendan know. What should I tell Clemenson?"

"Tell him that's where I'll be, and don't mention anything about my visitor. I want to share that surprise myself." Vargas punched out.

Abigail was stressed. She didn't like the idea of keeping things from Clemenson. Vargas dressed hurriedly, with Emma's assistance, and returned to her laptop to copy the stick. She deposited the original in her new belt pocket. Emma helped blow dry her hair, chasing her around, while Vargas sorted through the files from Pitts' safe and copied them on her printer/scanner. She wasn't sure who invented the cordless hair dryer, but it was a great idea. She returned the originals to the croc bag, dumping in the copied USB stick, and gave it to Emma.

"Keep this at your place, at least until I find out what's going on."

"Will do, Ms. Hamilton, and I'll get this mess cleaned up immediately. "

"Thank you," Vargas said. She turned and looked Emma squarely in the eyes. "Thank you very much, Emma." She squeezed the elderly lady's arm.

"Better get moving, my dear."

Vargas arrived at the saloon by taxi at seven forty-five and moved downstairs. She peeled five one hundred dollar notes off the cash-pack she kept from Colombia, and handed them to Art.

"I need a private spot tonight, completely private. I have a few friends joining me."

Art accepted the cash without a blink and led her to a small private room beyond the bar. It was a seldom used storage room, with a huge butcher-block table and numerous chairs, lamps, and candle holders jammed onto shelves. "How's this?"

"Perfect Art, thanks." Vargas hesitated. "You still have some of that Glenfarclas?"

"Sure do, Ms. Hamilton. You want a glass?"

"Five glasses and the bottle, please."

Again, he didn't blink. Art wiped down the heavy wooden table and slid five chairs into place around it. People who drop tips with hundred dollar bills get whatever they ask for.

"Scotch on the way. You want menus as well?"

"Just the scotch." She thought about the others for a moment. "And some ice."

As Art left to get the bottle, Vargas saw Clemenson walking down the length of the bar. She looked at him for a moment from her slightly concealed position in the back room. She was hunting his face for some clue as to where he stood. Pitts had exonerated him from any part in the drug import business, but the fact that the CIA knew their every move still tickled her intuition.

Art arrived with the bottle, ice, and glasses.

"Art, that gentleman standing at the bar, please direct him in here. Two more gentlemen and a cute redhead are on their way as well."

"Sure thing."

As Clemenson entered, Vargas saw Brendan and Rogers descending the stairs as well. They were both cleaned up and looking pretty, both clad in the usual black garb.

"What the hell is going on, Vargas?" Clemenson cut right to business.

"What, no hello, how are you, everyone okay, all that stuff?"

Clemenson sat down. It was not his nature to be ushered anywhere, anytime. He usually ran the show at his own whim, but something in Abigail's voice had swayed his decision to agree to this meeting. He wanted to know the whole Colombia report, in detail. Vargas slid a glass his way and then the bottle. Brendan and Rogers entered.

"Thank you, Art. Just missing a redhead now."

Art gave some sort of half salute to indicate he was on the lookout for her, as Vargas slid two more glasses to the recent arrivals. Brendan slid the R8 keys back across the table in return.

"I like that little jet," he said. "She definitely lets you know if there's a bump in the road."

"Yup, she's sensitive." Vargas winked back.

No one said anything. Finally, Vargas looked at Clemenson.

"Let's give Abby a second before we start."

Clemenson looked over at Brendan and Rogers. "How are you boys doing?"

"All good," Brendan replied, lifting his arm to demonstrate full mobility.

"I need some repair work on my left shoulder," Roger said, unable to lift his own.

Clemenson nodded, as if he understood. It was like he asked his question without really wanting an answer, leaning on the rhetorical to fill the silence.

Two minutes later, Abby was ushered in. Art closed the door on the way out.

"**P**itts is dead." Vargas said it without emotion. It was the least of her concerns at the moment.

"Shit," Clemenson muttered. He brought his hands to his face, providing a dry wash before pulling them back through his hair like a giant comb. "What happened?"

"He had a little difficulty navigating the Colombian terrain," Vargas said, looking Clemenson in the eyes. "He went sideway over a large cliff before we could corral him."

He stared back at Vargas, then at Brendan, who shrugged in quiet confirmation. Clemenson leaned back and he smiled.

"Thank god," he said, keeping his gaze directly at Vargas. He chuckled. "That gas would have severely fucked up this world."

Brendan looked at Vargas. She raised her eyebrows slightly. "No worries on that now," she replied.

"Not yet," Clemenson said. "But you can be damn sure Brenmar already has some scientists working hard to replicate the process."

"Not for long," Vargas said.

Clemenson looked up, surprised. "What's that mean?"

Vargas ignored his question.

"Our friend Mr. Pitts was off our radar because he only became Pitts about four years ago." She hoped for some reaction from

Clemenson, but none came. "You don't get it, boss?"

"Get what?"

Vargas could not have hoped for a more positive reaction. His ignorance to the situation reflected his innocence, more clearly that any conversation could have.

"Pitts was your man Wallach."

"What? Are you kidding me, how's that possible? How do you know? Are you sure?" He looked at Abigail. There was no surprise on her face. "You knew about this as well?"

Abigail nodded. "Just found out."

Vargas figured it was time to decide on Clemenson; either she trusted him or she didn't. It had to be trust; there was no other option. If he was dirty, PT1 was a lost cause anyway.

Vargas laid out the story as she knew it so far, including the discovery of Pitts' true identity, the original suspicion cast on Clemenson, the subsequent implication of Brenmar, and most importantly, the revelation about the CIA's entanglement with the Colombian government, with FARC, and the extensive drug trade they orchestrated.

Clemenson displayed a mixture of shock, revelation, curiosity, and even a little recognition when certain events were recounted. Vargas told him everything she had, getting the other members of PT1 fully apprised at the same time. Clemenson confirmed the fact that Wallach had brought him suspicions of CIA involvement in the drug trade, and that he had sent him back to Colombia to gather better intel on the situation. He also confirmed he told Brenmar about the revelation, unaware that he might be part of the deal. That would explain Wallach's original conclusion that Clemenson had arranged his attacker. Still, he must have discovered that Clemenson was a bystander in the scenario; after all, he had vindicated him prior to his demise.

Clemenson's reactions were tame compared to the umbrage he demonstrated when he realized it was Brenmar that had sent an assassination team to meet them in Cali. This definitely put the game on a new level, and the implications were not yet fully realized.

"Brenmar's a tough cookie," Clemenson said. He regained his composure, looking around at the team. "He has a low tolerance level, and I'm not really surprised that he would target his own men, if they leave the reservation, so to speak. But that ambush on you in Cali, if it was indeed his doing, breaks all the rules. I've told you all before that I'm on your side, and I guess it's time to make that clear."

The team was happy to hear those words.

"We don't have much time," Vargas said. Clemenson looked up. "There was a visitor waiting for me when I got home—with one of those nice Colt M4A1 assault rifles we practice with on the Farm." She paused momentarily. "Standard CIA issue."

Vargas glanced at Brendan. "We got the warning from Abby," he said, "but no encounters on our side."

Vargas leaned forward, her arms stretched out on the table towards Clemenson.

"Look, boss, Brenmar knows that we know, and he's going to do whatever he thinks necessary to keep us silent."

Clemenson leaned back. He looked around the room, engaging each of them in a short stare, gauging their position on the turn of events. He leaned forward and picked up the bottle of Glenfarclas. Not much remained, but he topped up everyone's glass, even a few drops for Abigail, who had barely touched her first drink. He leaned back again, swirling the scotch in his glass, staring at it for several seconds.

He finally spoke, almost a whisper, without raising his eyes. "What a mess. What an unbelievable fucking mess!"

He waited a few more seconds. No one else said a word. They wanted to know what their leader was going to do. If he was passive, it would indicate he was leery of taking on such a foe as Brenmar, with such a huge, and as yet unsubstantiated, finger of guilt.

Clemenson gulped down his scotch, slid the glass across the table towards Vargas, and stood up.

"I'm going to go see the president," he said. He stepped behind his chair and calmly slid it into place under the table top.

"It's late," Vargas said.

"He'll want to get up for this," Clemenson replied.

Vargas looked him in the eye. "I think I'll have to pay a visit to Brenmar."

Clemenson looked at her and nodded slightly. "It's late."

Vargas smiled. "He'll want to get up for this."

It was the first time Vargas had seen Clemenson express any real emotion. He was angry.

"I'll take care of that dog, Vargas" he said, obviously fighting back a more colorful response.

Vargas was cooler. She had taken the time to think this out. Rogers' comment about how it would take a huge chunk of people to run such an op was not far off.

"Look, Brenmar might appear to be the head honcho, but that isn't known for sure. Like Rogers kindly pointed out, managing a drug run of this size would take an army of people."

Clemenson nodded, his eyes slightly glazed. He paced slowly, walking around the table. Abby and Vargas exchanged glances.

"Don't chase Brenmar tonight, Vargas. Let me talk to the president first. He's got to be informed that the gas crisis has been resolved, even though he's going to freak about the death of Pitts. Let me drop the Brenmar drug bomb and see how he reacts. That might tell us a lot."

"Are you suggesting he might already know something about it?" Brendan asked.

"I can't believe he does, but ten minutes ago, I wouldn't have believed Brenmar was that deep in it either. I mean, he's an asshole, but a traitor, a drug runner... it just doesn't add up. Let me see how the president handles the news. We'll discuss it in more detail after that."

"Okay boss," Vargas said. She realized that the whole drug organization might indeed reach as high as the White House. *Christ, I hope not!* Clemenson looked at her, seeking reassurance that she would not take action before then.

"Not tonight, but let me meet with Brenmar in his office tomorrow morning, just him and me. Let me see what I can get out of him."

Her reputation for interrogation techniques was well established, but Clemenson didn't really think she was the right person to carry out such a Q&A with the director of the CIA. He started to protest the idea, but Vargas went on.

"It makes perfect sense. He's going to want to know what I know, what we know. We need to get this up front with him or we'll have a tag team waiting for us around every corner. And I mean ASAP. If not tonight, then tomorrow morning for sure."

"What are you thinking?" Clemenson asked, calmer now. He had made a full circle around the table and his hands were back on the top of his recessed chair.

"I'm thinking you'd better break the news to the president about losing Pitts and the formula, and I will make lovey-dovey with Brenmar in the morning. I don't know if he knows, that we know what he's into." Vargas looked around. "You know what I mean." She smiled.

"He's a dangerous man, Vargas," Clemenson said.

"Agreed. But wasn't it Colonel Younger that referred to me as the most dangerous woman in the world?"

Clemenson nodded. He turned to Abigail.

"You ready for a quick trip to the White House, young lady?"

"Whatever you need, boss."

After Clemenson left, Abby tight behind him and glancing back at the team, Vargas took out her iPhone and called the bar. Art brought in a second bottle of Glenfarclas. The team huddled around the fresh scotch as Vargas shared her ideas. Eventually they all agreed to a plan, though they admitted it was absolutely crazy.

They consumed most of the second bottle, wrapped up in recantations of the trip to Colombia, and comments on the plan Vargas had hatched. As Rogers began to question one particular aspect of the plan, Vargas suddenly held up her hand. He froze mid-sentence.

Vargas stood up, leveraging both her hands under the heavy table edge, and lifted it with one smooth action.

"Cover," she yelled. The table flew onto its side, scotch bottles and glasses scattered and shattered, and the door to the room burst open.

Rogers and Brendan dove behind the table. Vargas already had her Maxim 9 drawn. Several bursts of automatic weapons crashed into the tabletop, now acting as a shield, while other bullets sank into the wall behind them.

Vargas swung to her right, diving between a crouching Rogers and the lower edge of the table. She stuck her pistol out and began unloading rounds towards the door before she could see the entrance. As her slide finally brought the doorway into sight, she saw two men staggering from wounds. One was falling backwards, his grip sending automatic fire into the ceiling, as his hand tightened with the reflex of his imminent demise. Vargas concentrated on the second assailant, who was now looking directly towards her. He raised his weapon slowly with his wounded arm, but it was too late. Vargas popped two into his head before he blinked.

Brendan dove, rolled off the other side of the flipped table, and squeezed off several shots out into the room. The third assailant was dispatched without further incident.

Vargas rose cautiously, as she and Brendan simultaneously moved towards the doorway. Brendan was left of the entrance, flat on the floor with a clear sight line to the back of the whiskey room outside. Vargas was on the right with a complete view of the bar. People were flat on the floor, hands over their heads. One lady was screaming somewhere over near the stairs. She saw Art standing with his back against the wall of whiskey, his eyes shut, arms spread out like wings, and his hands flush against a bottle of Aultmore twenty-five-year-old on his left, and Bowmor Devil's Cask III on his right.

"Art," Vargas called. No reaction. He finally opened his eyes. They were terrified. "Anyone out there you don't know, Art?" she asked.

Art hesitated. He looked at Vargas, who waved her head sideways, indicating he should peruse the room. He looked around, then back at her.

"No."

Vargas stepped out into the room, Brendan kept cover from the doorway, and Rogers followed her. Three dead attackers and at least two injured guests, but there didn't seem to be any collateral casualties. Patrons began surfacing, all of them definitely bewildered. Vargas dialed the extraction number she had been given.

"Name?"

"Colestah."

"Code?"

"The Great Eight."

"What's the situation?"

"We need a serious clean up at Jack Rose Dining Saloon. You know the place?"

"No problem. What's the situation?"

Vargas thought about it for a second. This was probably a CIA line. She was probably calling in a clean-up job for dead CIA dudes. How ironic!

"Three down, dead; two civilians injured. Has to be a quiet run."

"No problem, Colestah. We'll be there in six minutes."

"I'll be gone."

"Where are you going to be?" he asked.

"I'm heading home," she said, knowing full well that information was heading straight to the large ear of the CIA brass.

Vargas hung up, tossed Art the rest of her roll of cash from Colombia, and waved Rogers and Brendan up and out.

"You never saw me, Art," she said as she moved to the stairs. He just looked on in disbelief.

They burst out onto the street.

"We've got three minutes before the cleanup team arrives," she said. She grabbed the door handle of her R8. "Rogers, jump in. Bren, meet us in the parking lot at 3121 South St."

She sped off. Rogers looked at her, but didn't say anything. He knew her well enough by now to realize she would speak when ready.

"I just called in a cleanup to the CIA, for the hit team the CIA sent for us." She looked at Rogers. He was shaking his head in disbelief. "I told him I'm going home. Let's see if they come to visit me there."

"They're probably already there," Rogers replied, his look one of near certainty.

Vargas sped down Florida Ave. Traffic was light, and she made the trip to South St. in less than seven minutes. Brendan arrived thirty seconds later. Vargas filled him in on the situation, and they headed on foot towards her building.

"I'm going through the front. Brendan, see if you can get around back. I'm the top floor, to your right. Watch out for these guys, there's probably more than one."

Brendan nodded, jumped up on the short stone wall at the property edge, and used the railing as a ladder to reach the higher side wall. It ran the length of the building, almost like a pedestrian walkway, right to the back courtyard.

Vargas crouched, motioning Rogers to do the same.

"You have a gun?" she asked.

"Nope."

"Are you kidding me?"

He shrugged. They moved to the front entrance and the first thing Vargas noticed was the dead security guard, a small patch on his left eye. He seemed like such a nice old guy. This probably meant that they were already here when the hit team attacked at the restaurant, just as Rogers had surmised. They had both locations covered.

She heard it before she spotted it: The black sedan in front, motor running. She moved silently up the driveway in a low crouch and slid along the passenger side. It definitely had bulletproof glass. Vargas stood and peered into the window. The driver turned to her, and after a moment of shock, reached for his gun. Vargas held hers down towards the asphalt and fired once, just for the popping sound effect. She winced visibly and then tumbled to the ground, as if she had been hit. She heard the driver's door open and saw his feet patter around the car. He probably figured one of his colleagues had caught her. As he rounded the front fender, her shot caught him just off center, under the chin, the bullet exiting slightly in front of his receding hairline. *Christ, where do they get these guys?*

Rogers moved in behind her. She picked up the driver's gun, reversed it in her hand, and gave it to Rogers.

"You'll probably need this," she said. She moved towards the entrance without waiting for a reply.

Rogers looked down at the gun and shook his head.

Brendan reached the back of the building and easily identified at least two intruders, high up on the balcony of Vargas' unit. He quietly descended the outside of the walkway wall and scurried to the building behind hers. Garbage can, drain pipe, window ledge, gutter, side overhang, and finally the shingled roof; the only flaw in his ascent being the creak of the gutter as the weight of his body bent it. He lay silent on the shingles, counting on the darkness and his black clothes to hide him.

Vargas and Rogers cleared the front door without incident. She pointed to the lobby couch.

"Get behind that. If anyone besides me comes out, shoot them." She hesitated before adding, "Anyone with a gun that is. Christ, don't shoot my neighbor walking her dog!"

Rogers smiled.

Vargas hit the staircase and leaped up, two stairs at a time. At the top floor, she peaked out the fire door and peered at the front of her penthouse. All appeared quiet. She moved over to the door and crouched in front. *If they're looking for a visitor, let me accommodate.*

She knocked.

As soon as she saw the shadow of an eye peering through the peep hole, she fired two shots where his esophagus would be, and spun sideways away from the door. She heard him hit the ground, as several rounds crashed back through the door in response. She was well clear by then. She hoped that her neighbor across the hall was not standing up. Now she knew there was at least one more inside. She moved down the hall to her next-door neighbor and knocked quietly. It was the same gentleman she had met early in the morning, a few days before.

"What the hell is going on?" he said.

Vargas pushed him back inside and dragged him over to the settee guarding his entrance foyer. He had the exact same unit as her. She wondered for a moment if he was with the CIA too, but dropped that thought from her mind.

"I'm the exterminator," she said, holding up the Maxim 9, looking him in the eye. "Big insects in my place next door. You'd better stay right here until they're dead."

He stared back, unsure what to make of his beautiful neighbor, slightly askew, brandishing a large suppressed pistol, barging through his door late at night. Just another night in Washington, DC.

Brendan climbed to the pinnacle of the building. It was still two-plus stories below Vargas' unit, and he began to doubt the validity of his decision to provide support from this vantage point. It was too late to change now though. Two figures remained on the balcony, both as shadowy outlines against the brick wall and dim windows.

Vargas went directly to her neighbor's bedroom closet, collecting a large, heavy table lamp on the way. She calculated that the other side of the wall must be her living room. She swung the lamp hard against the wall, easily breaking through the surface gyprock. Three more hard rams, a slight tear of some insulation, and she had a small hole clear through. She peered into her unit, just as a curious assassin came towards the noise. She slid the Maxim 9 through the opening and pulled off a few rounds. He was immediately dispatched. She wasn't sure how many were there, but she knew another angle of attack was required. As she left the bedroom, she heard the return fire crash through the closet wall. That confirmed there was at least one more inside.

She hurried towards the balcony, turning off the amber night-light that was bathing the room in a soft glow, and glancing back at her neighbor near the entrance. He was gone. She would have to worry about him later. He was probably hiding in the bathtub. She slid the balcony door open slightly and heard the ever familiar pop of Brendan's Glock, and the equally familiar thud as the next assassin crumpled to the ground.

"One more outside," Brendan yelled as the second man on Vargas' balcony swung and fired towards his voice. As soon as Vargas heard his gun discharge, she pushed her way onto the balcony and dove sideways, pumping two rounds into his side. There was still at least one more inside.

Suddenly, a loud bang echoed through the room behind her. She spun around, rolling sideways through instinct alone. Another CIA goon leaned sideways against the wall, part of his brain now dissemi-nated throughout the darkened living room. His blood spattered against the wall, guiding his body to a soft landing in a tidy heap on the ground. Vargas got to her knees and leaned into the room, gun first. Her elderly neighbor stood there with a huge golden Desert Eagle .50 caliber handgun, gently cradled in his two hands. *Christ, how can he even lift that thing?* He winked at her, his face barely visible in the darkness of the room.

"I guess some of those insects have crawled into my place as well," he said. "Must have come in through that new doorway you just added."

Vargas smiled. She had a sudden revelation: It took a lot of people to keep her alive! Wancheng, a couple of times, Bo, poor kid, Emma, and now her elderly neighbor. She made a mental note to find some way to thank them.

Shaking off the sentiment, she jumped up and headed back

towards the closet. If he came though there, anyone else in there is probably guarding the balcony. She retraced the brainless assassin's steps and climbed through the opening he had obviously enlarged in her living room wall. She silently moved through the kitchen to the balcony entrance and saw dummy assassin number six cautiously anticipating her arrival via the outside route. *Wait, is that six, or is that seven, if I count the driver downstairs?*

She moved directly behind him without a sound.

"Drop it," she said. She let he Maxim 9 touch the back of his head. He froze, letting his gun tumble to the ground.

"I always wanted to say that. It always works in the movies."

She used his own cuffs to secure his hands, and hoisted him to his feet.

Vargas leaned out the balcony door. "Front entrance," she called across to Brendan.

"Three minutes," he yelled back.

Vargas turned and started towards the door. Her elderly neighbor pushed through their new adjoining entrance and looked at her.

"That the last of them?" he asked, completely without emotion.

"I think we got them all." She smiled at the feistiness of this aging man. "What's your name?"

"John Handy," he replied.

"You certainly are that." Vargas nodded with thanks. "You have some place you can stay, John Handy? I don't think this will be suitable for a few days."

"Might be able to get Mrs. Hollyburn to put me up. She's a widow now." He cracked a large smile ear-to-ear. Vargas returned it. That was too bad, he would have been perfect for Emma!

"Okay, grab some stuff quick and head to her unit. Oh, and park that cannon somewhere safe. I have to get this guy to the police."

"I am the police," the sole surviving CIA agent said.

Vargas clipped him gently on the back of his head with her pistol. "Shut up."

She pushed him into the elevator and hit 'RC'. *Why don't they just call it 'L'?* Once they descended and the doors opened, she called to Rogers.

"It's just me and a friend," she said, loud enough to spook anyone in the lobby.

"Come on out," Rogers replied. "I'm here with a friend too."

Vargas marched her prisoner out. Rogers was on the couch, holding a small, artificially colored, blue Maltese dog. Beside him was an elderly lady, quite handsomely dressed for such a late night dog walk. Vargas looked at them and shook her head.

"Are you Mrs. Hollyburn, by any chance?"

The lady looked up, quite surprised. "I am indeed, young lady." She glanced at the CIA agent in cuffs.

"You have a visitor at your door, and he is in need of some support. I have to tell you, he was a true hero tonight."

Mrs. Hollyburn looked at her with more than a little surprise.

"Oh, my," she whispered. "Mr. Handy, no doubt."

She collected her dog from Rogers and headed to the elevator. She turned, took one more long look at the cuffed agent, then back at Rogers, and offered a parting remark. "Nice chatting with you, Mr. Smith."

"Likewise, Mrs. Hollyburn. Have a nice evening."

After the elevator closed, Vargas turned to Rogers. "Christ, what if I had been an assassin coming off the elevator?"

Rogers looked at her with his own grin. "When Mrs. Hollyburn entered, her little puppy sniffed me out right away. I mean, she offered to help me find whatever it was that I was looking for down behind the couch here." Vargas rolled her eyes. "So, I sat with her on the couch, figuring any bad guys coming out would not suspect me and this old lady. Figured I could easily get the drop on them." Vargas huffed a bit. "Just using the resources available."

Smart ass. This time Vargas smiled.

"Let's go," she said, motioning towards the door with her head and giving her prisoner a directional shove.

Outside, Brendan had already hoisted the dead driver into the back seat and was waiting behind the wheel. Vargas tried to connect with Abigail, but got no response. She was only off-line when she was with the president, so that answered question number one. She flipped her R8 keys to Rogers.

"Brendan, you and Rogers head to Abigail's. I'm going to return these guys to Brenmar first thing in the morning."

"We'll go with you," Brendan said, beginning to climb out of the car.

"Nope," she said. She looked at the cornflower blue dial of her Rolex Lady-Datejust. It wasn't a bad watch for forty thousand, and was still on time. "I'm going through the front door in six hours. Let's get these goons in the trunk and have a little nap at Abby's."

Brendan dragged the dead driver from the back seat and dumped him in. Before Vargas pushed her prisoner into the trunk, with his recently deceased friend, she cautioned him.

"I don't have any tape for your mouth, so just be quiet. If I hear any sound, I mean anything, even a cough, I'm putting six slugs through the trunk door. If they don't silence you, I'm pushing the car into the C&O Canal. Is that clear?"

"Yes, ma'am," he said.

Vargas put her finger to her lips.

"Just nod," she said. He did. She guided him into the trunk and slammed the door behind him.

"Breakfast at the diner on 18th St," Rogers said. It was a statement, not a question. Vargas looked at him. "We can't get into Abby's until she's finished with the president, and you can't see Brenmar for several hours."

"I guess a Diner Royale works," Vargas replied. "You can drive the baggage for now."

Rogers nodded and flipped the R8 keys back to her.

Vargas dialed the extraction number again. Time for the CIA to clean up the rest of their mess.

- END -